D1154643

O

The Many Worlds of
POUL ANDERSON

edited by
ROGER ELWOOD

THE MANY WORLDS OF POUL ANDERSON

Chilton Book Company

RADNOR
PENNSYLVANIA

LIBRARY OF CONGRESS CATALOGING IN PUBLICATION DATA

Elwood, Roger, comp.
  The many worlds of Poul Anderson.

  Includes bibliographical references.
  CONTENTS: Elwood, R.   Foreword.—Anderson, P.
Tomorrow's children.   The queen of air and darkness.—McGuire,
P.   Her strong enchantments failing. [etc.]
  1. Science fiction, American. 2. Anderson, Poul, 1926-   —
Criticism and interpretation.   I. Anderson, Poul, 1926-
II. Title.
PZ4.E522Man   [PS3551.N378]   813'.5'4   74-3445
ISBN 0-8019-5950-0

ACKNOWLEDGMENTS

TOMORROW'S CHILDREN Copyright © 1947 by Street and Smith
Publications, Inc. From *Astounding Science Fiction*. Reprinted by
permission of the author and author's agents, Scott Meredith Literary
Agency, Inc., 580 Fifth Avenue, New York, New York 10036.

THE QUEEN OF AIR AND DARKNESS Copyright © 1971 by Mercury
Press, Inc. From *Fantasy and Science Fiction*. Reprinted by permis-
sion of the author and author's agents, Scott Meredith Literary
Agency, Inc., 580 Fifth Avenue, New York, New York 10036.

EPILOGUE Copyright © 1962 by The Conde Nast Publications, Inc.
From *Analog*. Reprinted by permission of the author and author's
agents, Scott Meredith Literary Agency, Inc., 580 Fifth Avenue,
New York, New York 10036.

THE LONGEST VOYAGE Copyright © 1960 by Street and Smith Publications, Inc. From *Analog*. Reprinted by permission of the author
and author's agents, Scott Meredith Literary Agency, Inc., 580 Fifth
Avenue, New York, New York 10036.

JOURNEY'S END Copyright © 1957 by Fantasy House, Inc. Reprinted
by permission of the author and author's agents, Scott Meredith
Literary Agency, Inc., 580 Fifth Avenue, New York, New York
10036.

THE SHERIFF OF CANYON GULCH Originally appeared as HEROES ARE
MADE. Copyright © 1951 by Clark Publishing Co. From *Other
World Science Stories*. Reprinted by permission of the authors and
author's agents, Scott Meredith Literary Agency, Inc., 580 Fifth
Avenue, New York, New York 10036.

DAY OF BURNING Copyright © 1967 by The Conde Nast Publications, Inc. From *Analog*. Reprinted by permission of the author and
author's agents, Scott Meredith Literary Agency, Inc., 580 Fifth
Avenue, New York, New York 10036.

Foreword

The Many Worlds of Poul Anderson has been compiled for
several reasons: First, I wanted to bring together a group of
some of this author's finest stories, ranging from the relatively
short ("Tomorrow's Children") to those of much greater
length ("The Queen of Air and Darkness"). "Tomorrow's
Children" is also Poul's first published story, and though he
intimates that it has its flaws, it is certainly superior to most
first efforts.

Second, I sought to analyze Poul Anderson, in depth,
through major essays written by two authors who have followed
his career for a number of years. One of these, "Her Strong
Enchantments Failing" by Patrick McGuire, concentrates more
or less on a single work, while "Challenge and Response" by
Sandra Miesel takes on a broader perspective; both essays show
care, affection and insight.

Third, it seemed important to show the range of Poul's
talents, and thus, a wide variety of material was necessary—
from "The Sheriff of Canyon Gulch" (coauthored with Gordon
R. Dickson) to "The Longest Voyage" and others. While Poul
apparently is most at home with the so-called "epics," the
diversity herein shows that he handles other themes with
equal skill.

Fourth, Poul is a master at mapping out galactic battles,
even whole civilizations, anything indeed that requires an
almost omnipresent approach. Written especially for this book,
"A World Named Cleopatra" displays this ability at its most
impressive. One advance reaction to this material has been:

"tour de force." And that it is, a thorough construction of an entire world, even down to the minutest details of plant life and composition of the atmosphere.

Lastly, and encompassing all of the foregoing, *The Many Worlds of Poul Anderson* is intended as an honest-to-goodness tribute to one of the abiding geniuses of the science fiction genre. If every author were as good, consistently, as Poul, then science fiction would be even more highly regarded than it is. One can honestly say that Poul has never written a bad story; and when he is doing his very best, well, readers can rejoice.

Roger Elwood
Linwood, N. J.

Contents

The Many Worlds of
POUL ANDERSON

Tomorrow's Children

On the world's loom
Weave the Norns doom,
Nor may they guide it nor change.
— Wagner, *Siegfried*

Ten miles up, it hardly showed. Earth was a cloudy green and brown blur, the vast vault of the stratosphere reaching changelessly out to spatial infinities, and beyond the pulsing engine there was silence and serenity no man could ever touch. Looking down, Hugh Drummond could see the Mississippi gleaming like a drawn sword, and its slow curve matched the contours shown on his map. The hills, the sea, the sun and wind and rain, they didn't change. Not in less than a million slow-striding years, and human efforts flickered too briefly in the unending night for that.

Farther down, though, and especially where cities had been— The lone man in the solitary stratojet swore softly, bitterly, and his knuckles whitened on the controls. He was a big man, his gaunt rangy form sprawling awkwardly in the tiny pressure cabin, and he wasn't quite forty. But his dark hair was streaked with gray, in the shabby flying suit his shoulders stooped, and his long homely face was drawn into haggard lines. His eyes were black-rimmed and sunken with weariness, dark and dreadful in their intensity. He's seen too much, survived too much, until he began to look like most other people of the world. *Heir of the ages,* he thought dully.

Mechanically, he went through the motions of following his course. Natural landmarks were still there, and he had

§ 1

powerful binoculars to help him. But he didn't use them much. They showed too many broad shallow craters, their vitreous smoothness throwing back sunlight in the flat blank glitter of a snake's eye, the ground about them a churned and blasted desolation. And there were the worse regions of—deadness. Twisted dead trees, blowing sand, tumbled skeletons, perhaps at night a baleful blue glow of fluorescence. The bombs had been nightmares, riding in on wings of fire and horror to shake the planet with the death blows of cities. But the radioactive dust was worse than any nightmare.

He passed over villages, even small towns. Some of them were deserted, the blowing colloidal dust, or plague, or economic breakdown making them untenable. Others still seemed to be living a feeble half-life. Especially in the Midwest, there was a pathetic struggle to return to an agricultural system, but the insects and blights—

Drummond shrugged. After nearly two years of this, over the scarred and maimed planet, he should be used to it. The United States had been lucky. Europe, now—

Der Untergang des Abendlandes, he thought grayly. *Spengler foresaw the collapse of a topheavy civilization. He didn't foresee atomic bombs, radioactive-dust bombs, bacteria bombs, blight bombs—the bombs, the senseless inanimate bombs flying like monster insects over the shivering world. So he didn't guess the extent of the collapse.*

Deliberately he pushed the thoughts out of his conscious mind. He didn't want to dwell on them. He'd lived with them two years, and that was two eternities too long. And anyway, he was nearly home now.

The capital of the United States was below him, and he sent the stratojet slanting down in a long thunderous dive toward the mountains. Not much of a capital, the little town huddled in a valley of the Cascades, but the waters of the Potomac had filled the grave of Washington. Strictly speaking, there was no capital. The officers of the government were scattered over the country, keeping in precarious touch by plane and radio, but Taylor, Oregon, came as close to being the nerve center as any other place.

He gave the signal again on his transmitter, knowing with a faint spine-crawling sensation of the rocket batteries trained on him from the green of those mountains. When one plane could carry the end of a city, all planes were under suspicion. Not that anyone outside was supposed to know that that innocuous little town was important. But you never could tell. The war wasn't officially over. It might never be, with sheer personal survival overriding the urgency of treaties.

A light-beam transmitter gave him a cautious: "O.K. Can you land in the street?"

It was a narrow, dusty track between two wooden rows of houses, but Drummond was a good pilot and this was a good jet. "Yeah," he said. His voice had grown unused to speech.

He cut speed in a spiral descent until he was gliding with only the faintest whisper of wind across his ship. Touching wheels to the street, he slammed on the brake and bounced to a halt.

Silence struck at him like a physical blow. The engine stilled, the sun beating down from a brassy blue sky on the drabness of rude "temporary" houses, the total-seeming desertion beneath the impassive mountains—Home! Hugh Drummond laughed, a short harsh bark with nothing of humor in it, and swung open the cockpit canopy.

There were actually quite a few people, he saw, peering from doorways and side streets. They looked fairly well fed and dressed, many in uniform, they seemed to have purpose and hope. But this, of course, was the capital of the United States of America, the world's most fortunate country.

"Get out—quick!"

The peremptory voice roused Drummond from the introspection into which those lonely months had driven him. He looked down at a gang of men in mechanics' outfits, led by a harassed-looking man in captain's uniform. "Oh—of course," he said slowly. "You want to hide the plane. And, naturally, a regular landing field would give you away."

"Hurry, get out, you infernal idiot! Anyone, *anyone* might come over and see—"

"They wouldn't get unnoticed by an efficient detection system, and you still have that," said Drummond, sliding his booted legs over the cockpit edge. "And anyway, there won't be any more raids. The war's over."

"Wish I could believe that, but who are you to say? Get a move on!"

The grease monkeys hustled the plane down the street. With an odd feeling of loneliness, Drummond watched it go. After all, it had been his home for—how long?

The machine was stopped before a false house whose whole front was swung aside. A concrete ramp led downward, and Drummond could see a cavernous immensity below. Light within it gleamed off silvery rows of aircraft.

"Pretty neat," he admitted. "Not that it matters any more. Probably it never did. Most of the hell came over on robot rockets. Oh, well." He fished his pipe from his jacket. Colonel's insignia glittered briefly as the garment flipped back.

"Oh . . . sorry, sir!" exclaimed the captain. "I didn't know—"

" 'S O.K. I've gotten out of the habit of wearing a regular uniform. A lot of places I've been, an American wouldn't be very popular." Drummond stuffed tobacco into his briar, scowling. He hated to think how often he'd had to use the Colt at his hip, or even the machine guns in his plane, to save himself. He inhaled smoke gratefully. It seemed to drown out some of the bitter taste.

"General Robinson said to bring you to him when you arrived, sir," said the captain. "This way, please."

§

They went down the street, their boots scuffing up little acrid clouds of dust. Drummond looked sharply about him. He'd left very shortly after the two-month Ragnarok which had tapered off when the organization of both sides broke down too far to keep on making and sending the bombs, and maintaining order with famine and disease starting their ghastly ride over the homeland. At that time, the United States was a cityless, anarchic chaos, and he'd had only the briefest of radio exchanges since then, whenever he could get at a long-range set still in working order. They'd made remarkable progress meanwhile. How much, he didn't know, but the mere existence of something like a capital was sufficient proof.

Robinson— His lined face twisted into a frown. He didn't know the man. He'd been expecting to be received by the President, who had sent him and some others out. Unless the others had— No, he was the only one who had been in eastern Europe and western Asia. He was sure of that.

Two sentries guarded the entrance to what was obviously a converted general store. But there were no more stores. There was nothing to put in them. Drummond entered the cool dimness of an antechamber. The clatter of a typewriter, the Wac operating it— He gaped and blinked. That was— impossible! Typewriters, secretaries—hadn't they gone out with the whole world, two years ago? If the Dark Ages had returned to Earth, it didn't seem—*right*—that there should still be typewriters. It didn't fit, didn't—

He grew aware that the captain had opened the inner door for him. As he stepped in, he grew aware how tired he was. His arm weighed a ton as he saluted the man behind the desk.

"At ease, at ease," Robinson's voice was genial. Despite the five stars on his shoulders, he wore no tie or coat, and his round face was smiling. Still, he looked tough and competent underneath. To run things nowadays, he'd have to be.

"Sit down, Colonel Drummond." Robinson gestured to a chair near his and the aviator collapsed into it, shivering. His haunted eyes traversed the office. It was almost well enough outfitted to be a prewar place.

Prewar! A word like a sword, cutting across history with a brutality of murder, hazing everything in the past until it was a vague golden glow through drifting, red-shot black clouds. And—only two years. *Only two years!* Surely sanity was meaningless in a world of such nightmare inversions. Why, he could barely remember Barbara and the kids. Their faces were blotted out in a tide of other visages—starved faces, dead faces, human faces become beast-formed with want and pain and eating throttled hate. His grief was lost in the agony of a world, and in some ways he had become a machine himself.

"You look plenty tired," said Robinson.

"Yeah . . . yes, sir—"

"Skip the formality. I don't go for it. We'll be working pretty close together, can't take time to be diplomatic."

"Uh-huh. I came over the North Pole, you know. Haven't slept since— Rough time. But, if I may ask, you—" Drummond hesitated.

"I? I suppose I'm President. Ex officio, pro tem, or something. Here, you need a drink." Robinson got bottle and glasses from a drawer. The liquor gurgled out in a pungent stream. "Prewar Scotch. Till it gives out I'm laying off this modern hooch. *Gambai.*"

The fiery, smoky brew jolted Drummond to wakefulness. Its glow was pleasant in his empty stomach. He heard Robinson's voice with a surrealistic sharpness:

"Yes, I'm at the head now. My predecessors made the mistake of sticking together, and of traveling a good deal in trying to pull the country back into shape. So I think the sickness got the President, and I know it got several others. Of course, there was no means of holding an election. The armed forces had almost the only organization left, so we had to run things. Berger was in charge, but he shot himself when he learned he'd breathed radiodust. Then the command fell to me. I've been lucky."

"I see." It didn't make much difference. A few dozen more deaths weren't much, when over half the world was gone. "Do you expect to—continue lucky?" A brutally blunt question, maybe, but words weren't bombs.

"I do." Robinson was firm about that. "We've learned by experience, learned a lot. We've scattered the army, broken it into small outposts at key points throughout the country. For quite a while, we stopped travel altogether except for absolute emergencies, and then with elaborate precautions. That smothered the epidemics. The microorganisms were bred to work in crowded areas, you know. They were almost immune to known medical techniques, but without hosts and carriers they died. I guess natural bacteria ate up most of them. We still take care in traveling, but we're fairly safe now."

"Did any of the others come back? There were a lot like me, sent out to see what really had happened to the world."

"One did, from South America. Their situation is similar to ours, though they lacked our tight organization and have gone further toward anarchy. Nobody else returned but you."

It wasn't surprising. In fact, it was a cause for astonishment that anyone had come back. Drummond had volunteered after the bomb erasing St. Louis had taken his family, not expecting to survive and not caring much whether he did. Maybe that was why he had.

"You can take your time in writing a detailed report," said Robinson, "but in general, how are things over there?"

Drummond shrugged. "The war's over. Burned out. Europe has gone back to savagery. They were caught between America and Asia, and the bombs came both ways. Not many survivors, and they're starving animals. Russia, from what I saw, has managed something like you've done here, though they're worse off than we. Naturally, I couldn't find out much there. I didn't get to India or China, but in Russia I heard rumors— No, the world's gone too far into disintegration to carry on war."

"Then we can come out in the open," said Robinson softly. "We can really start rebuilding. I don't think there'll ever be another war, Drummond. I think the memory of this one will be carved too deeply on the race for us ever to forget."

"Can you shrug it off that easily?"

"No, no, of course not. Our culture hasn't lost its continuity, but it's had a terrific setback. We'll never wholly get over it. But—we're on our way up again."

The general rose, glancing at his watch. "Six o'clock. Come on, Drummond, let's get home."

"Home?"

"Yes, you'll stay with me. Man, you look like the original zombie. You'll need a month or more of sleeping between clean sheets, of home cooking and home atmosphere. My wife will be glad to have you; we see almost no new faces. And as long as we'll work together, I'd like to keep you handy. The shortage of competent men is terrific."

§

They went down the street, an aide following. Drummond was again conscious of the weariness aching in every bone and fiber of him. A home—after two years of ghost towns, of shattered chimneys above blood-dappled snow, of flimsy lean-tos housing starvation and death.

"Your plane will be mighty useful, too," said Robinson. "Those atomic-powered craft are scarcer than hens' teeth used to be." He chuckled hollowly, as at a rather grim joke. "Got you through close to two years of flying without needing fuel. Any other trouble?"

"Some, but there were enough spare parts." No need to tell of those frantic hours and days of slaving, of desperate improvisation with hunger and plague stalking him who stayed overlong. He'd had his troubles getting food, too, despite the plentiful supplies he'd started out with. He'd fought for scraps in the winters, beaten off howling maniacs who would have killed him for a bird he'd shot or a dead horse he'd scavenged. He hated that plundering, and would not have cared personally if they'd managed to destroy him. But he had a mission, and the mission was all he'd had left as a focal point for his life, so he'd clung to it with fanatic intensity.

And now the job was over, and he realized he couldn't rest. He didn't dare. Rest would give him time to remember. Maybe he could find surcease in the gigantic work of reconstruction. Maybe.

"Here we are," said Robinson.

Drummond blinked in new amazement. There was a car, camouflaged under brush, with a military chauffeur—*a car!* And in pretty fair shape, too.

"We've got a few oil wells going again, and a small patched-up refinery," explained the general. "It furnishes enough gas and oil for what traffic we have."

They got in the rear seat. The aide sat in front, a rifle ready. The car started down a mountain road.

"Where to?" asked Drummond a little dazedly.

Robinson smiled. "Personally," he said, "I'm almost the only lucky man on Earth. We had a summer cottage on Lake Taylor, a few miles from here. My wife was there when the war came, and stayed, and nobody came along till I brought the head offices here with me. Now I've got a home all to myself."

"Yeah. Yeah, you're lucky," said Drummond. He looked out the window, not seeing the sun-spattered woods. Presently he asked, his voice a little harsh: "How is the country really doing now?"

"For a while it was rough. Damn rough. When the cities went, our transportation, communication, and distribution systems broke down. In fact, our whole economy disintegrated, though not all at once. Then there was the dust and the plagues. People fled, and there was open fighting when over-crowded safe places refused to take in any more refugees. Police went with the cities, and the army couldn't do much patrolling. We were busy fighting the enemy troops that'd flown over the Pole to invade. We still haven't gotten them all. Bands are roaming the country, hungry and desperate outlaws, and there are plenty of Americans who turned to banditry when everything else failed. That's why we have this guard, though so far none have come this way.

"The insect and blight weapons just about wiped out our crops, and that winter everybody starved. We checked the pests with modern methods, though it was touch and go for a while, and next year got some food. Of course, with no distribution as yet, we failed to save a lot of people. And farming is still a tough proposition. We won't really have the bugs licked for a long time. If we had a research center as well equipped as those which produced the things— But we're gaining. We're gaining."

"Distribution—" Drummond rubbed his chin. "How about railroads? Horse-drawn vehicles?"

"We have some railroads going, but the enemy was as careful to dust most of ours as we were to dust theirs. As for horses, they were nearly all eaten that first winter. I know personally of only a dozen. They're on my place; I'm trying to breed enough to be of use, but"—Robinson smiled wryly—"by the time we've raised that many, the factories should have been going quite a spell."

"And so now—?"

"We're over the worst. Except for outlaws, we have the population fairly well controlled. The civilized people are fairly well fed, with some kind of housing. We have machine shops, small factories, and the like going, enough to keep our transportation and other mechanism 'level.' Presently we'll be able to expand these, begin actually increasing what we have. In another five years or so, I guess, we'll be integrated enough to drop martial law and hold a general election. A big job ahead, but a good one."

The car halted to let a cow lumber over the road, a calf trotting at her heels. She was gaunt and shaggy, and skittered nervously from the vehicle into the brush.

"Wild," explained Robinson. "Most of the real wild life was killed off for food in the last two years, but a lot of farm animals escaped when their owners died or fled, and have run free ever since. They—" He noticed Drummond's fixed gaze. The pilot was looking at the calf. Its legs were half the normal length.

"Mutant," said the general. "You find a lot of such animals. Radiation from bombed or dusted areas. There are even a lot of human abnormal births." He scowled, worry clouding his eyes. "In fact, that's just about our worst problem. It—"

The car came out of the woods onto the shore of a small lake. It was a peaceful scene, the quiet waters like molten gold in the slanting sunlight, trees ringing the circumference and all about them the mountains. Under one huge pine stood a cottage, a woman on the porch.

It was like one summer with Barbara—Drummond cursed under his breath and followed Robinson toward the little building. It wasn't, it wasn't, it could never be. Not ever again. There were soldiers guarding this place from chance marauders, and— There was an odd-looking flower at his foot. A daisy, but huge and red and irregularly formed.

A squirrel chittered from a tree. Drummond saw that its face was so blunt as to be almost human.

Then he was on the porch, and Robinson was introducing him to "my wife Elaine." She was a nice-looking young woman with eyes that were sympathetic on Drummond's exhausted face. The aviator tried not to notice that she was pregnant.

He was led inside, and reveled in a hot bath. Afterward there was supper, but he was numb with sleep by then, and hardly noticed it when Robinson put him to bed.

§

Reaction set in, and for a week or so Drummond went about in a haze, not much good to himself or anyone else. But it was surprising what plenty of food and sleep could do, and one evening Robinson came home to find him scribbling on sheets of paper.

"Arranging my notes and so on," he explained. "I'll write out the complete report in a month, I guess."

"Good. But no hurry." Robinson settled tiredly into an armchair. "The rest of the world will keep. I'd rather you'd just work at this off and on, and join my staff for your main job."

"O.K. Only what'll I do?"

"Everything. Specialization is gone; too few surviving specialists and equipment. I think your chief task will be to head the census bureau."

"Eh?"

Robinson grinned lopsidedly. "You'll *be* the census bureau, except for what few assistants I can spare you." He leaned forward, said earnestly: "And it's one of the most important jobs there is. You'll do for this country what you did for central Eurasia, only in much greater detail. Drummond, we have to *know*."

He took a map from a desk drawer and spread it out. "Look, here's the United States. I've marked regions known to be uninhabitable in red." His fingers traced out the ugly splotches. "Too many of 'em, and doubtless there are others we haven't found yet. Now, the blue X's are army posts." They were sparsely scattered over the land, near the centers of population groupings. "Not enough of those. It's all we can do to control the more or less well-off, orderly people. Bandits, enemy troops, homeless refugees—they're still running wild, skulking in the backwoods and barrens, and raiding whenever they can. And they spread the plague. We won't really have it licked till everybody's settled down, and that'd be hard to enforce. Drummond, we don't even have enough soldiers to start a feudal system for protection. The plague spread like a prairie fire in those concentrations of men.

"We have to *know*. We have to know how many people survived—half the population, a third, a quarter, whatever it is. We have to know where they are, and how they're fixed for supplies, so we can start up an equitable distribution system. We have to find all the small-town shops and labs and libraries still standing, and rescue their priceless contents before looters or the weather beat us to it. We have to locate doctors and engineers and other professional men, and put them to work rebuilding. We have to find the outlaws and round them up. We— I could go on forever. Once we have all that information, we can set up a master plan for redistributing population, agriculture, industry, and the rest most efficiently, for getting the country back under civil authority and police, for opening regular transportation and communication channels—for getting the nation back on its feet."

"I see," nodded Drummond. "Hitherto, just surviving and hanging on to what was left has taken precedence. Now you're in a position to start expanding, *if* you know where and how much to expand."

"Exactly." Robinson rolled a cigarette, grimacing. "Not much tobacco left. What I have is perfectly foul. Lord, that war was crazy!"

"All wars are," said Drummond dispassionately, "but technology advanced to the point of giving us a knife to cut our throats with. Before that, we were just beating our heads against the wall. Robinson, we can't go back to the old ways. We've *got* to start on a new track—a track of sanity."

"Yes. And that brings up—" The other man looked toward the kitchen door. They could hear the cheerful rattle of dishes there, and smell mouth-watering cooking odors. He lowered his voice. "I might as well tell you this now, but don't let Elaine know. She . . . she shouldn't be worried. Drummond, did you see our horses?"

"The other day, yes. The colts—"

"Uh-huh. There've been five colts born of eleven mares in the last year. Two of them were so deformed they died in a week, another in a few months. One of the two left has cloven hoofs and almost no teeth. The last one looks normal—so far. One out of eleven, Drummond."

"Were those horses near a radioactive area?"

"They must have been. They were rounded up wherever found and brought here. The stallion was caught near the site of Portland, I know. But if he were the only one with mutated genes, it would hardly show in the first generation, would it? I understand nearly all mutations are Mendelian recessives. Even if there were one dominant, it would show in all the colts, but none of these looked alike."

"Hm-m-m—I don't know much about genetics, but I do know hard radiation, or rather the secondary charged particles it produces, will cause mutation. Only mutants are rare, and tend to fall into certain patterns—"

"*Were* rare!" Suddenly Robinson was grim, something coldly frightened in his eyes. "Haven't you noticed the animals and plants? They're fewer than formerly, and . . . well, I've not kept count, but at least half those seen or killed have something wrong, internally or externally."

§

Drummond drew heavily on his pipe. He needed something to hang onto, in a new storm of insanity. Very quietly, he said:

"In my college biology course, they told me the vast majority of mutations are unfavorable. More ways of not doing something than of doing it. Radiation might sterilize an animal, or might produce several degrees of genetic change. You could have a mutation so violently lethal the possessor never gets born, or soon dies. You could have all kinds of more or less handicapping factors, or just random changes not making much difference one way or the other. Or in a few cases you might get something actually favorable, but you couldn't really say the possessor is a true member of the species. And favorable mutations themselves usually involve a price in the partial or total loss of some other function.

"Right." Robinson nodded heavily. "One of your jobs on the census will be to try and locate any and all who know genetics, and send them here. But your real task, which only you and I and a couple of others must know about, the job overriding all other considerations, will be to find the human mutants."

Drummond's throat was dry. "There've been a lot of them?" he whispered.

"Yes. But we don't know how many or where. We only know about those people who live near an army post, or have some other fairly regular intercourse with us, and they're only a few thousand all told. Among them, the birth rate has gone down to about half the prewar ratio. And over half the births they do have are abnormal."

"*Over half—*"

"Yeah. Of course, the violently different ones soon die, or are put in an institution we've set up in the Alleghenies. But what can we do with viable forms, if their parents still love them? A kid with deformed or missing or abortive organs, twisted internal structure, a tail, or something even worse . . . well, *it'll* have a tough time in life, but it can generally survive. And perpetuate itself—"

"And a normal-looking one might have some unnoticeable quirk, or a characteristic that won't show up for years. Or even a normal one might be carrying recessives, and pass them on— God!" The exclamation was half blasphemy, half prayer. "But how'd it happen? People weren't all near atom-hit areas."

"Maybe not, though a lot of survivors escaped from the outskirts. But there was that first year, with everybody on the move. One could pass near enough to a blasted region to be affected, without knowing it. And that damnable radiodust, blowing on the wind. It's got a long half-life. It'll be active for decades. Then, as in any collapsing culture, promiscuity was common. Still is. Oh, it'd spread itself, all right."

"I still don't see why it spread itself so much. Even here—"

"Well, I don't know why it shows up here. I suppose a lot of the local flora and fauna came in from elsewhere. This place is safe. The nearest dusted region is three hundred miles off, with mountains between. There must be many such islands of comparatively normal conditions. We have to find them too. But elsewhere—"

"Soup's on," announced Elaine, and went from the kitchen to the dining room with a loaded tray.

The men rose. Grayly, Drummond looked at Robinson and said tonelessly: "O.K. I'll get your information for you. We'll map mutation areas and safe areas, we'll check on our population and resources, we'll eventually get all the facts you want. But—what are you going to do then?"

"I wish I knew," said Robinson haggardly. "I wish I knew."

§

Winter lay heavily on the north, a vast gray sky seeming frozen solid over the rolling white plains. The last three winters had come early and stayed long. Dust, colloidal dust of the bombs, suspended in the atmosphere and cutting down the solar constant by a deadly percent or two. There had even been a few earthquakes, set off in geologically unstable parts of the world by bombs planted right. Half of California had been ruined when a sabotage bomb started the San Andreas Fault on a major slip. And that kicked up still more dust.

Fimbulwinter, thought Drummond bleakly. *The doom of the prophecy. But no, we're surviving. Though maybe not as men—*

Most people had gone south, and there overcrowding had made starvation and disease and internecine struggle the normal aspects of life. Those who'd stuck it out up here, and had luck with their pest-ridden crops, were better off.

Drummond's jet slid above the cratered black ruin of the Twin Cities. There was still enough radioactivity to melt the snow, and the pit was like a skull's empty eye socket. The man sighed, but he was becoming calloused to the sight of death. There was so much of it. Only the struggling agony of life mattered anymore.

He strained through the sinister twilight, swooping low over the unending fields. Burned-out hulks of farmhouses, bones of ghost towns, sere deadness of dusted land—but he'd heard travelers speak of a fairly powerful community up near the Canadian border, and it was up to him to find it.

A lot of things had been up to him in the last six months. He'd had to work out a means of search, and organize his few, overworked assistants into an efficient staff, and go out on the long hunt.

They hadn't covered the country. That was impossible. Their few planes had gone to areas chosen more or less at random, trying to get a cross section of conditions. They'd penetrated wildernesses of hill and plain and forest, establishing contact with scattered, still demoralized out-dwellers. On the whole, it was more laborious than anything else. Most were pathetically glad to see any symbol of law and order and the paradisical-seeming "old days." Now and then there was danger and trouble, when they encountered wary or sullen or outright hostile groups suspicious of a government they associated with disaster, and once there had even been a pitched battle with roving outlaws. But the work had gone ahead, and now the preliminaries were about over.

Preliminaries— It was a bigger job to find out exactly how matters stood than the entire country was capable of undertaking right now. But Drummond had enough facts for reliable extrapolation. He and his staff had collected most of the essential data and begun correlating it. By questioning, by observation, by seeking and finding, by any means that came to hand they'd filled their notebooks. And in the sketchy outlines of a Chinese drawing, and with the same stark realism, the truth was there.

Just this one more place, and I'll go home, thought Drummond for the—thousandth?—time. His brain was getting into a rut, treading the same terrible circle and finding no way out. *Robinson won't like what I tell him, but there it is.* And darkly, slowly: *Barbara, maybe it was best you and the kids went as you did. Quickly, cleanly, not even knowing it. This isn't much of a world. It'll never be our world again.*

He saw the place he sought, a huddle of buildings near the frozen shores of the Lake of the Woods, and his jet murmured toward the white ground. The stories he'd heard of this town weren't overly encouraging, but he supposed he'd get out all right. The others had his data anyway, so it didn't matter.

By the time he'd landed in the clearing just outside the village, using the jet's skis, most of the inhabitants were there waiting. In the gathering dusk they were a ragged and wild-looking bunch, clumsily dressed in whatever scraps of cloth and leather they had. The bearded, hard-eyed men were armed with clubs and knives and a few guns. As Drummond got out, he was careful to keep his hands away from his own automatics.

"Hello," he said. "I'm friendly."

"Y' better be," growled the big leader. "Who are you, where from, an' why?"

"First," lied Drummond smoothly, "I want to tell you I have another man with a plane who knows where I am. If I'm not back in a certain time, he'll come with bombs. But we don't intend any harm or interference. This is just a sort of social call. I'm Hugh Drummond of the United States Army."

They digested that slowly. Clearly, they weren't friendly to the government, but they stood in too much awe of aircraft and armament to be openly hostile. The leader spat. "How long you staying?"

"Just overnight, if you'll put me up. I'll pay for it." He held up a small pouch. "Tobacco."

Their eyes gleamed, and the leader said, "You'll stay with me. Come on."

Drummond gave him the bribe and went with the group. He didn't like to spend such priceless luxuries thus freely, but the job was more important. And the boss seemed thawed a little by the fragrant brown flakes. He was sniffing them greedily.

"Been smoking bark an' grass," he confided. "Terrible."

"Worse than that," agreed Drummond. He turned up his jacket collar and shivered. The wind starting to blow was bitterly cold.

"Just what y' here for?" demanded someone else.

"Well, just to see how things stand. We've got the government started again, and are patching things up. But we have to know where folks are, what they need, and so on."

"Don't want nothing t' do with the gov'ment," muttered a woman. "They brung all this on us."

"Oh, come now. We didn't ask to be attacked." Mentally, Drummond crossed his fingers. He neither knew nor cared who was to blame. Both sides, letting mutual fear and friction mount to hysteria— In fact, he wasn't sure the United States hadn't sent out the first rockets, on orders of some panicky or aggressive officials. Nobody was alive who admitted knowing.

"It's the jedgment o' God, for the sins o' our leaders," persisted the woman. "The plague, the fire-death, all that, ain't it foretold in the Bible? Ain't we living in the last days o' the world?"

"Maybe." Drummond was glad to stop before a long low cabin. Religious argument was touchy at best, and with a lot of people nowadays it was dynamite.

§

They entered the rudely furnished but fairly comfortable structure. A good many crowded in with them. For all their suspicion, they were curious, and an outsider in an aircraft was a blue-moon event these days.

Drummond's eyes flickered unobtrusively about the room, noticing details. Three women—that meant a return to concubinage. Only to be expected in a day of few men and strong-arm rule. Ornaments and utensils, tools and weapons of good quality—yes, that confirmed the stories. This wasn't exactly a bandit town, but it had waylaid travelers and raided other places when times were hard, and built up a sort of dominance of the surrounding country. That, too, was common.

There was a dog on the floor nursing a litter. Only three pups, and one of those was bald, one lacked ears, and one had more toes than it should. Among the wide-eyed children present, there were several two years old or less, and with almost no obvious exceptions, they were also different.

Drummond sighed heavily and sat down. In a way, this clinched it. He'd known for a long time, and finding mutation here, as far as any place from atomic destruction, was about the last evidence he needed.

He had to get on friendly terms, or he wouldn't find out much about things like population, food production, and whatever else there was to know. Forcing a smile to stiff lips, he took a flask from his jacket. "Prewar rye," he said. "Who wants a nip?"

"Do we!" The answer barked out in a dozen voices and words. The flask circulated, men pawing and cursing and grabbing to get at it. *Their homebrew must be pretty bad,* thought Drummond wryly.

The chief shouted an order, and one of his women got busy at the primitive stove. "Rustle you a mess o' chow," he said heartily. "An' my name's Sam Buckman."

"Pleased to meet you, Sam." Drummond squeezed the hairy paw hard. He had to show he wasn't a weakling, a conniving city slicker.

"What's it like, outside?" asked someone presently. "We ain't heard for so long—"

"You haven't missed much," said Drummond between bites. The food was pretty good. Briefly, he sketched conditions. "You're better off than most," he finished.

"Yeah. Mebbe so." Sam Buckman scratched his tangled beard. "What I'd give f'r a razor blade—! It ain't easy, though. The first year we weren't no better off 'n anyone else. Me, I'm a farmer, I kept some ears o' corn an' a little wheat an' barley in my pockets all that winter, even though I was starving. A bunch o' hungry refugees plundered my place, but I got away an' drifted up here. Next year I took an empty farm here an' started over."

Drummond doubted that it had been abandoned, but said nothing. Sheer survival outweighed a lot of considerations.

"Others came an' settled here," said the leader reminiscently. "We farm together. We have to; one man couldn't live by hisself, not with the bugs an' blight, an' the crops sproutin' into all new kinds, an' the outlaws aroun'. Not many up here, though we did beat off some enemy troops last winter." He glowed with pride at that, but Drummond wasn't particularly impressed. A handful of freezing starveling conscripts, lost and bewildered in a foreign enemy's land, with no hope of ever getting home, weren't formidable.

"Things getting better, though," said Buckman. "We're heading up." He scowled blackly, and a palpable chill crept into the room. "If 'twern't for the births—"

"Yes—the births. The new babies. Even the stock an' plants." It was an old man speaking, his eyes glazed with near madness. "It's the mark o' the beast. Satan is loose in the world—"

"Shut up!" Huge and bristling with wrath, Buckman launched himself out of his seat and grabbed the oldster by his scrawny throat. "Shut up 'r I'll bash y'r lying head in. Ain't no son o' mine being marked by the devil."

"Or mine—" "Or mine—" The rumble of voices ran about the cabin, sullen and afraid.

"It's God's jedgment, I tell you!" The woman was shrilling again. "The end o' the world is near. Prepare f'r the second coming—"

"An' you shut up too, Mag Schmidt," snarled Buckman. He stood bent over, gnarled arms swinging loose, hands flexing, little eyes darting red and wild about the room. "Shut y'r trap an' keep it shut. I'm still boss here, an' if you don't like it you can get out. I still don't think that gunny-looking brat o' y'rs fell in the lake by accident."

The woman shrank back, lips tight. The room filled with a crackling silence. One of the babies began to cry. It had two heads.

Slowly and heavily, Buckman turned to Drummond, who sat immobile against the wall. "You see?" he asked dully. "You see how it is? Maybe it is the curse o' God. Maybe the world is ending. I dunno. I just know there's few enough babies, an' most o' them *de*formed. Will it go on? Will all our kids be monsters? Should we . . . kill these an' hope we get some human babies? What is it? What to do?"

Drummond rose. He felt a weight as of centuries on his shoulders, the weariness, blank and absolute, of having seen that smoldering panic and heard that desperate appeal too often, too often.

"Don't kill them," he said. "That's the worst kind of murder, and anyway it'd do no good at all. It comes from the bombs, and you can't stop it. You'll go right on having such children, so you might as well get used to it."

By atomic-powered stratojet it wasn't far from Minnesota to Oregon, and Drummond landed in Taylor about noon the next day. This time there was no hurry to get his machine under cover, and up on the mountain was a raw scar of earth where a new airfield was slowly being built. Men were getting over their terror of the sky. They had another fear to face now, and it was one from which there was no hiding.

Drummond walked slowly down the icy main street to the central office. It was numbingly cold, a still, relentless intensity of frost eating through clothes and flesh and bone. It wasn't much better inside. Heating systems were still poor improvisations.

"You're back!" Robinson met him in the antechamber, suddenly galvanized with eagerness. He had grown thin and nervous, looking ten years older, but impatience blazed from him. "How is it? How is it?"

Drummond held up a bulky notebook. "All here," he said grimly. "All the facts we'll need. Not formally correlated yet, but the picture is simple enough."

Robinson laid an arm on his shoulder and steered him into the office. He felt the general's hand shaking, but he'd sat down and had a drink before business came up again.

"You've done a good job," said the leader warmly. "When the country's organized again, I'll see you get a medal for this. Your men in the other planes aren't in yet."

"No, they'll be gathering data for a long time. The job won't be finished for years. I've only got a general outline here, but it's enough. It's enough." Drummond's eyes were haunted again.

Robinson felt cold at meeting that too-steady gaze. He whispered shakily: "Is it—bad?"

"The worst. Physically, the country's recovering. But biolog-ically, we've reached a crossroads and taken the wrong fork."

"What do you mean? *What do you mean?*"

Drummond let him have it then, straight and hard as a bayonet thrust. "The birth rate's a little over half the prewar," he said, "and about seventy-five per cent of all births are mutant, of which possibly two-thirds are viable and pre-sumably fertile. Of course, that doesn't include late-maturing characteristics, or those undetectable by naked-eye observation, or the mutated recessive genes that must be carried by a lot of otherwise normal zygotes. And it's everywhere. There are no safe places."

"I see," said Robinson after a long time. He nodded, like a man struck a stunning blow and not yet fully aware of it. "I see. The reason—"

"Is obvious."

"Yes. People going through radioactive areas—"

"Why, no. That would only account for a few. But—"

"No matter. The fact's there, and that's enough. We have to decide what to do about it."

"And soon." Drummond's jaw set. "It's wrecking our cul-ture. We at least preserved our historical continuity, but even that's going now. People are going crazy as birth after birth is monstrous. Fear of the unknown, striking at minds still stunned by the war and its immediate aftermath. Frustration of parenthood, perhaps the most basic instinct there is. It's leading to infanticide, desertion, despair, a cancer at the root of society. We've got to act."

"How? How?" Robinson stared numbly at his hands.

"I don't know. You're the leader. Maybe an educational campaign, though that hardly seems practicable. Maybe an acceleration of your program for reintegrating the country. Maybe— I don't know."

§

Drummond stuffed tobacco into his pipe. He was near the end of what he had, but would rather take a few good smokes than a lot of niggling puffs. "Of course," he said thoughtfully, "it's probably not the end of things. We won't know for a generation or more, but I rather imagine the mutants can grow into society. They'd better, for they'll outnumber the humans. The thing is, if we just let matters drift there's no telling where they'll go. The situation is unprecedented. We may end up in a culture of specialized variations, which would be very bad from an evolutionary standpoint. There may be fighting between mutant types, or with humans. Interbreeding may produce worse freaks, particularly when accumulated recessives start showing up. Robinson, if we want any say at all in what's going to happen in the next few centuries, we have to act quickly. Otherwise it'll snowball out of all control."

"Yes. Yes, we'll have to act fast. And hard." Robinson straightened in his chair. Decision firmed his countenance, but his eyes were staring. "We're mobilized," he said. "We have the men and the weapons and the organization. They won't be able to resist."

The ashy cold of Drummond's emotions stirred, but it was with a horrible wrenching of fear. "What are you getting at?" he snapped.

"Racial death. All mutants and their parents to be sterilized whenever and wherever detected."

"You're crazy!" Drummond sprang from his chair, grabbed Robinson's shoulders across the desk, and shook him. "You . . . why, it's impossible! You'll bring revolt, civil war, final collapse!"

"Not if we go about it right." There were little beads of sweat studding the general's forehead. "I don't like it any better than you, but it's got to be done or the human race is finished. Normal births a minority—" He surged to his feet, gasping. "I've thought a long time about this. Your facts only confirmed my suspicions. This tears it. Can't you see? Evolution has to proceed slowly. Life wasn't meant for such a storm of change. Unless we can save the true human stock, it'll be absorbed and differentiation will continue till humanity is a collection of freaks, probably intersterile. Or . . . there must be a lot of lethal recessives. In a large population, they can accumulate unnoticed till nearly everybody has them, and then start emerging all at once. That'd wipe us out. It's happened before, in rats and other species. If we eliminate mutant stock now, we can still save the race. It won't be cruel. We have sterilization techniques which are quick and painless, not upsetting the endocrine balance. But it's got to be done." His voice rose to a raw scream, broke. "It's got to be done!"

Drummond slapped him, hard. He drew a shuddering breath, sat down, and began to cry, and somehow that was the most horrible sight of all. "You're crazy," said the aviator. "You've gone nuts and with brooding alone on this the last six months, without knowing or being able to act. You've lost all perspective.

"We can't use violence. In the first place, it would break our tottering, cracked culture irreparably, into a mad-dog finish fight. We'd not even win it. We're outnumbered, and we couldn't hold down a continent, eventually a planet. And remember what we said once, about abandoning the old savage way of settling things, that never brings a real settlement at all? We'd throw away a lesson our noses were rubbed in not three years ago. We'd return to the beast—to ultimate extinction.

"And anyway," he went on very quietly, "it wouldn't do a bit of good. Mutants would still be born. The poison is everywhere. Normal parents will give birth to mutants, somewhere along the line. We just have to accept that fact, and live with it. The *new* human race will have to."

"I'm sorry." Robinson raised his face from his hands. It was a ghastly visage, gone white and old, but there was calm on it. "I—blew my top. You're right. I've been thinking of this, worrying and wondering, living and breathing it, lying awake nights, and when I finally sleep I dream of it. I . . . yes, I see your point. And you're right."

"It's O.K. You've been under a terrific strain. Three years with never a rest, and the responsibility for a nation, and now this— Sure, everybody's entitled to be a little crazy. We'll work out a solution, somehow."

"Yes, of course." Robinson poured out two stiff drinks and gulped his. He paced restlessly, and his tremendous ability came back in waves of strength and confidence. "Let me see— Eugenics, of course. If we work hard, we'll have the nation tightly organized inside of ten years. Then . . . well, I don't suppose we can keep the mutants from interbreeding, but certainly we can pass laws to protect humans and encourage their propagation. Since radical mutations would probably be intersterile anyway, and most mutants handicapped one way or another, a few generations should see humans completely dominant again."

Drummond scowled. He was worried. It wasn't like Robinson to be unreasonable. Somehow, the man had acquired a mental blind spot where this most ultimate of human problems was concerned. He said slowly, "That won't work either. First, it'd be hard to impose and enforce. Second, we'd be repeating the old *Herrenvolk* notion. Mutants are inferior, mutants must be kept in their place—to enforce that, especially on a majority, you'd need a full-fledged totalitarian state. Third, that wouldn't work either, for the rest of the world, with almost no exceptions, is under no such control and we'll be in no position to take over that control for a long time— generations. Before then, mutants will dominate everywhere over there, and if they resent the way we treat their kind here, we'd better run for cover."

"You assume a lot. How do you know those hundreds or thousands of diverse types will work together? They're less like each other than like humans, even. They could be played off against each other."

"Maybe. But *that* would be going back onto the old road of treachery and violence, the road to Hell. Conversely, if every not-quite-human is called a 'mutant,' like a separate class, he'll think he is, and act accordingly against the lumped-together 'humans'. No, the only way to sanity—to *survival*— is to abandon class prejudice and race hate altogether, and work as individuals. We're all . . . well, Earthlings, and sub-classification is deadly. We all have to live together, and might as well make the best of it."

"Yeah . . . yeah, that's right too."

"Anyway, I repeat that all such attempts would be useless. All Earth is infected with mutation. It will be for a long time. The purest human stock will still produce mutants."

"Y-yes, that's true. Our best bet seems to be to find all such stock and withdraw it into the few safe areas left. It'll mean a small human population, but a *human* one."

"I tell you, that's impossible," clipped Drummond. "There is no safe place. Not one."

Robinson stopped pacing and looked at him as at a physical antagonist. "That so?" he almost growled. "Why?"

Drummond told him, adding incredulously, "Surely you knew that. Your physicists must have measured the amount of it. Your doctors, your engineers, that geneticist I dug up for you. You obviously got a lot of this biological information you've been slinging at me from him. They *must* all have told you the same thing."

Robinson shook his head stubbornly. "It can't be. It's not reasonable. The concentration wouldn't be great enough."

"Why, you poor fool, you need only look around you. The plants, the animals— Haven't there been any births in Taylor?"

"No. This is still a man's town, though women are trickling in and several babies are on the way—" Robinson's face was suddenly twisted with desperation. "Elaine's is due any time now. She's in the hospital here. Don't you see, our other kid died of the plague. This one's all we have. We want him to grow up in a world free of want and fear, a world of peace and sanity where he can play and laugh and become a man, not a beast starving in a cave. You and I are on our way out. We're the old generation, the one that wrecked the world. It's up to us to build it again, and then retire from it to let our children have it. The future's theirs. We've got to make it ready for them."

Sudden insight held Drummond motionless for long seconds. Understanding came, and pity, and an odd gentleness that changed his sunken bony face. "Yes," he murmured, "yes, I see. That's why you're working with all that's in you to build a normal, healthy world. That's why you nearly went crazy when this threat appeared. That . . . that's why you can't, just can't comprehend—"

He took the other man's arm and guided him toward the door. "Come on," he said. "Let's go see how your wife's making out. Maybe we can get her some flowers on the way."

§

The silent cold bit at them as they went down the street. Snow crackled underfoot. It was already grimy with town smoke and dust, but overhead the sky was incredibly clean and blue. Breath smoked whitely from their mouths and nostrils. The sound of men at work rebuilding drifted faintly between the bulking mountains.

"We couldn't emigrate to another planet, could we?" asked Robinson, and answered himself: "No, we lack the organization and resources to settle them right now. We'll have to make out on Earth. A few safe spots—there *must* be others besides this one—to house the true humans till the mutation period is over. Yes, we can do it."

"There are no safe places," insisted Drummond. "Even if there were, the mutants would still outnumber us. Does your geneticist have any idea how this'll come out, biologically speaking?"

"He doesn't know. His specialty is still largely unknown. He can make an intelligent guess, and that's all."

"Yeah. Anyway, our problem is to learn to live with the mutants, to accept anyone as—Earthling—no matter how he looks, to quit thinking anything was ever settled by violence or connivance, to build a culture of individual sanity. Funny," mused Drummond, "how the impractical virtues, tolerance and sympathy and generosity, have become the fundamental necessities of simple survival. I guess it was always true, but it took the death of half the world and the end of a biological era to make us see that simple little fact. The job's terrific. We've got half a million years of brutality and greed, superstition and prejudice, to lick in a few generations. If we fail, mankind is done. But we've got to try."

They found some flowers, potted in a house, and Robinson bought them with the last of his tobacco. By the time he reached the hospital, he was sweating. The sweat froze on his face as he walked.

The hospital was the town's biggest building, and fairly well equipped. A nurse met them as they entered.

"I was just going to send for you, General Robinson," she said. "The baby's on the way."

"How . . . is she?"

"Fine, so far. Just wait here, please."

Drummond sank into a chair and with haggard eyes watched Robinson's jerky pacing. *The poor guy. Why is it expectant fathers are supposed to be so funny? It's like laughing at a man on the rack. I know, Barbara, I know.*

"They have some anaesthetics," muttered the general. "They . . . Elaine never was very strong."

"She'll be all right." *It's afterward that worries me.*

"Yeah— Yeah— How long, though, how long?"

"Depends. Take it easy." With a wrench, Drummond made a sacrifice to a man he liked. He filled his pipe and handed it over. "Here, you need a smoke."

"Thanks." Robinson puffed raggedly.

The slow minutes passed, and Drummond wondered vaguely what he'd do when—it—happened. It didn't have to happen. But the chances were all against such an easy solution. He was no psychologist. Best just to let things happen as they would.

The waiting broke at last. A doctor came out, seeming an inscrutable high priest in his white garments. Robinson stood before him, motionless.

"You're a brave man," said the doctor. His face, as he removed the mask, was stern and set. "You'll need your courage."

"She—" It was hardly a human sound, that croak.

"Your wife is doing well. But the baby—"

A nurse brought out the little wailing form. It was a boy. But his limbs were rubbery tentacles terminating in boneless digits.

Robinson looked, and something went out of him as he stood there. When he turned, his face was dead.

"You're lucky," said Drummond, and meant it. He'd seen too many other mutants. "After all, if he can use those hands he'll get along all right. He'll even have an advantage in certain types of work. It isn't a deformity, really. If there's nothing else, you've got a good kid."

"*If!* You can't tell with mutants."

"I know. But you've got guts, you and Elaine. You'll see this through, together." Briefly, Drummond felt an utter personal desolation. He went on, perhaps to cover that emptiness:

"I see why you didn't understand the problem. You *wouldn't*. It was a psychological bloc, suppressing a fact you didn't dare face. That boy is really the center of your life. You couldn't think the truth about him, so your subconscious just refused to let you think rationally on that subject at all.

"Now you know. Now you realize there's no safe place, not on all the planet. The tremendous incidence of mutant births in the first generation could have told you that alone. Most such new characteristics are recessive, which means both parents have to have it for it to show in the zygote. But genetic changes are random, except for a tendency to fall into roughly similar patterns. Four-leaved clovers, for instance. Think how vast the total number of such changes must be, to produce so many corresponding changes in a couple of years. Think how many, *many* recessives there must be, existing only in gene patterns till their mates show up. We'll just have to take our chances of something really deadly accumulating. We'd never know till too late."

"The dust—"

"Yeah. The radiodust. It's colloidal, and uncountable other radiocolloids were formed when the bombs went off, and ordinary dirt gets into unstable isotopic forms near the craters. And there are radiogases too, probably. The poison is all over the world by now, spread by wind and air currents. Colloids can be suspended indefinitely in the atmosphere.

"The concentration isn't too high for life, though a physicist told me he'd measured it as being very near the safe limit and there'll probably be a lot of cancer. But it's everywhere. Every breath we draw, every crumb we eat and drop we drink, every clod we walk on, the dust is there. It's in the stratosphere, clear on down to the surface, probably a good distance below. We could only escape by sealing ourselves in air-conditioned vaults and wearing spacesuits whenever we got out, and under present conditions that's impossible.

"Mutations were rare before, because a charged particle has to get pretty close to a gene and be moving fast before its electromagnetic effect causes physico-chemical changes, and then that particular chromosome has to enter into reproduction. Now the charged particles, and the gamma rays producing still more, are everywhere. Even at the comparatively low concentration, the odds favor a given organism having so many cells changed that at least one will give rise to a mutant. There's even a good chance of like recessives meeting in the first generation, as we've seen. Nobody's safe, no place is free."

"The geneticist thinks some true humans will continue."

"A few, probably. After all, the radioactivity isn't too concentrated, and it's burning itself out. But it'll take fifty or a hundred years for the process to drop to insignificance, and by then the pure stock will be way in the minority. And there'll still be all those unmatched recessives, waiting to show up."

"You were right. We should never have created science. It brought the twilight of the race."

"I never said that. The race brought its own destruction, through misuse of science. Our culture was scientific anyway, in all except its psychological basis. It's up to us to take that last and hardest step. If we do, the race may yet survive."

Drummond gave Robinson a push toward the inner door. "You're exhausted, beat up, ready to quit. Go on in and see

Elaine. Give her my regards. Then take a long rest before going back to work. I still think you've got a good kid."

Mechanically, the *de facto* President of the United States left the room. Hugh Drummond stared after him a moment, then went out into the street.

POUL ANDERSON

The Queen of Air and Darkness

The last glow of the last sunset would linger almost until midwinter. But there would be no more day, and the northlands rejoiced. Blossoms opened, flamboyance on firethorn trees, steel-flowers rising blue from the brok and rainplant that cloaked all hills, shy whiteness of kiss-me-never down in the dales. Flitteries darted among them on iridescent wings; a crownbuck shook his horns and bugled. Between horizons the sky deepened from purple to sable. Both moons were aloft, nearly full, shining frosty on leaves and molten on waters. The shadows they made were blurred by an aurora, a great blowing curtain of light across half heaven. Behind it the earliest stars had come out.

A boy and a girl sat on Wolund's Barrow just under the dolmen it upbore. Their hair, which streamed halfway down their backs, showed startlingly forth, bleached as it was by summer. Their bodies, still dark from that season, merged with earth and bush and rock, for they wore only garlands. He played on a bone flute and she sang. They had lately become lovers. Their age was about sixteen, but they did not know this, considering themselves Outlings and thus indifferent to time, remembering little or nothing of how they had once dwelt in the lands of men.

His notes piped cold around her voice:

> "Cast a spell,
> weave it well
> of dust and dew
> and night and you."

§ 33

A brook by the grave mound, carrying moonlight down to a hill-hidden river, answered with its rapids. A flock of hellbats passed black beneath the aurora.

A shape came bounding over Cloudmoor. It had two arms and two legs, but the legs were long and claw-footed and feathers covered it to the end of a tail and broad wings. The face was half human, dominated by its eyes. Had Ayoch been able to stand wholly erect, he would have reached to the boy's shoulder.

The girl rose. "He carries a burden," she said. Her vision was not meant for twilight like that of a northland creature born, but she had learned how to use every sign her senses gave her. Besides the fact that ordinarily a pook would fly, there was a heaviness to his haste.

"And he comes from the south." Excitement jumped in the boy, sudden as a green flame that went across the constellation Lyrth. He sped down the mound. "Ohoi, Ayoch!" he called. "Me here, Mistherd!"

"And Shadow-of-a-Dream," the girl laughed, following.

The pook halted. He breathed louder than the soughing in the growth around him. A smell of bruised yerba lifted where he stood.

"Well met in winterbirth," he whistled. "You can help me bring this to Carheddin."

He held out what he bore. His eyes were yellow lanterns above. It moved and whimpered.

"Why, a child," Mistherd said.

"Even as you were, my son, even as you were. Ho, ho, what a snatch!" Ayoch boasted. "They were a score in yon camp by Fallowwood, armed, and besides watcher engines they had big ugly dogs aprowl while they slept. I came from above, however, having spied on them till I knew that a handful of dazedust—"

"The poor thing." Shadow-of-a-Dream took the boy and held him to her small breasts. "So full of sleep yet, aren't you?" Blindly, he sought a nipple. She smiled through the veil of her hair. "No, I am still too young, and you already too old.

But come, when you wake in Carheddin under the mountain, you shall feast."

"Yo-ah," said Ayoch very softly. "She is abroad and has heard and seen. She comes." He crouched down, wings folded. After a moment Mistherd knelt, and then Shadow-of-a-Dream, though she did not let go the child.

The Queen's tall form blocked off the moons. For a while she regarded the three and their booty. Hill and moor sounds withdrew from their awareness until it seemed they could hear the northlights hiss.

At last Ayoch whispered, "Have I done well, Starmother?"

"If you stole a babe from a camp full of engines," said the beautiful voice, "then they were folk out of the far south who may not endure it as meekly as yeomen."

"But what can they do, Snowmaker?" the pook asked. "How can they track us?"

Mistherd lifted his head and spoke in pride. "Also, now they too have felt the awe of us."

"And he is a cuddly dear," Shadow-of-a-Dream said. "And we need more like him, do we not, Lady Sky?"

"It had to happen in some twilight," agreed she who stood above. "Take him onward and care for him. By this sign," which she made, "is he claimed for the Dwellers."

Their joy was freed. Ayoch cartwheeled over the ground till he reached a shiverleaf. There he swarmed up the trunk and out on a limb, perched half hidden by unrestful pale foliage, and crowed. Boy and girl bore the child toward Carheddin at an easy distance-devouring lope which let him pipe and her sing:

"Wahaii, wahaii!
Wayala, laii!
Wing on the wind
high over heaven,
shrilly shrieking,
rush with the rainspears,
tumble through tumult,

drift to the moonhoar trees and the dream-heavy shadows
beneath them,
and rock in, be one with the clinking wavelets of lakes
where the starbeams drown."

§

As she entered, Barbro Cullen felt, through all grief and
fury, stabbed by dismay. The room was unkempt. Journals,
tapes, reels, codices, file boxes, bescribbled papers were piled
on every table. Dust filmed most shelves and corners. Against
one wall stood a laboratory setup, microscope and analytical
equipment. She recognized it as compact and efficient, but it
was not what you would expect in an office, and it gave the
air a faint chemical reek. The rug was threadbare, the furniture
shabby.

This was her final chance?

Then Eric Sherrinford approached. "Good day, Mrs. Cullen,"
he said. His tone was crisp, his handclasp firm. His faded
gripsuit didn't bother her. She wasn't inclined to fuss about
her own appearance except on special occasions. (And would
she ever again have one, unless she got back Jimmy?) What
she observed was a cat's personal neatness.

A smile radiated in crow's feet from his eyes. "Forgive my
bachelor housekeeping. On Beowulf we have—we had, at any
rate, machines for that, so I never acquired the habit myself,
and I don't want a hireling disarranging my tools. More convenient to work out of my apartment than keep a separate
office. Won't you be seated?"

"No, thanks. I couldn't," she mumbled.

"I understand. But if you'll excuse me, I function best in a
relaxed position."

He jackknifed into a lounger. One long shank crossed the
other knee. He drew forth a pipe and stuffed it from a pouch.
Barbro wondered why he took tobacco in so ancient a way.
Wasn't Beowulf supposed to have the up-to-date equipment
that they still couldn't afford to build on Roland? Well, of
course old customs might survive anyhow. They generally did

in colonies, she remembered reading. People had moved starward in the hope of preserving such outmoded things as their mother tongues or constitutional government or rational-technological civilization. . . .

Sherrinford pulled her up from the confusion of her weariness: "You must give me the details of your case, Mrs. Cullen. You've simply told me your son was kidnapped and your local constabulary did nothing. Otherwise, I know just a few obvious facts, such as your being widowed rather than divorced; and you're the daughter of outwayers in Olga Ivanoff Land, who nevertheless kept in close telecommunication with Christmas Landing; and you're trained in one of the biological professions; and you had several years' hiatus in field work until recently you started again."

She gaped at the high-cheeked, beak-nosed, black-haired and gray-eyed countenance. His lighter made a *scrit* and a flare which seemed to fill the room. Quietness dwelt on this height above the city, and winter dusk was seeping through the windows. "How in cosmos do you know that?" she heard herself exclaim.

He shrugged and fell into the lecturer's manner for which he was notorious. "My work depends on noticing details and fitting them together. In more than a hundred years on Roland, tending to cluster according to their origins and thought-habits, people have developed regional accents. You have a trace of the Olgan burr, but you nasalize your vowels in the style of this area, though you live in Portolondon. That suggests steady childhood exposure to metropolitan speech. You were part of Matsuyama's expedition, you told me, and took your boy along. They wouldn't have allowed any ordinary technician to do that; hence, you had to be valuable enough to get away with it. The team was conducting ecological research; therefore, you must be in the life sciences. For the same reason, you must have had previous field experience. But your skin is fair, showing none of the leatheriness one gets from prolonged exposure to this sun. Accordingly, you must have been mostly indoors for a good while before you went on your ill-fated trip.

As for widowhood—you never mentioned a husband to me, but you have had a man whom you thought so highly of that you still wear both the wedding and the engagement ring he gave you."

Her sight blurred and stung. The last of those words had brought Tim back; huge, ruddy, laughterful and gentle. She must turn from this other person and stare outward. "Yes," she achieved saying, "you're right."

The apartment occupied a hilltop above Christmas Landing. Beneath it the city dropped away in walls, roofs, archaistic chimneys and lamplit streets, goblin lights of human-piloted vehicles, to the harbor, the sweep of Venture Bay, ships bound to and from the Sunward Islands and remoter regions of the Boreal Ocean, which glimmered like mercury in the afterglow of Charlemagne. Oliver was swinging rapidly higher, a mottled orange disc a full degree wide; closer to the zenith which it could never reach, it would shine the color of ice. Alde, half the seeming size, was a thin slow crescent near Sirius, which she remembered was near Sol, but you couldn't see Sol without a telescope—

"Yes," she said around the pain in her throat, "my husband is about four years dead. I was carrying our first child when he was killed by a stampeding monocerus. We'd been married three years before. Met while we were both at the University —casts from School Central can only supply a basic education, you know— We founded our own team to do ecological studies under contract—you know, can a certain area be settled while maintaining a balance of nature, what crops will grow, what hazards, that sort of question— Well, afterward I did lab work for a fisher co-op in Portolondon. But the monotony, the . . . shut-in-ness . . . was eating me away. Professor Matsuyama offered me a position on the team he was organizing to examine Commissioner Hauch Land. I thought, God help me, I thought Jimmy—Tim wanted him named James, once the tests showed it'd be a boy, after his own father and because of 'Timmy and Jimmy' and —oh, I thought Jimmy could safely come along. I couldn't bear to leave him behind for months, not at his age.

We could make sure he'd never wander out of camp. What could hurt him inside it? *I* had never believed those stories about the Outlings stealing human children. I supposed parents were trying to hide from themselves the fact they'd been careless, they'd let a kid get lost in the woods or attacked by a pack of satans or—well, I learned better, Mr. Sherrinford. The guard robots were evaded and the dogs were drugged, and when I woke, Jimmy was gone."

He regarded her through the smoke from his pipe. Barbro Engdahl Cullen was a big woman of thirty or so (Rolandic years, he reminded himself, ninety-five percent of Terrestrial, not the same as Beowulfan years), broad-shouldered, long-legged, full-breasted, supple of stride; her face was wide, straight nose, straightforward hazel eyes, heavy but mobile mouth; her hair was reddish brown, cropped below the ears, her voice husky, her garment a plain street robe. To still the writhing of her fingers, he asked skeptically, "Do you now believe in the Outlings?"

"No. I'm just not so sure as I was." She swung about with half a glare for him. "And we have found traces."

"Bits of fossils," he nodded. "A few artifacts of a neolithic sort. But apparently ancient, as if the makers died ages ago. Intensive search has failed to turn up any real evidence for their survival."

"How intensive can search be, in a summer-stormy, winter-gloomy wilderness around the North Pole?" she demanded. "When we are, how many, a million people on an entire planet, half of us crowded into this one city?"

"And the rest crowding this one habitable continent," he pointed out.

"Arctica covers five million square kilometers," she flung back. "The Arctic Zone proper covers a fourth of it. We haven't the industrial base to establish satellite monitor stations, build aircraft we can trust in those parts, drive roads through the damned darklands and establish permanent bases and get to know them and tame them. Good Christ, generations of lonely outwaymen told stories about Graymantle, and the beast was never seen by a proper scientist till last year!"

"Still, you continue to doubt the reality of the Outlings?"

"Well, what about a secret cult among humans, born of isolation and ignorance, lairing in the wilderness, stealing children when they can for—" She swallowed. Her head drooped. "But you're supposed to be the expert."

"From what you told me over the visiphone, the Portolondon constabulary questions the accuracy of the report your group made, thinks the lot of you were hysterical, claims you must have omitted a due precaution, and the child toddled away and was lost beyond your finding."

His dry words pried the horror out of her. Flushing, she snapped, "Like any settler's kid? No. I didn't simply yell. I consulted Data Retrieval. A few too many such cases are recorded for accident to be a very plausible explanation. And shall we totally ignore the frightened stories about reappearances? But when I went back to the constabulary with my facts, they brushed me off. I suspect that was not entirely because they're undermanned. I think they're afraid too. They're recruited from country boys, and Portolondon lies near the edge of the unknown."

Her energy faded. "Roland hasn't got any central police force," she finished drably. "You're my last hope."

The man puffed smoke into twilight, with which it blent, before he said in a kindlier voice than hitherto: "Please don't make it a high hope, Mrs. Cullen. I'm the solitary private investigator on this world, having no resources beyond myself, and a newcomer to boot."

"How long have you been here?"

"Twelve years. Barely time to get a little familiarity with the relatively civilized coastlands. You settlers of a century or more—what do you, even, know about Arctica's interior?"

Sherrinford sighed. "I'll take the case, charging no more than I must, mainly for the sake of the experience," he said. "But only if you'll be my guide and assistant, however painful it will be for you."

"Of course! I dreaded waiting idle. Why me, though?"

"Hiring someone else as well qualified would be prohibitively expensive on a pioneer planet where every hand has a thousand urgent tasks to do. Besides, you have a motive. And I'll need that. As one who was born on another world altogether strange to this one, itself altogether strange to Mother Earth, I am too dauntingly aware of how handicapped we are."

Night gathered upon Christmas Landing. The air stayed mild, but glimmer-lit tendrils of fog, sneaking through the streets, had a cold look, and colder yet was the aurora where it shuddered between the moons. The woman drew closer to the man in this darkening room, surely not aware that she did, until he switched on a fluoropanel. The same knowledge of Roland's aloneness was in both of them.

§

One light-year is not much as galactic distances go. You could walk it in about 270 million years, beginning at the middle of the Permian Era, when dinosaurs belonged to the remote future, and continuing to the present day when spaceships cross even greater reaches. But stars in our neighborhood average some nine light-years apart, and barely one percent of them have planets which are man-habitable, and speeds are limited to less than that of radiation. Scant help is given by relativistic time contraction and suspended animation en route. These made the journeys seem short, but history meanwhile does not stop at home.

Thus voyages from sun to sun will always be few. Colonists will be those who have extremely special reasons for going. They will take along germ plasm for exogenetic cultivation of domestic plants and animals—and of human infants, in order that population can grow fast enough to escape death through genetic drift. After all, they cannot rely on further immigration. Two or three times a century, a ship may call from some other colony. (Not from Earth. Earth has long ago sunk into alien concerns.) Its place of origin will be an old settlement. The young ones are in no position to build and man interstellar vessels.

Their very survival, let alone their eventual modernization, is in doubt. The founding fathers have had to take what they could get, in a universe not especially designed for man.

Consider, for example, Roland. It is among the rare happy finds, a world where humans can live, breathe, eat the food, drink the water, walk unclad if they choose, sow their crops, pasture their beasts, dig their mines, erect their homes, raise their children and grandchildren. It is worth crossing three quarters of a light-century to preserve certain dear values and strike new roots into the soil of Roland.

But the star Charlemagne is of type F9, forty percent brighter than Sol, brighter still in the treacherous ultraviolet and wilder still in the wind of charged particles that seethes from it. The planet has an eccentric orbit. In the middle of the short but furious northern summer, which includes peri-astron, total insolation is more than double what Earth gets; in the depth of the long northern winter, it is barely less than Terrestrial average.

Native life is abundant everywhere. But lacking elaborate machinery, not yet economically possible to construct for more than a few specialists, man can only endure the high latitudes. A ten-degree axial tilt, together with the orbit, means that the northern part of the Arctican continent spends half its year in unbroken sunlessness. Around the South Pole lies an empty ocean.

Other differences from Earth might superficially seem more important, Roland has two moons, small but close, to evoke clashing tides. It rotates once in thirty-two hours, which is endlessly, subtly disturbing to organisms evolved through gigayears of a quicker rhythm. The weather patterns are alto-gether unterrestrial. The globe is a mere 9,500 kilometers in diameter; its surface gravity is 0.42×980 cm/sec^2; the sea level air pressure is slightly above one Earth atmosphere. (For actually, Earth is the freak, and man exists because a cosmic accident blew away most of the gas that a body its size ought to have kept, as Venus has done.)

However, Homo can truly be called sapiens when he practices his specialty of being unspecialized. His repeated attempts to freeze himself into an all-answering pattern or culture or ideology, or whatever he has named it, have repeatedly brought ruin. Give him the pragmatic business of making his living and he will usually do rather well. He adapts, within broad limits.

These limits are set by such factors as his need for sunlight and his being, necessarily and forever, a part of the life that surrounds him and a creature of the spirit within.

§

Portolondon thrust docks, boats, machinery, warehouses into the Gulf of Polaris. Behind them huddled the dwellings of its 5,000 permanent inhabitants: concrete walls, storm shutters, high-peaked tile roofs. The gaiety of their paint looked forlorn amidst lamps; this town lay past the Arctic Circle.

Nevertheless Sherrinford remarked, "Cheerful place, eh? The kind of thing I came to Roland looking for."

Barbro made no reply. The days in Christmas Landing, while he made his preparations, had drained her. Gazing out the dome of the taxi that was whirring them downtown from the hydrofoil that brought them, she supposed he meant the lushness of forest and meadows along the road, brilliant hues and phosphorescence of flowers in gardens, clamor of wings overhead. Unlike Terrestrial flora in cold climates, Arctican vegetation spends every daylit hour in frantic growth and energy storage. Not till summer's fever gives place to gentle winter does it bloom and fruit; and estivating animals rise from their dens and migratory birds come home.

The view was lovely, she had to admit: beyond the trees, a spaciousness climbing toward remote heights, silvery gray under a moon, an aurora, the diffuse radiance from a sun just below the horizon.

Beautiful as a hunting satan, she thought, and as terrible. That wilderness had stolen Jimmy. She wondered if she would at least be given to find his little bones and take them to his father.

Abruptly she realized that she and Sherrinford were at their hotel and that he had been speaking of the town. Since it was next in size after the capital, he must have visited here often before. The streets were crowded and noisy; signs flickered, music blared from shops, taverns, restaurants, sports centers, dance halls; vehicles were jammed down to molasses speed; the several-stories-high office buildings stood aglow. Portolondon linked an enormous hinterland to the outside world. Down the Gloria River came timber rafts, ores, harvest of farms whose owners were slowly making Rolandic life serve them, meat and ivory and furs gathered by rangers in the mountains beyond Troll Scarp. In from the sea came coastwise freighters, the fishing fleet, produce of the Sunward Islands, plunder of whole continents farther south where bold men adventured. It clanged in Portolondon, laughed, blustered, connived, robbed, preached, guzzled, swilled, toiled, dreamed, lusted, built, destroyed, died, was born, was happy, angry, sorrowful, greedy, vulgar, loving, ambitious, human. Neither the sun's blaze elsewhere nor the half year's twilight here—wholly night around midwinter—was going to stay man's hand.

Or so everybody said.

Everybody except those who had settled in the darklands. Barbro used to take for granted that they were evolving curious customs, legends, and superstitions, which would die when the outway had been completely mapped and controlled. Of late, she had wondered. Perhaps Sherrinford's hints, about a change in his own attitude brought about by his preliminary research, were responsible.

Or perhaps she just needed something to think about besides how Jimmy, the day before he went, when she asked him whether he wanted rye or French bread for a sandwich, answered in great solemnity—he was becoming interested in the alphabet—"I'll have a slice of what we people call the F bread."

She scarcely noticed getting out of the taxi, registering, being conducted to a primitively furnished room. But after she unpacked, she remembered Sherrinford had suggested a confidential conference. She went down the hall and knocked on his door. Her knuckles sounded less loud than her heart.

He opened the door, finger on lips, and gestured her toward a corner. Her temper bristled until she saw the image of Chief Constable Dawson in the visiphone. Sherrinford must have chimed him up and must have a reason to keep her out of scanner range. She found a chair and watched, nails digging into knees.

The detective's lean length refolded itself. "Pardon the interruption," he said. "A man mistook the number. Drunk, by the indications."

Dawson chuckled. "We get plenty of those." Barbro recalled his fondness for gabbing. He tugged the beard which he affected, as if he were an outwayer instead of a townsman. "No harm in them as a rule. They only have a lot of voltage to discharge, after weeks or months in the backlands."

"I've gathered that that environment—foreign in a million major and minor ways to the one that created man—I've gathered that it does do odd things to the personality." Sherrinford tamped his pipe. "Of course, you know my practice has been confined to urban and suburban areas. Isolated garths seldom need private investigators. Now that situation appears to have changed. I called to ask you for advice."

"Glad to help," Dawson said. "I've not forgotten what you did for us in the de Tahoe murder case." Cautiously: "Better explain your problem first."

Sherrinford struck fire. The smoke that followed cut through the green odors—even here, a paved pair of kilometers from the nearest woods—that drifted past traffic rumble through a crepuscular window. "This is more a scientific mission than a search for an absconding debtor or an industrial spy," he drawled. "I'm looking into two possibilities: that an organization, criminal or religious or whatever, has long been active and steals infants; or that the Outlings of folklore are real."

"Huh?" On Dawson's face Barbro read as much dismay as surprise. "You can't be serious!"

"Can't I?" Sherrinford smiled. "Several generations' worth of reports shouldn't be dismissed out of hand. Especially not when they become more frequent and consistent in the course of time, not less. Nor can we ignore the documented loss of babies and small children, amounting by now to over a hundred, and never a trace found afterward. Nor the finds which demonstrate that an intelligent species once inhabited Arctica and may still haunt the interior."

Dawson leaned forward as if to climb out of the screen. "Who engaged you?" he demanded. "That Cullen woman? We were sorry for her, naturally, but she wasn't making sense, and when she got downright abusive—"

"Didn't her companions, reputable scientists, confirm her story?"

"No story to confirm. Look, they had the place ringed with detectors and alarms, and they kept mastiffs. Standard procedure in country where a hungry sauroid or whatever might happen by. Nothing could've entered unbeknownst."

"On the ground. How about a flyer landing in the middle of camp?"

"A man in a copter rig would've roused everybody."

"A winged being might be quieter."

"A living flyer that could lift a three-year-old boy? Doesn't exist."

"Isn't in the scientific literature, you mean, Constable. Remember Graymantle; remember how little we know about Roland, a planet, an entire world. Such birds do exist on Beowulf—and on Rustum, I've read. I made a calculation from the local ratio of air density to gravity, and, yes, it's marginally possible here too. The child could have been carried off for a short distance before wing muscles were exhausted and the creature must descend."

Dawson snorted. "First it landed and walked into the tent

where mother and boy were asleep. Then it walked away, toting him, after it couldn't fly further. Does that sound like a bird of prey? And the victim didn't cry out, the dogs didn't bark!"

"As a matter of fact," Sherrinford said, "those inconsistencies are the most interesting and convincing features of the whole account. You're right, it's hard to see how a human kidnapper could get in undetected, and an eagle type of creature wouldn't operate in that fashion. But none of this applies to a winged intelligent being. The boy could have been drugged. Certainly the dogs showed signs of having been."

"The dogs showed signs of having overslept. Nothing had disturbed them. The kid wandering by wouldn't do so. We don't need to assume one damn thing except, first, that he got restless and, second, that the alarms were a bit sloppily rigged —seeing as how no danger was expected from inside camp— and let him pass out. And, third, I hate to speak this way, but we must assume the poor tyke starved or was killed."

Dawson paused before adding: "If we had more staff, we could have given the affair more time. And would have, of course. We did make an aerial sweep, which risked the lives of the pilots, using instruments which would've spotted the kid anywhere in a fifty-kilometer radius, unless he was dead. You know how sensitive thermal analyzers are. We drew a complete blank. We have more important jobs than to hunt for the scattered pieces of a corpse."

He finished brusquely. "If Mrs. Cullen's hired you, my advice is you find an excuse to quit. Better for her, too. She's got to come to terms with reality."

Barbro checked a shout by biting her tongue.

"Oh, this is merely the latest disappearance of the series," Sherrinford said. She didn't understand how he could maintain his easy tone when Jimmy was lost. "More thoroughly recorded than any before, thus more suggestive. Usually an outwayer family has given a tearful but undetailed account of their child who vanished and must have been stolen by the Old Folk. Sometimes, years later, they'd tell about glimpses of what they swore must have been the grown child, not really human any longer, flitting past in murk or peering through a window or working mischief upon them. As you say, neither the authorities nor the scientists have had personnel or resources to mount a proper investigation. But as I say, the matter appears to be worth investigating. Maybe a private party like myself can contribute."

"Listen, most of us constables grew up in the outway. We don't just ride patrol and answer emergency calls; we go back there for holidays and reunions. If any gang of . . . of human sacrificers was around, we'd know."

"I realize that. I also realize that the people you came from have a widespread and deep-seated belief in nonhuman beings with supernatural powers. Many actually go through rites and make offerings to propitiate them."

"I know what you're leading up to," Dawson flared. "I've heard it before, from a hundred sensationalists. The aborigines are the Outlings. I thought better of you. Surely you've visited a museum or three, surely you've read literature from planets which do have natives—or damn and blast, haven't you ever applied that logic of yours?"

He wagged a finger. "Think," he said. "What have we in fact discovered? A few pieces of worked stone; a few megaliths that might be artificial; scratchings on rock that seem to show plants and animals, though not the way any human culture would ever have shown them; traces of fires and broken bones; other fragments of bone that seem as if they might've belonged to thinking creatures, as if they might've been inside fingers or around big brains. If so, however, the owners looked nothing like men. Or angels, for that matter. Nothing! The most anthropoid reconstruction I've seen shows a kind of two-legged crocagator.

"Wait, let me finish. The stories about the Outlings—oh, I've heard them too, plenty of them. I believed them when I was a kid—the stories tell how there're different kinds, some winged, some not, some half human, some completely human except maybe for being too handsome— It's fairyland from ancient Earth all over again. Isn't it? I got interested once and dug into the Heritage Library microfiles, and be damned if I didn't find almost the identical yarns, told by peasants centuries before spaceflight.

"None of it squares with the scanty relics we have, if they are relics, or with the fact that no area the size of Arctica could spawn a dozen different intelligent species, or . . . hellfire, man, with the way your common sense tells you aborigines would behave when humans arrived!"

Sherrinford nodded. "Yes, yes," he said. "I'm less sure than you that the common sense of nonhuman beings is precisely like our own. I've seen so much variation within mankind. But, granted, your arguments are strong. Roland's too few scientists have more pressing tasks than tracking down the origins of what is, as you put it, a revived medieval superstition."

He cradled his pipe bowl in both hands and peered into the tiny hearth of it. "Perhaps what interests me most," he said softly, "is why—across that gap of centuries, across a barrier of machine civilization and its utterly antagonistic world view—no continuity of tradition whatsoever—why have hard-headed, technologically organized, reasonably well-educated colonists here brought back from its grave a belief in the Old Folk?"

"I suppose eventually, if the University ever does develop the psychology department they keep talking about, I suppose eventually somebody will get a thesis out of your question." Dawson spoke in a jagged voice, and he gulped when Sherrinford replied:

"I propose to begin now. In Commissioner Hauch Land, since that's where the latest incident occurred. Where can I rent a vehicle?"

"Uh, might be hard to do—"

"Come, come. Tenderfoot or not, I know better. In an economy of scarcity, few people own heavy equipment. But since it's needed, it can always be rented. I want a camper bus with a ground-effect drive suitable for every kind of terrain. And I want certain equipment installed which I've brought along, and the top canopy section replaced by a gun turret controllable from the driver's seat. But I'll supply the weapons. Besides rifles and pistols of my own, I've arranged to borrow some artillery from Christmas Landing's police arsenal."

"Hoy? Are you genuinely intending to make ready for . . . a war . . . against a myth?"

"Let's say I'm taking out insurance, which isn't terribly expensive, against a remote possibility. Now, besides the bus, what about a light aircraft carried piggyback for use in surveys?"

"No." Dawson sounded more positive than hitherto. "That's asking for disaster. We can have you flown to a base camp in a large plane when the weather report's exactly right. But the pilot will have to fly back at once, before the weather turns wrong again. Meteorology's underdeveloped on Roland; the air's especially treacherous this time of year, and we're not tooled up to produce aircraft that can outlive every surprise." He drew breath. "Have you no idea of how fast a whirly-whirly can hit, or what size hailstones might strike from a clear sky, or—? Once you're there, man, you stick to the ground." He hesitated. "That's an important reason our information is so scanty about the outway, and its settlers are so isolated."

Sherrinford laughed ruefully. "Well, I suppose if details are what I'm after, I must creep along anyway."

"You'll waste a lot of time," Dawson said. "Not to mention your client's money. Listen, I can't forbid you to chase shadows, but—"

The discussion went on for almost an hour. When the screen finally blanked, Sherrinford rose, stretched, and walked toward Barbro. She noticed anew his peculiar gait. He had come from a planet with a fourth again of Earth's gravitational drag, to one where weight was less than half Terrestrial. She wondered if he had flying dreams.

"I apologize for shuffling you off like that," he said. "I didn't expect to reach him at once. He was quite truthful about how busy he is. But having made contact, I didn't want to remind him overmuch of you. He can dismiss my project as a futile fantasy which I'll soon give up. But he might have frozen completely, might even have put up obstacles before us, if he'd realized through you how determined we are."

"Why should he care?" she asked in her bitterness.

"Fear of consequences, the worse because it is unadmitted—fear of consequences, the more terrifying because they are unguessable." Sherrinford's gaze went to the screen, and thence out the window to the aurora pulsing in glacial blue and white immensely far overhead. "I suppose you saw I was talking to a frightened man. Down underneath his conventionality and scoffing, he believes in the Outlings—oh, yes, he believes."

§

The feet of Mistherd flew over yerba and outpaced wind-blown driftweed. Beside him, black and misshapen, hulked Nagrim the nicor, whose earthquake weight left a swath of crushed plants. Behind, luminous blossoms of a firethorn shone through the twining, trailing outlines of Morgarel the wraith.

Here Cloudmoor rose in a surf of hills and thickets. The air lay quiet, now and then carrying the distance-muted howl of a beast. It was darker than usual at winterbirth, the moons being down and aurora a wan flicker above mountains on the northern world-edge. But this made the stars keen, and their numbers crowded heaven, and Ghost Road shone among them as if it, like the leafage beneath, were paved with dew.

"Yonder!" bawled Nagrim. All four of his arms pointed. The party had topped a ridge. Far off glimmered a spark. "Hoah, hoah! 'Ull we right off stamp dem flat, or pluck dem apart slow?"

We shall do nothing of the sort, bonebrain, Morgarel's answer slid through their heads. *Not unless they attack us, and they will not unless we make them aware of us, and her command is that we spy out their purposes.*

"Gr-r-rum-m-m. I know deir aim. Cut down trees, stick plows in land, sow deir cursed seed in de clods and in deir shes. 'Less we drive dem into de bitterwater, and soon, soon, dey'll wax too strong for us."

"Not too strong for the Queen!" Mistherd protested, shocked.

Yet they do have new powers, it seems, Morgarel reminded him. *Carefully must we probe them.*

"Den carefully can we step on dem?" asked Nagrim.

The question woke a grin out of Mistherd's own uneasiness. He slapped the scaly back. "Don't talk, you," he said. "It hurts my ears. Nor think; that hurts your head. Come, run!"

Ease yourself, Morgarel scolded. *You have too much life in you, human-born.*

Mistherd made a face at the wraith, but obeyed to the extent of slowing down and picking his way through what cover the country afforded. For he traveled on behalf of the Fairest, to learn what had brought a pair of mortals questing hither.

Did they seek that boy whom Ayoch stole? (He continued to weep for his mother, though less and less often as the marvels of Carheddin entered him.) Perhaps. A birdcraft had left them and their car at the now-abandoned campsite, from which they had followed an outward spiral. But when no trace of the cub had appeared inside a reasonable distance, they did not call to be flown home. And this wasn't because weather forbade the farspeaker waves to travel, as was frequently the case. No, instead the couple set off toward the mountains of Moonhorn. Their course would take them past a few outlying invader steadings and on into realms untrodden by their race.

So this was no ordinary survey. Then what was it?

Mistherd understood now why she who reigned had made her adopted mortal children learn, or retain, the clumsy language of their forebears. He had hated that drill, wholly foreign to Dweller ways. Of course, you obeyed her, and in time you saw how wise she had been. . . .

Presently he left Nagrim behind a rock—the nicor would only be useful in a fight—and crawled from bush to bush until he lay within man-lengths of the humans. A rainplant drooped over him, leaves soft on his bare skin, and clothed him in darkness. Morgarel floated to the crown of a shiverleaf, whose unrest would better conceal his flimsy shape. He'd not be much help either. And that was the most troublous, the almost appalling thing here. Wraiths were among those who could not just sense and send thought, but cast illusions. Morgarel had reported that this time his power seemed to rebound off an invisible cold wall around the car.

Otherwise the male and female had set up no guardian engines and kept no dogs. Belike they supposed none would be needed, since they slept in the long vehicle which bore them. But such contempt of the Queen's strength could not be tolerated, could it?

Metal sheened faintly by the light of their campfire. They sat on either side, wrapped in coats against a coolness that Mistherd, naked, found mild. The male drank smoke. The female stared past him into a dusk which her flame-dazzled eyes must see as thick gloom. The dancing glow brought her vividly forth. Yes, to judge from Ayoch's tale, she was the dam of the new cub.

Ayoch had wanted to come too, but the Wonderful One forbade. Pooks couldn't hold still long enough for such a mission.

The man sucked on his pipe. His cheeks thus pulled into shadow while the light flickered across nose and brow, he looked disquietingly like a shearbill about to stoop on prey.

"—No, I tell you again, Barbro, I have no theories," he was saying. "When facts are insufficient, theorizing is ridiculous at best, misleading at worst."

"Still, you must have some idea of what you're doing," she said. It was plain that they had threshed this out often before. No Dweller could be as persistent as she or as patient as he. "That gear you packed—that generator you keep running—"

"I have a working hypothesis or two, which suggested what equipment I ought to take."

"Why won't you tell me what the hypotheses are?"

"They themselves indicate that that might be inadvisable at

the present time. I'm still feeling my way into the labyrinth. And I haven't had a chance yet to hook everything up. In fact, we're really only protected against so-called telepathic influence—"

"What?" She started. "Do you mean . . . those legends about how they can read minds too—" Her words trailed off and her gaze sought the darkness beyond his shoulders.

He leaned forward. His tone lost its clipped rapidity, grew earnest and soft. "Barbro, you're racking yourself to pieces. Which is no help to Jimmy if he's alive, the more so when you may well be badly needed later on. We've a long trek before us, and you'd better settle into it."

She nodded jerkily and caught her lip between her teeth for a moment before she answered, "I'm trying."

He smiled around his pipe. "I expect you'll succeed. You don't strike me as a quitter or a whiner or an enjoyer of misery."

She dropped a hand to the pistol at her belt. Her voice changed; it came out of her throat like knife from sheath. "When we find them, they'll know what I am. What humans are."

"Put anger aside also," the man urged. "We can't afford emotions. If the Outlings are real, as I told you I'm provisionally assuming, they're fighting for their homes." After a short stillness he added: "I like to think that if the first explorers had found live natives, men would not have colonized Roland. But it's too late now. We can't go back if we wanted to. It's a bitter-end struggle, against an enemy so crafty that he's even hidden from us the fact that he is waging war."

"Is he? I mean, skulking, kidnapping an occasional child—"

"That's part of my hypothesis. I suspect those aren't harassments; they're tactics employed in a chillingly subtle strategy."

The fire sputtered and sparked. The man smoked awhile, brooding, until he went on:

"I didn't want to raise your hopes or excite you unduly while you had to wait on me, first in Christmas Landing, then in Portolondon. Afterward we were busy satisfying ourselves that

Jimmy had been taken farther from camp than he could have wandered before collapsing. So I'm only now telling you how thoroughly I studied available material on the . . . Old Folk. Besides, at first I did it on the principle of eliminating every imaginable possibility, however absurd. I expected no result other than final disproof. But I went through everything, relics, analyses, histories, journalistic accounts, monographs; I talked to outwayers who happened to be in town and to what scientists we have who've taken any interest in the matter. I'm a quick study. I flatter myself I became as expert as anyone— though God knows there's little to be expert on. Furthermore, I, a comparative stranger to Roland, maybe looked on the problem with fresh eyes. And a pattern emerged for me.

"If the aborigines had become extinct, why hadn't they left more remnants? Arctica isn't enormous, and it's fertile for Rolandic life. It ought to have supported a population whose artifacts ought to have accumulated over millennia. I've read that on Earth, literally tens of thousands of paleolithic hand axes were found, more by chance than archeology.

"Very well. Suppose the relics and fossils were deliberately removed, between the time the last survey party left and the first colonizing ships arrived. I did find some support for that idea in the diaries of the original explorers. They were too preoccupied with checking the habitability of the planet to make catalogues of primitive monuments. However, the remarks they wrote down indicate they saw much more than later arrivals did. Suppose what we have found is just what the removers overlooked or didn't get around to.

"That argues a sophisticated mentality, thinking in long-range terms, doesn't it? Which in turn argues that the Old Folk were not mere hunters or neolithic farmers."

"But nobody ever saw buildings or machines or any such thing," Barbro objected.

"No. Most likely the natives didn't go through our kind of metallurgic-industrial evolution. I can conceive of other paths to take. Their full-fledged civilization might have begun, rather than ended, in biological science and technology. It might have developed potentialities of the nervous system, which might be greater in their species than in man. We have those abilities to some degree ourselves, you realize. A dowser, for instance, actually senses variations in the local magnetic field caused by a water table. However, in us, these talents are maddeningly rare and tricky. So we took our business elsewhere. Who needs to be a telepath, say, when he has a visiphone? The Old Folk may have seen it the other way around. The artifacts of their civilization may have been, may still be unrecognizable to men."

"They could have identified themselves to the men, though," Barbro said. "Why didn't they?"

"I can imagine any number of reasons. As, they could have had a bad experience with interstellar visitors earlier in their history. Ours is scarcely the sole race that has spaceships. However, I told you I don't theorize in advance of the facts. Let's say no more than that the Old Folk, if they exist, are alien to us."

"For a rigorous thinker, you're spinning a mighty thin thread."

"I've admitted this is entirely provisional." He squinted at her through a roil of campfire smoke. "You came to me, Barbro, insisting in the teeth of officialdom that your boy had been stolen, but your own talk about cultist kidnappers was ridiculous. Why are you reluctant to admit the reality of nonhumans?"

"In spite of the fact that Jimmy's being alive probably depends on it," she sighed. "I don't know."

A shudder. "Maybe I don't dare admit it."

"I've said nothing thus far that hasn't been speculated about in print," he told her. "A disreputable speculation, true. In a hundred years, nobody has found valid evidence for the Outlings being more than a superstition. Still, a few people have declared it's at least possible that intelligent natives are at large in the wilderness."

"I know," she repeated. "I'm not sure, though, what has made you, overnight, take those arguments seriously."

"Well, once you got me started thinking, it occurred to me that Roland's outwayers are not utterly isolated medieval crofters. They have books, telecommunications, power tools, motor vehicles; above all, they have a modern science-oriented education. Why *should* they turn superstitious? Something must be causing it." He stopped. "I'd better not continue. My ideas go further than this; but if they're correct, it's dangerous to speak them aloud."

Mistherd's belly muscles tensed. There was danger for fair, in that shearbill head. The Garland Bearer must be warned. For a minute he wondered about summoning Nagrim to kill these two. If the nicor jumped them fast, their firearms might avail them naught. But no. They might have left word at home, or— He came back to his ears. The talk had changed course. Barbro was murmuring, "—why you stayed on Roland."

The man smiled his gaunt smile. "Well, life on Beowulf held no challenge for me. Heorot is—or was; this was decades past, remember—Heorot was densely populated, smoothly organized, boringly uniform. That was partly due to the lowland frontier, a safety valve that bled off the dissatisfied. But I lack the carbon dioxide tolerance necessary to live healthily down there. An expedition was being readied to make a swing around a number of colony worlds, especially those which didn't have the equipment to keep in laser contact. You'll recall its announced purpose, to seek out new ideas in science, arts, sociology, philosophy, whatever might prove valuable. I'm afraid they found little on Roland relevant to Beowulf. But I, who had wangled a berth, I saw opportunities for myself and decided to make my home here."

"Were you a detective back there, too?"

"Yes, in the official police. We had a tradition of such work in our family. Some of that may have come from the Cherokee side of it, if the name means anything to you. However, we also claimed collateral descent from one of the first private inquiry agents on record, back on Earth before spaceflight. Regardless of how true that may be, I found him a useful model. You see, an archetype—"

The man broke off. Unease crossed his features. "Best we go to sleep," he said. "We've a long distance to cover in the morning."

She looked outward. "Here is no morning."

They retired. Mistherd rose and cautiously flexed limberness back into his muscles. Before returning to the Sister of Lyrth, he risked a glance through a pane in the car. Bunks were made up, side by side, and the humans lay in them. Yet the man had not touched her, though hers was a bonny body, and nothing that had passed between them suggested he meant to do so.

Eldritch, humans. Cold and claylike. And they would overrun the beautiful wild world? Mistherd spat in disgust. It must not happen. It would not happen. She who reigned had vowed that.

§

The lands of William Irons were immense. But this was because a barony was required to support him, his kin and cattle, on native crops whose cultivation was still poorly understood. He raised some Terrestrial plants as well, by summerlight and in conservatories. However, these were a luxury. The true conquest of northern Arctica lay in yerba hay, in bathyrhiza wood, in pericoup and glycophyllon, and eventually, when the market had expanded with population and industry, in chalcanthemum for city florists and pelts of cage-bred rover for city furriers.

That was in a tomorrow Irons did not expect that he would live to see. Sherrinford wondered if the man really expected anyone ever would.

The room was warm and bright. Cheerfulness crackled in the fireplace. Light from fluoropanels gleamed off hand-carven chests and chairs and tables, off colorful draperies and shelved dishes. The outwayer sat solid in his high seat, stoutly clad, beard flowing down his chest. His wife and daughters brought coffee, whose fragrance joined the remnant odors of a hearty supper, to him, his guests, and his sons.

But outside, wind hooted, lightning flared, thunder bawled, rain crashed on roof and walls and roared down to swirl among the courtyard cobblestones. Sheds and barns crouched against hugeness beyond. Trees groaned, and did a wicked undertone of laughter run beneath the lowing of a frightened cow? A burst of hailstones hit the tiles like knocking knuckles.

You could feel how distant your neighbors were, Sherrinford thought. And nonetheless they were the people whom you saw oftenest, did daily business with by visiphone (when a solar storm didn't make gibberish of their voices and chaos of their faces) or in the flesh, partied with, gossiped and intrigued with, intermarried with; in the end, they were the people who would bury you. The lights of the coastal towns were monstrously farther away.

William Irons was a strong man. Yet when now he spoke, fear was in his tone. "You'd truly go over Troll Scarp?"

"Do you mean Hanstein Palisades?" Sherrinford responded, more challenge than question.

"No outwayer calls it anything but Troll Scarp," Barbro said.

And how had a name like that been reborn, light-years and centuries from Earth's Dark Ages?

"Hunters, trappers, prospectors—rangers, you call them—travel in those mountains," Sherrinford declared.

"In certain parts," Irons said. "That's allowed, by a pact once made 'tween a man and the Queen after he'd done well by a jack-o'-the-hill that a satan had hurt. Wherever the plumablanca grows, men may fare, if they leave man-goods on the altar boulders in payment for what they take out of the land. Elsewhere—" one fist clenched on a chair arm and went slack again—"'s not wise to go."

"It's been done, hasn't it?"

"Oh, yes. And some came back all right, or so they claimed, though I've heard they were never lucky afterward. And some didn't; they vanished. And some who returned babbled of wonders and horrors, and stayed witlings the rest of their lives. Not for a long time has anybody been rash enough to break the pact and overtread the bounds." Irons looked at Barbro almost entreatingly. His woman and children stared likewise, grown still. Wind hooted beyond the walls and rattled the storm shutters. "Don't you."

"I've reason to believe my son is there," she answered.

"Yes, yes, you've told and I'm sorry. Maybe something can be done. I don't know what, but I'd be glad to, oh, lay a double offering on Unvar's Barrow this midwinter, and a prayer drawn in the turf by a flint knife. Maybe they'll return him." Irons sighed. "They've not done such a thing in man's memory, though. And he could have a worse lot. I've glimpsed them myself, speeding madcap through twilight. They seem happier than we are. Might be no kindness, sending your boy home again."

"Like in the Arvid song," said his wife.

Irons nodded. "M-hm. Or others, come to think of it."

"What's this?" Sherrinford asked. More sharply than before, he felt himself a stranger. He was a child of cities and technics, above all a child of the skeptical intelligence. This family *believed*. It was disquieting to see more than a touch of their acceptance in Barbro's slow nod.

"We have the same ballad in Olga Ivanoff Land," she told him, her voice less calm than the words. "It's one of the traditional ones—nobody knows who composed them— that are sung to set the measure of a ring-dance in a meadow."

"I noticed a multilyre in your baggage, Mrs. Cullen," said the wife of Irons. She was obviously eager to get off the explosive topic of a venture in defiance of the Old Folk. A songfest could help. "Would you like to entertain us?"

Barbro shook her head, white around the nostrils. The oldest boy said quickly, rather importantly, "Well, sure, I can, if our guests would like to hear."

"I'd enjoy that, thank you." Sherrinford leaned back in his seat and stoked his pipe. If this had not happened spontaneously, he would have guided the conversation toward a similar outcome.

In the past he had had no incentive to study the folklore

of the outway, and not much chance to read the scanty references on it since Barbro brought him her trouble. Yet more and more he was becoming convinced that he must get an understanding—not an anthropological study, but a feel from the inside out—of the relationship between Roland's frontiersmen and those beings which haunted them.

A bustling followed, rearrangement, settling down to listen, coffee cups refilled and brandy offered on the side. The boy explained, "The last line is the chorus. Everybody join in, right?" Clearly he too hoped thus to bleed off some of the tension. Catharsis through music? Sherrinford wondered, and added to himself: No; exorcism.

A girl strummed a guitar. The boy sang, to a melody which beat across the storm noise:

> "It was the ranger Arvid
> rode homeward through the hills
> among the shadowy shiverleafs,
> along the chiming rills.
>> *The dance weaves under the firethorn.*

> "The night wind whispered around him
> with scent of brok and rue.
> Both moons rose high above him
> and hills aflash with dew.
>> *The dance weaves under the firethorn.*

> "And dreaming of that woman
> who waited in the sun,
> he stopped, amazed by starlight,
> and so he was undone.
>> *The dance weaves under the firethorn.*

> "For there beneath a barrow
> that bulked athwart a moon,
> the Outling folk were dancing
> in glass and golden shoon.
>> *The dance weaves under the firethorn.*

> "The Outling folk were dancing
> like water, wind, and fire
> to frosty-ringing harpstrings,
> and never did they tire.
>> *The dance weaves under the firethorn.*

"To Arvid came she striding
from where she watched the dance,
the Queen of Air and Darkness,
with starlight in her glance.
   The dance weaves under the firethorn.

"With starlight, love, and terror
in her immortal eye,
the Queen of Air and Darkness—"

"No!" Barbro leaped from her chair. Her fists were clenched and tears flogged her cheekbones. "You can't—pretend that—about the things that stole Jimmy!"

She fled from the chamber, upstairs to her guest bedroom.

§

But she finished the song herself. That was about seventy hours later, camped in the steeps where rangers dared not fare.

She and Sherrinford had not said much to the Irons family, after refusing repeated pleas to leave the forbidden country alone. Nor had they exchanged many remarks at first as they drove north. Slowly, however, he began to draw her out about her own life. After a while she almost forgot to mourn, in her remembering of home and old neighbors. Somehow this led to discoveries—that he, beneath his professorial manner, was a gourmet and a lover of opera and appreciated her femaleness; that she could still laugh and find beauty in the wild land around her—and she realized, half guiltily, that life held more hopes than even the recovery of the son Tim gave her.

"I've convinced myself he's alive," the detective said. He scowled. "Frankly, it makes me regret having taken you along, I expected this would be only a fact-gathering trip, but it's turning out to be more. If we're dealing with real creatures who stole him, they can do real harm. I ought to turn back to the nearest garth and call for a plane to fetch you."

"Like bottommost hell you will, mister," she said. "You

need somebody who knows outway conditions, and I'm a better shot than average."

"M-m-m . . . it would involve considerable delay too, wouldn't it? Besides the added distance, I can't put a signal through to any airport before this current burst of solar interference has calmed down."

Next "night" he broke out his remaining equipment and set it up. She recognized some of it, such as the thermal detector. Other items were strange to her, copied to his order from the advanced apparatus of his birthworld. He would tell her little about them. "I've explained my suspicion that the ones we're after have telepathic capabilities," he said in apology.

Her eyes widened. "You mean it could be true, the Queen and her people can read minds?"

"That's part of the dread which surrounds their legend, isn't it? Actually there's nothing spooky about the phenomenon. It was studied and fairly well defined centuries ago, on Earth. I dare say the facts are available in the scientific microfiles at Christmas Landing. You Rolanders have simply had no occasion to seek them out, any more than you've yet had occasion to look up how to build power-beamcasters or spacecraft."

"Well, how does telepathy work, then?"

Sherrinford recognized that her query asked for comfort as much as it did for facts, and he spoke with deliberate dryness: "The organism generates extremely long-wave radiation which can, in principle, be modulated by the nervous system. In practice, the feebleness of the signals and their low rate of information transmission make them elusive, hard to detect and measure. Our prehuman ancestors went in for more reliable senses, like vision and hearing. What telepathic transceiving we do is marginal at best. But explorers have found extraterrestrial species that got an evolutionary advantage from developing the system further, in their particular environments. I imagine such species could include one which gets comparatively little direct sunlight—in fact, appears to hide from broad day. It could even become so able in this regard that, at short range, it can pick up man's weak emissions and make man's primitive sensitivities resonate to its own strong sendings."

"That would account for a lot, wouldn't it?" Barbro said faintly.

"I've now screened our car by a jamming field," Sherrinford told her, "but it reaches only a few meters past the chassis. Beyond, a scout of theirs might get a warning from your thoughts, if you knew precisely what I'm trying to do. I have a well-trained subconscious which sees to it that I think about this in French when I'm outside. Communication has to be structured to be intelligible, you see, and that's a different enough structure from English. But English is the only human language on Roland, and surely the Old Folk have learned it."

She nodded. He had told her his general plan, which was too obvious to conceal. The problem was to make contact with the aliens, if they existed. Hitherto, they had only revealed themselves, at rare intervals, to one or a few backwoodsmen at a time. An ability to generate hallucinations would help them in that. They would stay clear of any large, perhaps unmanageable expedition which might pass through their territory. But two people, braving all prohibitions, shouldn't look too formidable to approach. And . . . this would be the first human team which not only worked on the assumption that the Outlings were real, but possessed the resources of modern, off-planet police technology.

Nothing happened at that camp. Sherrinford said he hadn't expected it would. The Old Folk seemed cautious this near to any settlement. In their own lands they must be bolder.

And by the following "night," the vehicle had gone well into yonder country. When Sherrinford stopped the engine in a meadow and the car settled down, silence rolled in like a wave.

They stepped out. She cooked a meal on the glower while he gathered wood, that they might later cheer themselves with a campfire. Frequently he glanced at his wrist. It bore no watch—instead, a radio-controlled dial, to tell what the instruments in the bus might register.

Who needed a watch here? Slow constellations wheeled beyond glimmering aurora. The moon Alde stood above a snowpeak, turning it argent, though this place lay at a goodly height. The rest of the mountains were hidden by the forest that crowded around. Its trees were mostly shiverleaf and feathery white plumablanca, ghostly amidst their shadows. A few firethorns glowed, clustered dim lanterns, and the underbrush was heavy and smelled sweet. You could see surprisingly far through the blue dusk. Somewhere nearby, a brook sang and a bird fluted.

"Lovely here," Sherrinford said. They had risen from their supper and not yet sat down again or kindled their fire.

"But strange," Barbro answered as low. "I wonder if it's really meant for us. If we can really hope to possess it."

His pipestem gestured at the stars. "Man's gone to stranger places than this."

"Has he? I . . . oh, I suppose it's just something left over from my outway childhood, but do you know, when I'm under them I can't think of the stars as balls of gas, whose energies have been measured, whose planets have been walked on by prosaic feet. No, they're small and cold and magical; our lives are bound to them; after we die, they whisper to us in our graves." Barbro glanced downward. "I realize that's nonsense."

She could see in the twilight how his face grew tight. "Not at all," he said. "Emotionally, physics may be a worse nonsense. And in the end, you know, after a sufficient number of generations, thought follows feeling. Man is not at heart rational. He could stop believing the stories of science if those no longer felt right."

He paused. "That ballad which didn't get finished in the house," he said, not looking at her. "Why did it affect you so?"

"I couldn't stand hearing *them*, well, praised. Or that's how it seemed. Sorry for the fuss."

"I gather the ballad is typical of a large class."

"Well, I never thought to add them up. Cultural anthropology is something we don't have time for on Roland, or more likely it hasn't occurred to us, with everything else there is to do. But—now you mention it, yes, I'm surprised at how many songs and stories have the Arvid motif in them."

"Could you bear to recite it?"

She mustered the will to laugh. "Why, I can do better than that if you want. Let me get my multilyre and I'll perform."

She omitted the hypnotic chorus line, though, when the notes rang out, except at the end. He watched her where she stood against moon and aurora.

> "—the Queen of Air and Darkness
> cried softly under sky:
>
> " 'Light down, you ranger Arvid,
> and join the Outling folk.
> You need no more be human,
> which is a heavy yoke.'
>
> "He dared to give her answer:
> 'I may do naught but run.
> A maiden waits me, dreaming
> in lands beneath the sun.
>
> " 'And likewise wait me comrades
> and tasks I would not shirk,
> for what is ranger Arvid
> if he lays down his work?
>
> " 'So wreak your spells you Outling,
> and cast your wrath on me.
> Though maybe you can slay me,
> you'll not make me unfree.'
>
> "The Queen of Air and Darkness
> stood wrapped about with fear
> and northlight-flares and beauty
> he dared not look too near.
>
> "Until she laughed like harpsong
> and said to him in scorn:
> 'I do not need a magic
> to make you always mourn.

" 'I send you home with nothing
except your memory
of moonlight, Outling music,
night breezes, dew, and me.

" 'And that will run behind you,
a shadow on the sun,
and that will lie beside you
when every day is done.

" 'In work and play and friendship
your grief will strike you dumb
for thinking what you are—and—
what you might have become.

" 'Your dull and foolish woman
treat kindly as you can.
Go home now, ranger Arvid,
set free to be a man!'

"In flickering and laughter
the Outling folk were gone.
He stood alone by moonlight
and wept until the dawn.
    The dance weaves under the firethorn."

She laid the lyre aside. A wind rustled leaves. After a long quietness Sherrinford said, "And tales of this kind are part of everyone's life in the outway?"

"Well, you could put it thus," Barbro replied. "Though they're not all full of supernatural doings. Some are about love or heroism. Traditional themes."

"I don't think your particular tradition has arisen of itself." His tone was bleak. "In fact, I think many of your songs and stories were not composed by human beings."

He snapped his lips shut and would say no more on the subject. They went early to bed.

Hours later, an alarm roused them.

§

The buzzing was soft, but it brought them instantly alert. They slept in gripsuits, to be prepared for emergencies. Skyglow lit them through the canopy. Sherrinford swung out of his bunk, slipped shoes on feet, and clipped gun holster to belt. "Stay inside," he commanded.

"What's here?" Her pulse thuttered.

He squinted at the dials of his instruments and checked them against the luminous telltale on his wrist. "Three animals," he counted. "Not wild ones happening by. A large one, homeothermic, to judge from the infrared, holding still a short ways off. Another . . . hm, low temperature, diffuse and unstable emission, as if it were more like a . . . a swarm of cells coordinated somehow . . . pheromonally? . . . hovering, also at a distance. But the third's practically next to us, moving around in the brush; and that pattern looks human."

She saw him quiver with eagerness, no longer seeming a professor. "I'm going to try to make a capture," he said. "When we have a subject for interrogation—Stand ready to let me back in again fast. But don't risk yourself, whatever happens. And keep this cocked." He handed her a loaded big game rifle.

His tall frame poised by the door, opened it a crack. Air blew in, cool, damp, full of fragrances and murmurings. The moon Oliver was now also aloft, the radiance of both unreally brilliant, and the aurora seethed in whiteness and ice-blue.

Sherrinford peered afresh at his telltale. It must indicate the directions of the watchers, among those dappled leaves. Abruptly he sprang out. He sprinted past the ashes of the campfire and vanished under trees. Barbro's hand strained on the butt of her weapon.

Racket exploded. Two in combat burst onto the meadow. Sherrinford had clapped a grip on a smaller human figure. She could make out by streaming silver and rainbow flicker that the other was nude, male, long haired, lithe, and young. He fought demoniacally, seeking to use teeth and feet and raking nails, and meanwhile he ululated like a satan.

The identification shot through her: A changeling, stolen in babyhood and raised by the Old Folk. This creature was what they would make Jimmy into.

"Ha!" Sherrinford forced his opponent around and drove stiffened fingers into the solar plexus. The boy gasped and sagged: Sherrinford manhandled him toward the car.

Out from the woods came a giant. It might itself have been a tree, black and rugose, bearing four great gnarly boughs; but earth quivered and boomed beneath its leg-roots, and its hoarse bellowing filled sky and skulls.

Barbro shrieked. Sherrinford whirled. He yanked out his pistol, fired and fired, flat whipcracks through the half-light. His free arm kept a lock on the youth. The troll shape lurched under those blows. It recovered and came on, more slowly, more carefully, circling around to cut him off from the bus. He couldn't move fast enough to evade it unless he released his prisoner—who was his sole possible guide to Jimmy—

Barbro leaped forth. "Don't!" Sherrinford shouted. "For God's sake, stay inside!" The monster rumbled and made snatching motions at her. She pulled the trigger. Recoil slammed her in the shoulder. The colossus rocked and fell. Somehow it got its feet back and lumbered toward her. She retreated. Again she shot, and again. The creature snarled. Blood began to drip from it and gleam oilily amidst dewdrops. It turned and went off, breaking branches, into the darkness that laired beneath the woods.

"Get to shelter!" Sherrinford yelled. "You're out of the jammer field!"

A mistiness drifted by overhead. She barely glimpsed it before she saw the new shape at the meadow edge. "Jimmy!" tore from her.

"Mother." He held out his arms. Moonlight coursed in his tears. She dropped her weapon and ran to him.

Sherrinford plunged in pursuit. Jimmy flitted away into the brush. Barbro crashed after, through clawing twigs. Then she was seized and borne away.

§

Standing over his captive, Sherrinford strengthened the fluoro output until vision of the wilderness was blocked off from within the bus. The boy squirmed beneath that colorless glare.

"You are going to talk," the man said. Despite the haggardness in his features, he spoke quietly.

The boy glared through tangled locks. A bruise was purpling on his jaw. He'd almost recovered ability to flee while Sherrinford chased and lost the woman. Returning, the detective had barely caught him. Time was lacking to be gentle, when Outling reinforcements might arrive at any moment. Sherrinford had knocked him out and dragged him inside. He sat lashed into a swivel seat.

He spat. "Talk to you, manclod?" But sweat stood on his skin, and his eyes flickered unceasingly around the metal which caged him.

"Give me a name to call you by."

"And have you work a spell on me?"

"Mine's Eric. If you don't give me another choice, I'll have to call you . . . m-m-m . . . Wuddikins."

"What?" However eldritch, the bound one remained a human adolescent. "Mistherd, then." The lilting accent of his English somehow emphasized its sullenness. "That's not the sound, only what it means. Anyway, it's my spoken name, naught else."

"Ah, you keep a secret name you consider to be real?"

"She does. I don't know myself what it is. She knows the real names of everybody."

Sherrinford raised his brows. "She?"

"Who reigns. May she forgive me, I can't make the reverent sign when my arms are tied. Some invaders call her the Queen of Air and Darkness."

"So." Sherrinford got pipe and tobacco. He let silence wax while he started the fire. At length he said:

"I'll confess the Old Folk took me by surprise. I didn't expect so formidable a member of your gang. Everything I could learn had seemed to show they work on my race— and yours, lad—by stealth, trickery, and illusion."

Mistherd jerked a truculent nod. "She created the first

nicors not long ago. Don't think she has naught but dazzlements at her beck."

"I don't. However, a steel-jacketed bullet works pretty well too, doesn't it?"

Sherrinford talked on, softly, mostly to himself: "I do still believe the, ah, nicors—all your half-humanlike breeds—are intended in the main to be seen, not used. The power of projecting mirages must surely be quite limited in range and scope as well as in the number of individuals who possess it. Otherwise she wouldn't have needed to work as slowly and craftily as she has. Even outside our mindshield, Barbro— my companion—could have resisted, could have remained aware that whatever she saw was unreal . . . if she'd been less shaken, less frantic, less driven by need."

Sherrinford wreathed his head in smoke. "Never mind what I experienced," he said. "It couldn't have been the same as for her. I think the command was simply given us, 'You will see what you most desire in the world, running away from you into the forest.' Of course, she didn't travel many meters before the nicor waylaid her. I'd no hope of trailing them; I'm no Arctican woodsman, and besides, it'd have been too easy to ambush me. I came back to you." Grimly: "You're my link to your overlady."

"You think I'll guide you to Starhaven or Carheddin? Try making me, clod-man."

"I want to bargain."

"I s'pect you intend more'n that." Mistherd's answer held surprising shrewdness. "What'll you tell after you come home?"

"Yes, that does pose a problem, doesn't it? Barbro Cullen and I are not terrified outwayers. We're of the city. We brought recording instruments. We'd be the first of our kind to report an encounter with the Old Folk, and that report would be detailed and plausible. It would produce action."

"So you see I'm not afraid to die," Mistherd declared, though his lips trembled a bit. "If I let you come in and do your manthings to my people, I'd have naught left worth living for."

"Have no immediate fears," Sherrinford said. "You're merely bait." He sat down and regarded the boy through a visor of calm. (Within, it wept in him: *Barbro, Barbro!*) "Consider. Your Queen can't very well let me go back, bringing my prisoner and telling about hers. She has to stop that somehow. I could try fighting my way through—this car is better armed than you know—but that wouldn't free anybody. Instead, I'm staying put. New forces of hers will get here as fast as they can. I assume they won't blindly throw themselves against a machine gun, a howitzer, a fulgurator. They'll parley first, whether their intentions are honest or not. Thus I make the contact I'm after."

"What d' you plan?" The mumble held anguish.

"First, this, as a sort of invitation." Sherrinford reached out to flick a switch. "There. I've lowered my shield against mind-reading and shape-casting. I daresay the leaders, at least, will be able to sense that it's gone. That should give them confidence."

"And next?"

"Next we wait. Would you like something to eat or drink?"

During the time which followed, Sherrinford tried to jolly Mistherd along, find out something of his life. What answers he got were curt. He dimmed the interior lights and settled down to peer outward. That was a long few hours.

They ended at a shout of gladness, half a sob, from the boy. Out of the woods came a band of the Old Folk.

Some of them stood forth more clearly than moons and stars and northlights should have caused. He in the van rode a white crownbuck whose horns were garlanded. His form was manlike but unearthly beautiful, silver blond hair falling from beneath the antlered helmet, around the proud cold face. The cloak fluttered off his back like living wings. His frost-colored mail rang as he fared.

Behind him, to right and left, rode two who bore swords whereon small flames gleamed and flickered. Above, a flying flock laughed and trilled and tumbled in the breezes. Near them drifted a half-transparent mistiness. Those others who passed among trees after their chieftain were harder to make out. But they moved in quicksilver grace and as it were to a sound of harps and trumpets.

"Lord Luighaid." Glory overflowed in Mistherd's tone. "Her master Knower—himself."

Sherrinford had never done a harder thing than to sit at the main control panel, finger near the button of the shield generator, and not touch it. He rolled down a section of canopy to let voices travel. A gust of wind struck him in the face, bearing odors of the roses in his mother's garden. At his back, in the main body of the vehicle, Mistherd strained against his bonds till he could see the oncoming troop.

"Call to them," Sherrinford said. "Ask if they will talk with me."

Unknown, flutingly sweet words flew back and forth. "Yes," the boy interpreted. "He will, the Lord Luighaid. But I can tell you, you'll never be let go. Don't fight them. Yield. Come away. You don't know what 'tis to be alive till you've dwelt in Carheddin under the mountain."

The Outlings drew nigh.

§

Jimmy glimmered and was gone. Barbro lay in strong arms, against a broad breast, and felt the horse move beneath her. It had to be a horse, though only a few were kept any longer on the steadings, and they only for special uses or love. She could feel the rippling beneath its hide, hear a rush of parted leafage and the thud when a hoof struck stone; warmth and living scent welled up around her through the darkness.

He who carried her said mildly, "Don't be afraid, darling. It was a vision. But he's waiting for us, and we're bound for him."

She was aware in a vague way that she ought to feel terror or despair or something. But her memories lay behind her— she wasn't sure just how she had come to be here—she was borne along in a knowledge of being loved. At peace, at peace, rest in the calm expectation of joy . . .

After a while the forest opened. They crossed a lea where boulders stood gray white under the moons, their shadows shifting in the dim hues which the aurora threw across them. Flitteries danced, tiny comets, above the flowers between. Ahead gleamed a peak whose top was crowned in clouds.

Barbro's eyes happened to be turned forward. She saw the horse's head and thought, with quiet surprise: "Why, this is Sambo, who was mine when I was a girl. She looked upward at the man. He wore a black tunic and a cowled cape, which made his face hard to see. She could not cry aloud, here. "Tim," she whispered.

"Yes, Barbro."

"I buried you—"

His smile was endlessly tender. "Did you think we're no more than what's laid back into the ground? Poor torn sweetheart. She who's called us is the All Healer. Now rest and dream."

"Dream," she said, and for a space she struggled to rouse herself. But the effort was weak. Why should she believe ashen tales about . . . atoms and energies, nothing else to fill a gape of emptiness . . . tales she could not bring to mind . . . when Tim and the horse her father gave her carried her on to Jimmy? Had the other thing not been the evil dream, and this her first drowsy awakening from it?

As if he heard her thoughts, he murmured, "They have a song in Outling lands. The Song of the Men:

"The world sails
to an unseen wind.
Light swirls by the bows.
The wake is night.
But the Dwellers have no such sadness."

"I don't understand," she said.

He nodded. "There's much you'll have to understand, darling, and I can't see you again until you've learned those truths. But meanwhile you'll be with our son."

She tried to lift her head and kiss him. He held her down. "Not yet," he said. "You've not been received among the Queen's people. I shouldn't have come for you, except that she was too merciful to forbid. Lie back, lie back."

Time blew past. The horse galloped tireless, never stumbling, up the mountain. Once she glimpsed a troop riding down it and thought they were bound for a last weird battle in the west against . . . who? . . . one who lay cased in iron and sorrow—Later she would ask herself the name of him who had brought her into the land of the Old Truth.

Finally spires lifted splendid among the stars, which are small and magical and whose whisperings comfort us after we are dead. They rode into a courtyard where candles burned unwavering, fountains splashed and birds sang. The air bore fragrance of brok and pericoup, of rue and roses, for not everything that man brought was horrible. The Dwellers waited in beauty to welcome her. Beyond their stateliness, pooks cavorted through the gloaming; among the trees darted children; merriment caroled across music more solemn.

"We have come—" Tim's voice was suddenly, inexplicably, a croak. Barbro was not sure how he dismounted, bearing her. She stood before him and saw him sway on his feet.

Fear caught her. "Are you well?" She seized both his hands. They felt cold and rough. Where had Sambo gone? Her eyes searched beneath the cowl. In this brighter illumination, she ought to have seen her man's face clearly. But it was blurred, it kept changing. "What's wrong, oh, what's happened?"

He smiled. Was that the smile she had cherished? She couldn't completely remember. "I, I must go," he stammered, so low she could scarcely hear. "Our time is not ready." He drew free of her grasp and leaned on a robed form which had appeared at his side. A haziness swirled over both their heads. "Don't watch me go . . . back into the earth," he pleaded. "That's death for you. Till our time returns—There, our son!"

She had to fling her gaze around. Kneeling, she spread wide her arms. Jimmy struck her like a warm, solid cannonball. She rumpled his hair; she kissed the hollow of his neck; she laughed and wept and babbled foolishness; and this was no ghost, no memory that had stolen off when she wasn't looking. Now and again, as she turned her attention to yet another hurt which might have come upon him—hunger, sickness, fear—and found none, she would glimpse their surroundings. The gardens were gone. It didn't matter.

"I missed you so, Mother. Stay?"

"I'll take you home, dearest."

"Stay. Here's fun. I'll show. But you stay."

A sighing went through the twilight. Barbro rose. Jimmy clung to her hand. They confronted the Queen.

Very tall she was in her robes woven of northlights, and her starry crown and her garlands of kiss-me-never. Her countenance recalled Aphrodite of Milos, whose picture Barbro had often seen in the realms of men, save that the Queen's was more fair and more majesty dwelt upon it and in the night-blue eyes. Around her the gardens woke to new reality, the court of the Dwellers and the heaven-climbing spires.

"Be welcome," she spoke, her speaking a song, "forever."

Against the awe of her, Barbro said, "Moonmother, let us go home."

"That may not be."

"To our world, little and beloved," Barbro dreamed she begged, "which we build for ourselves and cherish for our children."

"To prison days, angry nights, works that crumble in the fingers, loves that turn to rot or stone or driftweed, loss, grief, and the only sureness that of the final nothingness. No. You too, Wanderfoot who is to be, will jubilate when the banners of the Outworld come flying into the last of the cities and man is made wholly alive. Now go with those who will teach you."

The Queen of Air and Darkness lifted an arm in summons. It halted, and none came to answer.

For over the fountains and melodies lifted a gruesome growling. Fires leaped, thunders crashed. Her hosts scattered screaming before the steel thing which boomed up the mountainside. The pooks were gone in a whirl of frightened wings. The nicors flung their bodies against the unalive invader and were consumed, until their Mother cried to them to retreat.

Barbro cast Jimmy down and herself over him. Towers wavered and smoked away. The mountain stood bare under icy moons, save for rocks, crags, and farther off a glacier in whose depths the auroral light pulsed blue. A cave mouth darkened a cliff. Thither folk streamed, seeking refuge underground. Some were human of blood, some grotesques like the pooks and nicors and wraiths; but most were lean, scaly, long-tailed, long-beaked, not remotely men or Outlings.

For an instant, even as Jimmy wailed at her breast—perhaps as much because the enchantment had been wrecked as because he was afraid—Barbro pitied the Queen who stood alone in her nakedness. Then that one also had fled, and Barbro's world shivered apart.

The guns fell silent; the vehicle whirred to a halt. From it sprang a boy who called wildly, "Shadow-of-a-Dream, where are you? It's me, Mistherd, oh, come, come!"—before he remembered that the language they had been raised in was not man's. He shouted in that until a girl crept out of a thicket where she had hidden. They stared at each other through dust, smoke, and moonglow. She ran to him.

A new voice barked from the car, "Barbro, hurry!"

§

Christmas Landing knew day: short at this time of year, but sunlight, blue skies, white clouds, glittering water, salt breezes in busy streets, and the sane disorder of Eric Sherrinford's living room.

He crossed and uncrossed his legs where he sat, puffed on his pipes as if to make a veil, and said, "Are you certain you're recovered? You mustn't risk overstrain."

"I'm fine," Barbro Cullen replied, though her tone was flat. "Still tired, yes, and showing it, no doubt. One doesn't go through such an experience and bounce back in a week. But I'm up and about. And to be frank, I must know what's happened, what's going on, before I can settle down to regain my full strength. Not a word of news anywhere."

"Have you spoken to others about the matter?"

"No. I've simply told visitors I was too exhausted to talk. Not much of a lie. I assumed there's a reason for censorship."

Sherrinford looked relieved. "Good girl. It's at my urging. You can imagine the sensation when this is made public. The authorities agreed they need time to study the facts, think and debate in a calm atmosphere, have a decent policy ready to offer voters who're bound to become rather hysterical at first." His mouth quirked slightly upward. "Furthermore, your nerves and Jimmy's get their chance to heal before the journalistic storm breaks over you. How is he?"

"Quite well. He continues pestering me for leave to go play with his friends in the Wonderful Place. But at his age, he'll recover—he'll forget."

"He may meet them later anyhow."

"What? We didn't—" Barbro shifted in her chair. "I've forgotten too. I hardly recall a thing from our last hours. Did you bring back any kidnapped humans?"

"No. The shock was savage as it was, without throwing them straight into an . . . an institution. Mistherd, who's basically a sensible young fellow, assured me they'd get along, at any rate as regards survival necessities, till arrangements can be made." Sherrinford hesitated. "I'm not sure what the arrangements will be. Nobody is, at our present stage. But obviously they include those people—or many of them, especially those who aren't fullgrown—rejoining the human race. Though they may never feel at home in civilization. Perhaps in a way that's best, since we will need some kind of mutually acceptable liaison with the Dwellers."

His impersonality soothed them both. Barbro became able to say, "Was I too big a fool? I do remember how I yowled and beat my head on the floor."

"Why, no." He considered the big woman and her pride for a few seconds before he rose, walked over and laid a hand on her shoulder. "You'd been lured and trapped by a skillful play on your deepest instincts, at a moment of sheer nightmare. Afterward, as that wounded monster carried you off, evidently another type of being came along, one that could saturate you with close-range neuropsychic forces. On top of this, my arrival, the sudden brutal abolishment of every hallucination, must have been shattering. No wonder if you cried out in pain. Before you did, you competently got Jimmy and yourself into the bus, and you never interfered with me."

"What did you do?"

"Why, I drove off as fast as possible. After several hours, the atmospherics let up sufficiently for me to call Portolondon and insist on an emergency airlift. Not that that was vital. What chance had the enemy to stop us? They didn't even try.—But quick transportation was certainly helpful."

"I figured that's what must have gone on." Barbro caught his glance. "No, what I meant was, how did you find us in the backlands?"

Sherrinford moved a little off from her. "My prisoner was my guide. I don't think I actually killed any of the Dwellers who'd come to deal with me. I hope not. The car simply broke through them, after a couple of warning shots, and afterward outpaced them. Steel and fuel against flesh wasn't really fair. At the cave entrance, I did have to shoot down a few of those troll creatures. I'm not proud of it."

He stood silent. Presently: "But you were a captive," he said. "I couldn't be sure what they might do to you, who had first claim on me." After another pause: "I don't look for any more violence."

"How did you make . . . the boy . . . co-operate?"

Sherrinford paced from her to the window, where he stood staring out at the Boreal Ocean. "I turned off the mindshield," he said. "I let their band get close, in full splendor of illusion. Then I turned the shield back on, and we both saw them in their true shapes. As we went northward, I explained to Mistherd how he and his kind had been hoodwinked, used, made to live in a world that was never really there. I asked him if he wanted himself and whomever he cared about to go on till they died as domestic animals—yes, running in limited freedom on solid hills, but always called back to the dream-kennel." His pipe fumed furiously. "May I never see such bitterness again. He had been taught to believe he was free."

Quiet returned, above the hectic traffic. Charlemagne drew nearer to setting; already the east darkened.

Finally Barbro asked, "Do you know why?"

"Why children were taken and raised like that? Partly because it was in the pattern the Dwellers were creating; partly in order to study and experiment on members of our species—minds, that is, not bodies; partly because humans have special strengths which are helpful, like being able to endure full daylight."

"But what was the final purpose of it all?"

Sherrinford paced the floor. "Well," he said, "of course the ultimate motives of the aborigines are obscure. We can't do more than guess at how they think, let alone how they feel. But our ideas do seem to fit the data.

"Why did they hide from man? I suspect they, or rather their ancestors—for they aren't glittering elves, you know; they're mortal and fallible too—I suspect the natives were only being cautious at first, more cautious than human primitives, though certain of those on Earth were also slow to reveal themselves to strangers. Spying, mentally eavesdropping, Roland's Dwellers must have picked up enough language to get some idea of how different man was from them, and how powerful; and they gathered that more ships would be arriving, bringing settlers. It didn't occur to them that they might be conceded the right to keep their lands. Perhaps they're still more fiercely territorial than we. They determined to fight, in their own way. I dare say, once we begin to get insight into that mentality, our psychological science will go through its Copernican revolution."

Enthusiasm kindled in him. "That's not the sole thing we'll learn, either," he went on. "They must have science of their own, a nonhuman science born on a planet that isn't Earth. Because they did observe us as profoundly as we've ever observed ourselves; they did mount a plan against us, one that would have taken another century or more to complete. Well, what else do they know? How do they support their civilization without visible agriculture or aboveground buildings or mines or anything? How can they breed whole new intelligent species to order? A million questions, ten million answers!"

"*Can* we learn from them?" Barbro asked softly. "Or can we only overrun them as you say they fear?"

Sherrinford halted, leaned elbow on mantel, hugged his pipe and replied, "I hope we'll show more charity than that to a defeated enemy. It's what they are. They tried to conquer us and failed, and now in a sense we are bound to conquer them, since they'll have to make their peace with the civilization of the machine rather than see it rust away as they strove for. Still, they never did us any harm as atrocious as what we've inflicted on our fellow men in the past. And, I repeat, they could teach us marvelous things; and we could teach them, too, once they've learned to be less intolerant of a different way of life."

"I suppose we can give them a reservation," she said, and didn't know why he grimaced and answered so roughly:

"Let's leave them the honor they've earned! They fought to save the world they'd always known from that—" he made a chopping gesture at the city—"and just possibly we'd be better off ourselves with less of it."

He sagged a trifle and sighed, "However, I suppose if Elfland had won, man on Roland would at last—peacefully, even happily—have died away. We live with our archetypes, but can we live in them?"

Barbro shook her head. "Sorry, I don't understand."

"What?" He looked at her in a surprise that drove out melancholy. After a laugh: "Stupid of me. I've explained this to so many politicians and scientists and commissioners and Lord knows what, these past days, I forgot I'd never explained to you. It was a rather vague idea of mine, most of the time we were traveling, and I don't like to discuss ideas prematurely. Now that we've met the Outlings and watched how they work, I do feel sure."

He tamped down his tobacco. "In limited measure," he said, "I've used an archetype throughout my own working life. The rational detective. It hasn't been a conscious pose —much—it's simply been an image which fitted my personality and professional style. But it draws an appropriate response from most people, whether or not they've ever heard of the original. The phenomenon is not uncommon. We meet persons who, in varying degrees, suggest Christ or Buddha or the Earth Mother or, say, on a less exalted plane, Hamlet or d'Artagnan. Historical, fictional, and mythical, such figures crystallize basic aspects of the human psyche, and when we meet them in our real experience, our reaction goes deeper than consciousness."

He grew grave again: "Man also creates archetypes that are not individuals. The Anima, the Shadow—and, it seems, the Outworld. The world of magic, of glamour—which originally meant enchantment—of half-human beings, some like Ariel and some like Caliban, but each free of mortal frailties and sorrows—therefore, perhaps, a little carelessly cruel, more than a little tricksy; dwellers in dusk and moonlight, not truly gods but obedient to rulers who are enigmatic and powerful enough to be—Yes, our Queen of Air and Darkness knew well what sights to let lonely people see, what illusions to spin around them from time to time, what songs and legends to set going among them. I wonder how much she and her underlings gleaned from human fairy tales, how much they made up themselves, and how much men created all over again, all unwittingly, as the sense of living on the edge of the world entered them."

Shadows stole across the room. It grew cooler and the traffic noises dwindled. Barbro asked mutedly, "But what could this do?"

"In many ways," Sherrinford answered, "the outwayer *is* back in the Dark Ages. He has few neighbors, hears scanty news from beyond his horizon, toils to survive in a land he only partly understands, that may any night raise unforeseeable disasters against him, and is bounded by enormous wildernesses. The machine civilization which brought his ancestors here is frail at best. He could lose it as the Dark Ages nations had lost Greece and Rome, as the whole of Earth seems to have lost it. Let him be worked on, long, strongly, cunningly, by the archetypical Outworld, until he has come to believe in his bones that the magic of the Queen of Air and Darkness is greater than the energy of engines; and first his faith, finally his deeds will follow her. Oh, it wouldn't happen fast. Ideally, it would happen too slowly to be noticed, especially by self-satisfied city people. But when in the end a hinterland gone back to the ancient way turned from them, how could they keep alive?"

Barbro breathed, "She said to me, when their banners flew in the last of our cities, we would rejoice."

"I think we would have, by then," Sherrinford admitted. "Nevertheless, I believe in choosing one's destiny."

He shook himself, as if casting off a burden. He knocked the dottle from his pipe and stretched, muscle by muscle. "Well," he said, "it isn't going to happen."

She looked straight at him. "Thanks to you."

A flush went up his thin cheeks. "In time, I'm sure, somebody else would have—What matters is what we do next, and that's too big a decision for one individual or one generation to make."

She rose. "Unless the decision is personal, Eric," she suggested, feeling heat in her own face.

It was curious to see him shy. "I was hoping we might meet again."

"We will."

§

Ayoch sat on Wolund's Barrow. Aurora shuddered so brilliant, in such vast sheafs of light, as almost to hide the waning moons. Firethorn blooms had fallen; a few still glowed around the tree roots, amidst dry brok which crackled underfoot and smelled like woodsmoke. The air remained warm, but no gleam was left on the sunset horizon.

"Farewell, fare lucky," the pook called. Mistherd and Shadow-of-a-Dream never looked back. It was as if they didn't dare. They trudged on out of sight, toward the human camp whose lights made a harsh new star in the south.

Ayoch lingered. He felt he should also offer good-bye to her who had lately joined him that slept in the dolmen. Likely none would meet here again for loving or magic. But he could only think of one old verse that might do. He stood and trilled:

"Out of her breast
a blossom ascended.
The summer burned it.
The song is ended."

Then he spread his wings for the long flight away.

PATRICK L. MCGUIRE

"Her Strong Enchantments Failing"

"The Queen of Air and Darkness" displays many of the best
characteristics of Poul Anderson's writing. This fact earned the
novelette a first place in *The Magazine of Fantasy and Science
Fiction*'s special Anderson issue (April 1971), then a Nebula
award from the Science Fiction Writers of America and a
Hugo from the Thirtieth World Science Fiction Convention.
But the work does exhibit some of Anderson's characteristic
weaknesses as well, and is thus representative enough so that
a close examination of this one work should enhance the
appreciation of Anderson's production as a whole. We shall
approach "The Queen of Air and Darkness" with this larger
aim in mind.

But before we move on to analysis, it may be useful to
review some of the prominent features of the novelette's plot
and background: On the colony planet Roland, a young
widow, Barbro Cullen, comes to private detective Eric
Sherrinford for help. Barbro had taken her three-year-old son
Jimmy along on a scientific expedition to the polar Darklands.
When Jimmy disappears from camp, Barbro believes he must
have been stolen by the mysterious Outlings, known principally
from the colonists' folklore. This lore, however, portrays the
Outlings so much like elves or fairies of terrestrial tradition
that the authorities dismiss them as superstition—or defer to
them as supernatural beings. Whether or not supernatural, the
Outlings are real, as we learn from alternate scenes from the
viewpoint of kidnapped humans. The relatively warm but dark
polar region seems a sort of Rolandic fairyland, peopled by

various eldritch creatures, ruled by the majestic and beautiful Queen of Air and Darkness.

However, as the novelette progresses we learn that the Outling realm is in fact a sham, an illusion cast by Roland's hitherto-undiscovered aboriginal population, who intend to subvert the value system of the human civilization. Through such means as telepathic suggestion and induced hallucination, they gradually resurrect man's ancient superstitions, concretions of tendencies never deeply buried in the human mind, in the hope that this resurgence of an antiscientific way of thought will facilitate the absorption of the humans into the aborigines' biologically oriented, nonmechanical culture.

When Sherrinford's deductions have made at least some of the above clear to him, he ventures with Barbro into the Darklands in a ground-effect car shielded against telepathic interference. But when Sherrinford leaves the car to capture a changeling for interrogation, the nicor cuts off his return. Barbro leaves the jammer field to help him and is lured away.

We follow from her viewpoint as she is brought before the Queen, struggling feebly the while to regain her sense of reality despite an illusion of her late husband and other comforting visions from times past. In the nick of time, Sherrinford arrives at the rescue, and pits the ground-effect car's armament against the mere muscle of the Queen's guardians—"tanks" against "cavalry." The grand illusion dispels, and the Queen is revealed as a vaguely humanoid saurian.

Thus the aborigines' plot is undone; Sherrinford, however, expresses the hope that humankind will not be vindictive in its triumph. Roland was the "Outlings'" world first, after all, and in any case the aborigines have much to teach the colonists.

In the "personal subplot" typical of Anderson, Barbro comes to realize that life goes on outside the memory of her husband, while Sherrinford overcomes his Sherlock-Holmesian reserve toward women. At the conclusion of the novelette, there are hints of romance.

§

The image of the Queen of Air and Darkness pervades Anderson's novelette. The Queen-persona assumed by the aborigine leader is an "archetype," as is the Queen's realm, in approximately a Jungian sense. This accounts in part for the Outlings' power. As Sherrinford explains,

"We meet persons who, in varying degrees, suggest Christ or Buddha or the Earth Mother or, say, on a less exalted plane, Hamlet or d'Artagnan. Historical, fictional, and mythical, such figures crystallize basic aspects of the human psyche, and when we meet them in our real experience, our reaction goes deeper than consciousness.
. . . "Man also creates archetypes that are not individuals. The Anima, the Shadow—and, it seems, the Outworld. The world of magic, of glamour—which originally meant enchantment—of half-human beings . . ." (p. 82)[1]

In his introduction to the novelette (in the magazine publication), Anderson explains that mythological figures resembling the Queen can be found all over the world and as far back in prehistory as archeology can take us. The universality of the "Queen" archetype suggests what a close grip the concept has on human minds. Something of this power comes through even in a short description of the Queen:

Very tall she was in her robes woven of northlights, and her starry crown and her garlands of kiss-me-never. Her countenance recalled Aphrodite of Milos, whose picture Barbro had often seen in the realms of men, save that the Queen's was more fair and more majesty dwelt upon it and in the night-blue eyes. Around her the gardens woke to new reality, the court of the Dwellers and the heaven-climbing spires.
"Be welcome," she spoke, her speaking a song, "forever." (p. 76)

However universal the basic conception, the Queen must manifest herself in a particular form, and for this Anderson relies heavily on the medieval tradition of the Fairy Queen as recorded in ballads and romances. The Fairy Queen probably began as a powerful mother goddess,[2] but gradually the various European peoples modified their ideas. The Irish fairy-folk, the Tuatha Dé Danann, preserved the old conception in their name, which may be explained as "the people of the goddess Dana,"[3] but, powers once confined to a single goddess were distributed among numerous fay women. Even when Fairyland retains a queen, she often acquires a king: indeed, in some traditions, the most important woman fay is the *daughter* of the Fairy King.[4] Furthermore, in much of folklore, the role of the Fairy Queen as lover overshadows her role as mother. This notion too is very ancient, but perhaps its most familiar expression came with the almost-human fay ladies of medieval romance:

The fay of the Arthurian romance is essentially a super-natural woman, always more beautiful than imagination can possibly fancy her, untouched by time, unhampered by lack of resources for the accomplishment of her pleasure, superior to human necessity, in short, unlimited in her power.[5]

In his fantasy novels *The Broken Sword* and *Three Hearts and Three Lions,* Anderson portrays elf women much along medieval lines, and they do entice the heroes of those works into sexual entanglements; but this erotic element has almost entirely disappeared in "The Queen of Air and Darkness." The Queen is incomparably beautiful, but she is to be worshipped from afar.

Given the fact that the aborigines cannot maintain a perfect deception at short range (Barbro begins to see through the illusion of her husband), it would be out of the question for the Queen to take human lovers, but we may also look for some deeper significance here. We can, of course, refer to other relevant models, such as the Norwegian Huldra (beautiful from the front, hideous from the rear; like the aborigines possessing a tail), or the medieval cult of the Virgin. But beyond this, inaccessibility contributes to the definition of the Queen's persona in other ways, which we shall discuss below.

One reason for the aborigines' choice of the Fairy Queen archetype out of the many types available to them is her association with a call away from responsibility and rationality. This aspect of Fairyland has a long history—Circe's island; the tenth-century Irish *Imram Brain maic Febrail,* which tells of Bran Fabail-son's voyage to the Land of Women; Morgan's Avalon—but the idea remains attractive to a "modern" society.

In the first place, the Queen promises precious fellowship and security to the Rolandic colonist. The entire colony is horribly alone, tens of parsecs from other humans in an Einsteinian universe in which there is no faster-than-light travel. The million human colonists are not precisely beyond the help of other men—Sherrinford himself is an immigrant— but they are beyond the *assurance* of help. Such aid could, in any case, come only from other struggling settlements: "Two or three times a century, a ship may call from some other colony. (Not from Earth. Earth has long ago sunk into alien concerns.)" (p. 41)

This last sombre statement is virtually all we hear of Earth in "The Queen of Air and Darkness." However, Anderson also alludes to the planet Rustum (p. 46), and thereby both explains Roland's isolation from the mother planet and suggests the sort of disaster which may befall the colony.

The colonization of Rustum is the subject of Anderson's 1959–1961 series of novelettes collected as *Orbit Unlimited.* The series details the tribulations of a middle-class, largely North American group, the Constitutionalists, who stubbornly adhere to a scientific outlook and a libertarian theory of government on an Earth which has abandoned both concepts. The mother planet, under the weight of increasing population and diminishing resources, is sinking into ignorance and tyranny, and Earth's culture is shifting toward heavy drug use and toward Oriental mysticism. The Constitutionalists can find no way to protect their values except to escape. They pressure the government into allowing them to colonize a recently discovered habitable planet, Rustum. The characters of *Orbit Unlimited* believe that the colonization of Rustum probably represents Earth's last act in space. Obviously, in light of "The Queen of Air and Darkness," their fears were premature. In a manner characteristic of many dying cultures, Earth managed one last resurgence, lasting probably for several centuries (for in *Orbit Unlimited* no man-habitable worlds but Rustum had even been discovered), and planted other colonies. However, eventually the end foreseen in *Orbit Unlimited* must have come. After a severe struggle, Earth has succumbed to a Darkness similar to that which now threatens Roland's colonists.

Half of Roland's million human inhabitants live in the one city of Christmas Landing. This concentration presumably allows the colony to maintain the degree of specialization necessary for a technological society, and it may in some measure compensate for the isolation of the colony as a whole. But the other half of the population is spread out over the entire continent, largely on one-family farmsteads. These produce for the market, and while such commerce decreases their isolation, it may increase their insecurity: Roland has a largely capitalist economy and a decentralized government, so that it seems likely that farm incomes fluctuate widely from year to year. The farmsteads are tied to the outside world through telecommunication and by air travel, but even these are subject to disruption by Roland's erratic weather. An escape from this worry and this loneliness must seem enormously attractive, even an escape which must be purchased by the rejection of the influence of a scientific education. Once the countryside has gone over, the city must follow or starve.

But this psychological predisposition is not all the aborigines have working for them. Though entirely within a "realistic" framework, their land has a striking resemblance to Faerie. From a point of view within the plot, this provides an additional motive for the aborigines' adoption of the Fairy Queen archetype. From an "exterior" view, Anderson has provided a marvelously ingenious rationalization of the magical

—and not entirely as a game, but also for serious reasons which we shall discuss below.

Fairyland has certain specifications. There must be little or no sunlight, as Earthly legends tell us that fairies flee the sun. However, there must be some sort of eldritch illumination, both for the benefit of human visitors and because we know the fairies are not a gloomy folk. Faerie must have a location apart from usual human habitations, but one in which kidnapped humans can thrive. It should be ruled by a Queen who has at her command various sophont nonhuman creatures with abilities more or less specified by folklore. These include flight and spell-casting.[6]

The Rolandic north-polar lands—and North is the "inauspicious quarter; realm of darkness, night. Symbolizes the mysterious, the unknown"[7]—fit these specifications exactly.

There is indeed darkness. Roland has a highly eccentric orbit which will keep the arctic region in night through most of the year. This darkness is not intense and gloomy, for it is broken by bioluminescent plants, two moons, and brilliant auroras, which last are the result of the interaction between the atmosphere and the strong "wind" of charged particles emitted by Roland's type F9 sun. The high energy output of this star performs the further function of explaining the warmth of even the polar Darklands. Another factor contributing to this last effect is Roland's fairly slight axial tilt (10°) and small diameter (9500 km): the entire arctic circle must be only a little over five hundred miles (more nearly, 830 km) in radius. Masses of warmer air will constantly move into so small a region. Furthermore, the land area inside the circle is given as 1.25 million square kilometers (p. 39). This is just over half the total arctic area, so the rest must be ocean (the Gulf of Polaris), which further mitigates the climate.

The darkness of the polar regions is enough to make them unattractive to Roland's colonists, at least at so early a stage of economic development. But Roland's powerful sun provides a third service by adding further guarantees of the Queen's privacy. In conjunction with various planetary features, it

induces great atmospheric turbulence and sudden, unpre-
dictable storms. At the current level of development, this makes
regular air traffic impossible.

Roland has a surface gravity only 42% of Earth's, but it has
a nearly terrestrial air pressure. This is in accordance with
cosmological theories that "blame" Earth's large moon or some
such factor for reducing the amount of atmosphere our planet
retains, but beyond a contribution to verisimilitude, the function of endowing Roland with such a dense atmosphere is to
permit the existence of large flying creatures such as the
"pooks." In this way, the Queen gains her traditional winged
servants.

Even so, evidence on Earth suggests that one intelligent
species is likely to eliminate its close competitors, so that, as
the Portolondon Chief Constable says, " 'No area the size of
Arctica could spawn a dozen different intelligent species' "
(p. 49). The simplest solution is to suppose that the aborigines
themselves have "manufactured" multiple life-forms. This in
turn requires that the aborigines be masters of the biological
sciences.

A race that began with biology would have a rather different
view of life from one beginning with mechanics, a view which
could easily put them into conflict with "mechanico-technolog-
ical" humans. Anderson has previously explored this same
conflict in *The Star Ways* (1957)[8] and *After Doomsday*
(1962).

In his descriptions of the bioengineered inhabitants of the
Darklands, Anderson has modified the terrestrial traditions.
Presumably the form which the archetypal creatures take on
Roland is dictated partly by the restrictions of the aborigines'
biotechnology and partly by the culture of the human colonists.
The departure from folklore may also reinforce the reader's
feeling of verisimilitude—the story is "science fiction" rather
than "fantasy."

"Wraiths" are almost self-explanatory. They are the nearest
Rolandic equivalent of a disembodied spirit: " 'a swarm of cells
coordinated somehow . . . pheromonally?' " (p. 68). As befits

their "demonic" estate, wraiths have high intelligence and great telepathic power.

The word "pook" must be a derivative of "puck,"[9] and thence the Anglo-Saxon *puca*. Anderson uses the word for a winged creature somewhat like the small "degenerate" sprite of later folklore, although the one pook we know well, Ayoch, has a rather more phlegmatic character than one would expect of a winged fairy. After all, to speak scientifically, even on Roland a flying creature large enough to carry a child must be somewhat ponderous.

The creature Anderson terms the "nicor" is particularly interesting. *Nicor*, related to the modern "nix," is the Anglo-Saxon word for "water sprite" and also for "hippopotamus." Later the name seems to have become specific to one such being. His German equivalent, Nikard, stole newborn babes. In Yorkshire tradition he became the water sprite Nicobare, a halfwit who occasionally uttered profundities.[10] Anderson's nicors seem to have nothing to do with water; they look something like a cross between an elephant—or a hippopotamus?—and an Ent. But one of them, Nagrim, is involved in a kidnapping (Barbro's), and he is simultaneously stupid and wise. For example, he says of the colonists,

"I know deir aim. Cut down trees, stick plows in land, sow deir cursed seed in de clods and in deir shes. 'Less we drive dem into de bitterwater, and soon, soon, dey'll wax too strong for us." (p. 51)

We have seen that the "rational explanation" for most of the "magical" power of the Queen is telepathy and related parapsychological phenomena. As is true in the Flandry stories (which, however, are in a different "future history"), telepathy in turn reduces to the generation and reception by the nervous system of extremely long-wave electromagnetic radiation. Information transfer by radiation of this wavelength is slow, which explains why humans have so little telepathic ability, but in the dark homeland of the aborigines, the ability has had evolutionary advantage, and it has reached a fairly high level of development.

It is interesting to note that parapsychological researchers are themselves enmeshed in a debate as to whether the phenomena they study can be explained in terms of electromagnetic radiation. For a period of decades, it was generally accepted that they could not. The evidence in favor of cross-temporal phenomena, such as precognition, seemed as good as that for such phenomena as telepathy, which might be expected to more easily lend itself to an explanation in terms of current biological and physical theories. But more recently, researchers, especially Soviet, have again been examining "electromagnetic" theories, apparently with promising results. For "The Queen of Air and Darkness," Anderson has chosen to follow this more "pedestrian" explanation (which he does not in, for example, "Kyrie"): in "The Queen of Air and Darkness," the explanation should not only be *rational*; it should be as *familiar* to the reader as possible. Even in science fiction, emotional overtones are as important as logic.[11]

§

Although the aborigines make conscious use of archetypes on the grandest scale, so that the figure of the Queen of Air and Darkness must dominate the novelette, they are not the only ones to employ the technique. Sherrinford himself cultivates a resemblance to Sherlock Holmes, or rather to an archetypal Rational Detective:

"It hasn't been a conscious pose—much—it's simply been an image which fitted my personality and professional style. But it draws an appropriate response from most people, whether or not they've ever heard of the original." (p. 82)

A person may also fall into archetypal patterns unconsciously, as Barbro does when she assumes a sort of "devoted widow" role very familiar in literature. One of the advantages of conscious knowledge of archetypes, however, is that one has more freedom to move in and out of types at will. Thus Sherrinford allows himself to fall in love with Barbro even though this is out of Holmesian character. Barbro is also able to change her self-conception, with Sherrinford's help, but the novelette is half over before she has "realized, half guiltily, that life held more hopes than even the recovery of the son Tim gave her." (p. 62)

This is not, however, to suggest that knowledge guarantees a change for the better. Archetypes themselves are, as we shall see, symptomatic of deeper relationships, and as such are not easily or painlessly modified. At the end of the novelette it is Barbro who must draw Sherrinford out. Even the grand manipulators, the aborigines, seem to be prisoners of their own thought structures. If, instead of hiding themselves and obscuring all traces of their habitation, they had made themselves known to the first scouting expedition, humans never would have colonized Roland. Even afterward it would not seem terribly difficult to achieve some formal division of territory. The Darklands, plunged into night for over half the year, could never seem overwhelmingly attractive to humans. The aborigines, on the other hand, cannot endure the full light of day, and so have little incentive to move into what are now the lands of men. But somehow the aborigines cannot see this. Sherrinford notes,

"It didn't occur to them that they might be conceded the right to keep their lands. Perhaps they're still more fiercely territorial than we. They determined to fight, in their own way." (p. 80)[12]

However, Anderson also shows that self-direction can be won even against high odds. Sherrinford's allusion to the planet Rustum, already noted, is brought on by the fact that on that world, flying creatures large enough to carry a child are known to exist. A child-carrying bird does in fact play an important role in the *Orbit Unlimited* novelette "The Mills of the Gods," which also shares with "The Queen of Air and Darkness" the plot thread of a search for a lost little boy. One of the main concerns of the earlier story is how, after a decade of struggle, the Calvinist Joshua Coffin learns to break the rigid mold of his belief system and comes to a more "human" relationship with himself and with his family. By the end of "The Queen of Air and Darkness" a similar breakthrough seems possible for aborigine-human relations.

After all, the aboriginal methods of struggle have led to little bloodshed. A rational-technological society will be able to forgive the aborigines their subtler assault, recognizing that " 'they never did us any harm as atrocious as what we've inflicted on our fellow men in the past.' " (Sherrinford, p. 81) And while an accommodation between humans and aborigines will not be easy and may even prove impossible, the confrontation does present the two peoples with new opportunity. Not only can there be fruitful exchange between the aboriginal "biology technology" and the human "physics technology": more fundamentally, the alien perspective, with its own archetypes or other patterns of thought, should make possible a new understanding of the mind. " 'I daresay,' " says Sherrinford, " 'once we begin to get insight into that mentality, our psychological science will go through its Copernican revolution.' " (p. 80)

§

The concept of archetypes will be part of this new "psychological science," but it alone is clearly insufficient, as the failure of the aborigines' scheme demonstrates. And beyond this, it is obvious that secondhand Jungian psychology is not all that is needed to resolve the central philosophical conflict of the novelette.

Anderson shows a great deal of sympathy for, and appreciation of, the aboriginal way of life, but there is no doubt that on the margin his sympathies fall toward the "rational-technological" human culture. In one sense, he presents the conflict of societies as one between freedom and slavery.

But this is "slavery" only in a very special sense. In the

realm of the Queen of Air and Darkness, no one is compelled under pain of death to labor. There are no discontented slaves constantly looking for a means of escape, ready to make a break the moment the opportunity presents itself. Such relations between master and slave certainly do exist at times, and Anderson has dealt with them in other works.[13] But there is another condition of "slavery" which is perhaps more common. As van Rijn says in "The Master Key,"

"How many slaves have there been, in Earth's long history, that their masters could trust? Quite some! . . . And how many people today is domestic animals at heart? Wanting somebody else should tell them what to do, take care of their needfuls, protect them not just against their fellow men but against themselves?"

In order to draw a distinction between unwilling and willing servitude, we might reserve the term "slavery" for the first meaning, and call the second "enthrallment." A thrall is a slave, of course, but in modern English the former term has acquired a connotation of voluntary bondage.

This distinction between "slavery" and "enthrallment" is drawn with particular clarity in a theory of fundamental human relationships devised by Professor Manfred Halpern of the Politics Department of Princeton University. According to his theory, a coerced, unwilling master-slave relationship is an instance of what he terms "Subjection," while what we have called the master-thrall relation would be an instance of "Emanation." Halpern defines this latter as,

an encounter in which (1) one treats the other solely as an extension of one's own personality, one's own will and power as an embodiment of one's self. And (2) the other accepts his denial of his separate identity as legitimate because of the mysterious source or nature of the overwhelming power of the other.[14]

Additionally, in return for his denial of self, the "thrall" receives a sense of limitless security, a feeling of being loved and comforted. "Emanation" is, in fact, characteristic of relations between parents and young children, and it is one of the very few social tools available to primitive societies, which fact accounts for, among other things, the deification of many rulers. It also at least partially explains the at-times puzzling acquiescence of a people to a rule which seems tyrannical to the outsider.

In "The Queen of Air and Darkness," it would seem that a relationship of Emanation exists between the Queen and at least her nonaboriginal subjects—both kidnapped humans and the bioengineered beings. These individuals clearly see the Queen as possessing "overwhelming power" of a "mysterious source or nature." One of the aborigine-raised humans, Mistherd, reflects of the Queen, "Of course, you obeyed her, and in time you saw how wise she had been" (p. 52). Later, Sherrinford concludes that the Outlings are like folkloric fairies who are " 'not truly gods but obedient to rulers who are enigmatic and powerful enough to be.' " (p. 82)

Furthermore, the Queen does reward her servants with a sense of belonging, of love and comfort. After Barbro is kidnapped, the aborigines try to win her over by giving her a foretaste of this emotion: "she was borne along in a knowledge of being loved. At peace, at peace, rest in the calm expectation of joy." (p. 73)

It is not clear whether this psychology can be extended to the aborigines themselves. There is no obvious reason why their social patterns should be the same as those of humans and creatures designed to impress humans. On the other hand, it is possible to construct one or several explanations for their actions in human terms. One possible difference is that the aboriginal culture seems to lack Anderson's conception of freedom: the Queen seems unaware she is depriving the humans of anything.

Both of the Queen's aspects—awesome ruler and loving comforter—are reflected in the titles by which she is known among the humans and the bioengineered creatures: Starmother, Snowmaker, Lady Sky, the Fairest, All Healer, Moonmother, Garland Bearer, Wonderful One, Mother, Queen, Sister of Lyrth (Lyrth being a constellation visible from Roland).

But Anderson has dealt with simple personal "enthrallment" before: perhaps best in "The Master Key" and in the relationship between Djana and Ydwyr in *A Circus of Hells*. The treatment of the theme in "The Queen of Air and Darkness" is remarkable for the fact that here this personal "enthrallment" is almost explicitly identified with another sort of willing servitude: slavery to tradition, to that which maintains its awe of mystery simply because it is unexamined, slavery to the "collective unconscious." " 'We live with our archetypes, but can we live in them?' " (Sherrinford, p. 81)

Anderson has treated this second sort of "enthrallment" previously, perhaps best in "A Twelvemonth and a Day" (expanded version: *Let the Spacemen Beware!*), but the combination in "The Queen of Air and Darkness" is probably his best effort to show us that the two forms are essentially the same.[15] One can surrender one's rational will to beliefs or habits as easily as to individuals, for essentially the same reasons, and with essentially the same results. Ideas have a mystery and power of their own. They too can love and comfort. Barbro says,

". . . when I'm under them I can't think of the stars as balls of gas, whose energies have been measured, whose planets have been walked on by prosaic feet. No, they're small and cold and magical; our lives are bound to them; after we die, they whisper to us in our graves." (p. 65)

Later, during Barbro's kidnapping, as she struggles with telepathic suggestion:

Why should **she** believe ashen tales about . . . atoms and energies, nothing else to fill a gape of emptiness . . . tales she could not bring to mind . . . when Tim and the horse her father gave her carried her on to Jimmy? (p. 74)

But this quotation does more than to suggest that one can be "enthralled" by ideas. It also raises an important question. Why should anyone prefer the insecure search for truth to the comfort of sure belief? What does freedom have to offer which could induce anyone to reject the Queen of Air and Darkness and her world-view, to reject a sure route to a happy life in the aura of mystery and majesty?

§

While any final answers must be provided by each individual, Anderson takes us several steps in the inquiry. First, he reminds us that, as seen by an outsider, there is little difference between "enthrallment" and "real slavery." If the outsider is a contemporary Westerner, or if, like Sherrinford, he comes from a colony world founded expressly to preserve Western values, then in fact the "slave" awaiting the chance to resist his master will seem to retain more human dignity than the "thrall" who willingly submits. Furthermore, if the "thrall" can be brought to see his situation from this viewpoint even for a moment, it may break the spell. After such an insight, the psychological rewards of "enthrallment" cease, and the individual's subjective state reflects his objective condition of bondage.

After Barbro is kidnapped, Sherrinford tries to convince his own prisoner, Mistherd, to betray the Queen. The detective lures a group of "Outlings" within the range of his deactivated telepathy shield, and then turns it on, so that Mistherd for the first time sees the aborigines in their true guise. After the shock has made the youth ready to listen, Sherrinford explains his view of Mistherd's situation. The detective later comments, " 'May I never see such bitterness again. He had been taught to believe he was free.' " (p. 80)

An example such as this, where a subject comes to see "enthrallment" and "slavery" as the same thing, shows the working of a general rule: the elimination of mystery will bring a relationship of Emanation to an end. Mystery is in a way the guarantee of the boundlessness of the might of the ruler: power bound to reason must always have limitations, great though it may be. Consequently it is at least helpful that there exist (as we have seen) "rational explanations" for the seeming miracles of the Darklands.

Next, Anderson demonstrates that if one accepts a sham mystery as real, one has stopped or strayed in the search for truth, and truth has survival value. The net technological superiority of the human colonists over the aborigines—and the victories won through this technology—illustrate the point.

Of course, mere survival is no ultimate end, either for Anderson or more particularly for the Queen's subjects. People who see themselves as the extensions of a person or idea are often quite willing to be martyrs:

"So you see I'm not afraid to die," Mistherd declared, though his lips trembled a bit. "If I let you come in and do your manthings to my people, I'd have naught left worth living for." (p. 71)

Nevertheless, one of the rewards for the surrender of one's will is supposed to be a feeling of fundamental security, and the Queen cannot preserve this feeling in her subjects in opposition to man's engines:

The Queen of Air and Darkness lifted an arm in summons. It halted, and none came to answer.
For over the fountains and melodies lifted a gruesome growling. Fires leaped, thunders crashed. Her hosts scattered screaming before the steel thing which boomed up the mountainside. (p. 76)

Though a full description of freedom may be too much for one novelette (it could be argued that Anderson has devoted a career to the question), we can at least know some of freedom's characteristics and some of the things which it is not.

Anderson is not urging an abjuration of the unconscious. He does not advocate a stainless-steel-and-enamel pseudo-rationalism. Man can and should reject false divinities such as the Queen, but he remains "necessarily and forever, a part of the life that surrounds him and a creature of the spirit within" (p. 43). On the expedition which results in the downfall of the Queen, Sherrinford and Barbro indeed use a manufactured "glower" to cook food, but Sherrinford also gathers wood "that they might later cheer themselves with a campfire" (p. 64). It is Barbro's "irrational" love for her son— a love more irrational than most, since in it is bound up the memory of Jimmy's dead father—and Sherrinford's "irrational" pity, and later love, for Barbro which impel the expedition in the first place.[17]

Free, continuous choice promises the development of values which can never exist in the unreflective, carefree atmosphere of the Queen's realm. Mistherd, for example, cannot understand how a man and woman could possibly sleep close to one another without having sexual intercourse (p. 58). Earlier he has concluded of Sherrinford and Barbro that "no Dweller could be as persistent as she or as patient as he" (p. 53).[18]

It is nevertheless quite possible that the "free" suffer more than the "enthralled." Freedom brings responsibility and often guilt. It may indeed provide a deeper satisfaction and a richer life, but the evaluation of such rewards is a distressingly subjective process. Perhaps no argument in favor of liberty can satisfy the intellect; perhaps the best we can hope for is a shared emotional conviction. This could, indeed, help to explain why Anderson principally writes fiction.

§

Up to this point, most of our attention has been on the question of what Anderson is saying in "The Queen of Air and Darkness." Now perhaps it is time to devote some thought to the way in which he says it.

We quickly realize that we must deal with archetypes once again. We discussed above how, on the "plot level," the concept is consciously employed by various characters and how it provides motivation and explanation. We can find another usage, a "technique-level" employment intended to have its impact not on a character but on the reader. Often, of course, the same archetype can serve both functions.

Consider, for example, the lengths to which Anderson carries the resemblance between Eric Sherrinford and Sherlock Holmes. The first thing Barbro notices when she calls at Sherrinford's apartment/office is the contrast between its "sane disorder" (p. 77) and the detective's personal neatness. This is also characteristic of Holmes. Sherrinford smokes a pipe. He is tall, "high-cheeked, beak-nosed, black-haired, and gray-eyed" (p. 37). On their first meeting, he deduces Barbro's occupation and personal history from her appearance.

More than this, Sherrinford is a grandnephew several score times removed of Holmes himself. Or at least he says, "we also claimed collateral descent from one of the first private inquiry agents on record, back on Earth before spaceflight" (p. 57). Baring-Gould's pseudobiography gives "Sherrinford" as the maiden name of Holmes's mother.[19] "Sherrinford" was the Christian name of Holmes himself in the original draft of *A Study in Scarlet*.

It seems clear that this identification between Holmes and Eric Sherrinford is more than could be required by exingencies of plot alone. We can, however, easily discern at least two other purposes which this evocation serves. First, as a close approximation to an archetypal Rational Detective, Holmes serves as a symbol of the rational-technological age to place in opposition to the Queen of Air and Darkness. Second, implicit allusion to Holmes allows Anderson to be compact in his characterization. He has only to say, "basically, this fellow is a lot like Holmes, but with the following modifications . . ." Compactness in character portrayal holds great importance in science fiction, where so much other information must be worked into the narrative, and this is doubly true in a short work. Anderson's modifications, it must be added, are by no means insignificant. Sherrinford probably possesses a bit more kindness (a quality Anderson values highly), or at least sensitivity to the consequences of his actions, than did Conan Doyle's character. Holmes, as Watson somewhere puts it, had become a bit case-hardened. It may also be significant of the difference between the two characters that when Holmes could not find enough of a challenge to his intellect he turned to drugs, while Sherrinford, similarly bored by his job on the police force in the city of Heorot on the planet Beowulf, took ship on a scientific expedition which eventually brought him to Roland.

Other archetypes are added onto the Holmesian in the delineation of Sherrinford's character. The detective is part Cherokee and has a family tradition which makes him aware of this fact. Again this datum functions on two levels. It helps to explain the detective's sympathy for the Rolandic aborigines, and it invokes in the reader's mind a picture of the Vanishing Redman with associated sympathies. Both levels come into play at once in an exchange such as the following one between Barbro and Sherrinford:

"I suppose we can give them a reservation," she said, and didn't know why he grimaced and answered so roughly:
"Let's leave them the honor they've earned! They fought to save the world they'd always known from that—" he made a chopping gesture at the city— "and just possibly we'd be better off ourselves with less of it." (p. 81)

If we venture for a moment onto less certain ground, we may perceive a rather more oblique archetypal characterization of Sherrinford. All of the human-inhabited planets in this "future history" seem to be named after the heroes of national epics, and other celestial bodies and geographic places have related names. Thus Roland's sun is called Charlemagne, and Roland's moons are Oliver and Alde, after the hero's comrade and his betrothed. Heorot, mentioned above, is the hall of King Hrothgar in *Beowulf*. On Rustum (Rustum is the Persian national hero), many of the place-names come from Persian history, and the moon Raksh takes its name from Rustum's horse. This nomenclature—probably devised by the Astro-nautical Society of spaceship crewmen—bears no especial rela-tion to the nationality of the eventual colonists. Rustum is settled mostly by North Americans. French has never been spoken on Roland, but it is probably still a living language on Beowulf, since Sherrinford speaks it fluently (p. 64). If Anderson had any intention here beyond the provision of a plausible naming scheme, it may have been simply to empha-size the heroism implicit in the colonization of extrasolar planets. Still, if we bear in mind Sherrinford's planet of origin, we may find significance in the fact that, at least in the *chanson de geste* which bears his name, Roland has to deal only with human opponents, while Beowulf, like Sherrin-ford, is a slayer of monsters.

Barbro's "devoted widow" role—and the way she emerges from it by falling in love again—are of course also archetypal. However, again on this "technique" level, the only real com-petition to the Holmes archetype is that presented by the Queen of Air and Darkness and her realm.

As was true of Sherrinford/Holmes, the Queen of Air and Darkness archetype exerts a fascination on the imagination of the reader similar to her effect on the characters of the novelette. It must be this reader-effect which has motivated so many modern writers to introduce "Queen" figures into their works. Besides the literal "Queens of Air and Darkness" such as Morgause in T. H. White's *The Once and Future King,* or the otherwise unnamed lady in A. E. Housman's poem (III in *Last Poems*), the archetype is manifested in most modern uses of Morgan le Fay, or in Keats's "La Belle Dame sans Merci," or in the evil Narnian witch-queens of C. S. Lewis. These examples could be easily multiplied,[20] though, of course, every fairy queen is not Queen of Air and Darkness: consider the good Lady of the Lake, the traditional fairy god-mother, etc.

Archetypes pattern not only people and places. They also can shape action. The Outlings steal children (such as Jimmy) and mothers of young children (such as Barbro) because this is what fairies *do*. It is also simply of the nature of fairies that from time to time they invite humans to share their eldritch life.

This much is "plot-level" archetype. The Outlings have "reasonably" conformed to fairy practice because it reinforces the pattern in human minds and because they have uses for kidnapped humans. Young children are particularly suitable because they can be raised in the "Outling" life style, and mothers may be won over by manipulations of their maternal emotions. But we also see "technique-level" archetype here. The identification between aborigines and fairies tells us other things about the extraterrestrials, things they should rationally wish not to disclose or suggest. For example, as J. R. R. Tolkien reminds us, "It is often reported of fairies . . . that they are workers of illusion, that they are cheaters of men by 'fantasy.' "[21]

At least in the European tradition—this would not hold for, say, the Arabian Nights tales—one only rarely encounters stories which dwell on the marvels of Faerie without describing the price paid for them. Much more common—and more popular—are stories about people who have rejected the blandishments of Faerie, or first accepted them and later attempted escape, successfully or unsuccessfully. Sometimes simple homesickness motivates this rejection, but more often it is love for a wife or sweetheart left in the lands of men.[22] And despite the aborigines' plans, this latter drama is the one played out in "The Queen of Air and Darkness."

At the very least, this "double-leveled" archetype serves Anderson as a device for foreshadowing: the reader knows that the Outlings will prove to be deceitful and at least strongly suspects that their deceit will be successfully opposed.[23] But more than this, the very story of Escape from Elfland (as an instance of, in Halpern's terms, "breaking of Emanation") forms, in Sherrinford's words, a crystallization of basic aspects of the human psyche, and when we meet such an archetypal plot in fiction, our reaction goes deeper than consciousness.

§

There is, of course, more to fiction than the invocation and modification of archetypes (or of Halpern's basic relationships). Let us examine at least briefly the "surface" of Anderson's work, his choice of scenes and of wording.

Critics such as James Blish have long recognized that Anderson is a "poet," both literally and in his poetic use of prose. "The Queen of Air and Darkness" contains five poems, including one eighteen-stanza ballad,[24] a couplet in tetrameter which sounds almost Shakespearian, a song composed according to the rules of Scandinavian prosody, and a seventeen-syllable three-sentence poem which, Anderson insists, is *not* a haiku.[25] The prose is filled with poetic devices ranging from alliteration through metaphor even to one hyper-compound sentence consisting of fifteen verbs in a row followed immediately by nine adjectives, all with the same noun as grammatical referent. (p. 44)

One can find an excellent sample of his skill with prose in the opening paragraph of the novelette, where Anderson manages to establish an idyllic mood while at the same time conveying the alienness of the Rolandic setting. He coins names for extraterrestrial plants and animals which add to the pastoral spell instead of breaking it with unfamiliarity: firethorn, steel-flower, brok, rainplant, kiss-me-never, flittery, crownbuck.[26]

A little later in the story (p. 41), Anderson achieves one of the most graceful transitions from dialog to a long exposition of background to be found in science fiction. As Barbro holds her first conversation with Sherrinford, night gradually closes in, mirroring her anxiety. The scene ends with the sentences,

The woman drew closer to the man in this darkening room, surely not aware that she did, until he switched on a fluoropanel. The same knowledge of Roland's aloneness was in them both.

The passage of exposition then begins,

One light-year is not much as galactic distances go. You could walk it in about 270 million years, beginning at the middle of the Permian Era, when dinosaurs belonged to the remote future, and continuing to the present day when spaceships cross even greater reaches. . . .

Unfortunately, such instances are not as common as one could wish. For the most part, Anderson has resorted to his usual technique of "lectures." Anderson has considerably more conscience than some writers about having characters tell each other things they should already know; he invents excuses for such exercises, and even—on occasion—puts them to good dramatic use. However, after a while these cover-up attempts themselves become glaringly obvious:

"He shrugged and fell into the lecturer's manner for which he was notorious." (p. 37)

"To still the writhing of her fingers he asked skeptically . . ." (p. 39)

" 'I didn't want to raise your hopes or excite you unduly. . . . So I'm only now telling you how thoroughly I studied available material on the . . . Old Folk.' " (p. 55)

"Sherrinford recognized that her query asked for comfort as much as it did for facts, and he spoke with deliberate dryness. . . ." (p. 63)

This difficulty with the insertion of background material also relates to Anderson's general awkwardness with dialogue. The fault becomes most glaring in the speech of the three-year-old Jimmy. Story dialogue is not transcription, and whether or not any child ever used such an expression, it does not read convincingly when Jimmy, asked whether he wants French bread or rye, replies, " 'I'll have a slice of what we people call the F bread,' " (p. 45), or when, as he and his mother are reunited at the Queen's court, he says, " 'Stay. Here's fun. I'll show. But you stay.' " (p. 76)

Sometimes rather strange things happen to the plot so that

a particular conversation can occur at a particular moment. Rolanders, for example, are unaware of the electromagnetic nature of telepathy, and Sherrinford has to explain it to Barbro—and to the reader. He adds, " 'I daresay the facts are available in the scientific microfiles at Christmas Landing. You Rolanders have simply had no occasion to seek them out.' " (p. 63)

"Scientific microfiles" indeed! Even the two-dollar paperback *Columbia-Viking Desk Encyclopedia* has an article on telepathy, though as of its date of publication (1964) it can report nothing very definite on the topic. Are we to believe that Rolanders are so lacking in curiosity that they do not even reprint general reference works brought from Earth? Or that a topic so fascinating as telepathy could be completely passed over even in recreational reading?[27]

Again, the Rolandic government has imposed (or requested) temporary suspension of the story of the discovery of the aborigines in order to gain time to formulate policy. But no one has bothered to tell Barbro about this ban, so that only her own independent judgment keeps her from revealing the news. This gives Sherrinford, a week later, the chance to explain the reasons for the censorship, but it hardly adds to the story's credibility.

Neither of these cases presents an absolute impossibility. Before Sherrinford's deductions, no one had reason to connect the Outling "spells" with parapsychology. It is not beyond imagination that an interesting but seemingly irrelevant fact might, in a pioneer society, remain buried in the files. Similarly, governments, especially when confronted with unfamiliar problems, can be remarkably slipshod in their operation. Perhaps the Rolandic authorities could have overlooked Barbro. But in any case, instances such as these needlessly weaken verisimilitude. Furthermore, they may contribute to that vaguely "pulpish" odor which somehow clings to Anderson despite what should be ample proof of the real merit of his production.

§

One can indeed hope that Anderson will learn better to burnish even the "surface" of his work. Despite a quarter century as a published writer, and despite the current level of success indicated by two Nebulas, four Hugo awards (both figures as of this writing!), and consistent sales, Anderson remains concerned with expanding the scope and improving the quality of his creation.

In the meantime, however, the reader should not let superficial imperfections distract him. The stream of Anderson's art runs much deeper. It is continually replenished by tributaries drawing on the most diverse aspects of human experience, until at last it exhausts itself in a limitless expanse of Space, Time, and Mind.

ACKNOWLEDGMENTS

This article's citations do not fully reflect its intellectual debt to Professor Manfred Halpern, both for his published and as-yet-unpublished writings, and for course work. Nor do they indicate my even greater obligation to Sandra Miesel, for her articles on Anderson (especially the original version of "Challenge and Response" in *Riverside Quarterly* 4:2) and for fruitful discussion over a period of years. Poul Anderson was kind enough to answer a few more-or-less concrete questions, and to disabuse me of a number of notions which consequently do not appear in this paper. Poul Anderson, Judy Cohen (now Judy Carrick), Susan Glicksohn, Manfred Halpern, John Miesel, Sandra Miesel, Frieda Murray, and Alexei Panshin read and commented on one or another draft of this essay. Any remaining errors are, of course, my responsibility.

NOTES

1. In-text page citations for "The Queen of Air and Darkness" are to pages in this anthology.

2. Gertrude Jobes, *Dictionary of Mythology, Folklore, and Symbols,* (New York: Scarecrow Press, 1961), I, 545.

3. W. Y. Evans Wentz, *The Fairy-Faith in Celtic Countries,* (London: Oxford University Press, 1911), 283–4.

4. See for instance the Danish ballad "The Elven Shaft" in Axel Orlik, ed., *A Book of Danish Ballads,* trans. E. M. Smith-Dampier, (Princeton: Princeton University Press, 1939), 103–106. There is also a translation, "Sir Oluf and the Elf-King's Daughter," in the first volume of Francis James Child's *English and Scottish Ballads.*

5. Lucy Allen Paton, *Studies in the Fairy Mythology of Arthurian Romance,* Radcliffe College Monograph No. 13 (Boston: Ginn and Company, 1903), 3–4.

6. Fairyland often has in addition a time-rate different from that of the normal world. Anderson discards this feature—though the Outlings are "indifferent to time" (p. 33)—and a few others in "The Queen of Air and Darkness."

7. Jobes, II, 1180. The North is also the abode of the evil witch-queens in C. S. Lewis's Narnia series.

8. The plotline of *The Star Ways* is strikingly similar to that of "The Queen of Air and Darkness," though its development is altogether different.

9. This is the etymology given by Kipling's fairy in *Puck of Pook's Hill.*

10. Jobes, I, 545. Joseph Wright, ed., *The English Dialect Dictionary,* (New York: G. P. Putnam's Sons, 1903), IV, 264, 265.

11. A Soviet study putting forward a theory for telepathy strikingly like that used in "The Queen of Air and Darkness" is I. M. Kogan, *The Information Theory Aspect of Telepathy,* (Rand Corporation P-4145, 1969). Kogan reports positive results over ranges much longer than those Anderson permits the aborigines, but the same atmospheric conditions that upset radio communication on Roland might well do the same to telepathic transmissions.

12. Sherrinford's speculation about innate territoriality may well be incorrect, even within the terms of the novelette. Anderson has expressed his doubts about applying such theories to intelligent beings in *Is There Life on Other Worlds?,* (New York: Collier Books, 1963), 132–5.

13. For example, Flandry is for a while this sort of slave in *A Circus of Hells,* as are the crew of the *Franklin* in *After Doomsday,* and the elf women in *The Broken Sword.*

14. *Applying a New Theory of Human Relations to the Comparative Study of Racism,* (Denver: University of Denver Race and Nations Monograph Series I:1, 1969–70), 6.

15. The 1966 novel *The Ancient Gods (World Without Stars)* includes a somewhat similar identification. Anderson's 1966 novelette "Goat Song" did not see publication until the February 1972 issue of *Fantasy and Science Fiction,* which appeared while the original draft of this essay was in preparation. "Goat Song" provides corroboration for a number of ideas put forward in this paper; in particular, it presents a striking identification of the two types of "enthrallment." In the novelette, SUM, the non-self-aware computer, nothing more than a crystallization of the intentions of its builders, is rapidly taking on the attributes of personalistic

Godhood. Note that *sum* is Latin for "I Am," the name which God reveals to Moses (Exodus 3:14).

16. This quotation does not contradict the earlier contention that the aborigines do not understand freedom. It is exactly to the point that the aborigines equate this dependent freedom-from-material-want with "real" liberty.

17. This viewpoint also emerges strongly in other of Anderson's works. The hero of "Goat Song," after urging his followers to forsake SUM, tells them, " 'Seek out mystery; what else is the whole cosmos but mystery? Live bravely, die and be done, and you will be more than any machine. You may perhaps be God' " (p. 32). Similarly, in *The Ancient Gods,* Hugh Valland, who leads the opposition to the self-deified extraterrestrial Ai Chun, himself maintains, in cheerful disregard of his culture's permissive mores, a celibate devotion to a girl who died years before. Many Anderson heroes also adhere to one formal religion or another.

18. In *The Broken Sword,* Anderson presents a similar contrast between elven and human society. The elf-raised Scafloc reflects on the reaction of Freda to her family's murder: "The elves had not taught him about mourning such as this" (p. 68; [rev. ed., New York: Ballantine, 1971]).

Later in the book he tells her, " 'Elves know defeat only sometimes, fear seldom, and love never. But since meeting you, dear, I have found all three in myself.' "

Freda's reply is also significant: " 'And somewhat of elf has entered my blood. I fear that less and less do I think of what is right and holy, more and more of what is useful and pleasant. My sins grow heavy—' " (p. 117).

Finally even Imric, lord of all elves in Britain, concedes, " 'Happier are all men than the dwellers in Faerie—or the gods for that matter. . . . Better a life like a falling star, bright across the dark, than a deathlessness which can see naught above or beyond itself' " (p. 206).

The elven society of *The Broken Sword,* however, is much more complex than that of the Outlings in "The Queen of Air and Darkness." To explain the former in terms of Halpern's theory we would need to give important consideration to additional relationships such as "Subjection," "Direct Bargaining," and "Buffering."

19. William S. Baring-Gould, *Sherlock Holmes of Baker Street,* (New York: Clarkson N. Potter, 1962), 13.

20. One amusing "perversion" of the tradition is Robert A. Heinlein's *Glory Road,* which in outline is nothing but a typical fairy story: hero is enticed into Fairyland by beautiful woman who turns out to be Fairy Queen and whom he marries; hero performs feats of daring in Faerie, but gradually grows homesick, forsakes Queen and returns to "real world," after which he pines for Faerie.

Compare Heinlein's work especially to Yeats's *The Wanderings of Oisin.*

21. J. R. R. Tolkien, "On Fairy-Stories," *Tree and Leaf,* (Boston: Houghton Mifflin, 1965), 14.

22. Examples: The Irish "Cuchulain's Sickbed," "Tamlane" and its variants in the first volume of Child. In the Danish "The Elven Shaft" (cited above), and in Anderson's "Arvid Song" within the novelette itself, the hero, after rejecting Faerie in favor of an earthly sweetheart, pines for his lost opportunity. Nonetheless, even here the possibility of escape is affirmed.

23. Note also the role of the Holmesian archetype here. Consider Holmes's exposure of the "supernatural" Hound of the Baskervilles, or of the Cornish Horror in "The Adventure of the Devil's Foot." In fact, it may well be that the climax of the novelette is somewhat weakened by the obvious stacking of the archetypal cards against the Queen. By the time of Sherrinford's invasion of the Queen's court, no one can have the slightest doubt as to who will be the winner, and why. In the novelette's "future history," a philosophy similar to that of the Queen has actually triumphed on Earth; one suspects that the powers of Darkness should really have made a better fight of it on Roland.

24. The "Arvid Song" is based primarily on the rich medieval Danish ballad tradition. As was mentioned above, the plot of Anderson's poem closely parallels that of "The Elven Shaft." Anderson's meter and rhyme scheme, while not uncommon among Danish ballads [Johannes C. H. R. Steenstrup, *The Medieval Popular Ballad,* trans. Edward Godfrey Cox, (New York: Ginn and Company, 1914), 131–133], are also found in A. E. Housman's above-mentioned poem on the Queen of Air and Darkness (III in *Last Poems*).

25. Personal communication.

26. Compare these names, mostly English compounds, with the ones introduced later in the novelette, many of which have foreign roots, e.g., Greek: monocerus (one-horn), bathyrhiza (deeproot), glycephyllon (sweetleaf), chalcanthermum (copperflower); and Spanish: pumablanca (white-feather), yerba (grass, herb).

27. On the other hand, it must be admitted that the Kogan telepathy study cited above was sufficiently obscure that I myself ran across it entirely by accident when the original draft of this paper was almost complete. But in the novelette, the electromagnetic explanation is given as established fact, not as one of several competing theories; hence it should be more widely diffused and better known.

POUL ANDERSON

Epilogue

I

His name was a set of radio pulses. Converted into equivalent sound waves, it would have been an ugly squawk; so because he, like any consciousness, was the center of his own coordinate system, let him be called Zero.

He was out hunting that day. Energy reserves were low in the cave. That other who may be called One—being the most important dweller in Zero's universe—had not complained. But there was no need to. He also felt a dwindling potential. Accumulators grew abundantly in their neighborhood, but an undue amount of such cells must be processed to recharge One while she was creating. Motiles had more concentrated energy. And, of course, they were more highly organized. Entire parts could be taken from the body of a motile, needing little or no reshaping for One to use. Zero himself, though the demands on his functioning were much less, wanted a more easily assimilated charge than the accumulators provided.

In short, they both needed a change of diet.

Game did not come near the cave any more. The past hundred years had taught that it was unsafe. Eventually, Zero knew, he would have to move. But the thought of helping One through mile upon mile, steep, overgrown and dangerous, made him delay. Surely he could still find large motiles within a few days' radius of his present home. With One's help he fastened a carrier rack on his shoulders, took weapons in hand, and set forth.

§   114

That was near sunset. The sky was still light when he came on spoor: broken earth-crystals not yet healed, slabs cut from several boles, a trace of lubricant. Tuning his receptors to the highest sensitivity, he checked all the bands commonly made noisy by motiles. He caught a low-amplitude conversation between two persons a hundred miles distant, borne this far by some freak of atmospherics; closer by he sensed the impulses of small scuttering things, not worth chasing; a flier jetted overhead and filled his perception briefly with static. But no vibration of the big one. It must have passed this way days ago and now be out of receptor shot.

Well, he could follow the trail, and catch up with the clumsy sawyer in time. It was undoubtedly a sawyer—he knew these signs—and therefore worth a protracted hunt. He ran a quick check on himself. Every part seemed in good order. He set into motion, a long stride which must eventually overhaul anything on treads.

Twilight ended. A nearly full moon rose over the hills like a tiny cold lens. Night vapors glowed in masses and streamers against a purple black sky where stars glittered in the optical spectrum and hummed and sang in the radio range. The forest sheened with alloy, flashed with icy speckles of silicate. A wind blew through the radiation absorber plates overhead, setting them to ringing against each other; a burrower whirred, a grubber crunched through lacy crystals, a river brawled chill and loud down a ravine toward the valley below.

As he proceeded, weaving among trunks and girders and jointed rods with the ease of long practice, Zero paid most attention to his radio receptors. There was something strange in the upper communication frequencies tonight, an occasional brief note . . . set of notes, voice, drone, like nothing he had heard before or heard tell of . . . but the world was a mystery. No one had been past the ocean to the west or the mountains to the east. Finally Zero stopped listening and concentrated on tracking his prey. That was difficult, with his optical sensors largely nullified by the darkness, and he moved slowly. Once he tapped lubricant from a cylinder growth and once he thinned his acids with a drink of water. Several times he felt polarization in his energy cells and stopped for a while to let it clear away: he rested.

§

Dawn paled the sky over distant snowpeaks, and gradually turned red. Vapors rolled up the slopes from the valley, tasting of damp and sulfide. Zero could see the trail again, and began to move eagerly.

Then the strangeness returned—louder.

Zero slid to a crouch. His lattice swiveled upward. Yes, the pulses did come from above. They continued to strengthen. Soon he could identify them as akin to the radio noise associated with the functioning of a motile. But they did not sense like any type he knew. And there was something else, a harsh flickering overtone, as if he also caught leakage from the edge of a modulated shortwave beam—

The sound struck him.

At first it was the thinnest of whistles, high and cold above the dawn clouds. But within seconds it grew to a roar that shook the earth, reverberated from the mountains, and belled absorber plates until the whole forest rang. Zero's head became an echo chamber; the racket seemed to slam his brain from side to side. He turned dazzled, horrified sensors heavenward. And he saw the thing descending.

For a moment, crazily, he thought it was a flier. It had the long spindle-shaped body and the air fins. But no flier had ever come down on a tail of multicolored flame. No flier blocked off such a monstrous portion of sky. When the thing must be two miles away!

He felt the destruction as it landed, shattered frames, melted earth-crystals, a little burrower crushed in its den, like a wave of anguish through the forest. He hurled himself flat on the ground and hung on to sanity with all four hands. The silence which followed, when the monster had settled in place, was like a final thunderclap.

Slowly Zero raised his head. His perceptions cleared. An

arc of sun peered over the sierra. It was somehow outrageous that the sun should rise as if nothing had happened. The forest remained still, hardly so much as a radio hum to be sensed. The last echoes flew fading between the hills.

A measure of resolution: this was no time to be careful of his own existence. Zero poured full current into his transmitter. *"Alarm, alarm! All persons receiving, prepare to relay. Alarm!"*

Forty miles thence, the person who may as well be called Two answered, increasing output intensity the whole time: "Is that you, Zero? I noticed something peculiar in the direction of your establishment. What is the matter?"

Zero did not reply at once. Others were coming in, a surge of voices in his head, from mountaintops and hills and lowlands, huts and tents and caves, hunters, miners, growers, searakers, quarriers, toolmakers, suddenly became a unity. But he was flashing at his own home: "Stay inside, One. Conserve energy. I am unharmed, I will be cautious, keep hidden and stand by for my return."

"Silence!" called a stridency which all recognized as coming from Hundred. He was the oldest of them, he had probably gone through a total of half a dozen bodies. Irreversible polarization had slowed his thinking a little, taken the edge off, but the wisdom of his age remained and he presided over their councils. "Zero, report what you have observed."

The hunter hesitated. "That is not easy. I am at—" He described the location. ("Ah, yes," murmured Fifty-six, "near the large galena lick.") "The thing somewhat resembles a flier, but enormous, a hundred feet long or more. It came down about two miles north of here on an incandescent jet and is now quiet. I thought I overheard a beamed signal. If so, the cry was like nothing any motile ever made."

"In these parts," Hundred added shrewdly. "But the thing must have come from far away. Does it look dangerous?"

"Its jet is destructive," Zero said, "but nothing that size, with such relatively narrow fins, could glide about. Which makes me doubt it is a predator."

"Lure accumulators," said Eight.

"Eh? What about them?" asked Hundred.

"Well, if lure accumulators can emit signals powerful enough to take control of any small motile which comes near and make it enter their grinders, perhaps this thing has a similar ability. Then, judging from its size, its lure must have tremendous range and close up could overpower large motiles. Including even persons?"

Something like a shiver moved along the communication band.

"It is probably just a grazer," said Three. "If so—" His overt signal trailed off, but the thought continued in all their partly linked minds: *A motile that big! Megawatt-hours in its energy cells. Hundreds or thousands of usable part. Tons of metal. Hundred, did your great-grandcreator recall any such game, fabulous millennia ago?*

No.

If it is dangerous, it must be destroyed or driven off. If not, it must be divided among us. In either case: attacked!

Hundred rapped the decision forth. "All male persons take weapons and proceed to rendezvous at Broken Glade above the Coppertaste River. Zero, stalk as close as seems feasible, observe what you can, but keep silence unless something quite unforeseeable occurs. When we are gathered, you can describe details on which we may base a specific plan. Hasten!"

The voices toned away in Zero's receptor circuits. He was alone again.

§

The sun cleared the peaks and slanted long rays between the forest frames. Accumulators turned the black faces of their absorber plates toward it and drank thirstily of radiation. The mists dissipated, leaving boles and girders ashine with moisture. A breeze tinkled the silicate growths underfoot. For a moment Zero was astonishingly conscious of beauty. The wish that One could be here beside him, and the thought that soon he might be fused metal under the monster's breath, sharpened the morning's brightness.

Purpose congealed in him. Further down was a turmoil of frank greed. In all the decades since his activation there had been no such feast as this quarry should provide. Swiftly, he prepared himself. First he considered his ordinary weapons. The wire noose would never hold the monster, nor did he think the iron hammer would smash delicate moving parts— it did not seem to have any—or the steel bolts from his cross-bow pierce a thin plate to short out a crucial circuit. But the clawed, spear-headed pry bar might be of use. He kept it in one hand while two others unfastened the fourth and laid it with his extra armament in the carrier rack. Thereupon they deftly hooked his cutting torch in its place. No one used this artificial device except for necessary work or to finish off a big motile whose cells could replace the tremendous energy expended by the flame or in cases of dire need. But if the monster attacked him, that would surely constitute dire need. His only immediate intention was to spy on it.

Rising, he stalked among shadows and sun reflections, his camouflage-painted body nearly invisible. Such motiles as sensed him fled or grew very still. Not even the great slasher was as feared a predator as a hunting person. So it had been since that ancient day when some forgotten savage genius made the first crude spark gap and electricity was tamed.

Zero was about halfway to his goal, moving slower and more carefully with each step, when he perceived the newcomers.

He stopped dead. Wind clanked the branches above him, drowning out any other sound. But his electronic sensors told him of . . . two . . . three moving shapes, headed from the monster. And their emission was as alien as its own.

In a different way, Zero stood for a long time straining to sense and to understand what he sensed. The energy output of the three was small, hardly detectable even this close; a burrower or skitterer used more power to move itself. The output felt peculiar, too, not really like a motile's: too simple, as if a mere one or two circuits oscillated. Flat, cold, activity-less. But the signal output, on the other hand—it *must* be signal, that radio chatter—why, that was a shout. The things made such an uproar that receptors tuned at minimum could pick them up five miles away. As if they did not know about game, predators, enemies.

Or as if they did not care.

A while more Zero paused. The eeriness of this advent sent a tingle through him. It might be said he was gathering courage. In the end he gripped his pry bar more tightly and struck off after the three.

They were soon plain to his optical and radar senses among the tall growths. He went stock-still behind a frame and watched. Amazement shocked his very mind into silence. He had assumed, from their energy level, that the things were small. But they stood more than half as big as he did! And yet each of them had only one motor, operating at a level barely sufficient to move a person's arm. That could not be their power source. But what was?

Thought returned to him. He studied their outlandishness in some detail. They were shaped not altogether unlike himself, though two-armed, hunchbacked, and featureless. Totally unlike the monster, but unquestionably associated with it. No doubt it had sent them forth as spy eyes, like those employed by a boxroller. Certain persons had been trying for the last century or so to develop, from domesticated motiles, similar assistants for hunting persons. Yes, a thing as big and awkward as the monster might well need auxiliaries.

Was the monster then indeed a predator? Or even—the idea went like a lightning flash through Zero's entire circuitry— a thinker? Like a person? He struggled to make sense of the modulated signals between the three bipeds. No, he could not. But—

Wait!

Zero's lattice swung frantically back and forth. He could not shake off the truth. That last signal had come from the monster, hidden by a mile of forest. From the monster to the bipeds. And were they answering?

The bipeds were headed south. At the rate they were going, they might easily come upon traces of habitation, and follow those traces to the cave where One was, long before Hundred's males had gathered at Broken Glade.

The monster would know about One.

§

Decision came. Zero opened his transmitter to full output, but broadcast rather than beamed in any degree. He would give no clue where those were whom he called. "*Attention, attention!* Tune in on me: direct sensory linkage. I am about to attempt capture of these motiles."

Hundred looked through his optics, listened with his receptors, and exclaimed, "No, wait, you must not betray our existence before we are ready to act."

"The monster will soon learn of our existence in any event," Zero answered. "The forest is full of old campsites, broken tools, traps, chipped stones, slagheaps. At present I should have the advantage of surprise. If I fail and am destroyed, that ought still to provide you with considerable data. Stand alert!"

He plunged from behind the girders.

The three had gone past. They sensed him and spun about. He heard a jagged modulation of their signal output. A reply barked back, lower in frequency, the voice of the monster? There was no time to wonder about that. Slow and clumsy though they were, the bipeds had gotten into motion. The central one snatched a tube slung across its back. Pounding toward them, through shattering crystals and clangorous branches, Zero thought, *I have not yet made any overtly hostile move, but—* The tube flashed and roared.

An impact sent Zero staggering aside. He went to one knee. Ripped circuits overwhelmed him with destruction signals. As the pain throbbed toward extinction, his head cleared enough to see that half his upper left arm was blown off.

The tube was held steady on him. He rose. The knowledge of his danger flared in him. A second biped had its arms around the third, which was tugging a smaller object from a sheath.

Zero discharged full power through his effectors. Blurred to view by speed, he flung himself to one side while his remaining left hand threw the pry bar. It went meteorlike across a shaft of sunlight and struck the tube. The tube was pulled from the biped's grasp, slammed to the ground and buckled.

Instantly Zero was upon the three of them. He had already identified their communication system, a transmitter and antenna actually outside the skin! His one right hand smashed across a biped's back, tearing the radio set loose. His torch spat with precision. Fused, the communicator of a second biped went dead.

The third one tried to escape. Zero caught it in four strides, plucked off its antenna, and carried it wildly kicking under one arm while he chased the other two. When he had caught the second, the first stood its ground and battered forlornly at him with its hands. He lashed them all together with his wire rope. As a precaution, he emptied the carrier rack of the one which had shot him. Those thin objects might be dangerous even with the tube that had launched them broken. He stuffed the bipeds into his own carrier.

For a moment, then, he lingered. The forest held little sonic noise except the wind in the accumulators. But the radio spectrum clamored. The monster howled; Zero's own broadcast rolled between sky and mountainside, from person to person and so relayed across the land.

"No more talk now," he finished his report. "I do not want the monster to track me. I have prevented these auxiliaries from communicating with it. Now I shall take them to my cave for study. I hope to present some useful data at the rendezvous."

"This may frighten the monster off," Seventy-two said.

"So much the better," Hundred answered.

"In that case," Zero said, "I will at least have brought back something from my hunt."

He snapped off his transmission and faded into the forest shadows.

II

The boat had departed from the spaceship on a mere whisper of jets. Machinery inboard hummed, clicked, murmured, sucked in exhausted air and blew out renewed, busied itself with matters of warmth and light, computation and propulsion. But it made no more than a foundation for silence.

Hugh Darkington stared out the forward port. As the boat curved away from the mother ship's orbit, the great hull gleamed across his sky—fell astern and rapidly dwindled until lost to view. The stars which it had hidden sprang forth, icy-sharp points of glitter against an overwhelming blackness.

They didn't seem different to him. They were, of course. From Earth's surface the constellations would be wholly alien. But in space so many stars were visible that they made one chaos, at least to Darkington's eyes. Captain Thurshaw had pointed out to him, from the ship's bridge, that the Milky Way had a new shape, this bend was missing and that bay had not been there three billion years ago. To Darkington it remained words. He was a biologist and had never paid much attention to astronomy. In the first numbness of loss and isolation, he could think of nothing which mattered less than the exact form of the Milky Way.

Still the boat spiraled inward. Now the moon drifted across his view. In those eons since the *Traveler* left home, Luna had retreated from Earth: not as far as might have been predicted, because—they said—Bering Straits had vanished with every other remembered place; but nonetheless, now it was only a tarnished farthing. Through the ship's telescopes it had looked like itself. Some new mountains, craters, and maria, some thermal erosion of old features, but Thurshaw could identify much of what he once knew. It was grotesque that the moon should endure when everything else had changed.

Even the sun. Observed through a dimmer screen, the solar

disk was bloated and glaring. Not so much in absolute terms, perhaps. Earth had moved a little closer, as the friction of interplanetary dust and gas took a millennial toll. The sun itself had grown a little bigger and hotter, as nuclear reactions intensified. In three billion years, such things became noticeable even on the cosmic scale. To a living organism they totaled doomsday.

Darkington cursed under his breath and clenched a fist till the skin stretched taut. He was a thin man, long-faced, sharp-featured, his brown hair prematurely sprinkled with gray. His memories included beautiful spires above an Oxford squad, wonder seen through a microscope, a sailboat beating into the wind off Nantucket, which blew spray and a sound of gulls and church bells at him, comradeship bent over a chessboard or hoisting beer steins, forests hazy and ablaze with Indian summer: and all these things were dead. The shock had worn off, the hundred men and women aboard the *Traveler* could function again, but home had been amputated from their lives and the stump hurt.

Frederika Ruys laid her own hand on his and squeezed a little. Muscle by muscle he untensed himself, until he could twitch a smile in response to hers. "After all," she said, "we knew we'd be gone a long time. That we might well never come back."

"But we'd have been on a living planet," he mumbled.

"So we can still find us one," declared Sam Kuroki from his seat at the pilot console. "There's no less than six G-type stars within fifty light-years."

"It won't be the same," Darkington protested.

"No," said Frederika. "In a way, though, won't it be more? We, the last humans in the universe, starting the race over again?"

There was no coyness in her manner. She wasn't much to look at, plump, plain, with straight yellow hair and too wide a mouth. But such details had ceased to matter since the ship ended time acceleration. Frederika Ruys was a brave soul and a skilled engineer. Darkington felt incredibly lucky that she had picked him.

"Maybe we aren't the last, anyhow," Kuroki said. His flat features broke in one of his frequent grins; he faced immensity with a sparrow's cockiness. "Ought to've been other colonies than ours planted, oughtn't there? Of course, by now their descendants 'ud be bald-headed dwarfs who sit around thinking in calculus."

"I doubt that," Darkington sighed. "If humans had survived, anywhere else in the galaxy, don't you think they would at least have come back and . . . and reseeded this with life? The mother planet?" He drew a shaken breath. They had threshed this out a hundred times or more while the *Traveler* orbited about unrecognizable Earth, but they could not keep from saying the obvious again and again, as a man must keep touching a wound on his body. "No, I think the war really did begin soon after we left. The world situation was all set to explode."

§

That was why the *Traveler* had been built, and even more why it had departed in such haste, his mind went on. Fifty couples scrambling off to settle on Tau Ceti II before the missiles were unleashed. Oh, yes, officially they were a scientific team, and one of the big foundations had paid for the enterprise. But in fact, as everyone knew, the hope was to insure that a fragment of civilization would be saved, and some day return to help rebuild. (Even Panasia admitted that a total war would throw history back a hundred years; western governments were less optimistic.) Tension had mounted so horribly fast in the final months that no time was taken for a really careful check of the field drive. So new and little understood an engine ought to have had scores of test flights before starting out under full power. But . . . well . . . next year might be too late. And exploratory ships *had* visited the nearer stars, moving just under the speed of light, their crews experiencing only a few weeks of transit time. Why not the *Traveler*?

"The absolute war?" Frederika said, as she had done so often already. "Fought until the whole world was sterile? No. I won't believe it."

"Not in that simple and clean-cut a way," Darkington conceded. "Probably the war did end with a nominal victor; but he was more decimated and devastated than anyone had dared expect. Too impoverished to reconstruct, or even to maintain what little physical plant survived. A downward spiral into the Dark Ages."

"H-m-m, I dunno," Kuroki argued. "There were a lot of machines around. Automation, especially. Like those self-reproducing, sun-powered, mineral-collecting sea rafts. And a lot of other self-maintaining gadgets. I don't see why industry couldn't be revived on such a base."

"Radioactivity would have been everywhere," Darkington pointed out. "It's long-range effect on ecology— Oh, yes, the process may have taken centuries, as first one species changed or died, and then another dependent on it, and then more. But how could the human survivors recreate technology when biology was disintegrating around them?" He shook himself and stiffened his back, ashamed of his self-pity a minute ago, looking horror flatly in the face. "That's my guess. I could be wrong, but it seems to fit the facts. We'll never know for certain, I suppose."

Earth rolled into sight. The planetary disk was still edged with blueness darkening toward black. Clouds still trailed fleecy above shining oceans; they gleamed upon the darkness near the terminator as they caught the first light before sunrise. Earth was forever fair.

But the continental shapes were new, speckled with hard points of reflection upon black and ocher where once they had been softly green and brown. There were no polar caps; sea level temperatures ranged from eighty to two hundred degrees Fahrenheit. No free oxygen remained: the atmosphere was nitrogen, its oxides, ammonia, hydrogen sulfide, sulfur dioxide, carbon dioxide and steam. Spectroscopes had found no trace of chlorophyll or any other complex organic compound. The ground cover, dimly glimpsed through clouds, was metallic.

This was no longer Earth. There was no good reason why the *Traveler* should send a boat and three highly unexpendable humans down to look at its lifelessness. But no one had suggested leaving the Solar System without such a final visit. Darkington remembered being taken to see his grandmother when she was dead. He was twelve years old and had loved her. It was not her in the box, that strange unmeaningful mask, but where then was she?

"Well, whatever happened seems to be three billion years in the past," Kuroki said, a little too loudly. "Forget it. We got troubles of our own."

Frederika's eyes had not left the planet. "We can't ever forget, Sam," she said. "We'll always wonder and hope—they, the children at least—that it didn't happen to them too cruelly." Darkington started in surprise as she went on murmuring, very low, oblivious of the men:

> to tell you of the ending of the day.
> And you will see her tallness with surprise,
> and looking into gentle, shadowed eyes
> protest: it's not that late; you have to stay
> awake a minute more, just one, to play
> with yonder ball. But nonetheless you rise
> so they won't hear her say, 'A baby cries,
> but you are big. Put all your toys away.'
>
> She lets you have a shabby bear in bed,
> though frankly doubting that you two can go
> through dream-shared living rooms or wingless flight.
> She tucks the blankets close beneath your head
> and smooths your hair and kisses you, and so
> goes out, turns off the light. 'Good night, Sleep tight.'

Kuroki glanced around at her. The plaid shirt wrinkled across his wide shoulders. "Poems yet," he said. "Who wrote that?"

"Hugh," said Frederika. "Didn't you know he published poetry? Quite a bit. I admired his work long before I met him."

Darkington flushed. Her interest was flattering, but he regarded "Then Death Will Come" as a juvenile effort.

However, his embarrassment pulled him out of sadness. (On the surface. Down beneath, it would always be there, in every one of them. He hoped they would not pass too much of it on to their children. Let us not weep eternally for Zion.) Leaning forward, he looked at the planet with an interest that mounted as the approach curve took them around the globe. He hoped for a few answers to a hell of a lot of questions.

For one thing, why, in three billion years, had life not reevolved? Radioactivity must have disappeared in a few centuries at most. The conditions of primordial Earth would have returned. Or would they? What had been lacking, this time around?

§

He woke from his brown study with a jerk as Kuroki said, "Well, I reckon we can steepen our trajectory a bit." A surprising interval had passed. The pilot touched controls and the mild acceleration increased. The terrestrial disk, already enormous, swelled with terrifying velocity, as if tumbling down upon them.

Then, subtly, it was no longer to one side or above, but was beneath; and it was no longer a thing among the stars but the convex floor of bowl-shaped creation. The jets blasted more strongly. Kuroki's jaws clenched till knots of muscle stood forth. His hands danced like a pianist's.

He was less the master of the boat, Darkington knew, than its helper. So many tons, coming down through atmospheric turbulence at such a velocity, groping with radar for a safe landing spot, could not be handled by organic brain and nerves. The boat's central director—essentially a computer whose input came from the instruments and whose efferent impulses went directly to the controls—performed the basic operations. Its task was fantastically complex: very nearly as difficult as the job of guiding the muscles when a man walks. Kuroki's fingers told the boat, "Go that way," but the director could overrule him.

"I think we'll settle among those hills." The pilot had to shout now, as the jets blasted stronger. "Want to come down just east of the sunrise line, so we'll have a full day ahead of us, and yonder's the most promising spot in this region. The lowlands look too boggy."

Darkington nodded and glanced at Frederika. She smiled and made a thumbs-up sign. He leaned over, straining against his safety harness, and brushed his lips across hers. She colored with a pleasure that he found oddly moving.

Some day, on another planet—that possibly hadn't been born when they left Earth—

He had voiced his fears to her, that the engine would go awry again when they started into deep space, and once more propel them through time, uncontrollably, until fuel was exhausted. A full charge in the tanks was equivalent to three billion years, plus or minus several million; or so the physicists aboard had estimated. In six billion A.D. might not the sun be so swollen as to engulf them when they emerged?

She had rapped him across the knuckles with her slide rule and said no, but you'll have to take my word for it because you haven't got the math. I've studied it as far as differential equations, he said. She grinned and answered that then he'd never had a math course. It seemed, she said, that time acceleration was readily explained by the same theory which underlay the field drive. In fact, the effect had been demonstrated in laboratory experiments. Oh, yes, I know about that, he said; reactive thrust is rotated through a fourth dimension and gets applied along the temporal rather than a spatial axis. You do not know a thing about it, she said, as your own words have just proved. But never mind. What happened to us was that a faulty manifold generated the t-acceleration effect in our engine.

Now we've torn everything down and rebuilt from scratch. We know it'll work right. The tanks are recharged. The ship's ecosystem is in good order. Any time we want, we can take off for a younger sun, and travel fifty light-years without growing more than a few months older. After which, seing no one else was around, she sought his arms; and that was more comforting then her words.

A last good-bye to Grandmother Earth, he thought. *Then we can start the life over again that we got from her.*

The thrust upon him mounted. Toward the end he lay in his chair, now become a couch, and concentrated on breathing.

They reached ground.

Silence rang in their ears for a long while. Kuroki was the first to move. He unstrapped his short body and snapped his chair back upright. One hand unhooked the radio microphone, another punched buttons. "Boat calling *Traveler*," he intoned, "We're O.K. so far. Come in, *Traveler*. Hello, hello."

Darkington freed himself, stiffly, his flesh athrob, and helped Frederika rise. She leaned on him a minute. "Earth," she said. Gulping: "Will you look out the port first, dearest? I find I'm not brave enough."

He realized with a shock that none of them had yet glanced at the landscape. Convulsively, he made the gesture.

He stood motionless for so long that finally she raised her head and stared for herself.

III

They did not realize the full strangeness before they donned spacesuits and went outside. Then, saying very little, they wandered about looking and feeling. Their brains were slow to develop the gestalts which would allow them really to see what surrounded them. A confused mass of detail could not be held in the memory, the underlying form could not be abstracted from raw sense impressions. A tree is a tree, anywhere and anywhen, no matter how intricate its branching or how oddly shaped its leaves and blossoms. But what is a—

—Thick shaft of gray metal, planted in the sand, central to a labyrinthine skeleton of straight and curved girders, between which run still more enigmatic structures embodying helices and toruses and Möbius strips and less familiar geometrical elements; the entire thing some fifty feet tall; flaunting at the top several hundred thin metal plates whose black sides are turned toward the sun?

When you have reached the point of being able to describe it even this crudely, then you *have* apprehended it.

Eventually Darkington saw that the basic structure was repeated, with infinite variation of size and shape, as far as he could see. Some specimens tall and slender, some low and broad, they dominated the hillside. The deeper reaches were made gloomy by their overhang, but sun speckles flew piercingly bright within those shadows as the wind shook the mirror faces of the plates. That same wind made a noise of clanking and clashing and far-off booming, mile after metal mile.

There was no soil, only sand, rusty red and yellow. But outside the circle which had been devastated by the boat's jets, Darkington found the earth carpeted with prismatic growths, a few inches high, seemingly rooted in the ground. He broke one off for closer examination and saw tiny crystals, endlessly repeated, in some transparent siliceous material: like snowflakes and spiderwebs of glass. It sparkled so brightly, making so many rainbows, that he couldn't well study the interior. He could barely make out at the center a dark clump of . . . wires, coils, transistors? *No*, he told himself, *don't be silly*. He gave it to Frederika, who exclaimed at its beauty.

He himself walked across an open stretch, hoping for a view even vaguely familiar. Where the hillside dropped too sharply to support anything but the crystals—they made it one dazzle of diamonds—he saw eroded contours, the remote white sword of a waterfall, stewn boulders and a few crags like worn-out obelisks. The land rolled away into blue distances; a snowcapped mountain range guarded the eastern horizon. The sky overhead was darker than in his day, faintly greenish blue, full of clouds. He couldn't look near the fierce big sun.

Kuroki joined him. "What d'you think, Hugh?" the pilot asked.

"I hardly dare say. You?"

"Hell, I can't think with that bloody boiler factory clattering at me." Kuroki grimaced behind his faceplate. "Turn off your sonic mike and let's talk by radio."

Darkington agreed. Without amplification, the noise reached him through his insulated helmet as a far-off tolling. "We can take it for granted," he said, "that none of this is accidental. No minerals could simply crystallize out like this."

"Don't look manufactured to me, though."

"Well," said Darkington, "you wouldn't expect them to turn out their products in anything like a human machine shop."

"Them?"

"Whoever . . . whatever . . . made this. For whatever purpose."

Kuroki whistled. "I was afraid you'd say something like that. But we didn't see a trace of—cities, roads, anything —from orbit. I know the cloudiness made seeing pretty bad, but we couldn't have missed the signs of a civilization able to produce stuff on this scale."

"Why not? If the civilization isn't remotely like anything we've ever imagined?"

Frederika approached, leaving a cartful of instruments behind. "The low and medium frequency radio spectrum is crawling," she reported. "You never heard so many assorted hoots, buzzes, whirrs, squeals and whines in your life."

"We picked up an occasional bit of radio racket while in orbit," Kuroki nodded. "Didn't think much about it, then."

"Just noise," Frederika said hastily. "Not varied enough to be any kind of . . . of communication. But I wonder what's doing it?"

"Oscillators," Darkington said, "Incidental radiation from a variety of . . . oh, hell, I'll speak plainly . . . machines."

"But—" Her hand stole toward his. Glove grasped glove. She wet her lips. "No, Hugh, this is absurd. How could anyone be capable of making . . . what we see . . . and not have detected us in orbit and . . . and done something about us?"

Darkington shrugged. The gesture was lost in his armor. "Maybe they're biding their time. Maybe they aren't here at the moment. The whole planet could be an automated factory, you know. Like those ocean mineral harvesters we had in our time"—it hurt to say that—"which Sam mentioned on the way down. Somebody may come around periodically and collect the production."

"Where do they come from?" asked Kuroki in a rough tone.

"I don't know, I tell you. Let's stop making wild guesses and start gathering data."

Silence grew between them. The skeleton towers belled. Finally Kuroki nodded. "Yeah. What say we take a little stroll? We may come on something."

Nobody mentioned fear. They dared not.

§

Reentering the boat, they made the needful arrangements. The *Traveler* would be above the horizon for several hours yet. Captain Thurshaw gave his reluctant consent to an exploration on foot. The idea conflicted with his training, but what did survey doctrine mean under these conditions? The boat's director could keep a radio beam locked on the ship and thus relay communication between Earth and orbit. While Kuroki talked, Darkington and Frederika prepared supplies. Not much was needed. The capacitor pack in each suit held charge enough to power thermostat and air renewer for a hundred hours, and they only planned to be gone for three or four. They loaded two packboards with food, water, and the "buckets" used for such natural functions as eating, but that was only in case their return should be delayed. The assorted scientific instruments they took were more to the point. Darkington holstered a pistol. When he had finished talking, Kuroki put the long tube of a rocket gun and a rackful of shells on his own back. They closed their helmets anew and stepped out.

"Which way?" Frederika asked.

"Due south," Darkington said after studying the terrain. "We'll be following this long ridge, you see. Harder to get lost." There was little danger of that, with the boat emitting a continuous directional signal. Nonetheless they all had compasses on their wrists, and took note of landmarks as they went.

The boat was soon lost to view. They walked among surrealistic rods and frames and spirals, under ringing sheet metal. The crystals crunched beneath their tread and broke sunlight into hot shards of color. But not many rays pushed through the tangle overhead; shadows were dense and restless. Darkington began to recognize unrelated types of structure. They included long, black, seemingly telescopic rods, fringed with thin plates; glassy spheres attached to intricate grids; cables that looped from girder to girder. Frequently a collapsed object was seen crumbling on the ground.

Frederika looked at several disintegrated specimens, examined others in good shape, and said: "I'd guess the most important material, the commonest, is an aluminum alloy. Though . . . see here . . . these fine threads embedded in the core must be copper. And this here is probably manganese steel with a protective coating of . . . of . . . something more inert."

Darkington peered at the end of a broken strut through a magnifying glass. "Porous," he said. "Are these actually capillaries to transport water?"

"I thought a capillary was a hairy bug with lots of legs that turned into a butterfly," said Kuroki. He ducked an imaginary fist. "O.K., O.K., somebody's got to keep up morale."

The boat's radio relayed a groan from the monitor aboard the ship. Frederika said patiently, "No, Sam, the legs don't turn into a butterfly—" but then she remembered there would never again be bravely colored small wings on Earth and banged a hand against her faceplate as if she had been about to knuckle her eyes.

Darkington was still absorbed in the specimen he held. "I never heard of a machine this finely constructed," he declared. "I thought nothing but a biological system could—"

"Stop! Freeze!"

Kuroki's voice rapped in their earphones. Darkington laid a hand on his pistol butt. Otherwise only his head moved, turning inside the helmet. After a moment he saw the thing, too.

It stirred among shadows, behind a squat cylinder topped with the usual black-and-mirror plates. Perhaps three feet long, six or eight inches high . . . It came out into plain view. Darkington glimpsed a slim body and six short legs of articulated dull metal. A latticework swiveled at the front end like a miniature radio-radar beamcaster. Something glinted beadily beneath, twin lenses? Two thin tentacles held a metal sliver off one of the great stationary structures. They fed it into an orifice, and sparks shot back upward—

"Holy Moses," Kuroki whispered.

The thing stopped in its tracks. The front-end lattice swung toward the humans. Then the thing was off, unbelievably fast. In half a second there was nothing to see.

Nobody moved for almost a minute. Finally Frederika clutched Darkington's arm with a little cry. The rigidness left him and he babbled of experimental robot turtles in the early days of cybernetic research—very simple gadgets. A motor drove a wheeled platform, steered by a photoelectric unit that approached light sources by which the batteries might be recharged and, when this was done, became negatively phototropic and sought darkness. An elementary feedback circuit. But the turtles had shown astonishing tenacity, had gone over obstacles or even around . . .

"That beast there was a good deal more complicated," she interrupted.

"Certainly, certainly," Darkington said. "But—"

"I'll bet it heard Sam talk on the radio, spotted us with radar—or maybe eyes, if those socketed glass things were eyes—and took off."

"Very possibly, if you must use anthropomorphic language. However—"

"It was eating that strut." Frederika walked over to the piece of metal which the runner had dropped. She picked it up and came stiffly back with it. "See, the end has been ground away by a set of coarse emery wheels or something. You couldn't very well eat alloy with teeth like ours. You have to grind it. Either that or dissolve it in some chemical system."

"Hey!" Kuroki objected. "Let's not go completely off the deep end."

§

"What's happened down there?" called the man aboard the *Traveler*.

They resumed walking, in a dreamlike fashion, as they recounted what they had seen. Frederika concluded: "This . . . this arrangement might conceivably be some kind of automated factory—chemosynthetic or something—if taken by itself. But not with beasts like that one running loose."

"Now wait," Darkington said. "They could be maintenance robots, you know. Clear away rubbish and wreckage."

"A science advanced enough to build what we see wouldn't use such a clumsy system of maintenance," she answered. "Get off your professional caution, Hugh, and admit what's obvious."

Before he could reply, his earphones woke with a harsh jabber. He stopped and tried to tune in—it kept fading out, he heard it only in bursts—but the bandwidth was too great. What he did hear sounded like an electronic orchestra gone berserk. Sweat prickled his skin.

When the sound had stopped: "O.K.," breathed Kuroki, "you tell me."

"Could have been a language, I suppose," said Frederika,

dry throated. "It wasn't just a few simple oscillations like that stuff on the other frequencies."

Captain Thurshaw himself spoke from the orbiting ship. "You better get back to the boat and sit prepared for quick blastoff."

Darkington found his nerve. "No, sir. If you please. I mean, uh, if there are intelligences . . . if we really do want to contact them . . . now's the time. Let's at least make an effort."

"Well—"

"We'll take you back first, of course, Freddie."

"Nuts," said the girl. "I stay right here."

Somehow they found themselves pushing on. Once, crossing an open spot where only the crystals stood, they spied something in the air. Through binoculars, it turned out to be a metallic object shaped vaguely like an elongated manta. Apparently it was mostly hollow, upborne by air currents around the fins and propelled at low speed by a gas jet. "Oh, sure," Frederika muttered. "Birds."

They reentered the area of tall structures. The sonic amplifiers in their helmets were again turned high, and the clash of plates in the wind was deafening. Like a suit of armor, Darkington thought idiotically. Could be a poem in that. Empty armor on a wild horse, rattling and tossing as it galloped down an inexplicably deserted city street—symbol of . . .

The radio impulses that might be communication barked again in their earphones. "I don't like this," Thurshaw said from the sky. "You're dealing with too many unknowns at once. Return to the boat and we'll discuss further plans."

They continued walking in the same direction, mechanically. *We don't seem out of place here ourselves, in this stiff cold forest*, Darkington thought. *Let's turn around. Let's assert our dignity as organic beings. We aren't mounted on rails!*

"That's an order," Thurshaw stated.

"Very well, sir," Kuroki said. "And, uh, thanks."

The sound of running halted them. They whirled. Frederika screamed.

"What's the matter?" Thurshaw shouted. "What's the matter?" The unknown language ripped across his angry helplessness.

Kuroki yanked his rocket gun loose and put the weapon to his shoulder. "Wait!" Darkington yelled. But he grabbed at his own pistol. The oncomer rushed in a shower of crystal splinters, whipping rods and loops aside. Its gigantic weight shuddered in the ground.

Time slowed for Darkington; he had minutes or hours to tug at his gun, hear Frederika call his name, see Kuroki take aim and fire. The shape was mountainous before him. Nine feet tall, he estimated in a far-off portion of his rocking brain, three yards of biped four-armed monstrosity, head horned with radio lattice, eyes that threw back sunlight in a blank glitter, grinder orifice and— The rocket exploded. The thing lurched and half fell. One arm was in ruins.

"Ha!" Kuroki slipped a fresh shell into his gun. "Stay where you are, you!"

Frederika, wildly embracing Darkington, found time to gasp, "Sam, maybe it wasn't going to do any harm," and Kuroki snapped, "Maybe it was. Too big to take chances with." Then everything smashed.

Suddenly the gun was knocked spinning by a hurled iron bar they hadn't even noticed. And the giant was among them. A swat across Kuroki's back shattered his radio and dashed him to the ground. Flame spat and Frederika's voice was cut short in Darkington's receivers.

He pelted off, his pistol uselessly barking. "Run, Freddie!" he bawled into his sonic microphone. "I'll try and—" The machine picked him up. The pistol fell from his grasp. A moment later, Thurshaw's horrified oaths were gone: Darkington's radio antenna had been plucked out by the roots. Frederika tried to escape, but she was snatched up just as effortlessly. Kuroki, back on his feet, stood where he was and struck with ludicrous fists. It didn't take long to secure him either. Hog-tied, stuffed into a rack on the shoulders of the giant, the three humans were borne off southward.

IV

At first Zero almost ran. The monster must have known where its auxiliaries were and something of what had happened to them. Now that contact was broken, it might send forth others to look for them, better armed. Or it might even come itself, roaring and burning through the forest. Zero fled.

Only the monster's voice, raggedly calling for its lost members, pursued him. After a few miles he crouched in a road clump and strained his receptors. Nothing was visible but thickly growing accumulators and bare sky. The monster had ceased to shout. Though it still emitted an unmodulated signal, distance had dwindled this until the surrounding soft radio noise had almost obliterated that hum.

The units Zero had captured were making considerable sound-wave radiation. If not simply the result of malfunction in their damaged mechanism, it must be produced by some auxiliary system which they had switched on through interior control. Zero's sound receptors were not sensitive enough to tell him whether the emission was modulated. Nor did he care. Certain low forms of motile were known to have well-developed sonic parts, but anything so limited in range was useless to him except as a warning of occurrences immediately at hand. A person needed many square miles to support himself. How could there be a community of persons without the effortless ability to talk across trans-horizon distances?

Irrelevantly, for the first time in his century and a half of existence, Zero realized how few persons he had ever observed with his own direct optics. How few he had touched. Now and then, for this or that purpose, several might get together. A bride's male kin assisted her on her journey to the groom's dwelling. Individuals met to exchange the products of their labor. But still—this rally of all functional males at Broken Glade, to hunt the monster, would be the greatest assemblage in tradition. Yet not even Hundred had grasped its uniqueness.

For persons were always communicating. Not only practical questions were discussed. In fact, now that Zero thought about it, such problems were the least part of discourse. The major part was ritual, or friendly conversation, or art. Zero had seldom met Seven as a physical entity, but the decades in which they criticized each other's poetry had made them intimate. The abstract tone constructions of Ninety-six, the narratives of Eighty, the speculations about space and time of Fifty-nine—such things belonged to all.

Direct sensory linkage, when the entire output of the body was used to modulate the communication band, reduced still further the need for physical contact. Zero had never stood on the seashore himself. But he had shared consciousness with Fourteen, who lived there. He had perceived the slow inward movement of waves, their susurrus, the salt in the air; he had experienced the smearing of grease over his skin to protect it from corrosion, drawing an aquamotile from a net and feasting. For those hours, he and the searaker had been one. Afterward he had shown Fourteen the upland forest. . . .

What am I waiting for? Consciousness of his here-and-now jarred back into Zero. The monster had not pursued. The units on his back had grown quiescent. But he was still a long way from home. He rose and started off again, less rapidly but with more care to obliterate his traces.

As the hours passed, his interior sensors warned him increasingly of a need for replenishment. About midday he stopped and unloaded his three prizes. They were feebly squirming and one of them had worked an arm loose. Rather than lash them tight again, he released their limbs and secured them by passing the rope in successive loops around their middles and a tall stump, then welding everything fast with his torch.

That energy drain left him ravenous. He scouted the forest

in a jittery spiral until he found some accumulators of the calathiform sort. A quick slash with his pry bar exposed their spongy interiors, rich with energy storage cells and mineral salts. They were not very satisfying eaten unprocessed, but he was too empty to care. With urgency blunted, he could search more slowly and thoroughly. Thus he found the traces of a burrow, dug into the sand, and came upon a female digger. She was heavy with a half-completed new specimen and he caught her easily. This, too, would have been better if treated with heat and acid, but even raw the materials tasted good in his grinder.

Now to get something for One. Though she, better than he, could slow down her functioning when nourishment was scarce, a state of coma while the monster was abroad could be dangerous. After hunting for another hour, Zero had the good luck to start a rotor. It crashed off among the rods and crystals, faster than he could run, but he put a crossbow bolt through its hub. Dismembered and packed into his carrier, it made an immensely cheering burden.

He returned to his prizes. Moving quietly in comparison to the windy clatter of the forest, he came upon them unobserved. They had quit attempting to escape—he saw the wire was shiny where they had tried to saw it on a sharp rock—and were busy with other tasks. One of them had removed a boxlike object from its back and inserted its head (?) and arms through gasketed holes. A second was just removing a similar box from its lower section. The third had plugged a flexible tube from a bottle into its face.

Zero approached. "Let me inspect those," he said, before thinking how ridiculous it was to address them. They shrank away from him. He caught the one with the bottle and unplugged the tube. Some liquid ran out. Zero extended his chemical sensor and tasted cautiously. Water. Very pure. He did not recall ever having encountered water so free of dissolved minerals.

Thoughtfully, he released the unit. It stoppered the tube. So, Zero reflected, they required water like him, and carried a supply with them. That was natural; they—or, rather, the monster they served—could not know where the local springs and streams were. But why did they suck through a tube? Did they lack a proper liquid-ingestion orifice? Evidently. The small hole in the head, into which the tube had fitted, had automatically closed as the nipple was withdrawn.

The other two had removed their boxes. Zero studied these and their contents. There were fragments of mushy material in both, vaguely similar to normal body sludge. Nourishment or waste? Why such a clumsy system? It was as if the interior mechanism must be absolutely protected from contact with the environment.

He gave the boxes back and looked more thoroughly at their users. They were not quite so awkward as they seemed at first. The humps on their backs were detachable carriers like his. Some of the objects dangling at their waists or strapped to their arms must also be tools. (Not weapons or means of escape, else they would have used them before now. Specialized artificial attachments, then, analogous to a torch or a surgical ratchet.) The basic bipedal shape was smoother than his own, nearly featureless except for limb joints. The head was somewhat more complicated, though less so than a person's. Upon a cylindrical foundation grew various parts, including the sound-wave generators which babbled as he stood there watching. The face was a glassy plate, behind which moved . . . what? Some kind of jointed, partly flexible mechanism.

There was no longer any possibility of radio communication with—or through—them. Zero made a few experimental gestures, but the units merely stirred about. Two of them embraced. The third waved its arms and made sonic yelps. All at once it squatted and drew geometrical shapes in the sand, very much like the courtship figures drawn by a male dune-runner.

So . . . they not only had mechanical autonomy, like the spy eyes of a boxroller, but were capable of some independent behavior. They were more than simple remote-control limbs and sensors of the monster. Most probably they were domesticated motiles.

But if so, then the monster race had modified their type even more profoundly than the person race had modified the type of its own tamed motiles down in the lowlands. These bipeds were comically weak in proportion to size; they lacked grinders and liquid-ingestion orifices; they used sonics to a degree that argued their radio abilities were primitive; they required ancillary apparatus; in short, they were not functional by themselves. Only the care and shelter furnished by their masters allowed them to remain long in existence.

But what are the masters? Even the monster may well be only another motile. Certainly it appeared to lack limbs. The masters may be persons like us, come from beyond the sea or the mountains with great new skills.

But then what do they want? Why have they not tried to communicate with us? Have they come to take our land away? The question was jolting. Zero got hastily into motion. With his rack loaded, he had no room for his prizes. Besides, being crammed into it for hours was doubtless harmful to them; they moved a good deal more strongly now, after a rest, than when he first took them out. He simply left them tied together, cut the wire loose from the stump, and kept that end in one hand. Since he continued to exercise due caution about leaving a trail, he did not move too fast for them to keep up. From time to time they would stagger and lean on each other for support—apparently their energy cells polarized more quickly than his—but he found they could continue if he let them pause a while, lie down, use their curious artifacts.

§

The day passed. At this time of year, not long past the vernal equinox, the sun was up for about twenty hours. After dark, Zero's captives began stumbling and groping. He confirmed by direct sense perception that they had no radar. If they ever did, that part had been wrecked with their communicators. After some thought, he fashioned a rough seat from a toppled bole and nudged them to sit upon it. Thus he carried them in two hands. They made no attempt to escape, emitted few sounds, obviously they were exhausted. But to his surprise, they began to stir about and radiate sonics when he finally reached home and set them down. He welded the end of their rope to an iron block he kept for emergencies.

Part of him reflected that their mechanism must be very strange indeed, maybe so strange that they would not prove ingestible. Obviously their cells went to such extremes of polarization that they became comatose, which a person only did in emergencies. To them, such deactivation appeared to be normal, and they roused spontaneously.

He dismissed speculation. One's anxious voice had been rushing over him while he worked. "What has happened? You are hurt! Come closer, let me see, oh, your poor arm! Oh, my dear!"

"Nothing serious," he reassured her. "I shot a rotor. Prepare yourself a meal before troubling about me."

He lowered himself to the cave floor beside her great beautiful bulk. The glow globes, cultivated on the rough stone walls, shed luster on her skin and on the graceful tool tendrils that curled forth to embrace him. His chemical sensor brought him a hint of solvents and lubricants, an essence of femaleness. The cave mouth was black with night, save where one star gleamed bright and somehow sinister above the hills. The forest groaned and tolled. But here he had light and her touch upon his body. He was home.

She unshipped the rack from his shoulders but made no motion toward the food-processing cauldron. Most of her tools and all her attention were on his damaged arm. "We must replace everything below the elbow," she decided; and, as a modulation: *"Zero, you brave clever adored fool, why did you hazard yourself like that? Do you not understand, even yet, without you my world would be rust?"*

"I am sorry . . . to take so much from the new one," he apologized.

"No matter. Feed me some more nice large rotors like this and I will soon replace the loss, and finish all the rest, too." Her mirth fluttered toward shyness. "I want the new one activated soon myself, you know, so we can start another."

The memory of that moment last year, when his body pattern flowed in currents and magnetic fields through hers, when the two patterns heterodyned and deep within her the first crystallization took place, glowed in him. Sensory linkage was a wan thing by comparison.

What they did together now had a kindred intimacy. When she had removed the ruined forearm and he had thrust the stump into her repair orifice, a thousand fine interior tendrils enfolded it, scanning, relaying, and controlling. Once again, more subtly than in reproduction, the electrochemical-mechanical systems of One and Zero unified. The process was not consciously controllable, it was a female function; One was at this moment no different from the most primitive motile joined to her damaged mate in a lightless burrow.

It took time. The new person which her body was creating within itself was, of course, full size and, as it happened, not far from completion. (Had the case been otherwise, Zero would have had to wait until the new one did in fact possess a well-developed arm.) But it was not yet activated; its most delicate and critical synaptic pathways were still only half finished, gradually crystallizing out of solution. A part could not lightly nor roughly be removed.

But in the end, One's function performed the task. Slowly, almost reluctantly, Zero withdrew his new hand. His mind and hers remained intertwined a while longer. At last, with a shaky little overtone of humor, she exclaimed, "Well, how do your fingers wiggle? Is everything good? Then let us eat. I am famished!"

Zero helped her prepare the rotor for consumption. They threw the damaged forearm into the cauldron, too. While they processed and shared the meal, he recounted his experiences. She had shown no curiosity about the three bipeds. Like most females, she lacked any great interest in the world beyond her home, and had merely assumed they were some new kind of wild motile. As he talked, the happiness died in her. "Oh, no," she said, "you are not going out to fight the lightning breather, are you?"

"Yes, we must." He knew what image terrified her, himself smashed beyond hope of reconstruction, and added in haste: "If we leave it free, no tradition or instinct knows what it may do. But surely at the very least, so large a thing will cause extensive damage. Even if it is only a grazer, its appetite will destroy untold acres of accumulators; and it may be a predator. On the other hand, if we destroy it, what a hoard of nourishment! Your share and mine will enable us to produce a dozen new persons. The energy will let me range for hundreds of miles, thus gaining still more food and goods for us."

"If the thing can be assimilated," she said doubtfully. "It could be full of hydrofluoric acid or something, like a touch-me-not."

"Yes, yes. For that matter, the flier may be the property of intelligent beings: which does not necessarily mean we will not destroy and consume it. I intend to find out about that aspect right now. If the monster's auxiliaries are ingestible, the monster itself is almost sure to be."

"But if not—Zero, be careful!"

"I will. For your sake also." He stroked her and felt an answering vibration. It would have been pleasant to sit thus all night, but he must soon be on his way to rendezvous. And first he must dissect at least one specimen. He took up his pry bar.

v

Darkington awoke from a nightmare-ridden half sleep when he was dumped on the cave floor. He reached for Frederika and she came to him. For a space there was nothing but their murmuring.

Eventually they crouched on the sand and looked about. The giant that captured them had welded the free end of the wire rope to an immovable chunk of raw iron. Darkington was attached at that side, then the girl, and Kuroki on the outer end. They had about four feet of slack from one to the next. Nothing in the kit remaining to them would cut those strands.

"Limestone cave, I guess," Kuroki croaked. Behind the faceplate he was gaunt, bristly, and sunken-eyed. Frederika didn't look much better. They might not have survived the trip here if the robot hadn't carried them the last few hours. Nonetheless an odd dry clarity possessed Darkington's brain. He could observe and think as well as if he had been safe on shipboard. His body was one enormous ache, but he ignored that and focused on comprehending what had happened.

Here near the entrance, the cave was about twenty feet high and rather more wide. A hundred feet deeper inward, it narrowed and ended. That area was used for storage: a junk shop of mechanical and electronic parts, together with roughly fashioned metal and stone tools that looked almost homelike. The walls were overgrown with thin wires that sprouted scores of small crystalline globes. These gave off a cool white light that made the darkness outside appear the more elemental.

"Yes, a cave in a sheer hillside," said Frederika. "I saw that much. I kept more or less conscious all the way here, trying to keep track of our route. Not that that's likely to do us much good, is it?" She hugged her knees. "I've got to sleep soon . . . oh, but I have to sleep!"

"We have to get in touch." Kuroki's voice rose. (Thank heaven and some ages-dead engineer that sound mikes and earphones could be switched on by shoving your chin against the right button! With talk cut off, no recourse would have remained but to slip quietly into madness.) "I tried to show that tin nightmare we're intelligent. I drew diagrams and—" He checked himself. "Well, probably its builders don't monitor it. We'll have another go when they show up."

"Let's admit the plain facts, Sam," Frederika said tonelessly. "There aren't any builders. There never were any."

"Oh, no." The pilot gave Darkington a beggar's look. "You're the biologist, Hugh. Do you believe that?"

Darkington bit his lip. "I'm afraid she's right."

Frederika's laugh barked at them. "Do you know what that big machine is, there in the middle of the cave? The one the robot is fooling around with? I'll tell you. His wife!" She broke off. Laughter echoed too horribly in their helmets.

§

Darkington gazed in that direction. The second object had little in common with the biped shape, being low and wide —twice the bulk—and mounted on eight short legs which must lend very little speed or agility. A radio lattice, optical lenses, and arms—two, not four—were similar to the biped's. But numerous additional limbs were long goosenecks terminating in specialized appendages. Sleek blued metal covered most of the body.

And yet, the way those two moved—

"I think you may be right about that also," Darkington said at last.

Kuroki beat the ground with his fist and swore. "Sorry, Freddie," he gulped. "But won't you explain what you're getting at? This mess wouldn't be so bad if it made some sense."

"We can only guess," Darkington said.

"Well, guess, then!"

"Robot evolution," Frederika said. "After man was gone, the machines that were left began to evolve."

"No," said Kuroki, "That's nuts. Impossible!"

"I think what we've seen would be impossible any other way," Darkington said. "Metallic life couldn't arise spontaneously. Only carbon atoms make the long hookups needed for the chemical storage of biological information. But electronic storage is equally feasible. And . . . before the *Traveler* departed . . . self-reproducing machines were already in existence."

"I think the sea rafts must have been the important ones." Frederika spoke like someone in dream. Her eyes were fixed wide and unblinking on the two robots. "Remember? They were essentially motorized floating boxes, containing metallurgic processing plants and powered by solar batteries. They took dissolved minerals out of sea water, magnesium, uranium, whatever a particular raft was designed for. When it had a full cargo, it went to a point on shore where a depot received its load. Once empty, it returned to open waters for more. It had an inertial navigation device, as well as electronic sensors and various homeostatic systems, so it could cope with the normal vicissitudes of its environment.

"And it had electronic templates which bore full information on its own design. They controlled mechanisms aboard, which made any spare part that might be needed. Those same mechanisms also kept producing and assembling complete duplicate rafts. The first such outfit cost hundreds of millions of dollars to manufacture, let alone the preliminary research and development. But once made, it needed no further investment. Production and expansion didn't cost anyone a cent.

"And after man was gone from Earth . . . all life had vanished . . . the sea rafts were still there, patiently bringing their cargoes to crumbling docks on barren shores, year after year after meaningless year—"

She shook herself. The motion was violent enough to be seen in armor. "Go on, Hugh," she said, her tone turned harsh. "If you can."

§

"I don't know any details," he began cautiously. "You should tell me how mutation was possible to a machine. But if the templates were actually magnetic recordings on wire or tape, I expect that hard radiation would affect them, as it affects an organic gene. And for a while there was certainly plenty of hard radiation around. The rafts started making imperfect duplicates. Most were badly designed and, uh, foundered. Some, though, had advantages. For instance, they stopped going to shore and hanging about for decades waiting to be unloaded. Eventually some raft was made which had the first primitive ability to get metal from a richer source than the ocean: namely, from other rafts. Through hundreds of millions of years, an ecology developed. We might as well call it an ecology. The land was reconquered. Wholly new *types* of machines proliferated. Until today, well, what we've seen."

"But where's the energy come from?" Kuroki demanded.

"The sun, I suppose. By now, the original solar battery must be immensely refined. I'd make a guess at dielectric storage on the molecular level, in specialized units—call them cells—which may even be of microscopic size. Of course, productivity per acre must be a good deal lower than it was in our day. Alloys aren't as labile as amino acids. But that's offset to a large extent by their greater durability. And, as you can see in this cave, by interchangeability."

"Huh?"

"Sure. Look at those spare parts stacked in the rear. Some will no doubt be processed, analogously to our eating and digesting food. But others are probably being kept for use as such. Suppose you could take whole organs from animals you killed and install them in yourself to replace whatever was wearing out. I rather imagine that's common on today's Earth. The 'black box' principle was designed into most machines in our own century. It would be inherited."

"Where does the metal come from in the first place?"

"From lower types of machine. Ultimately from sessile types that break down ores, manufacture the basic alloys, and concentrate more dielectric energy than they use. Analogous to vegetation. I daresay the, uh, metabolism involves powerful reagents. Sulfuric and nitric acids in glass-lined compartments must be the least of them. I doubt if there are any equivalent of microbes, but the ecology seems to manage quite well without. It's a grosser form of existence than ours. But it works. It works."

"Even sex." Frederika giggled a little crazily.

Darkington squeezed her gauntleted hand until she grew calmer. "Well," he said, "quite probably in the more complex machines, reproduction has become the specialty of one form, while the other specializes in strength and agility. I daresay there are corresponding psychological differences."

"Psychological?" Kuroki bridled. "Wait a minute! I know there is . . . was . . . a lot of loose talk about computers being electronic brains and such rot, but—"

"Call the phenomenon what you like," Darkington shrugged. "But that robot uses tools which are made not grown. The problem is how to convince it that *we* think."

"Can't it see?" Frederika exclaimed. "We use tools, too. Sam drew mathematical pictures. What more does it want?"

"I don't know enough about this world to even guess," Darkington said tiredly. "But I suppose . . . well . . . we might once have seen a trained ape doing all sorts of elaborate things, without ever assuming it was more than an ape. No matter how odd it looked."

"Or maybe the robot just doesn't give a damn," Kuroki said. "There were people who wouldn't have."

"If Hugh's guess about the 'black box' is right," Frederika added slowly, "then the robot race must have evolved as hunters, instead of hunting being invented rather late in their evolution. As if men had descended from tigers instead of simians. How much psychological difference would that make?"

No one replied. She leaned forlornly against Darkington. Kuroki turned his eyes from them, perhaps less out of tact than loneliness. His girl was several thousand miles away, straight up, with no means for him to call her and say good-bye.

§

Thurshaw had warned the insistent volunteers for this expedition that there would be no rescue. He had incurred sufficient guilt in letting three people—three per cent of the human race—risk themselves. If anything untoward happened, the *Traveler* would linger a while in hopes the boat could somehow return. But in the end the *Traveler* would head for the stars. Kuroki's girl would have to get another father for the boy she might name Sam.

I wish Freddie were up there with her, Darkington thought. *Or do I? Isn't that simply what I'm supposed to wish?*

Cut that out. Start planning!

His brain spun like wheels in winter mud. What to do, what to do, what to do? His pistol was gone, so were Kuroki's rockets, nothing remained but a few tools and instruments. At the back of the cave there were probably stored some weapons with which a man could put up a moment's fight. (Only a moment, against iron and lightning; but that would end the present, ultimate horror, of sitting in your own fear-stink until the monster approached or the air renewal batteries grew exhausted and you strangled.) The noose welded around his waist, ending in a ton of iron, choked off any such dreams. They must communicate, somehow, anyhow, plead, threaten, promise, wheedle. But the monster hadn't cared about the Pythagorean theorem diagrammed in sand. What next, then? How did you say, "I am alive" to something that was not alive?

Though what was aliveness? Were proteins inherently and inescapably part of any living creature? If the ancient sea rafts had been nothing except complicated machines, at what point of further complication had their descendants come to life? *Now stop that, you're a biologist, you know perfectly well that any such question is empirically empty and anyhow it has nothing to do with preserving the continuity of certain protein chemistries which are irrationally much loved.*

"I think it talks by radio." Kuroki's slow voice sounded oddly through the thudding in Darkington's head. "It probably hasn't got any notion that sound waves might carry talk. Maybe it's even deaf. Ears wouldn't be any too useful in that rattletrap jungle. And our own radios are busted." He began to fumble in the girl's pack. "Freddie, I think I could cobble together one working set from the pieces of our three, if I can borrow some small tools and instruments. Once we make systematic noises on its talk band, the robot might get interested in trying to savvy us."

He began to lay out the job. Darkington, unable to help, ashamed that he had not thought of anything, turned attention back to the robots. They were coupled together, ignoring him.

Frederika dozed off. How slowly the night went. But Earth was old, rotating as wearily as . . . as himself. He slept.

A gasp awoke him.

The monster stood above them. Tall, tall, higher than the sky, it bestrode their awareness and looked down with blank eyes upon Kuroki's pitiful barely begun work. One hand was still a torch and another hand had been replaced; it was invulnerable and soulless as a god. For an instant Darkington's half aroused self groveled before it.

Then the torch spat, slashed the wire rope across and Kuroki was pulled free.

Frederika cried out. "Sam!"

"Not . . . so eager . . . pal," the pilot choked in the robot's arms. "I'm glad you like me, but . . . ugh . . . careful!"

With a free hand, the robot twisted experimentally at Kuroki's left leg. The suit joints turned. Kuroki shrieked. Darkington thought he heard the leg bones leave their sockets.

"No! You filthy machine!" He plunged forward. The rope stopped him cold. Frederika covered her faceplate and begged Kuroki to be dead.

He wasn't, yet. He wasn't even unconscious. He kept on screaming as the robot used a prying tool to drag the leg off his armor. Leakseal compound flowed from between the fabric layers and preserved the air in the rest of his suit.

The robot dropped him and sprang back, frantically fanning itself. A whiff of oxygen, Darkington realized amidst the red and black disintegration of his sanity. Oxygen was nearly as reactive as fluorine, and there had been no free oxygen on Earth since—Kuroki's agony jerked toward silence.

The robot reapproached with care, squatted above him,

poked at the exposed flesh, tore loose a chunk for examination and flung it aside. The metal off a joint seemed better approved.

§

Darkington realized vaguely that Frederika lay on the ground close to Kuroki and wept. The biologist himself was even nearer. He could have touched the robot as well as the body. Instead, though, he retreated, mumbling and mewing.

The robot had clearly learned a lesson from the gas, but was just as clearly determined to go on with the investigation. It stood up, moved a cautious distance away, and jetted a thin, intensely blue flame from its torch hand. Kuroki's corpse was divided across the middle.

Darkington's universe roared and exploded. He lunged again. The rope between him and Frederika was pulled across the fire beam. The strands parted like smoke.

The robot pounced at him, ran into the oxygen gushing from Kuroki's armor, and lurched back. Darkington grabbed the section of rope that joined him to the block. The torch was too bright to look at. If he touched its flame, that was the end of him, too. But there was no chance to think about such matters. Blindly and animally, he pulled his leash across the cutting jet.

He was free.

"Get out, Freddie!" he coughed, and ran straight toward the robot. No use trying to run from a thing that could overtake him in three strides. The torch had stopped spitting fire, but the giant moved in a wobbly, uncertain fashion, still dazed by the oxygen. By pain? Savagely, in the last spark of awareness, Darkington hoped so. *"Get out, Freddie!"*

The robot staggered in pursuit of him. He dodged around the other machine, the big one that they had called female. To the back of the cave. A weapon to fight with, gaining a moment where Frederika might escape. An extra pry bar lay on the floor. He snatched it and whirled. The huge painted shape was almost upon him.

He dodged. Hands clashed together just above his helmet. He pelted back to the middle of the cave. The female machine was edging into a corner. But slow, awkward—

Darkington scrambled on top of it.

An arm reached from below to pluck him off. He snarled and struck with the pry bar. The noise rang in the cave. The arm sagged, dented. This octopod had nothing like the biped's strength. Its tool tendrils, even more frail, curled away from him.

The male robot loomed close. Darkington smashed his weapon down on the radio lattice at his feet. It crumbled. He brandished the bar and howled senselessly, "Stand back, there! One step more and I'll give her the works! I'll kill her!"

The robot stopped. Monstrous it bulked, an engine that could tear apart a man and his armor, and raised its torch hand.

"Oh, no," Darkington rasped. He opened a bleeder valve on his suit, kneeling so the oxygen would flow across the front end of the thing on which he rode. Sensors ought to be more vulnerable than skin. He couldn't hear if the she-robot screamed as Kuroki had done. That would be on the radio band. But when he gestured the male back, it obeyed.

"Get the idea?" he panted, not as communication but as hatred. "You can split my suit open with your flame gun, but my air will pour all over this contraption here. Maybe you could knock me off her by throwing something, but at the first sign of any such move on your part, I'll open my bleeder valve again. She'll at least get a heavy dose of oxy. And meanwhile I'll punch the sharp end of this rod through one of those lenses. Understand? Well, then, stay where you are, machine!"

The robot froze.

Frederika came near. She had slipped the loop of cable joining her to Kuroki off what was left of his torso. The light shimmered on her faceplate so Darkington couldn't see through, and her voice was strained out of recognition. "Hugh, oh, Hugh!"

"Head back to the boat," he ordered. Rationality was returning to him.

"Without you? No."

"Listen, this is not the place for grandstand heroics. Your
first duty is to become a mother. But what I hope for, personally, is that you can return in the boat and fetch me. You're
no pilot, but they can instruct you by radio from the ship if
she's above the horizon. The general director does most of the
work in any event. You land here, and I can probably
negotiate a retreat for myself."

"But . . . but . . . the robot needed something like twenty
hours to bring us here. And it knew the way better than I do.
I'll have to go by compass and guess, mostly. Of course, I
won't stop as often as it did. No more than I have to. But still
. . . say twenty hours for me . . . you can't hold out that long!"

"I can try," he said. "You got any better ideas?"

"All right, then. Good-bye, Hugh. No, I mean so long. I
love you."

He grunted some kind of answer, but didn't see her go. He
had to keep watching the robot.

VI

"Zero!" his female called, just once, when the unit sprang
upon her back. She clawed at it. The pry bar smashed across
her arm. He felt the pain-surge within her sensors, broadcast
through her communicator, like a crossbow bolt in his body.

Wildly, he charged. The enemy unit crashed the bar down
on One's lattice. She shrilled in anguish. Affected by the
damage that crippled her radar, her communicator tone grew
suddenly, hideously different. Zero slammed himself to a halt.

Her sobbing, his own name blindly repeated, overwhelmed
the burning in him where the corrosive gas had flowed. He
focused his torch to narrow beam and took careful aim.

The unit knelt, fumbling with its free hand. One screamed
again, louder. Her tendrils flailed about. Numbly, Zero let his
torch arm droop. The unit rose and poised its weapon above

her lenses. A single strong thrust downward through the glass could reach her brain. The unit gestured him back. He obeyed.

"Help," One cried. Zero could not look at the wreckage of her face. There was no escaping her distorted voice. "Help, Zero. It hurts so much."

"Hold fast," he called in his uselessness. "I cannot do anything. Not now. The thing is full of poison. That is what you received." He managed to examine his own interior perceptions. "The pain will abate in a minute . . . from such a small amount. But if you got a large dose—I do not know. It might prove totally destructive. Or the biped might do ultimate mechanical damage before I could prevent it. Hold fast, One mine. Until I think of something."

"I am afraid," she rattled. "For the new one."

"Hold fast," he implored. "If that unit does you any further harm, I will destroy it slowly. I expect it realizes as much."

The other functional biped came near. It exchanged a few ululations with the first, turned and went quickly from the cave. "It must be going back to the flying monster," said One. The words dragged from her, now and then she whimpered as her perceptions of damage intensified, but she could reason again. "Will it bring the monster here?"

"I cannot give chase," said Zero unnecessarily. "But—" He gathered his energy. A shout blasted from his communicator. *"Alarm, alarm! All persons receiving, prepare to relay. Alarm!"*

Voices flashed in his head, near and far, and it was as if they poured strength into him. He and One were not alone in a night cave, a scuttling horror on her back and the taste of poison only slowly fading. Their whole community was here.

He reported the situation in a few phrases. "You have been rash," Hundred said, shaken. "May there be no further penalties for your actions."

"What else would you have had him do?" defended Seven. "We cannot deal randomly with a thing as powerful as the monster. Zero took upon himself the hazards of gathering information. Which he has succeeded in, too."

"Proving the danger is greater than we imagined," shuddered Sixteen.

"Well, that is a valuable datum."

"The problem now is, what shall we do?" Hundred interrupted. "Slow though you say it is, I expect the auxiliary that escaped can find the monster long before we can rendezvous and get up into the hills."

"Until it does, though, it cannot communicate, its radio being disabled," Zero said. "So the monster will presumably remain where it is, ignorant of events. I suggest that those persons who are anywhere near this neighborhood strike out directly toward that area. They can try to head off the biped."

"You can certainly capture it in a few minutes," Hundred said.

"I cannot leave this place."

"Yes, you can. The thing that has seized your female will not logically do anything more to her, unprovoked, lest she lose her present hostage value."

"How do you know?" Zero retorted. "In fact, I believe if I captured its companion, this unit would immediately attack One. What hope does it have except in the escape of the other, that may bring rescue?"

"Hope is a curious word to use in connection with an elaborated spy eye," Seven said.

"If it is," Zero said. "Their actions suggest to me that these bipeds are more than unthinking domesticated motiles."

"Let be!" Hundred said. "There is scant time to waste. We may not risk the entire community for the sake of a single member. Zero, go fetch back that biped."

Unmodulated radio buzzed in the night. Finally Zero said, "No." One's undamaged hand reached toward him, but she was too far away for them to touch each other. Nor could she caress him with radar.

"We will soon have you whole again," he murmured to her. She did not answer, with the community listening.

Hundred surrendered, having existed long enough to recognize unbendable negation. "Those who are sufficiently near the monster to reach it before dawn, report," he directed. When they had finished—about thirty all told—he said, "Very well, proceed there. Whenever feasible, direct your course to intercept the probable path of the escaped unit. If you capture it, inform us at once. The rest of us will rendezvous as planned."

§

One by one the voices died out in the night, until only Hundred, who was responsible, and Seven, who was a friend, were in contact with Zero. "How are you now, One?" Seven asked gently.

"I function somewhat," she said in a tired, uneven tone. "It is strange to be radar blind. I keep thinking that heavy objects are about to crash into me. When I turn my optics that way, there isn't anything." She paused. "The new one stirred a little bit just now. A motor impulse pathway must have been completed. Be careful, Zero," she begged.

"I cannot understand your description of the bipeds' interior," Hundred said practically. "Soft, porous material soaked in sticky red liquid; acrid vapors—How do they *work?* Where is the mechanism?"

"They are perhaps not functional at all," Seven proposed. "They may be purely artificial devices, powered by chemical action."

"Yet they act intelligently," Zero argued. "If the monster— or the monster's masters—do not have them under direct control—and certainly there is no radio involved . . ."

"There may be other means than radio to monitor an auxiliary," Seven said. "We know so little, we persons."

"In that case," Zero answered, "the monster has known about this cave all the time. It is watching me at this moment, through the optics of that thing on One's back."

"We must assume otherwise," Hundred said.

"I do," Zero said. "I act in the belief that these bipeds are out of contact with the flier. But if nevertheless they perform as they have been doing, then they certainly have independent function, including at least a degree of intelligence." A thought crashed through him, so stunning that he could not declare it at once. Finally: "They may be the monster's masters! It may be the auxiliary, they the persons!"

"No, no, that is impossible," Hundred groaned. Seven's temporary acceptance was quicker; he had always been able to leap from side to side of a discussion. He flashed:

"Let us assume that in some unheard-of fashion, these small entities are indeed the domesticators, or even the builders, of that flying thing. Can we negotiate with them?"

"Not after what has happened," Zero said bleakly. He was thinking less about what he had done to them than what they had done to One.

Seven continued: "I doubt it myself, on philosophical grounds. They are too alien. Their very functioning is deadly: the destruction wrought by their flier, the poison under their skins. Eventually, a degree of mutual comprehension may be achieved. But that will be a slow and painful process. Our first responsibility is to our own form of existence. Therefore we must unmistakably get the upper hand, before we even try to talk with them." In quick excitement, he added, "And I think we can."

Zero and Hundred meshed their intellects with his. The scheme grew like precipitation in a supersaturated pond. Slow and feeble, the strangers were only formidable by virtue of highly developed artifacts—or, possibly, domesticated motiles of radically modified type—the flier, the tube which had blown off Zero's arm, and other hypothetical weapons. But armament unused is no threat. If the flier could be immobilized—

Of course, presumably there were other dwarf bipeds inside it. Their voices had been heard yesterday. But Zero's trip here had proven that they lacked adequate nighttime senses. Well, grant them radar when in an undamaged condition. Radar can be confused, if one knows how.

Hundred's orders sprang forth across miles to the mountaineers now converging on the flier: "Cut the heaviest accumulator strands you can find in the forest. Twist them into cables.

Under cover of darkness, radar window and distraction objects, surround the monster. We believe now that it may not be sentient, only a flier. Weld your cables fast to deeply founded boles. Then, swiftly, loop them around the base of the flier. Tie it down!"

"No," said Twenty-nine, aghast. "We cannot weld the cables to its skin. It would annihilate us with one jetblast. We would have to make nooses first and—"

"So make the nooses," Zero said. "The monster is not a perfectly tapered spindle. The jets bulge out at the base. Slip the nooses around the body just above the jets. I hardly think it can rise then, without tearing its own tubes out."

"Easy for you to say, Zero, safe in your cave."

"If you knew what I would give to have matters other-wise—"

§

Abashed, the hunters yielded. Their mission was not really so dangerous. The nooses—two should be ample if the cable was heavy—could be laid in a broad circle around the area which the jets had flattened and devastated. They could be drawn tight from afar, and would probably slip upward by themselves, coming to rest just above the tubes, where the body of the flier was narrowest. If a cable did get stuck on something, someone would have to dash close and free it. A snort of jetfire during those few seconds would destroy him. But quite probably the flier, or its masters, could be kept from noticing him.

"And when we do have the monster leashed, what then?" asked Twenty-nine.

"We will do what seems indicated," Hundred said. "If the aliens do not seem to be reaching a satisfactory understanding with us—if we begin to entertain any doubts—we can erect trebuchets and batter the flier to pieces."

"That might be best," said Zero, with a revengeful look at One's rider.

"Proceed as ordered," said Hundred.

"But what about us?" Zero asked. "One and myself?"

"I shall come to you," Seven said. "If nothing else, we can stand watch and watch. You mentioned that the aliens polarize more easily than we do. We can wait until it drops from exhaustion."

"Good," said Zero. Hope lifted in him as if breaking through a shell. "Did you hear, One? We need only wait."

"Pain," she whispered. Then, resolutely: "I can minimize energy consumption. Comatose, I will not sense anything . . ." He felt how she fought down terror, and guessed what frightened her: the idea that she might never be roused.

"I will be guarding you all the time," he said. "You and the new one."

"I wish I could touch you, Zero —" Her radiation dimmed, second by second. Once or twice consciousness returned, kicked upward by fear; static gasped in Zero's perception; but she slipped again into blackness.

When she was quite inert, he stood staring at the unit on her—no, the entity. Somewhere behind that glass and horrible tissue, a brain peered back at him. He ventured to move an arm. The thing jerked its weapon aloft. It seemed indeed to have guessed that the optics were her most vulnerable spot. With immense care, Zero let his arm fall again. The entity jittered about, incapable of his own repose. Good. Let it drain its energy the faster.

He settled into his own thoughts. Hours wore away. The alien paced on One's broad back, sat down, sprang up again, slapped first one hand and then another against its body, made long noises that might possibly be intended to fight off coma. Sometimes it plugged the water tube into its face. Frequently Zero saw what looked like a good chance to catch it off guard—with a sudden rush and a flailing blow, or an object snatched off the floor and thrown, or even a snap shot with his torch—but he decided not to take the hazard. Time was his ally.

Besides, now that his initial rage had abated, he began to hope he might capture the entity undamaged. Much more could be learned from a functional specimen than from the thing which lay dismembered near the iron block. Faugh, the gases it was giving off! Zero's chemical sensor retracted in disgust.

The first dawnlight grayed the cave mouth.

"We have the flier!" Twenty-nine's exuberant word made Zero leap where he stood. The alien scrambled into motion. When Zero came no closer, it sagged again. "We drew two cables around its body. No trouble whatsoever. It never stirred. Only made the same radio hum."

"I thought—" someone else in his party ventured. "Not long ago . . . was there not a gibberish signal from above?"

"There might well be other fliers above the clouds," agreed Hundred from the valley. "Have a care. Disperse yourselves. Remain under cover. The rest of us will have rendezvoused by early afternoon. At that time we will confer afresh. Meanwhile, report if anything happens. And . . . good work, hunters."

Twenty-nine offered a brief sensory linkage. Thus Zero saw the place: the cindered blast area, and the upright spindle shining in the first long sunlight, and the cables that ran from its waist to a pair of old and mighty accumulator boles. Yes, the thing was captured for certain. Wind blew over the snow-peaks, set forest to chiming and scattered the little sunrise clouds. He had rarely known his land so beautiful.

The perception faded. He was in his cave again. Seven called: "I am getting close now, Zero. Shall I enter?"

"No, best not. You might alarm the alien into violence. I have watched its movements the whole night. They grow more slow and irregular each hour. It must be near collapse. Suppose you wait just outside. When I believe it to be comatose, I will have you enter. If it does not react to the sight of you, we will know it has lost consciousness."

"If it is conscious," mused Seven. "Despite our previous discussion, I cannot bring myself to believe quite seriously that these are anything but motiles or artifacts. Very ingenious and complex, to be sure . . . but *aware*, like a person?"

The unit made a long series of sonic noises. They were much weaker than hitherto. Zero allowed satisfaction to wax in him. Nevertheless, he would not have experienced this past night again for any profit.

§

Several hours later, a general alarm yanked his attention back outward. "The escaped auxiliary has returned! It has entered the flier!"

"What? You did not stop it?" Hundred demanded.

Twenty-nine gave the full report. "Naturally, after the change of plan, we were too busy weaving cables and otherwise preparing ourselves to beat the forest for the dwarf. After the flier was captured, we dispersed ourselves broadly as ordered. We made nothing like a tight circle around the blasted region. Moreover, our attention was directed at the flier, in case it tried to escape, and at the sky in case there should be more fliers. Various wild motiles were about, which we ignored, and the wind has gotten very loud in the accumulators. Under such circumstances, you will realize that probability actually favored the biped unit passing between us and reaching the open area unobserved.

"When it was first noticed, no person was close enough to reach the flier before it did. It slid a plate aside in one of the jacks which support the flier and pulled a switch. A portal opened in the body above and a ladder was extruded. By that time, a number of us had entered the clearing. The unit scrambled up the ladder. We hesitated, fearing a jetblast. None came. But how could we have predicted that? When at last we did approach, the ladder had been retracted and the portal was closed. I pulled the switch myself but nothing happened. I suppose the biped, once inside, deactivated that control by means of a master switch."

"Well, at least we know where it is," Hundred said. "Disperse again, if you have not already done so. The biped may try to escape, and you do not want to get caught in the jetblast. Are you certain the flier cannot break your cables?"

"Quite certain. Closely observed, the monster—the flier—
seems to have only a thin skin of light alloy. Nor would I
expect it to be strong against the unnatural kind of stresses
imposed by our tethers. If it tries to rise, it will pull itself in
two."

"Unless," said Fourteen, as he hastened through valley mists
toward Broken Glade, "some biped emerges with a torch and
cuts the cables."

"Just let it dare!" said Twenty-nine, anxious to redeem his
crew's failure.

"It may bring strong weapons," Zero warned.

"Ten crossbows are cocked and aimed at that portal. If a
biped shows itself, we will fill it with whetted steel."

"I think that will suffice," Zero said. He looked at the
drooping shape upon One. "They are not very powerful, these
things. Ugly, cunning, but weak."

Almost as if it knew it was being talked about, the unit
reeled to its feet and shook the pry bar at him. Even Zero
could detect the dullness in its noises. *Another hour,* he
thought, *and One will be free.*

Half that time had gone by when Seven remarked from
outside, "I wonder why the builders . . . whoever the ultimate
intelligences are behind these manifestations . . . why have
they come?"

"Since they made no attempt to communicate with us," Zero
said in renewed grimness, "we must assume their purpose is
hostile."

"And?"

"Teach them to beware of us."

He felt already the pride of victory. But then the monster
spoke.

Up over the mountains rolled the voice, driven by the power
which hurled those hundreds of tons through the sky. Roaring
and raging through the radio spectrum, louder than lightning,
enormous enough to shake down moon and stars, blasted that
shout. Twenty-nine and his hunters yelled as the volume
smote their receptors. Their cry was lost, drowned, engulfed

by the tide which seethed off the mountainsides. Here and there, where some accumulator happened to resonate, blue arcs of flame danced in the forest. Thirty miles distant, Zero and Seven still perceived the noise as a clamor in their heads. Hundred and his followers in the valley stared uneasily toward the ranges. On the seashore, females called, "What is that? What is that?" and aquamotiles dashed themselves about in the surf.

Seven forgot all caution. He ran into the cave. The enemy thing hardly moved. But neither Zero nor Seven observed that. Both returned to the entrance and gazed outward with terror.

The sky was empty. The forest rang in the breeze. Only that radio roar from behind the horizon told of anything amiss. "I did not believe—" stammered Seven. "I did not expect—a tone that loud. . . ."

Zero, who had One to think about, mustered decisiveness. "It is not hurting us," he said. "I am glad not to be as close as the hunters are, but even they should be able to endure it for a while. We shall see. Come, let us two go back inside. Once we have secured our prisoner—"

§

The monster began to talk.

No mere outrageous cry this time, but speech. Not words, except occasionally—a few images. But such occurrences were coincidental. The monster spoke in its own language, which was madness.

Seized along every radio receptor channel there was in him, total sensory and mental linkage, Zero became the monster.

DITditditdit DAH dit-nulnulnulnul-ditditDAHdah & the vector sum: infinitesimals infinitelyadded from nul-to-INFIN-ITY, dit—ditdit—DAH—ditditditnul (gammacolored chaos, *bang* goes a universe scattering stars&planets&bursts-of-fire BLOCK THAT NEUTRON BLOCK THAT NEUTRON BLOCK THAT NEUTRON BLOCK THAT BLOCK THAT BLOCK THAT NEUTRON) oneone*** nononul— DATTA—ditdit chitterchitterchitter burning suns & moons, burning stars & brains, burningburningburning. Burning DahditDahditDahdit give me fifty million logarithms this very microsecond or you will Burn ditditditdit—DAYADHVAM—DAMYATA

and one long wild logarithmic spiral down spacetimeenergy continuum of potentialgradient Xproduct i,j,k but multiply Time by the velocity of light in nothingness and the square root of minus one (two, three, four, five, six CHANGE for duodecimal computation zzzzzzzzzzz)

integral over sigma of del cross H d sigma equals one over c times integral over sigma partial of E with respect to t dot d sigma but correct for nonsphericalshapentropicoordinatetransformationtop&quantumelectrodynamichargelectricalephaselagradientemperature rising to burning Burning BURNING

dit-dit-chitterchitterchitter from eyrie to blind gnawer and back again O help the trunk is burningburningburning THEREFORE ANNUL in the name of the seven thunders

Everything-that-has-been, break up the roots of existence and strike flat the thick rotundity o' the world RRRIP spacetime across and throw it on the upleaping primordial energy for now all that was & will be, the very fact that it once *did* exist, is canceled and torn to pieces and

> Burning
> Burning
> Burning
> Burning

AND the binding energy of a lambda hyperon by a sigma —minus exploding

As the sun fell down the bowl of sky, and the sky cracked open, and the mountains ran like rivers forming faces that gaped and jeered, and the moon rose in the west and spat the grisliness of what he had done at him, Zero ran. Seven did not; could not; lay by the cave entrance, which was the gate of all horrors and corruptions, as if turned to salt. And when God descended, still shouting in His tongue which was madness, His fiery tail melted Seven to a pool.

Fifty million years later the star called Wormwood ascended to heaven; and a great silence fell upon the land.

Eventually Zero returned home. He was not surprised to find that the biped was gone. Of course it had been reclaimed by its Master. But when he saw that One was not touched, he stood mute for a long while indeed.

After he roused her, she—who had been unawake when the world was broken and refashioned—could not understand why he led her outside to pray that they be granted mercy, now and in the hour of their dissolution.

VII

Darkington did not regain full consciousness until the boat was in space. Then he pulled himself into the seat beside Frederika. "How did you do it?" he breathed.

Her attention remain focused on piloting. Even with the help of the director and radio instructions from the ship, it was no easy task for a novice. Absently, she answered, "I scared the robots away. They'd made the boat fast, you see. With cables too thick to pull apart. I had to go back out and cut them with a torch. But I'd barely gotten inside ahead of the pack. I didn't expect they would let me emerge. So I scared them off. After that, I went out, burned off the cables, and flew to get you."

"Barely in time," he shuddered. "I was about to pass out. I did keel over once I was aboard." A time went by with only the soft rushing noise of brake jets. "O.K.," he said, "I give up. I admit you're beautiful, a marvel of resourcefulness, and I can't guess how you shooed away the enemy. So tell me."

The director shut off the engine. They floated free. She turned her face, haggard, sweaty, begrimed, and dear, toward him and said diffidently, "I didn't have any inspiration. Just a guess and nothing to lose. We knew for pretty sure that the robots communicated by radio. I turned the boat's 'caster on full blast, hoping the sheer volume would be too much for them. Then something else occurred to me. If you have a radio transceiver in your head, hooked directly into your nervous system, wouldn't that be sort of like telepathy? I mean, it seems more direct somehow than routing everything we say through a larynx. Maybe I could confuse them by emitting unfamiliar signals. They'd be used to natural radio noise. But . . . well . . . the boat's general director includes a pretty complicated computer, carrying out millions of operations per second. Information is conveyed, not noise; but at the same time, it didn't seem to me like information that a bunch of semisavages could handle.

"Anyhow, there was no harm in trying. I hooked the broadcaster in parallel with the effector circuits, so the computer's output not only controlled the boat as usual but also modulated the radio emission. Then I assigned the computer a good tough problem in celestial navigation, put my armor back on, summoned every ounce of nerve I had and went outside. Nothing happened. I cut the cables without seeing any trace of the robots. I kept the computer 'talking' while I jockeyed the boat over in search of the cave. It must have been working frantically to compensate for my clumsiness; I hate to imagine what its output 'sounded' like. Felt like? Well, when I'd landed, I opened the air lock and, and you came inside, and—" Her fists doubled. "Oh, Hugh! How can we tell Sam's girl?"

He didn't answer.

With a final soft impulse, the boat nudged against the ship. As grapnels made fast, the altered spin of the vessels put Earth back in view. Darkington looked at the planet for minutes before he said:

"Good-bye. Good luck."

Frederika wiped her eyes with hands that left streaks of dirt in the tears. "Do you think we'll ever come back?" she wondered.

"No," he said. "It isn't ours anymore."

POUL ANDERSON

The Longest Voyage

When first we heard of the Sky Ship, we were on an island whose name, as nearly as Montalirian tongues can wrap themselves about so barbarous a noise, was Yarzik. That was almost a year after the *Golden Leaper* sailed from Lavre Town, and we judged we had come halfway round the world. So befouled was our poor caravel with weeds and shells that all sail could scarce drag her across the sea. What drinking water remained in the butts was turned green and evil, the biscuit was full of worms, and the first signs of scurvy had appeared on certain crewmen.

"Hazard or no," decreed Captain Rovic, "we must land somewhere." A gleam I remembered appeared in his eyes. He stroked his red beard and murmured, "Besides, it's long since we asked for the Aureate Cities. Perhaps this time they'll have intelligence of such a place."

Steering by that ogre planet which climbed daily higher as we bore westward, we crossed such an emptiness that mutinous talk broke out afresh. In my heart I could not blame the crew. Imagine, my lords. Day upon day upon day where we saw naught but blue waters, white foam, high clouds in a tropic sky; heard only the wind, *whoosh* of waves, creak of timbers, sometimes at night the huge sucking and rushing as a sea monster breached. These were terrible enough to common sailors, unlettered men who still thought the world must be flat. But then to have Tambur hang forever above the bowsprit, and climb, so that all could see we must eventually pass directly beneath that brooding thing . . . and what upbore it?

§ 170

the crew mumbled in the forecastle. Would an angered God not let fall down on us?

So a deputation waited on Captain Rovic. Very timid and respectful they were, those rough burly men, as they asked him to turn about. But their comrades massed below, muscled sun-blackened bodies taut in the ragged kilts, with daggers and belaying pins ready to hand. We officers on the quarterdeck had swords and pistols, true. But we numbered a mere six, including that frightened boy who was myself, and aged Froad the astrologue, whose robe and white beard were reverend to see but of small use in a fight.

Rovic stood mute for a long while after the spokesman had voiced this demand. The stillness grew, until the empty shriek of wind in our shrouds, the empty glitter of ocean out to the world's rim, became all there was. Most splendid our master looked, for he had donned scarlet hose and bell-tipped shoon when he knew the deputation was coming; as well as helmet and corselet polished to mirror brightness. The plumes blew around that blinding steel head and the diamonds on his fingers flashed against the rubies in his sword hilt. Yet when at last he spoke, it was not as a knight of the Queen's court, but in the broad Anday of his fisher boyhood.

"So 'tis back ye'd wend, lads? Wi' a fair wind an' a warm sun, liefer ye'd come about an' beat half round the globe? How ye're changed from yere fathers! Ken ye nay the legend, that once all things did as man commanded, an' 'twas an Andayman's lazy fault that now men must work? For see ye, 'twas nay too much that he told his ax to cut down a tree for him, an' told the faggots to walk home, but when he told 'em to carry him, then God was wroth an' took the power away. Though to be sure, as recompense God gave all Andaymen sea-luck, dice-luck, an' love-luck. What more d'ye ask for, lads?"

Bewildered at this reponse, the spokesman wrung his hands, flushed, looked at the deck, and stammered that we'd all perish miserably . . . starve, or thirst, or drown, or be crushed under that horrible moon, or sail off the world's edge . . . the

Golden Leaper had come farther than ship had sailed since the Fall of Man, and if we returned at once, our fame would live forever—

"But can ye eat fame, Etien?" asked Rovic, still mild and smiling. "We've had fights an' storms, aye, an' merry carouses too; but devil an Aureate City we've seen, though well ye ken they lie out here someplace, stuffed wi' treasure for the first bold man who'll come plunder 'em. What ails yere gutworks, lad? Is't nay an easy cruise? What would the foreigners say? How will yon arrogant cavaliers o' Sathayn, yon grubby chapmen o' Woodland, laugh—nay alone at us, but at all Montalir —did we turn back!"

Thus he jollied them. Only once did he touch his sword, half drawing it, as if absent-mindedly, when he recalled how we had weathered the hurricane off Xingu. But they remembered the mutiny that followed then, and how that same sword had pierced three armed sailors who attacked him together. His dialect told them he would let bygones lie forgotten: if they would. His bawdy promises of sport among lascivious heathen tribes yet to be discovered, his recital of treasure legends, his appeal to their pride as seamen and Montalirians, soothed fear. And then in the end, when he saw them malleable, he dropped the provincial speech. He stood forth on the quarterdeck with burning casque and tossing plumes, and the flag of Montalir blew its sea-faded colors above him, and he said as the knights of the Queen say:

"Now you know I do not propose to turn back until the great globe has been rounded and we bring to Her Majesty that gift which is most peculiarly ours to give. The which is not gold or slaves, nor even that lore of far places that she and her most excellent Company of Merchant Adventurers desire. No, what we shall lift in our hands to give her, on that day when again we lie by the long docks of Lavre, shall be our achievement: that we did this thing which no men have dared in all the world erenow, and did it to her glory."

A while longer he stood, through a silence full of the sea's noise. Then he said quietly, "Dismissed," turned on his heel and went back into his cabin.

§

So we continued for some days more, the men subdued but not uncheerful, the officers taking care to hide their doubts. I found myself busied, not so much with the clerical duties for which I was paid or the study of captaincy for which I was apprenticed—both these amounting to little by now—as with assisting Froad the astrologue. In these balmy airs he could carry on his work even on shipboard. To him it scarce mattered whether we sank or swam; he had lived more than a common span of years already. But the knowledge of the heavens to be gained here, that was something else. At night, standing on the foredeck with quadrant, astrolabe, and telescope, drenched in the radiance from above, he resembled some frosty-bearded saint in the windows of Provien Minster.

"See there, Zhean." His thin hand pointed above seas that glowed and rippled with light, past the purple sky and the few stars still daring to show themselves, toward Tambur. Huge it was in full phase at midnight, sprawling over seven degrees of sky, a shield or barry of soft vert and azure, splotched with angry sable that could be seen to move across its face. The firefly moon we had named Siett twinkled near the hazy edge of the giant. Balant, espied rarely and low on the horizon in our part of the world, here stood high: a crescent, but with the dark part of the disk tinged by luminous Tambur.

"Observe," declared Froad, "there's no doubt left, one can *see* how it rotates on an axis, and how storms boil up in its air. Tambur is no longer the dimmest of frightened legends, nor a dreadful apparition seen to rise as we entered unknown waters; Tambur is real. A world like our own. Immensely bigger, certes, but still a spheroid in space: around which our own world moves, always turning the same hemisphere to her monarch. The conjectures of the ancients are triumphantly confirmed. Not merely that our world is round, *pouf,* that's obvious to anyone . . . but that we move about a greater center, which in turn has an annual path about the sun. But, then, how big is the sun?"

"Siett and Balant are inner satellites of Tambur," I rehearsed, struggling for comprehension. "Vieng, Darou, and the other moons commonly seen at home, have paths outside our own world's. Aye. But what holds it all up?"

"That I don't know. Mayhap the crystal sphere containing the stars exerts an inward pressure. The same pressure, maybe, that hurled mankind down onto the earth, at the time of the Fall From Heaven."

That night was warm, but I shivered, as if those had been winter stars. "Then," I breathed, "there may also be men on . . . Siett, Balant, Vieng . . . even on Tambur?"

"Who knows? We'll need many lifetimes to find out. And what lifetimes they'll be! Thank the good God, Zhean, that you were born in this dawn of the coming age."

Froad returned to making measurements. A dull business, the other officers thought; but by now I had learned enough of the mathematic arts to understand that from these endless tabulations might come the true size of the earth, of Tambur, sun and moons and stars, the path they took through space and the direction of Paradise. So the common sailors, who muttered and made signs against evil as they passed our instruments, were closer to fact than Rovic's gentlemen: for indeed Froad practiced a most potent gramarye.

§

At length we saw weeds floating on the sea, birds, towering cloud masses, all the signs of land. Three days later we raised an island. It was an intense green under those calm skies. Surf, still more violent than in our hemisphere, flung against high cliffs, burst in a smother of foam and roared back down again. We coasted carefully, the palomers aloft to seek an approach, the gunners standing by our cannon with lighted matches. For not only were there unknown currents and shoals—familiar hazards—but we had had brushes with canoe-

sailing cannibals in the past. Especially did we fear the
eclipses. My lords can visualize how in that hemisphere the
sun each day must go behind Tambur. In that longitude the
occurrence was about midafternoon and lasted nearly ten minutes. An awesome sight: the primary planet—for so Froad now
called it, a planet akin to Diell or Coint, with our own world
humbled to a mere satellite thereof!—become a black disk
encircled with red, up in a sky suddenly full of stars. A cold
wind blew across the sea, and even the breakers seemed
hushed. Yet so impudent is the soul of man that we continued
about our duties, stopping only for the briefest prayer as the
sun disappeared, thinking more about the chance of shipwreck
in the gloom than of God's Majesty.

So bright is Tambur that we continued to work our way
around the island at night. From sunup to sunup, twelve
mortal hours, we kept the *Golden Leaper* slowly moving.
Toward the second noon, Captain Rovic's persistence was
rewarded. An opening in the cliffs revealed a long fjord.
Swampy shores overgrown with saltwater trees told us that
while the tides rose high in that bay, it was not one of those
roosts so dreaded by mariners. The wind being against us,
we furled sail and lowered the boats, towing in our caravel
by the power of oars. This was a vulnerable moment, especially
since we had perceived a village within the fjord. "Should we
not stand out, master, and let them come first to us?" I
ventured.

Rovic spat over the rail. "I've found it best never to show
doubt," said he. "If a canoe fleet should assail us, we'll give
'em a whiff of grapeshot and trust to break their nerve. But I
think, thus showing ourselves fearless of them from the very
first, we're less likely to meet treacherous ambuscade later."

He proved right.

In the course of time, we learned we had come upon the
eastern end of a large archipelago. The inhabitants were
mighty seafarers, considering that they had only outrigger dug-
outs to travel in. These, however, were often a hundred feet
long. With forty paddles, or with three bast-sailed masts, such

a vessel could almost match our best speed, and was more maneuverable. However, the small cargo space limited their range of travel.

Though they lived in houses of wood and thatch, possessing only stone tools, the natives were cultivated folk. They farmed as well as fished; their priests had an alphabet. Tall and vigorous, somewhat darker and less hairy than we, they were impressive to behold: whether nude as was common, or in full panoply of cloth and feathers and shell ornaments. They had formed a loose empire throughout the archipelago, raided islands lying farther north and carried on a brisk trade within their own borders. Their whole nation they called the Hisagazi, and the island on which we had chanced was Yarzik.

This we learned slowly, as we mastered somewhat their tongue. For we were several weeks at that town. The duke of the island, Guzan, made us welcome, supplying us with food, shelter, and helpers as we required. For our part, we pleased them with glassware, bolts of Wondish cloth, and suchlike trade goods. Nonetheless we encountered many difficulties. The shore above high-water mark being too swampy for beaching a vessel as heavy as ours, we must build a dry-dock before we could careen. Numerous of us took a flux from some disease, though all recovered in time, and this slowed us further.

"Yet I think our troubles will prove a blessing," Rovic told me one night. As had become his habit, once he learned I was a discreet amanuensis, he confided certain thoughts in me. The captain is ever a lonely man; and Rovic, fisher lad, freebooter, self-taught navigator, victor over the Grand Fleet of Sathayn and ennobled by the Queen herself, must have found the keeping of that necessary aloofness harder than would a gentleman born.

I waited silent, there in the grass hut they had given him. A soapstone lamp threw wavering light and enormous shadows over us; something rustled the thatch. Outside, the damp ground sloped past houses on stilts and murmurous fronded trees, to the fjord where it shimmered under Tambur. Faintly

I heard drums throb, a chant and stamping of feet around some sacrificial fire. Indeed the cool hills of Montalir seemed far.

Rovic leaned back his muscular form, y-clad in a mere seaman's kilt in this heat. He had had them fetch him a civilized chair from the ship. "For see you, young fellow," he continued, "at other times we'd have established just enough communication to ask about gold. Well, we might also try to get a few sailing directions. But all in all, we'd hear little except the old story— 'aye, foreign lord, indeed there's a kingdom where the very streets are paved with gold . . . a hundred miles west'— anything to get rid of us, eh? But in this prolonged stay, I've asked out the duke and the idolater priests more subtly. I've been so coy about whence we came and what we already know, that they've let slip a gobbet of knowledge they'd not otherwise have disgorged on the rack itself."

"The Aureate Cities?" I cried.

"Hush! I'd not have the crew get excited and out of hand. Not yet."

His leathery, hooknosed face turned strange with thought. "I've always believed those cities an old wives' tale," he said. My shock must have been mirrored to his gaze, for he grinned and went on, "A useful one. Like a lodestone on a stick, it's dragging us around the world." His mirth faded. Again he got that look, which was not unlike the look of Froad considering the heavens. "Aye, of course I want gold, too. But if we find none on this voyage, I'll not care. I'll just capture a few ships of Eralia or Sathayn when we're back in home waters, and pay for the voyage thus. I spoke God's truth that day on the quarterdeck, Zhean, that this journey was its own goal; until I can give it to Queen Odela, who once gave me the kiss of ennoblement."

He shook himself out of his reverie and said in a brisk tone: "Having led him to believe I already knew the most of it, I teased from Duke Guzan the admission that on the main island of this Hisagazi empire is something I scarce dare think about. A ship of the gods, he says, and an actual live god who came from the stars therein. Any of the natives will tell you this much. The secret reserved to the noble folk is that this is no legend or mummery, but sober fact. Or so Guzan claims. I know not what to think. But . . . he took me to a holy cave and showed me an object from that ship. It was some kind of clockwork mechanism, I believe. What, I know not. But of a shining silvery metal such as I've never seen before. The priest challenged me to break it. The metal was not heavy; must have been thin. But it blunted my sword, splintered a rock I pounded with, and my diamond ring would not scratch it."

I made signs against evil. A chill went along me, spine and skin and scalp, until I prickled all over. For the drums were muttering in a jungle dark, and the waters lay like quicksilver beneath gibbous Tambur, and each afternoon that planet ate the sun. Oh, for the bells of Provien, across wind-swept Anday downs!

§

When the *Golden Leaper* was seaworthy again, Rovic had no trouble gaining permission to visit the Hisagazian emperor on the main island. He would, indeed, have found difficulty in not doing so. By now the canoes had borne word of us from one end of the realm to another, and the great lords were all agog to see these blue-eyed strangers. Sleek and content once more, we disentangled ourselves from the arms of tawny wenches and embarked. Up anchor, up sail, with chanties whose echoes sent sea birds whirling above the steeps, and we stood out to sea. This time we were escorted. Guzan himself was our pilot, a big middle-aged man whose handsomeness was not much injured by the livid green tattoos his folk affected on face and body. Several of his sons spread their pallets on our decks, while a swarm of warriors paddled alongside.

Rovic summoned Etien the boatswain to him in his cabin. "You're a man of some wit," he said. "I give you charge of keeping our crew alert, weapons ready, however peaceful this may look."

"Why, master!" The scarred brown face sagged with near dismay. "Think you the natives plot a treachery?"

"Who can tell?" said Rovic. "Now, say naught to the crew. They've no skill in dissembling. Did greed or fear rise among 'em, the natives would sense as much, and grow uneasy—which would worsen the attitude of our own men, until none but God's Daughter could tell what'd happen. Only see to it, as casually as you're able, that our arms are ever close by and that our folk stay together."

Etien collected himself, bowed, and left the cabin. I made bold to ask what Rovic had in mind.

"Nothing, yet," said he. "However, I did hold in these fists a piece of clockwork such as the Grand Ban of Giair never imagined; and yarns were spun me of a Ship which flew down from heaven, bearing a god or a prophet. Guzan thinks I know more than I do, and hopes we'll be a new, disturbing element in the balance of things, by which he may further his own ambitions. He did not take all those fighting men along by accident. As for me . . . I intend to learn more about this."

He sat a while at his table, staring at a sunbeam which sickled up and down the wainscot as the ship rocked. Finally: "Scripture tells us man dwelt beyond the stars before the Fall. The astrologues of the past generation or two have told us the planets are corporeal bodies like this earth. A traveler from Paradise—"

I left with my head in a roar.

We made an easy passage among scores of islands. After several days we raised the main one, Ulas-Erkila. It is about a hundred miles long, forty miles across at the widest, rising steep and green toward central mountains dominated by a volcanic cone. The Hisagazi worship two sorts of gods, watery and fiery, and believe this Mount Ulas houses the latter. When I saw that snowpeak afloat in the sky above emerald ridges, staining the blue with smoke, I could feel what the pagans did. The holiest act a man can perform among them is to cast himself into the burning crater of Ulas, and many an aged warrior is carried up the mountain that he may do so. Women are not allowed on the slopes.

Nikum, the royal seat, is situated at the head of a fjord like the village where we had been staying. But Nikum is rich and extensive, being about the size of Roann. Many houses are made from timber rather than thatch; there is also a massive basalt temple atop a cliff, overlooking the city, with orchards, jungle, and mountains at its back. So great are the tree trunks available to them for pilings, the Hisagazi have built here a regular set of docks like those at Lavre—instead of moorings and floats that can rise or fall with the tides, such as most harbors throughout the world are content with. We were offered a berth of honor at the central wharf, but Rovic made the excuse that our ship was awkward to handle and got us tied at the far end.

"In the middle, we'd have the watchtower straight above us," he muttered to me. "And they may not have discovered the bow here, but their javelin throwers are good. Also, we'd have an easy approach to our ship, plus a clutter of moored canoes between us and the bay mouth. Here, though, a few of us could hold the pier whilst the others ready for quick departure."

"But have we anything to fear, master?" I asked.

He gnawed his mustache. "I know not. Much depends on what they really believe about this god-ship of theirs . . . as well as what the truth is. But come all death and hell against us, we'll not return without that truth for Queen Odela."

§

Drums rolled and feathered spearmen leaped as our officers disembarked. A royal catwalk had been erected above high-water level. (Common townsfolk in this realm swim from house to house when the tide laps their thresholds, or take a coracle if they have burdens to carry.) Across the graceful span of vines and canes lay the palace, which was a long building made from logs, the roof pillars carved into fantastic god-shapes.

Iskilip, Priest-Emperor of the Hisagazi, was an old and corpulent man. A soaring headdress of plumes, a feather robe, a wooden scepter topped with a human skull, his own facial tattoos, his motionlessness, all made him seem unhuman. He sat on a dais, under sweet-smelling torches. His sons sat cross-legged at his feet, his courtiers on either side. Down the long walls were ranged his guardsmen. They had not our custom of standing to attention; but they were big supple young men, with shields and corselets of scaly sea-monster leather, with flint axes and obsidian spears that could kill as easily as iron. Their heads were shaven, which made them look the fiercer.

Iskilip greeted us well, called for refreshment, bade us be seated on a bench not much lower than his dais. He asked many perceptive questions. Wide-ranging, the Hisagazi knew of islands far beyond their own chain. They could even point the direction and tell us roughly the distance of a many-castled country they named Yurakadak, though only one of them had traveled that far himself. Judging by their third-hand description, what could this be but Giair, which the Wondish adventurer Hanas Tolasson had reached overland? It blazed in me that we were indeed rounding the world. Only after that glory had faded a little did I again heed the talk.

"As I told Guzan," Rovic was saying, "another thing which drew us hither was the tale that you were blessed with a Ship from heaven. And he showed me this was true."

A hissing went down the hall. The princes grew stiff, the courtiers blanked their countenances, even the guardsmen stirred and muttered. Remotely through the walls I heard the rumbling, nearing tide. When Iskilip spoke, through the mask of himself, his voice had gone whetted: "Have you forgotten that these things are not for the uninitiate to see, Guzan?"

"No, Holy One," said the duke. Sweat sprang forth among the devils on his face, but it was not the sweat of fear. "However, this captain knew. His people also . . . as nearly as I could learn . . . he still has trouble speaking so I can understand . . . his people are initiate too. The claim seems reasonable, Holy One. Look at the marvels they brought. The hard, shining stone-which-is-not-stone, as in this long knife I was given, is that not like the stuff of which the Ship is built? The tubes which make distant things look close at hand, such as he has given you, Holy One, is this not akin to the far-seer the Messenger possesses?"

Iskilip leaned forward, toward Rovic. His scepter hand trembled so much that the pegged jaws of the skull clattered together. "Did the Star People themselves teach you to make all this?" he cried. "I never imagined . . . The Messenger never spoke of any others—"

Rovic held up both palms. "Not so fast, Holy One, I pray you," said he. "We are poorly versed in your tongue. I couldn't recognize a word just now."

This was his deceit. All his officers had been ordered to feign a knowledge of Hisagazi less than they really possessed. (We had improved our command of it by secret practicing with each other.) Thus he had an unimpeachable device for equivocation.

"Best we talk of this in private, Holy One," suggested Guzan, with a glance at the courtiers. They returned him a jealous glare.

Iskilip slouched in his gorgeous regalia. His words fell blunt enough, but in the weak tone of an old, uncertain man. "I know not. If these strangers are already initiate, certes we can show them what we have. But otherwise—if profane ears heard the Messenger's own tale—"

§

Guzan raised a dominator's hand. Bold and ambitious, long thwarted in his petty province, he had taken fire this day. "Holy One," he said, "why has the full story been withheld all these years? In part to keep the commoners obedient, aye. But also, did you and your councillors not fear that all the world might swarm hither, greedy for knowledge, if it knew, and we should then be overwhelmed? Well, if we let the blue-eyed men go home with curiosity unsatisfied, I think they are sure to return in strength. So we have naught to lose by revealing the truth to them. If they have never had a Messenger of their own, if they can be of no real use to us, time enough to kill them. But if they have indeed been visited like us, what might we and they not do together!"

This was spoken fast and softly, so that we Montalirians should not understand. And indeed our gentlemen failed to do so. I, having young ears, got the gist; and Rovic preserved such a fatuous smile of incomprehension that I knew he was seizing every word.

So in the end they decided to take our leader—and my insignificant self, for no Hisagazian magnate goes anywhere quite unattended—up to the temple. Iskilip led the way in person, with Guzan and two brawny princes behind. A dozen spearmen brought up the rear. I thought Rovic's blade would be scant use if trouble came, but set my lips firmly together and made myself walk behind him. He looked as eager as a child on Thanksgiving Morning, teeth agleam in the pointed beard, a plumed bonnet slanted rakish over his brow. None would have thought him aware of any peril.

We left about sundown; in Tambur's hemisphere, folk make less distinction between day and night than our people must. Having observed Siett and Balant in high tide position, I was not surprised that Nikum lay nearly drowned. And yet, as we wound up the cliff trail toward the temple, methought I had never seen a view more alien.

Below us lay a sheet of water, on which the long grass roofs of the city appeared to float; the crowded docks, where our own ship's masts and spars raked above heathen figureheads; the fjord, winding between precipices toward its mouth, where the surf broke white and terrible on the skerries. The heights above us seemed altogether black, against a fire-colored sunset that filled nigh half the sky and bloodied the waters. Wan through those clouds I glimpsed the thick crescent of Tambur, banded in a heraldry no man could read. A basalt column chipped into the shape of a head loomed in outline athwart the planet. Right and left of the path grew sawtoothed grasses, summer-dry. The sky was pale at the zenith, dark purple in the east, where the first few stars had appeared. Tonight I found no comfort in the stars. We all walked silent. The bare native feet made no noise. My own shoes went *pad-pad* and the bells on Rovic's toes raised a tiny jingle.

The temple was a bold piece of work. Within a quadrangle of basalt walls guarded by tall stone heads lay several buildings of the same material. Only the fresh-cut fronds that roofed them were alive. With Iskilip to lead us, we brushed past acolytes and priests to a wooden cabin behind the sanctum. Two guardsmen stood watch at its door, but they knelt for Iskilip. The emperor rapped with his curious scepter.

My mouth was dry and my heart thunderous. I expected almost any being hideous or radiant to stand in the doorway as it was opened. Astonishing, then, to see just a man, and of no great stature. By lamplight within I discerned his room, clean, austere, but not uncomfortable; this could have been any Hisagazian dwelling. He himself wore a simple bast skirt. The legs beneath were bent and thin, old man's shanks. His body was also thin, but still erect, the white head proudly carried. In complexion he was darker than a Montalirian, lighter than a Hisagazian, with brown eyes and thin beard. His visage differed subtly, in nose and lips and slope of jaw, from any other race I had ever encountered. But he was human.

Naught else.

§

We entered the cabin, shutting out the spearmen. Iskilip doddered through a half-religious ceremony of introduction. I saw Guzan and the princes shift their stance, restless and unawed. Their class had long been party to this. Rovic's face was unreadable. He bowed with full courtliness to Val Nira, Messenger of Heaven, and explained our presence in a few words. But as he spoke, their eyes met and I saw him take the star man's measure.

"Aye, this is my home," said Val Nira. Habit spoke for him; he had given this account to so many young nobles that the edges were worn off it. As yet he had not observed our metallic instruments, or else had not grasped their significance to him. "For . . . forty-three years, is that right, Iskilip? I have been treated as well as might be. If at times I was near screaming from loneliness, that is what an oracle must expect."

The emperor stirred, uneasy in his robe. "His demon left him," he explained. "Now he is simple human flesh. That's the real secret we keep. It was not ever thus. I remember when he first came. He prophesied immense things, and all the people wailed and went on their faces. But sithence his demon has gone back to the stars, and the once potent weapon he bore has equally been emptied of its force. The people would not believe this, however, so we still pretend otherwise, or there would be unrest among them."

"Affecting your own privileges," said Val Nira. His tone was tired and sardonic. "Iskilip was young then," he added to Rovic, "and the imperial succession was in doubt. I gave him my influence. He promised in return to do certain things for me."

"I tried, Messenger," said the monarch. "Ask all the sunken canoes and drowned men if I did not try. But the will of the gods was otherwise."

"Evidently," Val Nira shrugged. "These islands have few ores, Captain Rovic, and no person capable of recognizing those I required. It's too far to the mainland for Hisagazian canoes. But I don't deny you tried, Iskilip . . . then." He cocked an eyebrow back at us. "This is the first time foreigners have been taken so deeply into the imperial confidence, my friends. Are you certain you can get back out again, alive?"

"Why, why, why, they're our guests!" blustered Iskilip and Guzan, almost in each other's mouths.

"Besides," smiled Rovic, "I had most of the secret already. My own country has secrets of its own, to set against this.

Yes, I think we might well do business, Holy One."

The emperor trembled. His voice cracked across. "Have you indeed a Messenger too?"

"What?" For a numbed moment Val Nira stared at us. Red and white pursued each other across his countenance. Then he sat down on the bench and began to weep.

"Well, not precisely." Rovic laid a hand on the shaking shoulder, "I confess no heavenly vessel had docked at Montalir. But we've certain other secrets, belike equally valuable." Only I, who knew his moods somewhat, could sense the tautness in him. He locked eyes with Guzan and stared the duke down as a wild animal tamer does. And all the while, motherly gentle, he spoke with Val Nira. "I take it, friend, your Ship was wrecked on these shores, but could be repaired if you had certain materials?"

"Yes . . . yes . . . listen—" Stammering and gulping at the thought he might see his home again ere he died, Val Nira tried to explain.

The doctrinal implications of what he said are so astounding, even dangerous, that I feel sure my lords would not wish me to repeat much. However, I do not believe they are false. If the stars are indeed suns like our own, each attended by planets like our own, this demolishes the crystal-sphere theory. But Froad, when he was told later, did not think that mattered to the true religion. Scripture has never said in so many words that Paradise lies directly above the birthplace of God's Daughter; this was merely assumed, during those centuries when the earth was believed to be flat. Why should Paradise not be those planets of other suns, where men dwell in magnificence, men who possess all the ancient arts and flit from star to star as casually as we might go from Lavre to West Alayn?

Val Nira believed our ancestors had been cast away on this world, several thousand years ago. They must have been fleeing the consequences of some crime or heresy, to come so far from any human domain. Somehow their ship was wrecked, the survivors went back to savagery, only by degrees have their descendants regained a little knowledge. I cannot see where this explanation contradicts the dogma of the Fall. Rather, it amplifies it. The Fall was not the portion of all mankind, but only of a few—our own tainted blood—while the others continued to dwell prosperous and content in the heavens.

Even today, our world lies far off the trade lanes of the Paradise folk. Very few of them nowadays have any interest in seeking new worlds. Val Nira, though, was such a one. He traveled at hazard for months until he chanced upon our earth. Then the curse seized him, too. Something went wrong. He descended upon Ulas-Erkila, and the Ship would fly no more.

"I know what the damage is," he said ardently. "I've not forgotten. How could I? No day has passed in all these years that I didn't recite to myself what must be done. A certain subtle engine in the Ship requires quicksilver." (He and Rovic must spend some time talking ere they deduced this must be what he meant by the word he used.) "When the engine failed, I landed so hard that its tanks burst. All the quicksilver, what I had in reserve as well as what I was employing, poured forth. So much, in that hot enclosed space, would have poisoned me. I fled outside, forgetting to close the doorway. The deck being canted, the quicksilver ran after me. By the time I had recovered from blind panic, a tropical rainstorm had carried off all the fluid metal. A series of unlikely accidents, yes, that's what's condemned me to a life's exile. It really would have made more sense to perish outright!"

He clutched Rovic's hand, staring up from his seat at the captain who stood over him. "Can you actually get quicksilver?" he begged. "I need no more than the volume of a man's head. Only that, and a few repairs easily made with tools in the Ship. When this cult grew up around me, I must needs release certain things I possessed, that each provincial temple might have a relic. But I took care never to give away anything important. Whatever I need is all there. A gallon of quicksilver, and— Oh, God, my wife may even be alive, on Terra!"

§

Guzan, at least, had begun to understand the situation. He gestured to the princes, who hefted their axes and stepped a little closer. The door was shut on the guard escort, but a shout would bring their spears into this cabin. Rovic looked from Val Nira to Guzan, whose face was grown ugly with tension. My captain laid hand on hilt. In no other way did he seem to feel any nearness of trouble.

"I take it, milord," he said lightly, "you're willing that the Heaven Ship be made to fly again."

Guzan was jarred. He had never expected this. "Why, of course," he exclaimed. "Why not?"

"Your tame god would depart you. What then becomes of your power in Hisagazi?"

"I . . . I'd not thought of that," Iskilip stuttered.

Val Nira's eyes shuttled among us, as if watching a game of paddleball. His thin body shook. "No," he whimpered. "You can't. You can't keep me!"

Guzan nodded. "In a few more years," he said, not unkindly, "you would depart in death's canoe anyhow. If meanwhile we held you against your will, you might not speak the right oracles for us. Nay, be at ease; we'll get your flowing stone." With a slitted glance at Rovic: "Who shall fetch it?"

"My own folk," said the knight. "Our ship can readily reach Giair, where there are civilized nations who surely have the quicksilver. We could return within a year, I think."

"Accompanied by a fleet of adventurers, to help you seize the sacred vessel?" asked Guzan bluntly. "Or . . . once out of our islands . . . you might not proceed to Yurakadak at all. You might continue the whole way home, and tell your Queen, and return with all the power she commands."

Rovic lounged against a roof post, like a big pouncecat at its ease in ruffles and hose and scarlet cape. His right hand continued to rest on his sword pommel. "Only Val Nira could make that Ship go, I suppose," he drawled. "Does it matter who aids him in making repairs? Surely you don't think either of our nations could conquer Paradise!"

"The Ship is very easy to operate," chattered Val Nira. "Anyone can fly it in air. I showed many nobles what levers to use. Its navigating among the stars which is more difficult. No nation on this world could even reach my people unaided —let alone fight them—but why should you think of fighting? I've told you a thousand times, Iskilip, the dwellers in the Milky Way are dangerous to none, helpful to all. They have so much wealth they're hard put to find a use for most of it. Gladly would they spend large amounts to help all the peoples on this world become civilized again." With an anxious, half hysterical look at Rovic: "Fully civilized, I mean. We'll teach you our arts. We'll give you engines, automata, homunculi, that do all the toilsome work; and boats that fly through the air; and regular passenger service on those ships that ply between the stars—"

"These things you have promised for forty years," said Iskilip. "We've only your word."

"And, finally, a chance to confirm his word," I blurted.

Guzan said with calculated grimness: "Matters are not that simple, Holy One. I've watched these men from across the ocean for weeks, while they lived on Yarzik. Even on their best behavior, they're a fierce and greedy lot. I trust them no further than my eyes reach. This very night I see how they've befooled us. They know our language better than they ever admitted. And they misled us to believe they might have some inkling of a Messenger. If the Ship were indeed made to fly again, with them in possession, who knows what they might choose to do?"

Rovic's tone softened still further, "What do you propose, Guzan?"

"We can discuss that another time."

I saw knuckles tighten around stone axes. For a moment, only Val Nira's unsteady breathing was heard. Guzan stood heavy in the lamplight, rubbing his chin, the small black eyes turned downward in thoughtfulness. At last he shook himself.

"Perhaps," he said crisply, "a crew mainly Hisagazian could sail your ship, Rovic, and fetch the flowing stone. A few of your men could go along to instruct ours. The rest could remain here as hostages."

My captain made no reply. Val Nira groaned, "You don't understand! You're squabbling over nothing! When my people come here, there'll be no more war, no more oppression, they'll cure you of all such diseases. They'll show friendship to all and favor to none. I beg you—"

"Enough," said Iskilip. His own words fell ragged. "We shall sleep on all this. If anyone can sleep after so much strangeness."

Rovic looked past the emperor's plumes, into the face of Guzan. "Before we decide anything—" His fingers tightened on the sword hilt till the nails turned white. Some thought had sprung up within him. But he kept his tone even. "First I want to see that Ship. Can we go there tomorrow?"

Iskilip was the Holy One, but he stood huddled in his feather robe. Guzan nodded agreement.

§

We bade our goodnights and went forth under Tambur. The planet was waxing toward full, flooding the courtyard with cold luminance, but the hut was shadowed by the temple. It remained a black outline, with a narrow lamplight rectangle of doorway in the middle. There was etched the frail body of Val Nira, who had come from the stars. He watched us till we had gone out of sight.

On the way down the path, Guzan and Rovic bargained in curt words. The Ship lay two days' march inland, on the slopes of Mount Ulas. We would go in a joint party to inspect it, but a mere dozen Montalirians were to be allowed. Afterward we would debate our course of action.

Lanthorns glowed yellow at our caravel's poop. Refusing Iskilip's hospitality, Rovic and I returned thither for the night. A pikeman on guard at the gangway inquired what I had learned. "Ask me tomorrow," I said feebly. "My head's in too much of a whirl."

"Come into my cabin, lad, for a stoup ere we retire," the captain invited me.

God knows I needed wine. We entered the low little room, crowded with nautical instruments, with books, and with printed charts that looked quaint to me now I had seen a little of those spaces where the cartographer drew mermaids and windsprites. Rovic sat down behind his table, gestured me to a chair opposite, and poured from a carafe into two goblets of Quaynish crystal. Then I knew he had momentous thoughts in his head—far more than the problem of saving our lives.

We sipped a while, unspeaking. I heard the *lap-lap* of wavelets on our hull, the tramp of men on watch, the rustle of distant surf: otherwise nothing. At last Rovic leaned back, staring at the ruby wine on the table. I could not read his expression.

"Well, lad," said he, "what do you think?"

"I know not what to think, master."

"You and Froad are a little prepared for this idea that the stars are other suns. You're educated. As for me, I've seen so much eldritch in my day that this seems quite believable. The rest of our people, though—"

"An irony that barbarians like Guzan should long have been familiar with the concept—having had the old man from the sky to preach it privily to their class for more than forty years— Is he indeed a prophet, master?"

"He denies it. He plays prophet because he must, but it's evident all the dukes and earls of this realm know it's a trick. Iskilip is senile, more than half converted to his own artificial creed. He was mumbling about prophecies Val Nira made long ago, true prophecies. Bah! Tricks of memory and wishfulness. Val Nira is as human and fallible as I am. We Montalirians are the same flesh as these Hisagazi, even if we have learned the use of metal before they did. Val Nira's people know more in turn than us; but they're still mortals, by Heaven. I *must* remember that they are."

"Guzan remembers."

"Bravo, lad!" Rovic's mouth bent upward, one-sidedly. "He's a clever one, and bold. When he came, he saw his chance to stop stagnating as the petty lord of an outlying island. He'll not let that chance slip without a fight. Like many a double-dealer before him, he accuses us of plotting the very things he hopes to do."

"But what does he hope for?"

"My guess would be, he wants the Ship for himself. Val Nira said it was easy to fly. Navigation between the stars would be too difficult for anyone save him; nor could any man in his right mind hope to play pirate along the Milky Way. However . . . if the Ship stayed right here, on this earth, rising no higher than a mile above ground . . . the warlord who used it might conquer more widely than Lame Darveth himself."

I was aghast. "Do you mean Guzan would not even try to seek out Paradise?"

Rovic scowled so blackly at his wine that I saw he wanted aloneness. I stole off to my bunk in the poop.

The captain was up before dawn, readying our folk. Plainly he had reached some decision, and it was not pleasant. But once he set a course, he seldom left it. He was long in conference with Etien, who came out of the cabin looking frightened. As if to reassure himself, the boatswain ordered the men about all the more harshly.

Our allowed dozen were to be Rovic, Froad, myself, Etien, and eight crewmen. All were supplied with helmets and corselets, muskets and edged weapons. Since Guzan had told us there was a beaten path to the Ship, we assembled a supply cart on the dock. Etien supervised its lading. I was astonished to see that nearly all it carried, till the axles groaned, was barrels of gunpowder. "But we're not taking cannon!" I protested.

"Skipper's orders," rapped Etien. He turned his back on me. After a glance at Rovic's face, no one ventured to ask him the reason. I remembered we would be going up a mountainside.

A wagonful of powder, with lit fuse, set rolling down toward a hostile army, might win a battle. But did Rovic anticipate open conflict so soon?

Certes his orders to the men and officers remaining behind suggested as much. They were to stay aboard the *Golden Leaper,* holding her ready for instant fight or flight.

As the sun rose, we said our morning prayers to God's Daughter and marched down the docks. The wood banged hollow under our boots. A few thin mists drifted on the bay; Tambur's crescent hung wan above. Nikum Town was hushed as we passed through.

Guzan met us at the temple. A son of Iskilip was supposedly in charge, but the duke ignored that youth as much as we did. They had a hundred guardsmen with them, scaly-coated, shaven-headed, tattooed with storms and dragons. The early sunlight gleamed off obsidian spearheads. Our approach was watched in silence. But when we drew up before those disorderly ranks, Guzan trod forth. He was also y-clad in leather, and carried the sword Rovic had given him on Yarzik. The dew shimmered on his feather cloak. "What have you in that wagon?" he demanded.

"Supplies," Rovic answered.

"For four days?"

"Send home all but ten of your men," said Rovic coolly, "And I'll send back this cart."

Their eyes clashed, until Guzan turned and gave his orders. We started off, a few Montalirians surrounded by pagan warriors. The jungle lay ahead of us, a deep and burning green, rising halfway up the slope of Ulas. Then the mountain became naked black, up to the snow that edged its smoking crater.

Val Nira walked between Rovic and Guzan. Strange, I thought, that the instrument of God's will for us was so shriveled. He ought to have walked tall and haughty, with a star on his brow.

During the day, at night when we made camp, and again the next day, Rovic and Froad questioned him eagerly about his home. Of course, all their talk was in fragments. Nor did I hear everything, since I must take my turn at pulling our wagon along that narrow, upward, damnable trail. The Hisagazi have no draft animals, therefore they make very little use of the wheel and have no proper roads. But what I did hear kept me long awake.

§

Ah, greater marvels than the poets have imagined for Elf Land! Entire cities built in a single tower half a mile high. The sky made to glow so that there is no true darkness after sunset. Food not grown in the earth, but manufactured in alchemical laboratories. The lowest peasant owning a score of machines which serve him more subtly and humbly than might a thousand slaves—owning an aerial carriage which can fly him around his world in less than a day—owning a crystal window on which theatrical images appear, to beguile his abundant leisure. Argosies between suns, stuffed with the wealth of a thousand planets; yet every ship unarmed and unescorted, for there are no pirates and this realm has long ago come to such good terms with the other starfaring nations that war has also ceased. (These other countries, it seems, are more akin to the supernatural than Val Nira's, in that the races composing them are not human, though able to speak and reason.) In this happy land there is little crime. When it does occur, the criminal is soon captured by the arts of the provost corps; yet he is not hanged, nor even transported overseas. Instead, his mind is cured of the wish to violate any law. He returns home to live as an especially honored citizen, since all know he is now completely trustworthy. As for the government—but here I lost the thread of discourse. I believe it is in form a republic, but in practice a devoted fellowship of men, chosen by examination, who see to the welfare of everyone else.

Surely, I thought, this was Paradise!

Our sailors listened with mouths agape. Rovic's mien was reserved, but he gnawed his mustaches incessantly. Guzan, to whom this was an old tale, grew rough of manner. Plain to see, he disliked our intimacy with Val Nira, and the ease wherewith we grasped ideas that were spoken.

But then, we came of a nation which has long encouraged natural philosophy and improvement of all mechanic arts. I myself, in my short lifetime, had witnessed the replacement of the waterwheel in regions where there are few streams, by the modern form of windmill. The pendulum clock was invented the year before I was born. I had read many romances about the flying machines which no few men have tried to devise. Living at such a dizzy pace of progress, we Montalirians were well prepared to entertain still vaster concepts.

At night, sitting up with Froad and Etien around a campfire, I spoke somewhat of this to the savant. "Ah," he crooned, "today Truth stood unveiled before me. Did you hear what the starman said? The three laws of planetary motion about a sun, and the one great law of attraction which explains them? Dear saints, that law can be put in a single short sentence, and yet the development will keep mathematicians busy for three hundred years!"

He stared past the flames, and the other fires around which the heathen men slept, and the jungle gloom, and the angry volcanic glow in heaven. I started to query him. "Leave be, lad," grunted Etien. "Can ye nay tell when a man's in love?"

I shifted my position, a little closer to the boatswain's stolid, comforting bulk. "What do you think of all this?" I asked, softly, for the jungle whispered and croaked on every side.

"Me, I stopped thinking a while back," he said. "After yon day on the quarterdeck, when the skipper jested us into sailing wi' him though we went off the world's edge an' tumbled down in foam amongst the nether stars . . . well, I'm but a poor sailor man, an' my one chance o' regaining home is to follow the skipper."

"Even beyond the sky?"

"Less hazard to that, maybe, than sailing on around the world. The little man swore his vessel was safe, an' that there're no storms between the suns."

"Can you trust his word?"

"Oh, aye. Even a knocked-about old palomer like me has seen enough o' men to ken when a one's too timid an' eagersome to stand by a lie. I fear not the folk in Paradise, nor does the skipper. Except in some way—" Etien rubbed his bearded jaw, scowling. "In some way I can nay wholly grasp, they affright Rovic. He fears nay they'll come hither wi' torch an' sword; but there's somewhat else about 'em that frets him."

I felt the ground shudder, ever so faintly. Ulas had cleared his throat. "It does seem we'd be daring God's anger—"

"That's nay what gnaws on the skipper's mind. He was never an over-pious man." Etien scratched himself, yawned, and climbed to his feet. "Glad I am to be nay the skipper. Let him think over what's best to do. Time ye an' me was asleep."

§

But I slept little that night.

Rovic, I think, rested well. Yet as the next day wore on, I could see haggardness on him. I wondered why. Did he think the Hisagazi would turn on us? If so, why had he come at all? As the slope steepened, the wagon grew so toilsome to push and drag that my fears died for lack of breath.

Yet when we came upon the Ship, toward evening, I forgot my weariness. And after one amazed volley of oaths, our mariners rested silent on their pikes. The Hisagazi, never talkative, crouched low in token of awe. Only Guzan remained erect among them. I glimpsed his expression as he stared at the marvel. It was a look of lust.

Wild was that place. We had gone above timberline, so the land was a green sea below us, edged with silvery ocean. Here we stood among tumbled black boulders, with cinders and spongy tufa underfoot. The mountain rose in steeps and scarps and ravines, up to the snows and the smoke, which rose another mile into a pale chilly sky. And here stood the Ship.

And the Ship was beauty.

I remember. In length—height, rather, since it stood on its tail—it was about equal to our own caravel, in form not unlike a lance head, in color a shining white untarnished after forty years. That was all. But words are paltry, my lord. What can they show of clean soaring curves, of iridescence on burnished metal, of a thing which was proud and lovely and in its very shape aquiver to be off? How can I conjure back the glamor which hazed that Ship whose keel had cloven starlight?

We stood there a long time. My vision blurred. I wiped my eyes, angry to be seen so affected, until I noticed one tear glisten in Rovic's red beard. But the captain's visage was quite blank. When he spoke, he said merely, in a flat voice, "Come, let's make camp."

The Hisagazian guardsmen dared approach no closer than these several hundred yards, to so potent an idol as the Ship had become. Our own mariners were glad enough to maintain the same distance. But after dark, when all else was in order, Val Nira led Rovic, Froad, Guzan, and myself to the vessel.

As we approached, a double door in the side swung noiselessly open and a metal gangplank descended therefrom. Glowing in Tambur's light, and in the dull clotted red reflected off the smoke clouds, the Ship was already as strange as I could endure. When it thus opened itself to me, as if a ghost stood guard, I whimpered and fled. The cinders crunched beneath my boots; I caught a whiff of sulfurous air.

But at the edge of camp I rallied myself enough to look again. The dark ground blotted all light, so that the Ship appeared alone with its grandeur. Presently I went back.

The interior was lit by luminous panels, cool to the touch. Val Nira explained that the great engine which drove it—as if the troll of folklore were put on a treadmill—was intact, and would furnish power at the flick of a lever. As nearly as I could understand what he said, this was done by changing the metallic part of ordinary salt into light . . . so I do not understand after all. The quicksilver was required for a part of the controls, which channeled power from the engine into another mechanism that hurtled the Ship skyward. We inspected the broken container. Enormous indeed had been the impact of landing, to twist and bend that thick alloy so. And yet Val

Nira had been shielded by invisible forces, and the rest of the ship had not suffered important damage. He fetched some tools, which flamed and hummed and whirled, and demonstrated a few repair operations on the broken part. Obviously he would have no trouble completing the work—and then he need only pour in a gallon of quicksilver, to bring his vessel alive again.

Much else did he show us that night. I shall say naught of this, for I cannot even remember such strangeness very clearly, let alone find words. Suffice it that Rovic, Froad, and Zhean spent a few hours in Elf Hill.

So, too, did Guzan. Though he had been taken here once before, as part of his initiation, he had never been shown this much erenow. Watching him, however, I saw less marveling in him than greed.

No doubt Rovic observed the same. There was little which Rovic did not observe. When we departed the Ship, his silence was not stunned like Froad's or my own. At the time, I thought in a vague fashion that he fretted over the trouble Guzan was certain to make. Now, looking back, I believe his mood was sadness.

Sure it is that long after we others were in our bedrolls, he stood alone, looking at the planet-lit Ship.

§

Early in a cold dawn, Etien shook me awake. "Up, lad, we've work to do. Load yere pistols an' belt on yere dirk."

"What? What's to happen?" I fumbled with a hoarfrosted blanket. Last night seemed a dream.

"The skipper's nay said, but plainly he awaits a fight. Report to the wagon an' help us move into yon flying tower." Etien's thick form heel-squatted a moment longer beside me. Then, slowly: "Methinks Guzan has some idea o' murdering us all, here on the mountain. One officer an' a few crewmen can be made to sail the *Golden Leaper* for him, to Giair an' back. The rest o' us would be less trouble to him wi' our weasands slit."

I crawled forth, teeth clattering in my head. After arming

myself, I snatched some food from the common store. The Hisagazi on the march carry dried fish and a sort of bread made from a powdered weed. Only the saints knew when I'd next get a chance to eat. I was the last to join Rovic at the cart. The natives were drifting sullenly toward us, unsure what we intended.

"Let's go, lads," said Rovic. He gave his orders. Four men started manhandling the wagon across the rocky trail toward the Ship, where this gleamed among mists. We others stood by, weapons ready. Almost at once Guzan hastened toward us, with Val Nira toiling in his wake.

Anger darkened his countenance. "What are you doing?" he barked.

Rovic gave him a calm stare. "Why, milord, as we may be here for some time, inspecting the wonders aboard the Ship—"

"What?" interrupted Guzan. "What do you mean? Have you not seen enough for one visit? We must get home again, and prepare to sail after the flowing stone."

"Go if you wish," said Rovic. "I choose to linger. And since you don't trust me, I reciprocate the feeling. My folk will stay in the Ship, which can be defended if necessary."

Guzan stormed and raged, but Rovic ignored him. Our men continued hauling the cart over the uneven ground. Guzan signaled his spearmen, who approached in a disordered but alert mass. Etien spoke a command. We fell into line. Pikes slanted forward, muskets took aim.

Guzan stepped back. We had demonstrated firearms for him at his own home island. Doubtless he could overwhelm us with sheer numbers, were he determined enough, but the cost would be heavy. "No reason to fight, is there?" purred Rovic. "I am only taking a sensible precaution. The Ship is a most valuable prize. It could bring Paradise for all . . . or dominion over this earth for one. There are those who'd prefer the latter. I've not accused you of being among them. However, in prudence I'd liefer keep the Ship for my hostage and my fortress, as long as it pleases me to remain here."

I think then I was convinced of Guzan's real intentions, not as a surmise of ours but as plain fact. Had he truly wished to attain the stars, his one concern would have been to keep the Ship safe. He would not have reached out, snatched little Val Nira in his powerful hands, and dragged the starman backward like a shield against our fire. Not that his intent matters, save to my own conscience. Wrath distorted his patterned visage. He screamed at us, "Then I'll keep a hostage too! And much good may your shelter do you!"

The Hisagazi milled about, muttering, hefting their spears and axes, but not prepared to follow us. We grunted our way across the black mountainside. The sun strengthened. Froad twisted his beard. "Dear me, master captain," he said, "think you they'll lay siege to us?"

"I'd not advise anyone to venture forth alone," said Rovic dryly.

"But without Val Nira to explain things, what use for us to stay at the Ship? Best we go back. I've mathematic texts to consult—my head's aspin with the law that binds the turning planets—I must ask the man from Paradise what he knows of—"

Rovic interrupted with a gruff order to three men, that they help lift a wheel wedged between two stones. He was in a savage temper. I confess his action seemed mad to me. If Guzan intended treachery, we had gained little by immobilizing ourselves in the Ship, where he could starve us. Better to let him attack in the open, where we would have a chance of fighting our way through. On the other hand, if Guzan did not plan to fall on us in the jungle—or any other time—then this was senseless provocation on our part. But I dared not question.

§

When we had brought our wagon up to the Ship, its gangplank again descended for us. The sailors started and cursed. Rovic forced himself out of his own bitterness, to speak soothing words. "Easy, lads. I've been aboard already, ye ken.

Naught harmful within. Now we must tote our powder thither, an' stow it as I've planned."

Being slight of frame, I was not set to carrying the heavy casks, but put at the foot of the gangplank to watch the Hisagazi. We were too far away to distinguish words, but I saw how Guzan stood up on a boulder and harangued them. They shook their weapons at us and whooped. But they did not venture to attack. I wondered wretchedly what this was all about. If Rovic had foreseen us besieged, that would explain why he brought so much powder along . . . no, it would not, for there was more than a dozen men could shoot off in weeks of musketry, even had we had enough lead along . . . and we had almost no food! I looked past the poisonous volcano clouds, to Tambur where storms raged that could engulf all our earth, and wondered what demons lurked here to possess men.

I sprang to alertness at an indignant shout from within. Froad! Almost, I ran up the gangway, then remembered my duty. I heard Rovic roar him down and order the crewfolk to carry on. Froad and Rovic must have gone alone into the pilot's compartment and talked for an hour or more. When the old man emerged, he protested no longer. But as he walked down the gangway, he wept.

Rovic followed, grimmer of countenance than I had ever seen a man erenow. The sailors filed after, some looking appalled, some relieved, but chiefly watching the Hisagazian camp. They were simple mariners; the Ship was little to them save an alien and disquieting thing. Last came Etien, walking backward down the metal plank as he uncoiled a long string.

"Form square!" barked Rovic. The men snapped into position. "Best get within, Zhean and Froad," said the captain. "You can better carry extra ammunition than fight." He placed himself in the van.

I tugged Froad's sleeve. "Please, I beg you, master, what's happening?" But he sobbed too much to answer.

Etien crouched with flint and steel in his hands. He heard me—for otherwise we were all deathly silent—and said in a hard voice: "We placed casks o' powder throughout this hull, lad, wi' powder trains to join 'em. Here's the fuse to the whole."

I could not speak, could not even think, so monstrous was this. As if from immensely far away, I heard the click of stone on steel in Etien's fingers, heard him blow on the spark and add: "A good idea, methinks. I said t'other eventide, I'd follow the skipper wi'out fear o' God's curse—but better 'tis not to tempt Him overmuch."

"Forward march!" Rovic's sword blazed clear of the scabbard.

Our feet scrunched loud and horrible on the mountain as we quick-stepped away. I did not look back. I could not. I was still fumbling in a nightmare. Since Guzan would have moved to intercept us anyhow, we proceeded straight toward his band. He stepped forward as we halted at the camp's edge. Val Nira slunk shivering after him. I heard the words dimly:

"Well, Rovic, what now? Are you ready to go home?"

"Yes," said the captain. His voice was dull. "All the way home."

Guzan squinted in rising suspiciousness. "Why did you abandon your wagon? What did you leave behind?"

Supplies. Come, let's march."

Val Nira stared at the cruel shapes of our pikes. He must wet his lips a few times ere he could quaver, "What are you talking about? There's no reason to leave food there. It would spoil in all the time until . . . until—" He faltered as he looked into Rovic's eyes. The blood drained from him.

"What have you done?" he whispered.

Suddenly Rovic's free hand went up, to cover his face. "What I must," he said thickly. "Daughter of God, forgive me."

The starman regarded us an instant more. Then he turned and ran. Past the astonished warriors he burst, out onto the cindery slope, toward his Ship.

"Come back!" bellowed Rovic. "You fool you'll never—"

He swallowed hard. As he looked after that small, stumbling, lonely shape, hurrying across a fire mountain toward the

Beautiful One, the sword sank in his grasp. "Perhaps it's best," he said, like a benediction.

Guzan raised his own sword. In scaly coat and blowing feathers, he was a figure as impressive as steel-clad Rovic. "Tell me what you've done," he snarled, "or I'll kill you this moment!"

He paid our muskets no heed. He, too, had had dreams.

He, too, saw them end, when the Ship exploded.

§

Even that adamantine hull could not withstand a wagonload of carefully placed gunpowder, set off at one time. There came a crash that knocked me to my knees, and the hull cracked open. White-hot chunks of metal screamed across the slopes. I saw one of them strike a boulder and split it in twain. Val Nira vanished, destroyed too quickly to have seen what happened; so in the ultimate, God was merciful to him. Through the flames and smokes and the doomsday noise which followed, I saw the Ship fall. It rolled down the slope, strewing its own mangled guts behind. Then the mountainside grumbled and slid in pursuit, and buried it, and dust hid the sky.

More than this, I have no heart to remember.

The Hisagazi shrieked and fled. They must have thought all hell came to earth. Guzan stood his ground. As the dust enveloped us, hiding the grave of the Ship and the white volcano crater, turning the sun red, he sprang at Rovic. A musketeer raised his weapon. Etien slapped it down. We stood and watched those two men fight, up and over the shaken cinder land, and knew in our private darkness that this was their right. Sparks flew where the blades clamored together. At last Rovic's skill prevailed. He took Guzan in the throat.

We gave Guzan decent burial and went down through the jungle.

That night the guardsmen rallied their courage enough to attack us. We were aided by our muskets, but must chiefly use sword and pike. We hewed our way through them because we had no other place to go than the sea.

They gave up, but carried word ahead of us. When we reached Nikum, all the forces Iskilip could raise were besieging the *Golden Leaper* and waiting to oppose Rovic's entry. We formed a square again, and no matter how many thousands they had, only a score or so could reach us at any time. Nonetheless, we left six good men in the crimsoned mud of those streets. When our people on the caravel realized Rovic was coming back, they bombarded the town. This ignited the thatch roofs and distracted the enemy enough that a sortie from the ship was able to effect a juncture with us. We chopped our way to the pier, got aboard, and manned the capstan.

Outraged and very brave, the Hisagazi paddled their canoes up to our hull, where our cannon could not be brought to bear. They stood on each other's shoulders to reach our rail. One band forced itself aboard, and the fight was fierce which cleared them from the decks. That was when I got the shattered collarbone which plagues me to this day.

But in the end, we came out of the fjord. A fresh east wind was blowing. With all sail aloft, we outran the foe. We counted our dead, bound our wounds, and slept.

Next dawning, awakened by the pain of my shoulder and the worse pain within, I mounted the quarterdeck. The sky was overcast. The wind had stiffened; the sea ran cold and green, whitecaps out to a cloud-gray horizon. Timbers groaned and rigging skirled. I stood an hour facing aft, into the chill wind that numbs pain.

When I heard boots behind me, I did not turn around. I knew they were Rovic's. He stood beside me a long while, bareheaded. I noticed that he was starting to turn gray.

Finally, not yet regarding me, still squinting into the air that lashed tears from our eyes, he said: "I had a chance to talk Froad over, that day. He was grieved, but owned I was right. Has he spoken to you about it?"

"No," I said.

"None of us are ever likely to speak of it much," said Rovic. After another time: "I was not afraid Guzan or anyone else would seize the Ship and try to turn conqueror. We men of Montalir should well be able to deal with any such rogues. Nor was I afraid of the Paradise dwellers. That poor little man could only have been telling truth. They would never have harmed us . . . willingly. They would have brought precious gifts, and taught us their own esoteric arts, and let us visit all their stars."

"Then why?" I got out.

"Someday Froad's successors will solve the riddles of the universe," he said. "Someday our descendants will build their own Ship, and go forth to whatever destiny they wish."

Spume blew up and around us, until our hair was wet. I tasted the salt on my lips.

"Meanwhile," said Rovic, "we'll sail the seas of this earth, and walk its mountains, and chart and subdue and come to understand it. Do you see, Zhean? That is what the Ship would have taken from us."

Then I was also made able to weep. He laid his hand on my uninjured shoulder and stood with me while the *Golden Leaper*, all sail set, proceeded westward.

SANDRA MIESEL

Challenge and Response

Poul Anderson has a unique gift for designing worlds and beings to dwell upon them. From the parameters of orbits to the scents of flowers he delights in presenting sensuous, plausible details which are all the more vivid for incorporating authentic data. Mastery of science and history join with a firsthand knowledge of the lands and peoples of our own globe to impart a sturdy vitality to Anderson's fiction that no uninformed imagination can match. He makes us nostalgic for marvels we have never seen.

But whether the setting be a misty vale in Faerie or a glittering metallic forest on Earth three billion years hence, the environment in an Anderson story is more than a mere backdrop; it is essential to the drama. The interaction of consciousness with the real universe is the author's principal and most characteristic theme. The interaction between man— and all other rational beings—and Nature can be summarized in the formula "challenge and response." Anderson maintains: (1) man needs challenge, (2) man must respond to challenge, (3) man must accept responsibility for his response.

Of course the author has not always been absolutely consistent in his opinions. No human being could be. Nevertheless he has persistently upheld the importance of "challenge and response" during more than a quarter century as a professional writer. Publication dates will be cited at the first mention of each work to demonstrate this continuity.[1]

Anderson's first proposition, men need challenge if they are to remain human, is concisely stated in "We Have Fed Our

Sea"/*The Enemy Stars* (1958): "No people live long, who offer their young men naught but fatness and security."

The external, physical world is an indispensable source of challenge:

A civilization which just sat down and stared at its own inwardness—how soon would it become stagnant, caste-ridden, poor, and nasty? You can't think unless you have something to think about. And this has to come from outside. Doesn't it? The universe is immeasurably larger than any mind.

(*There Will Be Time* 1973)

So essential is challenge both for the species and the individual that an artificial one can serve as effectively as a real one. For example: a nonexistent criminal wrecks a dictatorship in "Sam Hall" (1953); contrived political pressure changes society in "Robin Hood's Barn" (1959); and alien conquerors try to provoke a healthy counterreaction from their human subjects in "Inside Earth" (1951). As the hero of the last-mentioned story explains:

'Valgolia [Terra's overlord] is the great and lonely enemy, the self-appointed Devil, since none of us can be angels. It is the source of challenge and adversity such as has always driven intelligence onward and upward, in spite of itself.'

In essays, speeches, and fiction the author repeatedly stresses space exploration as the future's greatest real challenge. This would provide a safety valve and a psychological stimulus for the entire species just as other frontiers have throughout history. Besides the intellectual, practical, and even aesthetic potential of space, Anderson feels that "our enterprise beyond the sky will keep alive that sense of bravery . . . and achievement without which man would hardly be himself" (*Is There Life on Other Worlds?* 1963). Or as expressed in "Marque and Reprisal" (1965):

That's why we've got to move into space. . . . Room. A chance to get out of this horrible huddle on Earth, walk free, be our own men, try out new ways to live, work, think, create, wonder.

Dispersal into space would also insure survival of humankind if Earth were destroyed. "The Children of Fortune" (1961), "The Day After Doomsday"/*After Doomsday* (1961), "Epilogue" (1962), and *Tau Zero* (1970) are based on this premise. Anderson places an exceedingly high value on racial propagation because it guarantees a kind of immortality—the only demonstrably certain kind. The narrator of "The Man Who Came Early" (1956) states this from the pagan Norse viewpoint: " 'The house and the blood . . . are holy. Men die and women weep, but while the kindred live our names are remembered.' "

The author's concern with perpetuation ignites into glory in *Tau Zero*. In this novel an Einsteinian starship malfunctions and cannot decelerate to complete its colonization mission. As it accelerates closer and closer to the speed of light eons speed by in heartbeats. The expedition outlives this cycle of creation and beholds the reforging of the stars. The now-repaired vessel is brought to rest on a planet in the new universe. Could not future ships repeat this feat, forever and ever, human world without end? The race can make itself—if not its members—immortal.

Yet "there can be too great a price for survival" ("Turning Point" 1963). It is by no means the ultimate value.

But there were limits. . . . Some things were more important than survival. Than even the survival of a cause.
It came to Sverdlov that this was another way a man might serve his planet: just by being the right kind of man, maybe a better way than planning the extinction of people who happened to live somewhere else.

("We Have Fed Our Sea")

Or as the hero of "The Mills of the Gods" (1961) reminds us: " 'Honor wasn't enough. Survival wasn't enough. You had to be kind as well.' "

Mere purposeless prolongation of life, whether of the race or the individual, is a futile goal, as the moody elves in *The Broken Sword* (1954) and the immortal men in "The Star Beast" (1950) realize to their sorrow. One of the latter muses: " 'Death is the longest voyage of all. Without death there is no evolution, no real meaning to life, the ultimate adventure has been snatched away.' " Men need to be liberated from the paralyzing fear of death and enslavement to a promise of synthetic resurrection in "Goat Song" (1972). On the other hand, immortality does not corrupt men in "The Ancient Gods"/*World Without Stars* (1966) because they are still willing to risk their lives and can die bravely when they must.

The quality rather than the quantity of life is what matters. The composite picture of good living which emerges from Anderson's stories has undeniable appeal. It features robust enjoyment of such things as sailing, scotch, and Mozart (which is to say: nature, conviviality, and the arts). Anderson is interested in how well, how creatively, how intensely, people live. Men require the stimulation of constant challenge to attain excellence. A perfect world from which challenge had been excluded would be soul destroying. The antitechnological Outworld in "The Queen of Air and Darkness" (1971) is a cruel delusion as are the fantasy realms of Faerie in *The Broken Sword* and *Three Hearts and Three Lions* (1961).

But technology is more usually the villain. In "Quixote and the Windmill" (1950), complete automation has robbed ordinary people of the opportunity to create and feel useful, resulting in mass ennui. The same craving for meaningful work is reiterated in "What Shall It Profit?" (1956). Material satiety produces mindless hedonism, apathy, and ultimately decadence in "The Star Beast" and "Conversation in Arcady" (1963). A totally planned society causes evolutionary reversal in "The High Ones" (1958), since the absence of challenge obviates the necessity for intelligence.

Technological anti-utopias abound in Anderson's writing (e.g., the UN-Man series, 1953ff.;[2] "Ghetto" 1954; "The Long Way Home"/*No World of Their Own* 1955; "Inside Straight"

1955; "We Have Fed Our Sea"; "Time Lag" 1961; *Orbit Unlimited* 1961; the Gearchy series, 1965ff.;[3] "Fortune Hunter" 1973). The author was an active environmentalist long before ecology became fashionable. He denounces the world-ravaging, dehumanizing effects of existing technic civilization. Men, he says in "License" (1957), do not want to be "crowded together, and chained to one tiny spot of the earth's surface, and be an anonymous unit, bossed and herded and jammed into an iron desert of a city, subordinating food and sleep and digestion and love and play to a single monotonous job." The issue is also debated in "Progress" (1962).

'If industrialism can feed and clothe people better, though, doesn't it deserve to win out?'
'Who says it can? It can feed and clothe more people, yes. But not necessarily better. And are sheer numbers any measure of quality?'

But since there can be no turning back now, he proposes alternatives. The crudest one is some marvelous invention which will permit individual economic independence and therefore personal freedom. Examples are the protective force field in *Shield* (1962) and a cheap universal power source in "Snowball" (1955).

It is far more difficult to rechannel human nature by internal conversion. This is unsuccessfully attempted by alien intruders in "No Truce With Kings" (1963) and by the Psychotechnic Institute in the UN-Man series. This approach can more easily harm than heal. The aliens' secret efforts to modify humanity incite war and discredit their unwitting human agents, and while the Institute initially uses its techniques of individual mental-physical conditioning and group sociodynamics to fight tyranny, it eventually mistakes means for ends and perishes through pride. Saving men against their will is no true salvation.

Some pressures of contemporary civilization could be eased by extraterrestrial colonization as in *The Star Fox* (1966),

Tales of the Flying Mountains (1970), and *Is There Life on Other Worlds?*. But the best solution would be a radical, voluntary restructuring, for "civilization was not material technology but a thought-pattern and an understanding" (*The Star Ways* (1956). New possibilities are suggested: in *The Byworlder* (1971) and its essay version, "More Futures Than One," and in "The People of the Wind" (1973) and its fore-shadow, "Outpost of Empire" (1967). The former pair describe a near-future mosaic society in which technology has become the handmaiden of ecology. The latter two stories are set on colonial planets where human and alien cultures have successfully melded.

If experimentation fails, improvements may still result from a cleansing catastrophe. A drastic, abrupt increase in human and animal intelligence shatters society in *Brain Wave* (1954), but it also transfigures man and sends him spacefaring. After global holocausts men rediscover benevolent feudalism and local autonomy ("No Truce With Kings"), exploit mutant physical and mental powers plus a new style of logic (*Twilight World* 1961), wed science to magic ("Superstition" 1956), and develop an ecologically sensitive neo-Polynesian civilization ("The Sky People" 1959 and "Progress") which first restores the earth and then yields to a new interstellar cosmopolitanism (*There Will Be Time* 1972). A voluntary mutual aid organization is a more benign replacement for the fallen Terran Empire in "Starfog" (1967). When Bronze Age Crete and the contemporary West go down in blood and fire, even higher civilizations replace them according to *The Dancer From Atlantis* (1972). The utterly indomitable heroine of this last novel declares:

'We have our victory—for it was a victory, that we and those in our care outlived the end of a world and even saved much of it for the world which is to follow. . . . I see now that we were never slaves to fate, because our own wills were what made that destiny for us.'

All these stories imply that the emergence of a healthier successor society at least partly compensates for the disaster that brought it forth.

Obviously, adaptation without such painful stimulus is preferable. Since Anderson has described his utopia so often—at least two dozen times in twenty years—a general description is easy. Except for unspoiled aliens who have avoided technological deformation altogether ("Green Thumb" 1953, "Sister Planet" 1959, and *The Star Ways*), his utopians are human colonists on a marvelously beautiful world. (Of course he has also shown vigorous societies on harsh worlds such as Vixen, Kraken, Lochlanna, and Kirkasant in the Terran Empire series,[4] but the ideal case is at issue here.) Utopia's population is extremely low—typically ten million—and stable. Government is minimal and decentralized. Individual citizens possess exceptional initiative, resourcefulness, and stability. They are adept at fine arts, crafts, and athletics. They have a great reverence for tradition and a deep emotional attachment for their planet. A sophisticated understanding of ecology enables the colonists to enjoy nature without ruining it. Their vigorous culture is that of their ancient Terran ancestors modified by a fresh environment. The entire system might be termed "scientific pastoralism."

"Time Lag" is an excellent example of utopia and anti-utopia locked in mortal combat. The "Finnish" Vaynamoans defeat the invading "Russian" Chertokians despite a 1:500 population disparity because the former surpass the latter in scientific achievement, cultural vitality, and most of all, courage. Vaynamo is lush and unspoiled. Man's presence enhances rather than diminishes the beauty of the landscape:

Ahead stretched grainfields and pastures, still wet from winter but their shy green deepening toward summer hues, on down to the great metallic sheet of Lake Rovaniemi and then across the opposite horizon, where the High Mikkela reared into a sky as tall and blue as itself.

Chertoki is a planet-sized slum:

The city grew bigger, smokier, uglier. . . . The desert could no longer be seen, even from the highest towers, only the abandoned mine and slag mountains, in the process of conversion into tenements.

The Vaynamoans are both energetic and tradition minded. The heroine describes herself:

'I'm the Magnate's daughter and the Freeholder's wife, I have a University degree and a pistol-shooting medal, as a girl I sailed through hurricanes and skindove into grottoes where fanfish laired, as a woman I brought a son into the world. . . .' . . . 'I'm a true daughter of Vaynamo, . . . whatever is traditional, full of memories, whatever has been looked at and been done by all the generations before me, I hold dear. The Chertokians don't care. They haven't any past worth remembering.'

Right prevails in "Time Lag" and the brave remain free. Vaynamo has to repel one expansionist neighbor, but Avalon in "The People of the Wind" resists annexation by the mighty Terran Empire. In this latter story the will to resist and the wit to prepare defenses again bring victory.

Not all of Anderson's utopias fare as fortunately. They can be destroyed by Nature ("The Pirate" 1968), willingly abandoned ("Turning Point" 1963 and "Gypsy" 1950), forcibly evacuated ("The Chapter Ends" 1954 and "The Disinherited" 1966), perverted ("The Helping Hand" 1950), or disrupted by new social developments (forthcoming sequels to *Orbit Unlimited*). Even if undisturbed, human imperfection must inevitably spoil these fair domains, thus initiating new cycles of collapse and recovery and generating perennial historical challenges. Awareness of evil does not drive Anderson to despair. He remains unquenchably optimistic over man's capacity to meet whatever demands the universe presents.

Anderson's second principle requires that challenges be promptly faced, however they may arise. This theme of immediate response has appeared so often it is difficult to select the most representative examples. "The High Crusade" (1960), "No Truce With Kings," *The Star Fox*, and the UN-Man series all stress the importance of solving current problems rather than bequeathing them to future generations. The hero of "Brake" declares: " 'Well, it'll only be us who die now. Not a hundred million people twenty or thirty years from now.' " Indifference to the well-being of its descendants is a sign of the Terran Empire's decadence.

To hell with it. Let civilization hang together long enough for Dominic Flandry to taste a few more vintages, ride a few more horses, kiss a lot more girls and sing another ballad or two, that would suffice. At least it was all he dared hope for.
("Hunters of the Sky Cave"/*We Claim These Stars!* 1959)

When Flandry tries on fashionable cynicism for size, he finds it a less than perfect fit. But he is unwilling to acknowledge his hidden altruism even to himself.

Challenge must not only be met briskly, it must be met freely. Anderson's concept of freedom is positive—it is the presence of opportunity, not the absence of restraint. Violating the freedom of rational beings by domesticating or manipulating them is a heinous crime. What the author calls "domestication" is exploitation by shielding from challenge. The free will, individuality, and self-awareness of one group is damped by another until these essential properties atrophy: "A slave may or may not obey. But a domestic animal has got to obey. His genes won't let him do any different" ("The Master Key" 1964). The threat of domestication plainly alarms the author. He fears the emasculating consequences of some contemporary trends: loss of option, initiative, and meaningful work; collectivization and homogenization; decline of rationality, taste, and competence. First introduced in *Brain Wave*, Anderson reiterated this problem in *The Star Ways*, "The Children of Fortune," "Turning Point," "No Truce With Kings," *The Star Fox*, "Satan's World" (1968), "The Queen of Air and Darkness," and "Goat Song." It also generated the plots of "The Master Key" and "The Ancient Gods."

In "The Master Key" traders from the Polesotechnic League encounter a race of radically unsocial aliens which controls another intelligent species to be its servants. Unable to comprehend human civilization, the dominant Yildivians cannot decide if men are free "wild" beings like themselves or runaway "domesticated" beings like their Lugals. Actually, men can be either.

'We here in this room are wild,' Van Rijn said. 'We do what we do because we want to or because it is right. . . . But how many slaves have there been in earth's long history, that their masters could trust? . . . And how many people today is domestic animals at heart? Wanting somebody else should tell them what to do, take care of their needfuls, and protect them not just against their fellow men but against themselves? And why has every free human society been so short-lived? Is this not because the wild-animal men are born so heartbreakingly seldom?'

Anderson presents the curse of domestication even more sharply in "The Ancient Gods." The Ai Chun are an incredibly old race with psychic powers who believe themselves to be gods and demand worship from other beings. By eons of selective breeding they raise another species to sentience and enslave them. A few of these escape and develop their own social structure and monotheistic religion. A crew of marooned spacemen aids the free Pack against the Ai Chun, but a psychological flaw causes one man to defect to the enemy. Having surrendered his will and identity to the aliens, he stubbornly prefers bondage to manly struggle and dies with his masters. In contrast, Valland, the *de facto* leader of the humans is a splendidly free man. He is considerate, loyal, tenacious, and talented. With serene independence he rejects the permissive sexual mores of his society for a lifetime of heroic chastity. To Anderson freedom is a painful glory; it is no cloak for selfishness.

Manipulation denies men the opportunity to decide their own response to challenges. The best intentions and loftiest objectives cannot avert disaster as the history of Anderson's Psychotechnic Institute illustrates. Established in the aftermath of World War III to improve individuals and society, the Institute develops techniques to shape history to its own specifications. It no longer suffices to "meet the future when it gets here" argues an Institute supporter: " 'That is what man has always done. And that is why the race has always blundered from one catastrophe to the next. This may be our last chance to change the pattern' " ("Marius").

But two generations later when the world has recovered, the Institute still considers itself the only savior of mankind. This period is described in "The Sensitive Man" (a story with a protagonist as smugly self-righteous as the supermen in Heinlein's "Gulf").

'I take it you favor libertarian government,' he said. 'In the past it's always broken down sooner or later and the main reason has been that there aren't enough people with the intelligence, alertness, and toughness to resist the inevitable encroachments of power on liberty.'

A critic replies:

'But what sort of person is needed? Who decides it? You've decided *you* are the almighty arbiters. Your superior wisdom is going to lead poor mankind up the road to heaven. I say it's down the road to hell!'

Read in isolation, "The Sensitive Man" seems inconsistent with the rest of Anderson's work. But in the context of its series, it is ironic: the objections blithely dismissed in "The Sensitive Man" eventually prove correct. In "Question and Answer" set a century later, the Institute is so intoxicated with its plan for man's future it plots to forestall stellar exploration —man is still too "uncivilized" to "deserve" the stars. An Institute agent says:

'It will take a thousand years of slow, subtle, secret direction
. . . to evolve the culture we want. . . . Men won't be blind,
greedy, pushing, ruthless animals; there will be restraint, and
dignity, and contentment . . . .'

A spaceman replies:

'I claim that man crawling into his own little shell to think
pure thoughts and contemplate his navel is no longer man. . . .
I like man as he is and not man as a bunch of theorists thinks
he ought to be. . . . Personally, I believe that no small group
has the right to impose its own will on everybody else. . . .
I vote for telling the truth, going out to the stars, and taking
the consequences. Good, bad, or indifferent. I want to see what
the consequences are, and I think most men do.'

The mighty Institute is discredited and outlawed: *hubris,*
nemesis, até. "The tragic flaw in the character of Institute
personnel was only that they were human" ("The Snows of
Ganymede").

These same issues are vividly summarized in "No Truce
With Kings." Here a small group of aliens secretly attempts to
redesign post-Armageddon society. They try to force a central-
ized state and a passive, collectivized society upon men "for
their own good." But the patronizing aliens actually fear
human vitality. Their race wants no competition from other
civilizations. Their role is discovered during a war they insti-
gated to further their plan. One of the soldiers who exposed
the conspiracy reacts:

'If you'd come openly, like honest folk, you'd had found some
to listen to you. Maybe enough, even. But no, your do-gooding
had to be subtle and crafty. You knew what was right for us.
We weren't entitled to any say in the matter.' . . .
. . . 'Sure we make some ghastly blunders, we humans. But
they're our own. And we learn from them. You're the ones
who won't learn.'

Subversion in "No Truce With Kings" depends on superior
material technology and social manipulation. In *The Star*
Ways and "The Queen of Air and Darkness" enemy strategy

relies chiefly on illusion, suggestion, and psychic phenomena. Not only do the aliens delude men, they make them enjoy being deluded. Unmasking these conspiracies leaves despair in the deceivers and outrage in the deceived. But if the aliens can overcome their aversion for human ways, willing partnership can replace secret aggression to the benefit of both sides.

Even public, benevolent interference can be deadly. The hero of "The Longest Voyage" (1960) rejects premature interstellar contact lest his own world be deprived of an exciting stage in its development and thereby forfeit its own uniqueness. "The Helping Hand" contrasts the reactions of two war-ravaged alien societies to proferred Terran aid. Lush Cundaloa is corrupted by accepting and loses its creativity. Grim Skontar rebuilds itself single-handedly without sacrificing its dignity.

The most poignant example of this theme is *Let the Spacemen Beware!* (1963). Explorers who rediscover the lost Terran colony Gwydion admire the uncanny serenity of its inhabitants. But the idyllic life of the Gwydiona is punctuated with periods of biochemically induced schizophrenia. The expedition's military head, who is deeply grounded in archaic traditions, can understand their myth-saturated culture. The technocratic civilian chief, his rival in love, is completely baffled. Despite the former's warnings, the latter attempts to interfere during the madness and thereby triggers needless slaughter. The soldier gives his life so that his comrades and his Gwydiona beloved can escape. She will never even remember how he died.

However, the powerful statements all these stories make on the dangers of intervention must be reconciled with the author's approval of interfering agencies like the Galactic Patrol and the Time Patrol. The unsubtle Galactic Patrol series ("The Double-Dyed Villains" 1949, "Enough Rope" 1953, and "The Live Coward" 1956) relates this organization's efforts to keep peace in the galaxy through deceit, bribery, blackmail, or any other unscrupulous method so long as they do not cause the death of a single rational being. The Patrol's ethics are simply based on choosing the lesser evils. As one member explains:

'And I, for one, would rather break any number of arbitrary laws and moral rules, and wreck a handful of lives of idiots who think with a blaster, than see a planet go up in flames or . . . see one baby killed in a war it never even heard about.'
("The Double-Dyed Villains")

The men of the Time Patrol (*The Guardians of Time* 1960 and "My Object All Sublime" 1961) face more complex issues. They are charged with guarding the timeline that leads to the indescribably evolved men of the far distant future who discover time travel. They eliminate anachronisms that weaken the temporal fabric, apprehend fugitives from future justice, and correct changes made by time-criminals. Intervening to preserve history as it has been seems permissible even though it means leaving suffering unrelieved.

He had seen enough human misery in all the ages. You got case hardened after a while, but down underneath, when a peasant stared at you with sick brutalized eyes, or a soldier screamed with a pike through him, or a city went up in radio-active flame, something wept. He could understand the fanatics who tried to change events. It was only that their work was so unlikely to make anything better.
("Delenda Est" 1955)

But the temporal agents can also be ordered to change "real" history to suit their superiors' needs. Historical reality is, in the end, merely relative. The dilemma of contradictory interests stated in "The Only Game in Town" (1960) is not solved there nor is it solved in unrelated stories like "Progress" and "Turning Point." Collisions between equally sincere men are inevitable as in *Let the Spacemen Beware!*, *The Rebel Worlds*, and "The People of the Wind." Anderson does not see any clear answers. He sees the pain choice must bring. Here lies the distinction between licit and illicit intervention: those who would change the course of the universe must bear the guilt.

What guards the guardians is their humility and the anguish they endure for their deeds.

Finally, when men meet any challenge, they must accept responsibility. Power without responsibility is tyranny. Therefore Anderson's rulers suffer. Leadership is kingship—*de jure* or *de facto*. Its splendor is sorrowful. The heroes of *Tau Zero* and *There Will Be Time* accept their royal roles only during crises. They are anxious to be freed of their crowns once the need has passed.

Not unexpectedly, the ancient myth of the king's saving death inspires some stories. A secret agent characterizes his work: " 'We are the kings who die for the people so that little boys with shoeshine kits may not be fried on molten streets' " ("State of Assassination" 1959). In "Kings Who Die" (1962) spacemen's deaths in an endless, stalemated war between America and Unasia serve as ritual sacrifice to preserve the rest of mankind. The hero explains:

'Today the machine age has developed its own sacrificial kings. We are the chosen of the race. The best it can offer, none gainsays us. We may have what we choose, pleasure, luxury, women, adulation—only not the simple pleasures of wife and child and home, for we must die that the people may live.'

When an American and a Russian attempt to replace the slaughter with peaceful exploration, their collaboration fails. Bloodshed continues unabated.

Anderson's elites—spacemen or witches, secret agents or feudal lords—exist ideally to serve. Two good examples occur in the UN-Man series and *Brain Wave*.

The UN-Men are a band of identical exogenetic brothers, created and trained as special UN operatives by the Psychotechnic Institute. They are amply endowed with all the author's favorite skills: mental, physical, linguistic, and artistic. They are also considerate, humble, perceptive, dependable, and good-humored. They are more remarkable for the full and balanced development of all their abilities than for any specific outstanding talent. Although performing invaluable services for the world, they do not share the Institute's delusions of superiority or its tragic fall. Some of the Brothers eventually join another elite service group, the semimonastic Order of Engineers.

In *Brain Wave*, an exponential increase in human intelligence suddenly makes men mentally superior to every other race they find in the galaxy. But these transcendent geniuses have no wish to conquer or domesticate other beings. They envision their future role:

'We will not be gods, or even guides. But we will—some of us—be givers of opportunity. We will see that evil does not flourish too strongly, and that hope and chance happen when they are most needed, to all those millions of sentient creatures who live and love and fight and laugh and weep and die, just as man once did. No, we will not be embodied Fate; but perhaps we can be Luck. And even, it may be, Love.'

This benevolence stands in violent contrast to the contemptuous attitudes of "Genius" (1948), Anderson's third published story. A colony of "pure geniuses" not only reviles the rest of humanity, but plots to rule it:

The genius is forced into the straightjacket of the mediocre man's and the moron's mentality. That he can expand any distance at all beyond his prison is a tribute to the supreme power of high intellect. . . .
. . . The ordinary man is just plain stupid. . . . He follows, or rather accepts what the creative or dominant minority does, but it is haltingly and unwillingly.

This wretched story is an anomaly and a present embarrassment to its author. He has kept to the path of compassion ever since.

Anderson's hero can be defined as "the man who pays the price." His endowments, motives, or even virtues are irrelevant. Readiness to bear burdens for some good purpose is all that matters. A man's willingness to suffer—not what he suffers—is the measure of heroism. Other writers see things differently. Heinlein heroes, untroubled by guilt or regret, are supremely confident of themselves and their causes. They have no sense of ambivalence. Delany's tolerant heroes suffer but never have to grapple with vices within themselves or make agonizing ethical decisions.

The Anderson hero has pragmatic ethics. The end justifies the means *if* one can stand the cost. As James Blish observes, "For Anderson, the tragic hero is a man . . . who is driven partly by circumstances, but mostly by his own conscience, to do the wrong thing for the right reason—and then has to live with the consequences."[5] Two particularly cruel examples of this occur in "The Burning Bridge" (1960) and "Sister Planet."

Spacefleet commander Joshua Coffin, a bleak Puritan with an aching sense of duty, saves Earth's first (and perhaps last) interstellar colonization effort from failure with a lie that could cost a man's life. Overcome by guilt, he retires from spacefaring, which is the only thing he loves. A long grim decade will pass before he learns to live with himself again.

"Sister Planet" presents a complicated set of moral dilemmas. Human explorers on Venus discover a way to terraform that planet. They decide to suppress their discovery since it would doom the indigenous race. After ravaging their own world men have no right to colonize at the expense of another intelligent species. But no knowledge can be permanently suppressed and human society is growing so brutal it would not shrink from planetary genocide. Realizing this, the hero teaches the innocent natives to fear men by bombing their holy place and forestalls future expeditions by murdering all his companions and blaming the natives for this crime. Although Venus is spared, he is seared by excruciating pangs of guilt: "Oh God . . . please exist. Please make a hell for me." Remorse over killing his friends drives him to suicide.

Elegant Dominic Flandry is also a price-paying hero. He is committing spiritual suicide—trading off bits of his soul for success in vital intelligence missions. From his earliest adventure, *Ensign Flandry* (1966), in which he deliberately beguiles and betrays a courtesan who loves him, the weight of his guilt grows. Yet his costly efforts are not entirely in vain, for worlds he helps save survive the fall of the Terran Empire.

Purely private heroism also exacts its price. It may require rejecting marriage for the good of the beloved (*Shield* and "Starfog"), or remaining in an unsatisfactory marriage ("Brave to be a King" 1959 and *Three Worlds to Conquer* 1964), or reconciling conflicting loves ("No Truce With Kings," *The Rebel Worlds* and *The Dancer From Atlantis*). "Escape From Orbit" (1962) depicts this best. A NASA ground controller who had resigned from astronaut training to care for his sick wife suffers gnawing regret, constant pressure, and involuntary celibacy. His professional problems can be solved, his personal ones only endured. But his sense of family responsibility allows no self-pity.

One obvious obstacle to heroism is the refusal to suffer. "The Disinherited" reverses the situation in "Sister Planet." Terran scientists studying an idyllic planet enjoy living there so much, they refuse to return to overcrowded Earth although the future good of the autochthones and their own descendants demands it. An envoy from Earth pleads for responsible action:

'I have so much pride [in being a man] that I will not see my race guilty of the ultimate crime. We are not going to make anyone else pay for our mistakes. We are going home and see if we cannot amend them ourselves.'

But the scientists defy him and must be evacuated by force.

A subtler pitfall is false asceticism—the overvaluing of suffering. In "The Mills of the Gods," dour Joshua Coffin slowly comes to realize the limits of austerity as a path to virtue. In *Rogue Sword* (1960), the ruthless Aragonese knight En Jaime refuses to accept this: " 'But do you really believe that nothing more is required of man than . . . than kindness?' "

The stupendous effects of intelligently directed kindness are demonstrated in "The Sharing of Flesh." The heroine forces herself to be merciful despite the pressures of cultural conditioning and personal inclination. She forgives her husband's murderer and reveals how the people of his planet can be freed from a genetic compulsion to cannibalism. Had she withheld the information out of revenge, her sin would have been infinitely worse than anything the natives had done. The gentler, more "liberal" explorers pity the natives, but their tender feelings are mingled with revulsion and do nothing to help correct the situation.

Anderson's hero is no Übermensch:

In so far as human qualities are important in war or less violent conflict, they tend to be courage and steadiness of purpose rather than intellectual complexity.

(*Is There Life on Other Worlds?*)

Instead, his heroes are often typical members of a group or class distinguished principally by willingness to seize the initiative. A minor bureaucrat starts a successful revolution in "Sam Hall." The heroines of "Time Lag," *We Claim These Stars!*, and "The Sharing of Flesh" are representative women of their planets. A timid, effete-looking alien thwarts human space pirates in "A Little Knowledge" (1972). A witch, a bobtailed werewolf, and a tomcat harrow Hell in *Operation Chaos* (1972). (The werewolf-hero cites this as an example of God's sense of humor.)

Three Hearts and Three Lions depicts a humble man who is in actuality an epic hero. In our world he is quiet Holger Carlson:

We were all his friends. He was an amiable, slow-spoken fellow, thoroughly down to earth, with simple tastes in living style and humor. . . . As an engineer he was satisfactory if unspectacular, his talents running more toward rule-of-thumb practicality than the analytical approach. . . . All in all, Holger was a nice average guy, what was later called a good Joe.

But in the alternate universe of Faerie he is the fabulous Carolingian paladin Holger Danske. After ordeals in Faerie he recognizes his true identity and takes up his role as

Defender of mankind to break the hosts of Chaos.

The hero realizes his own limitations:

James Mackenzie knew he was not much more than average bright under the best of conditions. . . . His achievements amounted to patchwork jobs carried out in utter confusion or to slogging like this and wishing only for an end to the whole mess. . . . Hero? What an all-time laugh!

("No Truce With Kings")

There is no glamor in heroic adventures: war is only "hunger, thirst, exhaustion, terror, mutilation, death, and forever the sameness, boredom grinding you down like an ox" ("No Truce With Kings"). The lack of glamor in heroism is such a common Anderson motif that it even occurs in a colorful action tale like "The High Crusade." Even David Falkayn, the Polesotechnic popinjay (*The Trouble Twisters* 1966), and Dominic Flandry find their exploits more grubby than glamorous in the execution.

Personal virtue is not a prerequisite for heroism. A man need not be a saint to perform useful, and even great deeds. In "Robin Hood's Barn," a waspish, conniving government commissioner provides an escape hatch for faltering humanity by deceit. Pleasure-loving MacLaren and brutish Sverdlov are just as heroic as their more "respectable" crewmates in "We Have Fed Our Sea."

Moreover, good men are not necessarily the most effective heroes. The rebel admiral's moral righteousness brings himself and his followers to ruin in *The Rebel Worlds*. Wily, self-indulgent Nicholas Van Rijn solves the problems in "The Man Who Counts"/*War of the Wing-Men* (1958). Therefore the heroine bestows herself on him, rather than his clean-cut, conventionally "heroic" young subordinate. The considerable good accomplished by Van Rijn's escapades is always presented as an incidental byproduct of his greed. Not until "Satan's World" does he awkwardly admit concern for the welfare of others.

To Anderson fanaticism is "the ugliest sin of all," for the

well-meaning fanatic has been the cause of most human misery.
" 'Don't you realize that deliberate scoundrels do little harm,
but that the evil wrought by sincere fools is incalculable?' "
asks the hero of "The Double-Dyed Villains" in echo of
Ortega y Gasset. Fanatics are also the villains in the UN-Man
series, "Progress," "A Plague of Masters"/*Earthman, Go
Home!* (1961), *Shield*, "No Truce With Kings," *The Star
Fox*, "Operation Changeling" (1969), and *There Will Be
Time*. No amount of sincerity can justify the fanatic's crimes.
He knows no mercy, compassion, or self-doubt. "The face in
the screen grew altogether inhuman. It was a face Banning
knew—millennia of slaughter-house history knew it—the face
of embodied Purpose" ("Brake"). And unlike Delany, Anderson does not allow his evil fanatics the excuse of insanity.
They are fully culpable for their wrongdoing.

Men must bear the responsibility for their deeds and this
responsibility inevitably entails guilt. After leading a military
coup against his best friend, "Fourré reached out and closed
the darkened eyes. He wondered if he would ever be able to
close them within himself" ("Marius"). Even alien manipulators feel remorse: " 'Do you think . . . when we see the final
result . . . will the blood wash off us?' 'No. We pay the
heaviest price of all' " ("No Truce With Kings"). Pain is ines-
capable. Good is always flawed. "I didn't know. Wherever I
turned, there were treason and injustice. However hard I tried
to do right, I had to wrong somebody" ("Inside Earth"). Computer simulations demonstrate the impossibility of social per-
fection in "The Fatal Fulfillment" (1970). Man can devise
no one set of rigid answers to ease his struggles.

Sunt lacrimae rerum . . . . The tears of things pervade the
cosmos. The terror of infinite spaces haunts the silent stars.
Planets reproach their conquerors in every windsong. The
more time and circumstance change man, the more he remains
the same—frail and sadly fallible.

The enemy was old and strong and crafty, it took a million
forms and could never be quite slain. For it was man himself—

the madness and sorrow of the human soul, the revolt of a primitive animal against the unnatural state called civilization and freedom.

("The UN-Man")

What then is a man to do? "We must try, or stop claiming to be men" ("What'll You Give?"/"Que Donn'rez Vous?" 1963). The unending challenge must be met with steadfast dignity. A devout Protestant declares: " 'Our part is to take what God sends us and still hold ourselves up on both feet' " ("We Have Fed Our Sea").

Anderson's superb Norse fantasy *The Broken Sword* is a forceful statement of one man's response to fate. The hero is absolutely unflinching in the best pagan tradition: " 'There is no other road than the one we take, hard though it be. And no man outlives his weird. Best to meet it bravely face to face.' " His courage illuminates his tragic life. When he perishes, he dies neither as a pawn of the Aesir nor of destiny. He dies an indomitable man.

Valiant effort matters more than success, for no victory is eternal. Anderson gives "one grey command: Endure" ("The UN-Man"). But in the last analysis, why bother? Life, as stated in *The Star Ways*, "has no extrinsic purpose or meaning; it's just another phenomenon of the physical universe, it simply *is*." Or as the author says in his own voice: "There is no scientific reason to believe that life was ever intended; it is simply a property of matter under certain conditions" (*Is There Life on Other Worlds?*).

Viewing intelligence as a purely pragmatic development rather than a mystical goal of Nature means rejecting such ideas as those of Teilhard de Chardin. Instead, Anderson favors a nonrigorous, intuitive response which is not an answer.

I still see the same blind cosmos governed by the same blind laws. But suddenly it matters. It matters terribly, and means something. What, I haven't figured out yet. I probably never will. But I have a reason for living, or dying if need be. Maybe that's the whole purpose of life: purpose itself.

("We Have Fed Our Sea")

Anderson's heroes find the meaning of life in the living and the seeking of mystery and beauty and love. Boldly living, bravely dying, man finds his purpose in struggling against the endless challenges life provides: "Our pride is that nevertheless, now and then, we do our best. A few times we succeed. What more dare we ask for?" (*Ensign Flandry*).

ACKNOWLEDGMENTS
for "Challenge and Response":
A slightly different version of this essay appeared in the *Riverside Quarterly*, IV, No. 2 (January 1970), pp. 80–95.
I would like to thank Patrick McGuire for helpful criticism.

NOTES
Footnotes to "Challenge and Response":
1. Titles and dates given are those of the first *complete* publication with title changes indicated as necessary.
2. In internal chronological order: "Marius" (1957), "The UN-Man" (1953), "The Sensitive Man" (1953), "The Big Rain" (1954), "Quixote and the Windmill" (1950), "Out of the Iron Womb" (1955), "Cold Victory" (1957), "The Snows of Ganymede" (1955), "Brake" (1957), "The Troublemakers" (1953), and "Question and Answer"/*Planet of No Return* (1954). The last story was not intended to be part of the series, but it fits in nevertheless. The author has allowed it to be added, *post hoc*.
3. "The Life of Your Time" (1965), "In the Shadow" (1967), "The Alien Enemy" (1968).
4. "The Star Plunderer" (1952), "Sargasso of Lost Starships" (1952), "The People of the Wind" (1973), *Ensign Flandry* (1966), "Outpost of Empire" (1967), *A Circus of Hells* (1969), *The Rebel Worlds* (1969), *The Day of Their Return* (1973), *Agent of the Terran Empire* (1965), *Flandry of Terra* (1965), "A Tragedy of Errors" (1968), *Let the Spacemen Beware!* (1963), "The Sharing of Flesh" (1968), and "Starfog" (1967).
5. James Blish, "Poul Anderson: The Enduring Explosion," *The Magazine of Fantasy and Science Fiction*, April 1971, 54.

○

POUL ANDERSON

Journeys End

*—doctor bill & twinges in chest but must be all right maybe
indigestion & dinner last night & wasn't audrey giving me the
glad eye & how the hell is a guy to know & maybe i can try
and find out & what a fool i can look if she doesn't—*

*—goddam idiot & they shouldn't let some people drive & oh
all right so the examiner was pretty lenient with me i haven't
had a bad accident yet & christ blood all over my blood let's
face it i'm scared to drive but the buses are no damn good &
straight up three paces & man in a green hat & judas i ran
that red light—*

In fifteen years a man got used to it, more or less. He could
walk down the street and hold his own thoughts to himself
while the surf of unvoiced voices was a nearly ignored mumble
in his brain. Now and then, of course, you got something very
bad, it stood up in your skull and shrieked at you.

Norman Kane, who had come here because he was in love
with a girl he had never seen, got to the corner of University
and Shattuck just when the light turned against him. He
paused, fetching out a cigarette with nicotine-yellowed fingers
while traffic slithered in front of his eyes.

It was an unfavorable time, four-thirty in the afternoon,
homeward rush of nervous systems jangled with weariness and
hating everything else on feet or wheels. Maybe he should
have stayed in the bar down on San Pablo. It had been pleas-
antly cool and dim, the bartender's mind an amiable cud-
chewing somnolence, and he could have suppressed awareness
of the woman.

No, maybe not. When the city had scraped your nerves raw, they didn't have much resistance to the slime in some heads.

Odd, he reflected, how often the outwardly polite ones were the foully twisted inside. They wouldn't dream of misbehaving in public, but just below the surface of consciousness . . . Better not think of it, better not remember. Berkeley was at least preferable to San Francisco or Oakland. The bigger the town, the more evil it seemed to hold, three centimeters under the frontal bone. New York was almost literally uninhabitable.

There was a young fellow waiting beside Kane. A girl came down the sidewalk, pretty, long yellow hair and a well-filled blouse. Kane focused idly on her: yes, she had an apartment of her own, which she had carefully picked for a tolerant superintendent. Lechery jumped in the young man's nerves. His eyes followed the girl, Cobean-style, and she walked on . . . simple harmonic motion.

Too bad. They could have enjoyed each other. Kane chuckled to himself. He had nothing against honest lust, anyhow not in his liberated conscious mind; he couldn't do much about a degree of subconscious puritanism. Lord, you can't be a telepath and remain any kind of prude. People's lives were their own business, if they didn't hurt anyone else too badly.

—*the trouble is,* he thought, *they hurt me. but i can't tell them that. they'd rip me apart and dance on the pieces. the government /the military/ wouldn't like a man to be alive who could read secrets but their fear-inspired anger would be like a baby's tantrum beside the red blind amok of the common man (thoughtful husband considerate father good honest worker earnest patriot) whose inward sins were known. you can talk to a priest or a psychiatrist because it is only talk & he does not live your failings with you*—

The light changed and Kane started across. It was clear fall weather, not that this area had marked seasons, a cool sunny day with a small wind blowing up the street from the water. A few blocks ahead of him, the University campus was a splash of manicured green under brown hills.

—*flayed & burningburningburning moldering rotted flesh &*

the bones the white hard clean bones coming out gwtjklfmx—

Kane stopped dead. Through the vertigo he felt how sweat was drenching into his shirt.

And it was such an ordinary-looking man!

"Hey, there, buster, wake up! Ya wanna get killed?"

Kane took a sharp hold on himself and finished the walk across the street. There was a bench at the bus stop and he sat down till the trembling was over.

Some thoughts were unendurable.

He had a trick of recovery. He went back to Father Schliemann. The priest's mind had been like a well, a deep well under sun-speckled trees, its surface brightened with a few gold-colored autumn leaves . . . but there was nothing bland about the water, it had a sharp mineral tang, a smell of the living earth. He had often fled to Father Schliemann, in those days of puberty when the telepathic power had first wakened in him. He had found good minds since then, happy minds, but never one so serene, none with so much strength under the gentleness.

"I don't want you hanging around that papist, boy, do you understand?" It was his father, the lean implacable man who always wore a black tie. "Next thing you know, you'll be worshiping graven images just like him."

"But they *aren't*—"

His ears could still ring with the cuff. "Go up to your room! I don't want to see you till tomorrow morning. And you'll have two more chapters of Deuteronomy memorized by then. Maybe that'll teach you the true Christian faith."

Kane grinned wryly and lit another cigarette from the end of the previous one. He knew he smoked too much. And drank—but not heavily. Drunk, he was defenseless before the horrible tides of thinking.

He had had to run away from home at the age of fourteen. The only other possibility was conflict ending with reform school. It had meant running away from Father Schliemann too, but how in hell's red fire could a sensitive adolescent dwell in the same house as his father's brain? Were the psychologists now admitting the possibility of a sadistic masochist? Kane *knew* the type existed.

Give thanks for this much mercy, that the extreme telepathic range was only a few hundred yards. And a mind-reading boy was not altogether helpless; he could evade officialdom and the worst horrors of the underworld. He could find a decent elderly couple at the far end of the continent and talk himself into adoption.

Kane shook himself and got up again. He threw the cigarette to the ground and stubbed it out with his heel. A thousand examples told him what obscure sexual symbolism was involved in the act, but what the deuce . . . it was also a practical thing. Guns are phallic too, but at times you need a gun.

Weapons: he could not help wincing as he recalled dodging the draft in 1949. He'd traveled enough to know this country was worth defending. But it hadn't been any trick at all to hoodwink a psychiatrist and get himself marked hopelessly psychoneurotic—which he would be after two years penned with frustrated men. There had been no choice, but he could not escape a sense of dishonor.

—haven't we all sinned / every one of us / is there a single human creature on earth without his burden of shame?—

A man was coming out of the drugstore beside him. Idly, Kane probed his mind. You could go quite deeply into anyone's self if you cared to, in fact you couldn't help doing so. It was impossible merely to scan verbalized thinking: the organism is too closely integrated. Memory is not a passive filing cabinet, but a continuous process beneath the level of consciousness; in a way, you are always reliving your entire past. And the more emotionally charged the recollection is, the more powerfully it radiates.

The stranger's name was—no matter. His personality was as much an unchangeable signature as his fingerprints. Kane had gotten into the habit of thinking of people as such-and-such a multidimensional symbolic topography; the name was an arbitrary gabble.

The man was an assistant professor of English at the University. Age forty-two, married, three children, making payments on a house in Albany. Steady sober type, but convivial, popular with his colleagues, ready to help out most friends. He was thinking about tomorrow's lectures, with overtones of a movie he wanted to see and an undercurrent of fear that he might have cancer after all, in spite of what the doctor said.

Below, the list of his hidden crimes. As a boy: tormenting a cat, well-buried Oedipean hungers, masturbation, petty theft . . . the usual. Later: cheating on a few exams, that ludicrous fumbling attempt with a girl which came to nothing because he was too nervous, the time he crashed a cafeteria line and had been shoved away with a cold remark (and praises be, Jim who had seen that was now living in Chicago) . . . still later: wincing memories of a stomach uncontrollably rumbling at a formal dinner, that woman in his hotel room the night he got drunk at the convention, standing by and letting old Carver be fired because he didn't have the courage to protest to the dean . . . now: youngest child a nasty whining little snotnose, but you can't show anyone what you really think, reading Rosamond Marshall when alone in his office, disturbing young breasts in tight sweaters, the petty spite of academic politics, giving Simonson an undeserved good grade because the boy was so beautiful, disgraceful sweating panic when at night he considered how death would annihilate his ego—

And what of it? This assistant professor was a good man, a kindly and honest man, his inwardness ought to be between him and the Recording Angel. Few of his thoughts had ever become deeds, or ever would. Let him bury them himself, let him be alone with them. Kane ceased focusing on him.

The telepath had grown tolerant. He expected little of anyone; nobody matched the mask, except possibly Father Schliemann and a few others . . . and those were human too, with human failings; the difference was that they knew peace. It was the emotional overtones of guilt which made Kane wince. God knew he himself was no better. Worse, maybe, but then his life had thrust him to it. If you had an ordinary human sex drive, for instance, but could not endure to cohabit with the thoughts of a woman, your life became one of fleeting encounters; there was no help for it, even if your austere boyhood training still protested.

"Pardon me, got a match?"

—lynn is dead / i still can't understand it that i will never see her again & eventually you learn how to go on in a chopped-off fashion but what do you do in the meantime how do you get through the nights alone—

"Sure."*—maybe that is the worst: sharing sorrow and unable to help & only able to give him a light for his cigarette—*

Kane put the matches back in his pocket and went on up University, pausing again at Oxford. A pair of large campus buildings jutted up to the left; others were visible ahead and to the right, through a screen of eucalyptus trees. Sunlight and shadow damascened the grass. From a passing student's mind he discovered where the library was. A good big library—perhaps it held a clue, buried somewhere in the periodical files. He had already arranged for permission to use the facilities: prominent young author doing research for his next novel.

Crossing wistfully named Oxford Street, Kane smiled to himself. Writing was really the only possible occupation: he could live in the country and be remote from the jammed urgency of his fellow men. And with such an understanding of the soul as was his, with any five minutes on a corner giving him a dozen stories, he made good money at it. The only drawback was the trouble of avoiding publicity, editorial summonses to New York, autographing parties, literary teas . . . he didn't like those. But you could remain faceless if you insisted.

They said nobody but his agent knew who B. Traven was. It had occurred, wildly, to Kane that Traven might be another like himself. He had gone on a long journey to find out. . . . No. He was alone on earth, a singular and solitary mutant, except for—

It shivered in him, again he sat on the train. It had been three years ago, he was in the club car having a nightcap while the streamliner ran eastward through the Wyoming darkness. They passed a westbound train, not so elegant a one. His drink leaped from his hand to the floor and he sat for a moment in stinging blindness. That flicker of thought, brushing his mind and coming aflame with recognition and then borne away again . . . Damn it, damn it, he should have pulled the emergency cord and so should *she*. They should have halted both trains and stumbled through cinders and sagebrush and found each other's arms.

Too late. Three years yielded only a further emptiness. Somewhere in the land there was, or there had been, a young woman, and she was a telepath and the startled touch of her mind had been gentle. There had not been time to learn anything else. Since then he had given up on private detectives. (How could you tell them: "I'm looking for a girl who was on such-and-such a train the night of—"?) Personal ads in all the major papers had brought him nothing but a few crank letters. Probably she didn't read the personals; he'd never done so till his search began, there was too much unhappiness to be found in them if you understood humankind as well as he did.

Maybe this library here, some unnoticed item . . . but if there are two points in a finite space and one moves about so as to pass through every infinitesimal volume dV, it will encounter the other one in finite time *provided* that the other point is not moving too.

Kane shrugged and went along the curving way to the gatehouse. It was slightly uphill. There was a bored cop in the shelter, to make sure that only authorized cars were parked on campus. The progress paradox: a ton or so of steel, burning irreplaceable petroleum to shift one or two human bodies around, and doing the job so well that it becomes universal and chokes the cities which spawned it. A telepathic society would be more rational. When every little wound in the child's soul could be felt and healed . . . when the thick burden of guilt was laid down, because everyone knew that everyone else had done the same . . . when men could not kill, because soldier and murderer felt the victim die . . .

—adam & eve? you can't breed a healthy race out of two people. but if we had telepathic children/ & we would be bound to do so i think because the mutation is obviously recessive/ then we could study the heredity of it & the gift would be passed on to other bloodlines in logical distribution & every generation there would be more of our kind until we could come out openly & even the mindmutes could be helped by our psychiatrists & priests & each would be fair and clean and sane—

There were students sitting on the grass, walking under the Portland Cement Romanesque of the buildings, calling and laughing and talking. The day was near an end. Now there would be dinner, a date, a show, maybe some beer at Robbie's or a drive up into the hills to neck and watch the lights below like trapped stars and the mighty constellation of the Bay Bridge . . . or perhaps, with a face-saving grumble about midterms, an evening of books, a world suddenly opened. It must be good to be young and mindmute. A dog trotted down the walk and Kane relaxed into the simple wordless pleasure of being a healthy and admired collie.

—so perhaps it is better to be a dog than a man? no/ surely not/ for if a man knows more grief he also knows more joy & so it is to be a telepath: more easily hurt yes but /god/ think of the mindmutes always locked away in aloneness and think of sharing not only a kiss but a soul with your beloved—

The uphill trend grew steeper as he approached the library, but Kane was in fair shape and rather enjoyed the extra effort. At the foot of the stairs he paused for a quick cigarette before entering. A passing woman flicked eyes across him and he learned that he could also smoke in the lobby. Mind reading had its everyday uses. But it was good to stand here in the sunlight. He stretched, reaching out physically and mentally.

—let's see now the integral of log x dx will make a substitution suppose we call y equal to log x then this is interesting i wonder who wrote that line about euclid has looked on beauty bare—

Kane's cigarette fell from his mouth.

It seemed that the wild hammering of his heart must drown out the double thought that rivered in his brain, the thought of a physics student, a very ordinary young man save that he was quite wrapped up in the primitive satisfaction of hounding down a problem, and the other thought, the one that was listening in.

—she—

He stood with closed eyes, asway on his feet, breathing as if he ran up a mountain. *—are You there? are You there?—*

—not daring to believe: what do i feel?—

—i was the man on the train—

—& i was the woman—

A shuddering togetherness.

"Hey! Hey, mister, is anything wrong?"

Almost, Kane snarled. Her thought was so remote, on the very rim of indetectability, he could get nothing but sub-vocalized words, nothing of the self, and this busybody—"No, thanks, I'm O.K., just a, a little winded."—*where are You, where can i find You o my darling?—*

—image of a large white building/right over here & they call it dwinelle hall & i am siting on the bench outside & please come quickly please be here i never thought this could become real—

Kane broke into a run. For the first time in fifteen years, he was unaware of his human surroundings. There were startled looks, he didn't see them, he was running to her and she was running too.

—my name is norman kane & i was not born to that name but took it from people who adopted me because i fled my father (horrible how mother died in darkness & he would not let her have drugs though it was cancer & he said drugs were sinful and pain was good for the soul & he really honestly believed that & when the power first appeared i made slips and he beat me and said it was witchcraft & i have searched all my life since & i am a writer but only because i must live but it was not aliveness until this moment—

—o my poor kicked beloved/ i had it better/ in me the

power grew more slowly and i learned to cover it & i am twenty years old & came here to study but what are books at this moment—

He could see her now. She was not conventionally beautiful, but neither was she ugly, and there was kindness in her eyes and on her mouth.

—what shall i call you? to me you will always be You but there must be a name for the mindmutes & i have a place in the country among old trees & such few people as live nearby are good folk/ as good as life will allow them to be—

—then let me come there with you & never leave again—

They reached each other and stood a foot apart. There was no need for a kiss or even a handclasp . . . not yet. It was the minds which leaped out and enfolded and became one.

—I REMEMBER THAT AT THE AGE OF THREE I DRANK OUT OF THE TOILET BOWL/ THERE WAS A PECULIAR FASCINATION TO IT & I USED TO STEAL LOOSE CHANGE FROM MY MOTHER THOUGH SHE HAD LITTLE ENOUGH TO CALL HER OWN SO I COULD SNEAK DOWN TO THE DRUGSTORE FOR ICE CREAM & I SQUIRMED OUT OF THE DRAFT & THESE ARE THE DIRTY EPISODES INVOLVING WOMEN—

—AS A CHILD I WAS NOT FOND OF MY GRANDMOTHER THOUGH SHE LOVED ME AND ONCE I PLAYED THE FOLLOWING FIENDISH TRICK ON HER & AT THE AGE OF SIXTEEN I MADE AN UTTER FOOL OF MYSELF IN THE FOLLOWING MANNER & I HAVE BEEN PHYSICALLY CHASTE CHIEFLY BECAUSE OF FEAR BUT MY VICARIOUS EXPERIENCES ARE NUMBERED IN THE THOUSANDS—

Eyes watched eyes with horror.

—it is not that you have sinned for i know everyone has done the same or similar things or would if they had our gift & i know too that it is nothing serious or abnormal & of course you have decent instincts & are ashamed—

—just so/ it is that you know what i have done & you know every last little wish & thought & buried uncleanness & in the top of my head i know it doesn't mean anything but down underneath is all which was drilled into me when i was just

a baby & i will not admit to ANYONE *else that such things exist
in* ME—

A car whispered by, homeward bound. The trees talked in
the light sunny wind.

A boy and girl went hand in hand.

The thought hung cold under the sky, a single thought in
two minds.

—get out i hate your bloody guts.—

POUL ANDERSON

A World Named Cleopatra

The planetary system lies in Ursa Major, 398 light-years from Sol. This causes certain changes in the appearance of the heavens. Northerly constellations are "spread out" and most of the familiar stars in them show brighter than at Earth, though some have left the configurations because, seen from here, they now lie in a southerly direction. Fainter stars in them, invisible at Earth, have become naked-eye objects. These changes are the greater the nearer one looks toward Ursa Major. It is itself modified quite out of recognition by the untrained eye, as are the constellations closest to it. The further away one looks, around the celestial sphere, the less distortion. Southern constellations are comparatively little affected. Those near the south celestial pole of Earth, such as Octans, keep their shapes the best, though they exhibit the most shrinkage in angular size. Various of their fainter stars (as seen from Earth) are now invisible—Sol is too—but they have been replaced by others which (as seen from Earth) "originally" were northern.

Thus to a native of the Terrestrial northern hemisphere the sky seems considerably changed around the Dippers, Cassiopeia, etc. But Orion, for example, is still identifiable; and the constellations that an Australian or Argentinian is used to are not much altered.

However—the celestial hemispheres of Cleopatra are not identical with those of Earth. In fact, the Cleopatran north pole points toward Pisces, which is almost 90° from the direction of the Terrestrial axis. ("North" and "south" are defined so as to make the sun rise in the east.) There is no definite lodestar, but Pisces turns around a point in its own middle, accompanied by neighbors such as Virgo, Pegasus, and Aquarius. The south celestial pole is near Crater. The constellations that Earthmen are accustomed to seeing high in either sky are here—insofar as they are recognizable—always low, and many are only to be observed at given seasons.

Under these circumstances, it may be most convenient for colonists to redraw the star map entirely, making new constellations out of what they see. Or perhaps this will happen of itself in the course of generations.

THE SUN

The sun was named Caesar, mythology having been used up closer to home. It is of type F7, which means it is hotter and whiter than Sol. Its mass is 1.2, its total luminosity 2.05 Sol. The diameter is little greater, but spots, prominences, corona, and output of charged particles (solar wind) are fewer. It is a younger star than ours, though by less than a billion years. Either because of this, or because of variations in galactic distribution, the proportion of heavy elements in it and its planets is somewhat more than for the Solar System.

In general, the Caesarian System is a normal one. Besides asteroids, it contains eleven planets. In outward order, these have been christened Agrippa (small, hot, nearly airless); Antony (about Earth size, with an atmosphere, but not habitable by man); Cleopatra (the sole terrestroid member); Enobarbus (smaller than Earth, larger than Mars, ruddy like the latter); Pompey (a gas giant, somewhat more massive than Jupiter); four lesser giants (Lepidus, Cornelia, Calpurnia and Julia); and finally, remote Marius and Sulla (the latter really just a huge comet which has never moved into the inner system). There are two distinct asteroid belts separating Enobarbus, Pompey and Lepidus.

Seen from Cleopatra, Agrippa and Antony are morning or evening stars, though the former is usually lost in sun glare. The latter is brilliant, its iridescence often apparent to the naked eye as solar wind causes its upper atmosphere to fluoresce. Enobarbus glows red, Pompey and Lepidus tawny white. Pale-green Cornelia can occasionally be seen without instruments.

THE PLANET

Cleopatra moves around Caesar in an orbit of slight eccentricity, at an average distance of 1.24 astronomical units. Its year is 1.26 times that of Earth, about 15 months long, and the sun in its sky has only 0.87 the angular diameter of ours. Nevertheless, because of its brightness, Caesar gives Cleopatra 1.33 times the total irradiation that Earth gets. A larger proportion of this energy is in the shorter wavelengths; Caesar appears a bit more bluish white than yellowish white to human vision. The lesser apparent size is not particularly noticeable, since no prudent person looks anywhere near it without eye protection, let alone straight at it. Shadows on the ground tend to be sharper than on Earth and to have more of a blue tinge. All color values are subtly different, though one quickly gets used to this.

Theoretically, the mean temperature at a given latitude on Cleopatra should be some 20°C higher than the corresponding value for Earth. In practice, the different spectral distribution and the atmosphere and hydrosphere, modify things considerably. Cleopatra *is* warmer, and lacks polar icecaps. But then, this was true of Earth throughout most of its existence. Even at the equator, some regions are balmy rather than hot, while the latitudes comfortable to man reach further north and south than on present-day Earth. People simply avoid the furnace-like deserts found here and there.

They also take precautions against the higher level of ultraviolet light, especially in the tropics. Again, this poses no severe problem. One can safely sunbathe in the temperate zones, and do so well into the polar regions in summer. Usually there is no undue glare of light; the more extensive atmosphere (vide infra) helps in scattering and softening illumination. Winter nights are usually ornamented by fantastically bright and beautiful auroras, down to lower latitudes than is the case on Earth—in spite of Cleopatra's strong magnetic field. To be sure, solar-atmospheric interference with radio and the like can get pretty bad, especially at a peak of the sunspot cycle (for Caesar, about 14 Earth-years long, as opposed to Sol's 11). But once installed, laser transceivers aren't bothered.

Cleopatra is smaller than Earth. In terms of the latter planet, its mass is 0.528, its radius 0.78 (or 4960 km at the equator), its mean density 1.10 (or 6.1 times that of water), and its surface gravity 0.86. This last means that, for example, a human who weighed 80 kg on Earth weighs 68.5 here; he himself soon adjusts to that—though he is well advised to maintain a lifetime program of thorough physical exercise to avoid various atrophies and circulation problems— but engineering is affected. (For instance, aircraft need less wing area but ground vehicles need more effective brakes.) An object falling through a given distance takes 1.07 times as long to do so as on Earth and gains 0.93 the velocity; a pendulum of given length has 1.14 the period; the speed of a wave on deep water is 0.93 what it is on Earth.

Standing on a flat plain or sea, a man of normal height observes the horizon as being about 7 km off, compared to about 8 on Earth—not a terribly striking difference, especially in rugged topography or hazy weather.

Despite its lesser dimensions, Cleopatra has a quite terrestroid atmosphere. In fact, the sea level pressures on the two planets are almost identical. It is thought that this is due to the hot, dense mass of the planet outgassing more than Earth did, early in their respective histories, and to the fact that, ever since, the strong magnetic field has helped keep too many molecules from getting kicked away into space by solar and cosmic ray particles.

Air pressure drops with altitude more slowly than on Earth, because of the lower gravity. On Earth, at about 5.5 km the pressure is one-half that at sea level; but on Cleopatra, one must go up 6.35 km to find this. Not only does that moderate surface conditions, it extends life zones higher, and offers more possibilities to flyers both living and mechanical.

There having been less tidal friction acting on it through most of its existence, Cleopatra spins faster than Earth: once in 17 hr 21 m 14.8 s, or about 17.3 hr or 0.72 Earth diurnal period. Its year therefore lasts 639 of its own days, give or take a little bit because of trepidation, precession, etc.

The axial tilt is 28°, somewhat more than Earth's. However, the climate of high latitudes is not necessarily more extreme on that account. Certainly winters are less cold. It is the difference in the length of seasons—a fourth again as much—which is most important. Likewise, the seasonal variation of day and night lengths is more marked than on Earth, and the Arctic and Antarctic Circles come nearer to the equator.

The stronger sun, which supplies more energy; the longer year, which gives more time to overcome thermal lag; the smaller size, which brings zones closer together; the larger axial tilt, which exaggerates the differences between them; the quicker spin, which generates more potent cyclonic forces; the lower pressures but the longer distance up to a stratosphere, which make for more extensive air masses moving at a given time under given conditions—all these create "livelier" weather than on Earth. Storms are more common and violent, though they tend to be short-lived. Huge thunderstorms in the river valleys, twisters on the plains, hurricanes in the tropics, and blizzards near the poles are things which colonists must expect; they have to build stoutly and maintain an alert meteorological service.

But this seeming drawback has its good side. With such variability, both droughts and deluges are rare; chilly fogs don't linger; inversion layers break up before they accumulate unpleasant gases; daytime cloud patterns can be gorgeous to watch, while nights are brilliantly clear more often than not, in most areas of the planet.

Turning back to the globe itself: Its greater mean density than Earth's is due to a higher percentage of heavy elements, especially those later in the periodic table than iron. This leads to a particularly hot core which, combined with the rapid rotation, is the source of the magnetic field screening the atmosphere from solar wind. (Of course, the field is far weaker than in any generator—roughly twice as strong as Earth's—but it reaches way out.) Having not only more interior heat but a smaller volume, Cleopatra radiates more strongly.

This means that it is geologically, or planetologically, more active. There are more hot springs, geysers, volcanoes, quakes, and tsunamis, especially along the leading edges of continents and in midocean (vide infra). There is faster mountain-building, aided by the lower gravity which permits higher upheavals and steeper slopes. (The same is true of sand dunes.) Erosion proceeds more rapidly too; hence spectacularly sculptured uplands are quite common.

With the crustal plates more mobile than on Earth, we get an overall situation—there are many local exceptions, of course—about as follows. No continent is as big as Eurasia; the largest is comparable to North America. Their shelves drop sharply off to more profound depths than Terrestrial. They define—in the same rough way as on Earth—four major oceans, each surrounded by its "ring of fire" and marked down the middle by archipelagos of which numerous islands are volcanic. Elsewhere are smaller, shallower seas. Along with the tide patterns (vide infra), these factors tend to inhibit the generation of great ocean currents, and thus to somewhat isolate the latitudes fom each other. That isn't all bad; if "Norway" has no "Gulf Stream" to warm it, neither does the "Pacific Northwest" have a "Kuroshio" to chill it, and marine life is even more varied than on Earth.

The proportion of land to water surface is slightly higher than Terrestrial, mainly because of the powerful upthrust of crustal masses—though doubtless the splitting of H_2O molecules by ultraviolet quanta, before there was a protective ozone layer, also has a good deal to do with this. However, there is no water shortage; in fact, the smaller size of individual land blocs and the vigorous air circulation make for better distribution of this substance and keep continental interiors reasonably temperate.

The abundance of heavy metals is a boon to industry, yet not altogether a blessing. Some of these elements and their compounds are poisonous to man. Concentrated in certain areas, they make the soil, or organisms living there, dangerous. But again, this is by no means the universal case, and precautions are not hard to take once people have been warned. Several beautiful minerals and gemstones appear to be unique to this planet.

SATELLITES

Cleopatra has no moon in the usual sense. Perhaps it once did, or perhaps an asteroid was captured. In any event, at some point in the fairly recent past (estimated 10 million years ago), this body (estimated mass, 0.001 that of Luna) came within the Roche limit and was pulled asunder by tidal forces.

Numerous fragments fell. The biggest left traces in the form of huge circular lakes, bays and valleys. Meteorites are still coming down as perturbation maneuvers them out of orbit. So there are many pitted rocks, many craters great and small, on Cleopatra, the newest sharply defined, the oldest blurred by erosion. On any clear night, shooting stars may be seen delightfully often.

But most of the disrupted mass formed a ring, at a mean distance of some 7500 km from the surface, which is still around and will probably last for millions of years to come. It is not like the ring(s) of Saturn, the latter consisting of tiny ice particles. Cleopatra is surrounded by a belt of stony and metallic fragments, ranging in size down to gravel and fine dust. There is considerable space between the average pair of rocks, though of course this varies.

Except for Charmian and Iras (vide infra), the satellites are too small to be seen by day against sun glare. Moreover, being nearly in the equatorial plane, the ring shows best in the tropics. In high latitudes one sees it low in the sky, often obscured by mountains, woods, or haze; and one cannot see it at all in the polar regions (above latitude 66°) aside from a few isolated, far-out particles.

The ring is at its most spectacular at equatorial midnight around the time of solstice. Then a band of hundreds of glittering, twinkling fireflies streams across the sky from west to east, the faster (nearer) overtaking the slower (further out) though all move swiftly. Irregular in shape, scoured and scored by dust, many sparkle in prismatic hues as well as white. The dust itself forms a dimly glowing background, through which stars can be seen. Though the band has no constant or definite boundaries, it averages about 10° wide, brightest at the middle, fading out toward the edges.

The mean synodic period of a particle, i.e., the time for a complete cycle from rising to rising as observed on the ground, is 7.5 hr or about 0.43 Cleopatran day. This is 48° per hr, or rather more than three times as fast as Sol or Luna crosses the Terrestrial sky. However, the ring is too close in for the entire half arc to be visible anywhere on the planet, so the maximum time observed (at the equator) is 1 hr 22 m.

That time is really only interesting as concerns the two members of the ring which are so big that they may be called tiny moons. They have, indeed, been given names, Charmian and Iras. (At the nomenclature conference, one faction wanted a Ftaatateeta but was voted down.) Charmian is the larger and slightly closer. In fact, it seems just about the same size as Luna does on Earth, though its actual mean diameter is not quite 70 km. Iras has about half the linear cross section and moves a little slower. (The respective synodic periods are 7.6 and 8.2 hr, which means that Charmian overtakes Iras every 102 hr or 5.9 Cleopatran days. These figures are subject to some oscillation because of assorted gravitational influences.) The two orbits are so skewed that, while they come near, the moonlets seldom overlap.

In other words, they move along the ring approximately four times in a Cleopatran day and night, going through approximately 5.6 phase-change cycles as they do; but most of this cannot be seen from any single place on the ground.

Neither looks much like Luna. Charmian is only roughly spheroidal, Iras still less so. They show angles, facets, promontories and markings as they orbit the planet while spinning in a wobbly fashion. They both resemble Luna in being large and reflective enough to remain visible during an eclipse.

This eclipse is due to the fact that Cleopatra's shadow crosses the rings. There is sufficient axial tilt that at a solstice, only a small "bite" is taken out of the lower edge of the band at its lowest point—and the band is irregular, fluctuating, and vaguely defined enough for this not to be particularly noticeable. But as the planet moves on around its sun, the geometry changes. About 23 Cleopatran days after solstice, the shadow arc entirely bisects the ring. By equinox, ca. 160 days after solstice (ca. 115 Earth days), the eclipse is at a maximum.

At this season, when watched from the equator, the ring—including the two moons—streams upward from the west as before. But at an azimuth of about 52°, not quite 60% of the way up to the zenith, the particles blank out. They do not reappear until they are correspondingly near the eastern horizon and descending. Charmian, Iras, and a few of the largest meteoroids remain visible but turn dull coppery red from atmosphere-refracted light, as they transit the dark gap.

This cycle of eclipse and full illumination is repeated twice in the course of a year. The precise appearance of the ring, as well as its position in the heavens, depends on time and location of the observer.

But at any season—what with auroras, background skyglow, stars, ring, and the frequently seen changeable moonlets—Cleopatran nights are not unduly dark. In clear weather, a human can make his way around pretty well without artificial light.

The tidal pull of Caesar is small, about one-third that of Sol on Earth or less than one-fifth the total of what Earth gets. Were the ring particles concentrated in one mass, the total heave would be enormous, about 18 times what Luna gives to Earth. Scattered as they are, they produce only minor effects individually. But the resultants are complex and variable. The seas do not get stagnant, and crosscurrents often make them choppy.

GENERAL BIOLOGY

Given a planet this similar to Earth, it is not surprising that here too life arose, based on proteins in water solution, and in time developed photosynthesizing plants which formed and now maintain an oxynitrogen atmosphere. It *is* unusual to have so many details duplicated. (To be sure, given the vast number of worlds in the galaxy, this must happen once in a while.) Here too life uses predominantly levoamino acids and dextro sugars. Many lipids, carbohydrates, hydrocarbons, pyrroles, etc. are the same as on Earth, chlorophyl and hemoglobin included (with some minor variations). In like manner, we find viruses, bacteria, protozoa, vegetable and animal kingdoms.

Now it would be too improbable for every detail to be the same, considering how many are the consequence of random "choice" among numerous possibilities. Much Cleopatran life can be eaten by man, is nourishing and tasty; but some of it is poisonous, and all of it lacks certain vitamins and other nutrients. Hence one can live only temporarily on an exclusive diet of it. This is not a great handicap. In fact, basically it is desirable, because it works both ways. Native germs cannot function in the human body, native viruses are not equipped to take over human genetic machinery—in short, to man this is an infection-free world.

And of course he can introduce his own plants and animals. Given a start—e.g., by eradication of deadly weeds from a range—they will flourish. Soon the problem will be to save the Cleopatran ecology. Once established, Terrestrial life will spread fast and overwhelmingly unless it is controlled. For it is further evolved.

After all, Cleopatra is younger than Earth. If anything, it

is surprising how far life has developed, in so much less time. Conceivably the energetic sun, the higher lever of actinic radiation and electrical discharge, promoted rapid development of the primitive protobiology and later microorganisms. But afterward, perhaps, the weak tides—making for a sharper division between sea and land—delayed the conquest of the latter.

At any rate, though inaccurate, it is helpful to think of this world as being in a "Mesozoic" era.

PLANTS

Angiosperms have not yet developed. There are primitive equivalents of the spermatophytes, including some gymnosperms. These are most common in the drier inland and upland regions. The coasts, marshes, etc. are dominated by types similar to Terrestrial bryophytes and pteridophytes, more elaborated than on present-day Earth. Because of certain rootlike structures, they are known as dactylophytes.

Nothing like grass or flowers exists. Moist areas are carpeted with low, dense, intensely green vegetation resembling moss. Species of this phylum have developed protection against drying out and are therefore found elsewhere as ground cover in paler and stiffer versions. Many trees and shrubs (if one may call them that) have colorful pseudoblooms, analogous to those of our poinsettias, to lure pollinators.

Among the more picturesque plants are: The misnamed dinobryons, huge dactylophytes in wet regions which suggest spongy green many-branched coral growths; the aquatic weirplant and its land relatives, the dichtophytes, carnivorous species which grow in the form of great nets to trap sizable prey; the Venus mirror, a bush named for its highly reflective leaves, which attract glitterwings; the chameleon plant, which exhibits changes of shade and even to some degree color, according to lighting conditions—a camouflage against eaters; the sarissa, resembling sharp-pointed bamboo but growing in clusters which bristle almost horizontally outward, supported by roots along the stalks; the grenade, a bush whose round pods explode spectacularly, though harmlessly, to scatter seeds; the Christmas memory, a primitive evergreen whose roughly shaped but brilliant red cones are like oraments; and the delicious sugarroot.

No one region has all kinds. Some genera are circumpolar, others not. This is likewise true in the zoological field.

ANIMALS

A biologist would vehemently deny that Cleopatra has insects, fish, amphibians, reptiles, birds, mammals, or anything else Terrestrial, other than what man may import. There are too many differences of detail, some quite fundamental. Nevertheless, resemblances are close enough—when similar environments have selected for similar characteristics—that pioneers are not inclined to split every semantic hair.

The colonists do use scientific names for the broad classes. But "worm" has so wide a meaning even on Earth that it can reasonably be applied to numerous legless invertebrates on Cleopatra. One interesting family is that of the arthroscholes, whose segments carry articulated, chitinoidal blue armor. Thus protected, they may grow to lengths of more than a meter.

"Insectoid" soon became shortened in daily language to "secto," and is as loosely applied as ever "insect" and "bug" were on Earth. There are countless kinds of secto. Among the famous are the glitterwing, like a moth whose wings are almost mirrorlike because of tiny metallic particles; a long, many-legged, bulge-eyed scuttler called the I-spy; and the smidgin, which travels in swarms that darken the air, accompanied by flyers that leisurely feast on them.

Marine invertebrates include the drifting gorgon with its mesh of lethal streamers. The big polypus has no definite number of tentacles, for injury causes more than one new one to sprout. When it has grown inconveniently many, the animal develops a second head and set of interior organs, and fissions into two—an alternative to its usual sexual reproduction. Biologists are fascinated by the problem of how this is possible in something of that size and complexity.

Besides male-female sexuality and paired eyes, parallel evolution has produced Cleopatran vertebrates which, like the Terrestrial, have just four true limbs.

Piscoids include the great, sleek, swift, carnivorous pirate and the miter-headed, grotesquely ululating sea preacher. Among marine sauroids is the macrotrach, remarkably similar in appearance to the ancient plesiosaur.

The land is dominated by sauroids. Many of them are more highly developed than any Terrestrial reptile, having efficient hearts, giving live birth and caring for their young, even showing an almost mammalian capacity to learn by experience. This is probably due to the fact that, on generally warmer Cleopatra, being homeothermic ("warm-blooded") confers less relative advantage than on Earth; there do not seem ever to have been any glacial periods. Thus poikilothermic ("cold-blooded") animals have had more chance to flourish and evolve new capabilities.

The best-known ones include: the hipposaur, a hoofed grazer of plains and mountains, as big as a big horse; the king gator, a dry-land carnivore with long legs but otherwise rather crocodilian; the hoplite, a two-meter-wide walking dome of bony armor and spiky tail; the faber, eerily caricaturing humanity in appearance and certain behavior patterns; and the huge-winged flying deltasoar.

The homeothermic beasts remain primitive. They have hair, whose possible colors include a bright green, but no mammary glands. Most young are born with full sets of teeth, immediately able to eat the same as the parents. Where this is not the case, feeding is by regurgitation. Thus even some ground-dwelling animals have beaks rather than snouts, and none have lips.

They are furthest developed in the aerial forms, the ptenoids or pseudobirds. Though none of these quite compare to Terrestrial avians in capabilities, they number some handsome species, like the colorfully plumed jackadandy. The rich-furred (not feathered) flier and diver known as the cinnamon bat is, however, a theroid.

No theroid is very large. A common forest dweller is the tree spook, suggestive of a parrot-billed lemur. On one continent, the carnivorous hootinanny runs in packs which make hideous loud noises in their throat pouches to stampede the prolific herbivorous jumping Toms; both species are rabbit-sized. In arctic regions, the snow snake has shed legs and belly fur in order to go more effectively after its own burrowing prey; with its white pelt everywhere else on the body and its affectionate ways, it makes an excellent pet. Of course, this is only a partial list.

In fact, all these remarks are quite superficial and incomplete. Any planet is a world, and therefore inexhaustible.

POUL ANDERSON AND GORDON R. DICKSON

The Sheriff of Canyon Gulch

It had been a very near thing. Alexander Jones spent several
minutes enjoying the simple pleasure of still being alive.

Then he looked around.

It could almost have been Earth—almost, indeed, his own
North America. He stood on a great prairie whose dun grasses
rolled away beneath a high windy sky. A flock of birds,
alarmed by his descent, clamored upward; they were not so
very different from the birds he knew. A line of trees marked
the river, a dying puff of steam the final berth of his scoutboat.
In the hazy eastern distance he saw dim blue hills. Beyond
those, he knew, were the mountains, and then the enormous
dark forests, and finally the sea near which the *Draco* lay. A
hell of a long ways to travel.

Nevertheless, he was uninjured, and on a planet almost the
twin of his own. The air, gravity, biochemistry, the late-
afternoon sun, could only be told from those of home with
sensitive instruments. The rotational period was approximately
24 hours, the sidereal year nearly 12 months, the axial tilt
a neat but not gaudy 11½ degrees. The fact that two small
moons were in the sky and a third lurking somewhere else,
that the continental outlines were an alien scrawl, that a snake
coiled on a nearby rock had wings, that he was about five
hundred light-years from the Solar System—all this was mere
detail. The veriest bagatelle. Alex laughed at it.

The noise jarred so loud in this emptiness that he decided
a decorous silence was more appropriate to his status as an
officer and, by Act of Parliament as ratified locally by the

United States Senate, a gentleman. Therefore he straightened his high-collared blue naval tunic, ran a nervous hand down the creases of his white naval trousers, buffed his shining naval boots on the spilled-out naval parachute, and reached for his emergency kit.

He neglected to comb his rumpled brown hair, and his lanky form did not exactly snap to attention. But he was, after all, quite alone.

Not that he intended to remain in that possibly estimable condition. He shrugged the heavy packsack off his shoulders. It had been the only thing he grabbed besides the parachute when his boat failed, and the only thing he really needed. His hands fumbled it open and he reached in for the small but powerful radio which would bring help.

He drew out a book.

It looked unfamiliar, somehow . . . had they issued a new set of instructions since he was in boot camp? He opened it, looking for the section on Radios, Emergency, Use of. He read the first page he turned to:

"—apparently incredibly fortunate historical development was, of course, quite logical. The relative decline in politico-economic influence of the Northern Hemisphere during the later twentieth century, the shift of civilized dominance to a Southeast Asia–Indian Ocean region with more resources, did not, as alarmists at the time predicted, spell the end of Western civilization. Rather did it spell an upsurge of Anglo-Saxon democratic and libertarian influence, for the simple reason that this area, which now held the purse strings of Earth, was in turn primarily led by Australia and New Zealand, which nations retained their primordial loyalty to the British Crown. The consequent renascence and renewed growth of the British Commonwealth of Nations, the shaping of its councils into a truly world—even interplanetary—government, climaxed as it was by the American Accession, has naturally tended to fix Western culture, even in small details of everyday life, in the mold of that particular time, a tendency which was accentuated by the unexpectedly early invention of the faster-than-light

secondary drive and repeated contact with truly different men-
talities, and has produced in the Solar System a social stability
which our forefathers would have considered positively
Utopian and which the Service, working through the Inter-
being League, has as its goal to bring to all sentient races—"

"*Guk!*" said Alex.

He snapped the book shut. Its title leered up at him:

EMPLOYEES' ORIENTATION MANUAL
by Adalbert Parr, Chief Control Commissioner
Cultural Development Service
Foreign Ministry of the United Commonwealths
League City, N.Z., Sol III

"Oh, no!" said Alex.

Frantically, he pawed through the pack. There *must* be a
radio . . . a ray thrower . . . a compass . . . one little can of
beans?

He extracted some five thousand tightly bundled copies of
CDS Form J-16-LKR, to be filled out in quadruplicate by
applicant and submitted with attached Forms G-776802 and
W-2-ZGU.

Alex's snub-nosed face sagged open. His blue eyes revolved
incredulously. There followed a long, dreadful moment in
which he could only think how utterly useless the English
language was when it came to describing issue-room clerks.

"Oh, hell," said Alexander Jones.

He got up and began to walk.

§

He woke slowly with the sunrise and lay there for a while
wishing he hadn't. A long hike on an empty stomach followed
by an uneasy attempt to sleep on the ground, plus the prospect
of several thousand kilometers of the same, is not conducive
to joy. And those animals, whatever they were, that had been
yipping and howling all night sounded so damnably *hungry*.

"He looks human."

"Yeah. But he ain't dressed like no human."

Alex opened his eyes with a wild surmise. The drawling voices spoke . . . English!

He closed his eyes again, immediately. "No," he groaned.

"He's awake, Tex." The voices were high-pitched, slightly unreal. Alex curled up into the embryonic position and reflected on the peculiar horror of a squeaky drawl.

"Yeah. Git up, stranger. These hyar parts ain't healthy right now, nohow."

"No," gibbered Alex. "Tell me it isn't so. Tell me I've gone crazy, but deliver me from its being real!"

"I dunno." The voice was uncertain. "He don't talk like no human."

Alex decided there was no point in wishing them out of existence. They looked harmless, anyway—to everything except his sanity. He crawled to his feet, his bones seeming to grate against each other, and faced the natives.

The first expedition, he remembered, had reported two intelligent races, Hokas and Slissii, on this planet. And these must be Hokas. For small blessings, give praises! There were two of them, almost identical to the untrained Terrestrial eye: about a meter tall, tubby and golden-furred, with round blunt-muzzled heads and small black eyes. Except for the stubby-fingered hands, they resembled nothing so much as giant teddy bears.

The first expedition had, however, said nothing about their speaking English with a drawl. Or about their wearing the dress of Earth's nineteenth-century West.

All the American historical stereofilms he had ever seen gabbled in Alex's mind as he assessed their costumes. They wore—let's see, start at the top and work down and try to keep your reason in the process—ten-gallon hats with brims wider than their own shoulders, tremendous red bandanas, checked shirts of riotous hues, levis, enormously flaring chaps, and high-heeled boots with outsize spurs. Two sagging cartridge belts on each plump waist supported heavy Colt six-shooters which almost dragged on the ground.

One of the natives was standing before the Earthman, the other was mounted nearby, holding the reins of the first one's —well—his animal. The beasts were about the size of a pony, and had four hoofed feet . . . also whiplike tails, long necks with beaked heads, and scaly green hides. But of course, thought Alex wildly, of course they bore Western saddles with lassos at the horns. Of course. Who ever heard of a cowboy without a lasso?

"Wa'l, I see yo're awake," said the standing Hoka. "Howdy, stranger, howdy." He extended his hand. "I'm Tex and my pardner here is Monty."

"Pleased to meet you," mumbled Alex, shaking hands in a dreamlike fashion. "I'm Alexander Jones."

"I dunno," said Monty dubiously. "He ain't named like no human."

"Are yo' human, Alexanderjones?" asked Tex.

The spaceman got a firm grip on himself and said, spacing his words with care: "I am Ensign Alexander Jones of the Terrestrial Interstellar Survey Service, attached to HMS *Draco*." Now it was the Hokas who looked lost. He added wearily: "In other words, I'm from Earth. I'm human. Satisfied?"

"I s'pose," said Monty, still doubtful. "But we'd better take yo' back to town with us an' let Slick talk to yo'. He'll know more about it. Cain't take no chances in these hyar times."

"Why not?" said Tex, with a surprising bitterness. "What we got to lose, anyhow? But come on, Alexanderjones, we'll go on to town. We shore don't want to be found by no Injun war parties."

"Injuns?" asked Alex.

"Shore. They're comin', you know. We'd better sashay along. My pony'll carry double."

Alex was not especially happy at riding a nervous reptile in a saddle built for a Hoka. Fortunately, the race was sufficiently broad in the beam for their seats to have spare room for a slim Earthman. The "pony" trotted ahead at a surprisingly fast and steady pace. Reptiles on Toka—so-called by the first expedition from the word for "earth" in the language of the most advanced Hoka society—seemed to be more highly evolved than in the Solar System. A fully developed four-chambered heart and a better nervous system made them almost equivalent to mammals.

Nevertheless, the creature stank.

Alex looked around. The prairie was just as big and bare, his ship just as far away.

" 'Tain't none o' my business, I reckon," said Tex, "but how'd yo' happen to be hyar?"

"It's a long story," said Alex absent-mindedly. His thoughts at the moment were chiefly about food. "The *Draco* was out on Survey, mapping new planetary systems, and our course happened to take us close to this star, your sun, which we knew had been visited once before. We thought we'd look in and check on conditions, as well as resting ourselves on an Earth-type world. I was one of the several who went out in scout-boats to skim over this continent. Something went wrong, my engines failed and I barely escaped with my life. I parachuted out, and as bad luck would have it, my boat crashed in a river. So—well—due to various other circumstances, I just had to start hiking back toward my ship."

"Won't yore pardners come after yo'?"

"Sure, they'll search—but how likely are they to find a shattered wreck on the bottom of a river, with half a continent to investigate? I could, perhaps have grubbed a big SOS in the soil and hoped it would be seen from the air, but what with the necessity of hunting food and all . . . well, I figured my best chance was to keep moving. But now I'm hungry enough to eat a . . . a buffalo."

"Ain't likely to have buffalo meat in town," said the Hoka imperturbably. "But we got good T-bone steaks."

"Oh," said Alex.

"Yo' wouldn't'a lasted long, hoofin' it," said Monty. "Ain't got no gun."

"No, thanks to—never mind!" said Alex. "I thought I'd try to make a bow and some arrows."

"Bow an' arrers—Say!" Monty squinted suspiciously at him. "What yo' been doin' around the Injuns?"

"I ain't—I haven't been near any Injuns, dammit!"

"Bows an' arrers is Injun weapons, stranger."

"I wish they was," mourned Tex. "We didn't have no trouble back when only Hokas had six-guns. But now the Injuns got 'em too, it's all up with us." A tear trickled down his button nose.

If the cowboys are teddy bears, thought Alex, *then who— or what—are the Indians?*

"It's lucky for yo' me an' Tex happened to pass by," said Monty. "We was out to see if we couldn't round up a few more steers afore the Injuns get here. No such luck, though. The greenskins done rustled 'em all."

Greenskins! Alex remembered a detail in the report of the first expedition: two intelligent races, the mammalian Hokas and the reptilian Slissii. And the Slissii, being stronger and more warlike, preyed on the Hokas—

"Are the Injuns Slissii?" he asked.

"Wa'l, they're ornery, at least," said Monty.

"I mean . . . well . . . are they big tall beings, bigger than I am, but walking sort of stooped over . . . tails and fangs and green skins, and their talk is full of hissing noises?"

"Why, shore. What else?" Monty shook his head, puzzled. "If yo're a human, how come yo' don't even know what a Injun is?"

They had been plop-plopping toward a large and noisy dust cloud. As they neared, Alex saw the cause, a giant herd of— uh—

"Longhorn steers," explained Monty.

Well . . . yes . . . one long horn apiece, on the snout. But at least the red-haired, short-legged, barrel-bodied "cattle" were mammals. Alex made out brands on the flanks of some. The entire herd was being urged along by fast-riding Hoka cowboys.

"That's the X Bar X outfit," said Tex. "The Lone Rider

decided to try an' drive 'em ahead o' the Injuns. But I'm afeered the greenskins'll catch up with him purty soon."

"He cain't do much else," answered Monty. "All the ranchers, just about, are drivin' their stock off the range. There just ain't any place short o' the Devil's Nose whar we can make a stand. I shore don't intend tryin' to stay in town an' hold off the Injuns, an' I don't think nobody else does either, in spite o' Slick an' the Lone Rider wantin' us to."

"Hey," objected Alex. "I thought you said the, er, Lone Rider was fleeing. Now you say he wants to fight. Which is it?"

"Oh, the Lone Rider what owns the X Bar X is runnin', but the Lone Rider o' the Lazy T wants to stay. So do the Lone Rider o' Buffalo Stomp, the Really Lone Rider, an' the Loneliest Rider, but I'll bet they changes their minds when the Injuns gets as close to them as the varmints is to us right now."

Alex clutched his head to keep it from flying off his shoulders. "How many Lone Riders are there, anyway?" he shouted.

"How should I know?" shrugged Monty. "I knows at least ten myself. I gotta say," he added exasperatedly, "that English shore ain't got as many names as the old Hoka did. It gets gosh-awful tiresome to have a hundred other Montys around, or yell for Tex an' be asked which one."

They passed the bawling herd at a jog trot and topped a low rise. Beyond it lay a village, perhaps a dozen small frame houses and a single rutted street lined with square-built false-fronted structures. The place was jammed with Hokas—on foot, mounted, in covered wagons and buggies—refugees from the approaching Injuns, Alex decided. As he was carried down the hill, he saw a clumsily lettered sign:

WELCOME TO CANYON GULCH
Pop. Weekdays 212
Saturdays 1000

"We'll take yo' to Slick," said Monty above the hubbub. "He'll know what to do with yo'."

They forced their ponies slowly through the swirling, pressing, jabbering throng. The Hokas seemed to be a highly excitable race, given to arm-waving and shouting at the top of their lungs. There was no organization whatsoever to the evacuation, which proceeded slowly with its traffic tie-ups, arguments, gossip exchange, and exuberant pistol shooting into the air. Quite a few ponies and wagons stood deserted before the saloons, which formed an almost solid double row along the street.

Alex tried to remember what there had been in the report of the first expedition. It was a brief report, the ship had only been on Toka for a couple of months. But—yes—the Hokas were described as friendly, merry, amazingly quick to learn . . . and hopelessly inefficient. Only their walled seacoast towns, in a state of bronze-age technology, had been able to stand off the Slissii; otherwise the reptiles were slowly but steadily conquering the scattered ursinoid tribes. A Hoka fought bravely when he was attacked, but shoved all thought of the enemy out of his cheerful mind whenever the danger was not immediately visible. It never occurred to the Hokas to band together in a massed offensive against the Slissii; such a race of individualists could never have formed an army anyway.

A nice, but rather ineffectual little people. Alex felt somewhat smug about his own height, his dashing spaceman's uniform, and the fighting, slugging, persevering human spirit which had carried man out to the stars. He felt like an elder brother.

He'd have to do something about this situation, give these comic-opera creatures a hand. Which might also involve a promotion for Alexander Braithwaite Jones, since Earth wanted a plentiful supply of planets with friendly dominant species, and the first report on the Injuns—Slissii, blast it!—made it unlikely that they could ever get along with mankind.

A. Jones, hero. Maybe then Tanni and I can—

He grew aware that a fat, elderly Hoka was gaping at him, together with the rest of Canyon Gulch. This particular one wore a large metal star pinned to his vest.

"Howdy, sheriff," said Tex, and snickered.

"Howdy, Tex, old pal," said the sheriff obsequiously. "An' my good old sidekick Monty too. Howdy, howdy, gents! Who's this hyar stranger—not a *human*?"

"Yep, that's what he says. Whar's Slick?"

"Which Slick?"

"*The* Slick, yo'—yo' sheriff!"

The fat Hoka winced. "I think he's in the backroom o' the Paradise Saloon," he said. And humbly: "Uh, Tex . . . Monty . . . yo'll remember yore old pal come *ee*-lection day, won't yo'?"

"Reckon we might," said Tex genially. "Yo' been sheriff long enough."

"Oh, thank yo', boys, thank yo'! If only the others will have yore kind hearts—" The eddying crowd swept the sheriff away.

"What off Earth?" exclaimed Alex. "What the *hell* was he trying to get you to do?"

"Vote ag'in him come the next *ee*-lection, o' course," said Monty.

"Against him? But the sheriff . . . he runs the town . . . maybe?"

Tex and Monty looked bewildered. "Now I really wonder if yo're human after all," said Tex. "Why, the humans themselves taught us the sheriff is the dumbest man in town. Only we don't think it's fair a man should have to be called that all his life, so we chooses him once a y'ar."

"Buck there has been *ee*-lected sheriff three times runnin'," said Monty. "He's *really* dumb!"

"But who is this Slick?" cried Alex a trifle wildly.

"The town gambler, o' course."

"What have I got to do with a town gambler?"

Tex and Monty exchanged glances. "Look, now," said Monty with strained patience, "we done allowed for a lot with yo'. But when yo' don't even know what the officer is what runs a town, that's goin' just a little too far."

"Oh," said Alex. "A kind of city manager, then."

"Yo're plumb loco," said Monty firmly. "*Ever'body* knows a town is run by a town gambler!"

§

Slick wore the uniform of his office: tight pants, a black coat, a checked vest, a white shirt with wing collar and string tie, a diamond stickpin, a Derringer in one pocket and a pack of cards in the other. He looked tired and harried; he must have been under a tremendous strain in the last few days, but he welcomed Alex with eager volubility and led him into an office furnished in vaguely nineteenth-century style. Tex and Monty came along, barring the door against the trailing, chattering crowds.

"We'll rustle up some sandwiches for yo'," beamed Slick. He offered Alex a vile purple cigar of some local weed, lit one himself, and sat down behind the rolltop desk. "Now," he said, "when can we get help from yore human friends?"

"Not soon, I'm afraid," said Alex. "The *Draco* crew doesn't know about this. They'll be spending all their time flying around in search of me. Unless they chance to find me here, which isn't likely, they won't even learn about the Injun war."

"How long they figger to be here?"

"Oh, they'll wait at least a month before giving me up for dead and leaving the planet."

"We can get yo' to the seacoast in that time, by hard ridin', but it'd mean takin' a shortcut through some territory which the Injuns is between us and it." Slick paused courteously while Alex untangled that one. "Yo'd hardly have a chance to sneak through. So, it looks like the only way we can get yo' to yore friends is to beat the Injuns. Only we can't beat the Injuns without help from yore friends."

Gloom.

To change the subject, Alex tried to learn some Hoka history. He succeeded beyond expectations, Slick proving surprisingly intelligent and well informed.

The first expedition had landed thirty-odd years ago. At the time, its report had drawn little Earthly interest; there were so many new planets in the vastness of the galaxy. Only now, with the *Draco* as a forerunner, was the League making any attempt to organize this frontier section of space.

The first Earthmen had been met with eager admiration by the Hoka tribe near whose village they landed. The autochthones were linguistic adepts, and between their natural abilities and modern psychography had learned English in a matter of days. To them, the humans were almost gods, though like most primitives they were willing to frolic with their deities.

Came the fatal evening. The expedition had set up an outdoor stereoscreen to entertain itself with films. Hitherto the Hokas had been interested but rather puzzled spectators. Now, tonight, at Wesley's insistence, an old film was reshown. It was a Western.

Most spacemen develop hobbies on their long voyages. Wesley's was the old American West. But he looked at it through romantic lenses, he had a huge stack of novels and magazines but very little factual material.

The Hokas saw the film and went wild.

The captain finally decided that their delirious, ecstatic reaction was due to this being something they could understand. Drawing-room comedies and interplanetary adventures meant little to them in terms of their own experience, but here was a country like their own, heroes who fought savage enemies, great herds of animals, gaudy costumes—

And it occurred to the captain and to Wesley that this race could find very practical use for certain elements of the old Western culture. The Hokas had been farmers, scratching a meager living out of prairie soil never meant to be plowed; they went about on foot, their tools were bronze and stone— they could do much better for themselves, given some help.

The ship's metallurgists had had no trouble reconstructing the old guns, Colt and Derringer and carbine. The Hokas had to be taught how to smelt iron, make steel and gunpowder, handle lathes and mills; but here again, native quickness and psychographic instruction combined to make them learn easily. Likewise they leaped at the concept of domesticating the wild beasts they had hitherto herded.

Before the ship left, Hokas were breaking "ponies" to the saddle and rounding up "longhorns." They were making treaties with the more civilized agricultural and maritime cities of the coast, arranging to ship meat in exchange for wood, grain, and manufactured goods. And they were gleefully slaughtering every Slissii warband that came against them.

As a final step, just before he left, Wesley gave his collection of books and magazines to the Hokas.

None of this had been in the ponderous official report Alex read: only the notation that the ursinoids had been shown steel metallurgy, the use of chemical weapons, and the benefits of certain economic forms. It had been hoped that with this aid they could subdue the dangerous Slissii, so that if man finally started coming here regularly, he wouldn't have a war on his hands.

Alex could fill in the rest. Hoka enthusiasm had run wild. The new way of life was, after all, very practical and well adapted to the plains—so why not go all the way, be just like the human godlings in every respect? Talk English with the stereofilm accent, adopt human names, human dress, human mannerisms, dissolve the old tribal organizations and replace them with ranches and towns—it followed very naturally. And it was so much more fun.

The books and magazines couldn't circulate far; most of the new gospel went by word of mouth. Thus certain oversimplifications crept in.

Three decades passed. The Hokas matured rapidly; a second generation which had been born to Western ways was already prominent in the population. The past was all but forgotten. The Hokas spread westward across the plains, driving the Slissii before them.

Until, of course, the Slissii learned how to make firearms

too. Then, with their greater military talent, they raised an army of confederated tribes and proceeded to shove the Hokas back. This time they would probably continue till they had sacked the very cities of the coast. The bravery of individual Hokas was no match for superior numbers better organized.

And one of the Injun armies was now roaring down on Canyon Gulch. It could not be many kilometers away, and there was nothing to stop it. The Hokas gathered their families and belongings from the isolated ranch houses and fled. But with typical inefficiency, most of the refugees fled no further than this town; then they stopped and discussed whether to make a stand or hurry onward, and meanwhile they had just one more little drink. . . .

§

"You mean you haven't even *tried* to fight?" asked Alex.

"What could we do?" answered Slick. "Half the folks 'ud be ag'in the idea an' wouldn't have nothin' to do with it. Half o' those what did come would each have their own little scheme, an' when we didn't follow it they'd get mad an' walk off. That don't leave none too many."

"Couldn't you, as the leader, think of some compromise— some plan which would satisfy everybody?"

"O' course not," said Slick stiffly. "My own plan is the only right one."

"Oh, Lord!" Alex bit savagely at the sandwich in his hand. The food had restored his strength and the fluid fire the Hokas called whiskey had given him a warm, courageous glow.

"The basic trouble is, your people just don't know how to arrange a battle," he said. "Humans do."

"Yo're a powerful fightin' outfit," agreed Slick. There was an adoration in his beady eyes which Alex had complacently noticed on most of the faces in town. He decided he rather liked it. But a demi-god has his obligations.

"What you need is a leader whom everyone will follow without question," he went on. "Namely me."

"Yo' mean—" Slick drew a sharp breath. "*Yo'?*"

Alex nodded briskly. "Am I right, that the Injuns are all on foot? Yes? Good. Then I know, from Earth history, what to do. There must be several thousand Hoka males around, and they all have some kind of firearms. The Injuns won't be prepared for a fast, tight cavalry charge. It'll split their army wide open."

"Wa'l, I'll be hornswoggled," murmured Slick. Even Tex and Monty looked properly awed.

Suddenly Slick began turning handsprings about the office. "Yahoo!" he cried. "I'm a rootin', tootin' son of a gun, I was born with a pistol in each hand an' I teethed on rattlesnakes!" He did a series of cartwheels. "My daddy was a catamount and my mother was a alligator. I can run faster backward than anybody else can run forrad, I can jump over the outermost moon with one hand tied behind me, I can fill an inside straight every time I draw, an' if any sidewinder here says it ain't so I'll fill him so full o' lead they'll mine him!"

"What the hell?" gasped Alex, dodging.

"The old human war cry," explained Tex, who had apparently resigned himself to his hero's peculiar ignorances.

"Let's go!" whooped Slick, and threw open the office door. A tumultuous crowd surged outside. The gambler filled his lungs and roared squeakily:

"Saddle yore hosses, gents, an' load yore six-guns! We got us a human, an' he's gonna lead us all out to wipe the Injuns off the range!"

The Hokas cheered till the false fronts quivered around them, danced, somersaulted, and fired their guns into the air. Alex shook Slick and wailed: "—no, no, you bloody fool, not *now*! We have to study the situation, send out scouts, make a plan—"

Too late. His impetuous admirers swept him out into the street. He couldn't be heard above the falsetto din, he tried to keep his footing and was only vaguely aware of anything else. Someone gave him a six-shooter, he strapped it on as if in a dream. Someone else gave him a lasso, and he made out the voice: "Rope yoreself a bronc, Earthman, an' let's go!"

"Rope—" Alex grew groggily aware that there was a corral just behind the saloon. The half-wild reptile ponies galloped about inside it, excited by the noise. Hokas were deftly whirling their lariats forth to catch their personal mounts.

"Go ahead!" urged the voice. "Ain't got no time to lose."

Alex studied the cowboy nearest him. Lassoing didn't look so hard. You held the rope here and here, then you swung the noose around your head like *this*—

He pulled and came crashing to the ground. Through whirling dust, he saw that he had lassoed himself.

Tex pulled him to his feet and dusted him off. "I . . . I don't ride herd at home," he mumbled. Tex made no reply.

"I got a bronc for yo'," cried another Hoka, reeling in his lariat. "A real spirited mustang!"

Alex looked at the pony. It looked back. It had an evilly glittering little eye. At the risk of making a snap judgment, he decided he didn't like it very much. There might be personality conflicts between him and it.

"Come on, let's git goin'!" cried Slick impatiently. He was astraddle a beast which still bucked and reared, but he hardly seemed to notice.

Alex shuddered, closed his eyes, wondered what he had done to deserve this, and wobbled over to the pony. Several Hokas had joined to saddle it for him. He climbed aboard. The Hokas released the animal. There was a personality conflict.

Alex had a sudden feeling of rising and spinning on a meteor that twisted beneath him. He grabbed for the saddle horn. The front feet came down with a ten-gee thump and he lost his stirrups. Something on the order of a nuclear shell seemed to explode in his vicinity.

Though it came up and hit him with unnecessary hardness, he had never known anything so friendly as the ground just then.

"Oof!" said Alex and lay still.

A shocked, unbelieving silence fell on the Hokas. The human hadn't been able to use a rope—now he had set a new record for the shortest time in a saddle—*what sort of human was this, anyway?*

Alex sat up and looked into a ring of shocked fuzzy faces. He gave them a weak smile. "I'm not a horseman either," he said.

"What the hell are yo', then?" stormed Monty. "Yo' cain't rope, yo' cain't ride, yo' cain't talk right, yo' cain't shoot—"

"Now hold on!" Alex climbed to somewhat unsteady feet. "I admit I'm not used to a lot of things here, because we do it differently on Earth. But I can out-shoot any man . . . er, any Hoka of you any day in the week and twice on Sundays!"

Some of the natives looked happy again, but Monty only sneered. "Yeah?"

"Yeah. I'll prove it." Alex looked about for a suitable target. For a change, he had no worries. He was one of the best ray-thrower marksmen in the Fleet. "Throw up a coin. I'll plug it through the middle."

The Hokas began looking awed. Alex gathered that they weren't very good shots by any standards but their own. Slick beamed, took a silver dollar from his pocket, and spun it into the air. Alex drew and fired.

Unfortunately, ray-throwers don't have recoil. Revolvers do.

Alex went over on his back. The bullet broke a window in the Last Chance Bar & Grill.

The Hokas began to laugh. It was a bitter kind of merriment.

"Buck!" cried Slick. "Buck . . . yo' thar, sheriff . . . c'mere!"

"Yes, sir, Mister Slick, sir?"

"I don't think we need yo' for sheriff no longer, Buck. I think we just found ourselves another one. Gimme yore badge!"

When Alex regained his feet, the star gleamed on his tunic. And, of course, his proposed counterattack had been forgotten.

§

He mooched glumly into Pizen's Saloon. During the past few hours, the town had slowly drained itself of refugees as the Injuns came horribly closer; but there were still a few delaying for one more drink. Alex was looking for such company.

Being official buffoon wasn't too bad in itself. The Hokas weren't cruel to those whom the gods had afflicted. But—well —he had just ruined human prestige on this continent. The Service wouldn't appreciate that.

Not that he would be seeing much of the Service in the near future. He couldn't possibly reach the *Draco* now before she left—without passing through territory held by the same Injuns whose army was advancing on Canyon Gulch. It might be years till another expedition landed. He might even be marooned here for life. Though come to think of it, that wouldn't be a lot worse than the disgrace which would attend his return.

Gloom.

"Here, sheriff, let me buy yo' a drink," said a voice at his elbow.

"Thanks," said Alex. The Hokas did have the pleasant rule that the sheriff was always treated when he entered a saloon. He had been taking heavy advantage of the custom, though it didn't seem to lighten his depression much.

The Hoka beside him was a very aged specimen, toothless and creaky. "I'm from Childish way," he introduced himself. "They call me the Childish Kid. Howdy, sheriff."

Alex shook hands, dully.

They elbowed their way to the bar. Alex had to stoop under Hoka ceilings, but otherwise the rococo fittings were earnestly faithful to their fictional prototypes—including a small stage where three scantily clad Hoka females were going through a song-and-dance number while a bespectacled male pounded a rickety piano.

The Childish Kid leered. "I know those gals," he sighed. "Some fillies, hey? Stacked, don't yo' think?"

"Uh . . . yes," agreed Alex. Hoka females had four mammaries apiece. "Quite."

"Zunami an' Goda an' Torigi, that's their names. If I warn't so danged old—"

"How come they have, er, non-English names?" inquired Alex.

"We had to keep the old Hoka names for our wimmin," said the Childish Kid. He scratched his balding head. "It's bad enough with the men, havin' a hundred Hopalongs in the same county . . . but how the hell can yo' tell yore wimmin apart when they're all named Jane?"

"We have some named 'Hey, you' as well," said Alex grimly. "And a lot more called 'Yes, dear.' "

His head was beginning to spin. This Hoka brew was potent stuff.

Nearby stood two cowboys, arguing with alcoholic loudness. They were typical Hokas, which meant that to Alex their tubby forms were scarcely to be distinguished from each other. "I know them two, they're from my old outfit," said the Childish Kid. "That one's Slim, an' t'other's Shorty."

"Oh," said Alex.

Brooding over his glass, he listened to the quarrel for lack of anything better to do. It had degenerated to the name-calling stage. "Careful what yo' say, Slim," said Shorty, trying to narrow his round little eyes. "I'm a powerful dangerous hombre."

"You ain't no powerful dangerous hombre," sneered Slim.

"I am so too a powerful dangerous hombre!" squeaked Shorty.

"Yo're a fathead what ought to be kicked by a jackass," said Slim, "an' I'm just the one what can do it."

"When yo' call me that," said Shorty, "smile!"

"I said yo're a fathead what ought to be kicked by a jack-ass," repeated Slim, and smiled.

Suddenly the saloon was full of the roar of pistols. Sheer reflex threw Alex to the floor. A ricocheting slug whanged nastily by his ear. The thunder barked again and again. He hugged the floor and prayed.

Silence came. Reeking smoke swirled through the air. Hokas

crept from behind tables and the bar and resumed drinking, casually. Alex looked for the corpses. He saw only Slim and Shorty, putting away their emptied guns.

"Wa'l, that's that," said Shorty. "I'll buy this round."

"Thanks, pardner," said Slim. "I'll get the next one."

Alex bugged his eyes at the Childish Kid. "Nobody was hurt!" he chattered hysterically.

"O' course not," said the ancient Hoka. "Slim an' Shorty is old pals." He spread his hands. "Kind o' a funny human custom, that. It don't make much sense that every man should sling lead at every other man once a month. But I reckon maybe it makes 'em braver, huh?"

"Uh-huh," said Alex.

Others drifted over to talk with him. Opinion seemed about equally divided over whether he wasn't a human at all or whether humankind simply wasn't what the legends had cracked it up to be. But in spite of their disappointment, they bore him no ill will and stood him drinks. Alex accepted thirstily. He couldn't think of anything else to do.

It might have been an hour later, or two hours or ten, that Slick came into the saloon. His voice rose over the hubbub: "A scout just brung me the latest word, gents. The Injuns ain't no more'n five miles away an' comin' fast. We'll all have to git a move on."

The cowboys swallowed their drinks, smashed their glasses, and boiled from the building in a wave of excitement. "Gotta calm the boys down," muttered the Childish Kid, "or we could git a riot." With great presence of mind, he shot out the lights.

"Yo' fool!" bellowed Slick. "It's broad daylight outside!"

Alex lingered aimlessly by the saloon, until the gambler tugged at his sleeve. "We're short o' cowhands an' we got a big herd to move," ordered Slick. "Get yoreself a *gentle* pony an' see if yo' can help."

"Okay," hiccoughed Alex. It would be good to know he was doing something useful, however little. Maybe he would be defeated at the next election.

He traced a wavering course to the corral. Someone led forth a shambling wreck of a mount, too old to be anything but docile. Alex groped after the stirrup. It evaded him. "C'mere," he said sharply. "C'mere, shtirrup. Ten-*shun!* For'ard marsh!"

"Here yo' are." A Hoka who flickered around the edges . . . ghost Hoka? Hoka Superior? the Hoka after Hoka? . . . assisted him into the saddle. "By Pecos Bill, yo're drunk as a skunk!"

"No," said Alex. "I am shober. It's all Toka whish ish drunk. So only drunks on Toka ish shober. Tha's right. Y'unnershtan'? Only shober men on Toka ish uh drunks—"

His pony floated through a pink mist in some or other direction. "I'm a lo-o-o-one cowboy!" sang Alex. "I'm thuh loneliesh lone cowboy in these here parts."

He grew amorphously aware of the herd. The cattle were nervous, they rolled their eyes and lowed and pawed the ground. A small band of Hokas galloped around them, swearing, waving their hats, trying to get the animals going in the right path.

"I'm an ol' cowhand, from thuh Rio Grande!" bawled Alex.

"Not so loud!" snapped a Tex-Hoka. "These critters are spooky enough as it is."

"You wanna get 'em goin', don'cha?" answered Alex. "We gotta get going. The greenskins are coming. Simple to get going. Like this. See?"

He drew his six-shooter, fired into the air, and let out the loudest screech he had in him. "Yahoo!"

"*Yo' crazy fool!*"

"Yahoo!" Alex plunged toward the herd, shooting and shouting. "Ride 'em, cowboy! Get along, little dogies! Yippee!"

The herd, of course, stampeded.

Like a red tide, it suddenly broke past the thin Hoka line. The riders scattered, there was death in those thousands of hoofs, their universe was filled with roaring and rushing and thunder. The earth shook!

"Yahoo!" caroled Alexander Jones. He rode behind the long-horns, still shooting. "Git along, git along! Hi-yo, Silver!"

"Oh, my God," groaned Slick. "Oh, my God! The tumble-weed-headed idiot's got 'em stampeded *straight toward the Injuns*—"

"After 'em!" shouted a Hopalong-Hoka. "Mebbe we can still turn the herd! We cain't let the Injuns git all that beef!"

"An' we'll have a little necktie party, too," said a Lone Rider-Hoka. "I'll bet that thar Alexanderjones is a Injun spy planted to do this very job."

The cowboys spurred their mounts. A Hoka-brain had no room for two thoughts at once. If they were trying to head off a stampede, the fact that they were riding full tilt toward an overwhelming enemy simply did not occur to them.

"Whoopee-ti-yi yo-o-o-o!" warbled Alex, somewhere in the storm of dust.

Caught by the peculiar time-sense of intoxication, he seemed almost at once to burst over a long low hill. And beyond were the Slissii.

The reptile warriors went afoot, not being built for riding—but they could outrun a Hoka pony. Their tyrannosaurian forms were naked, save for war paint and feathers such as primitives throughout the galaxy wear, but they were armed with guns as well as lances, bows, and axes. Their host formed a great compact mass, tightly disciplined to the rhythm of the thudding signal drums. There were thousands of them . . . and a hundred cowboys, at most, galloped blindly toward their ranks.

Alex saw none of this. Being behind the stampede, he didn't see it hit the Injun army.

Nobody really did. The catastrophe was just too big.

When the Hokas arrived on the scene, the Injuns—such of them as had not simply been mashed flat—were scattered over the entire visible prairie. Slick wondered if they would ever stop running.

"At 'em, boys!" he yelled. "Go mop 'em up!"

The Hoka band sped forward. A few small Injun groups

sounded their war-hisses and tried to rally for a stand, but it was too late, they were too demoralized, the Hokas cut them down. Others were chased as they fled, lassoed and hog-tied by wildly cheering teddy bears.

Presently Tex rode up to Slick. Dragging behind his pony at a lariat's end was a huge Injun, still struggling and cursing. "I think I got their chief," he reported.

The town gambler nodded happily. "Yep, you have. He's wearin' a high chief's paint. Swell! With him for a hostage, we can make t'other Injuns talk turkey—not that they're gonna bother this hyar country for a long time to come."

As a matter of fact, Canyon Gulch has entered the military textbooks with Cannae, Waterloo, and Xfisthgung as an example of total and crushing victory.

Slowly, the Hokas began to gather about Alex. The old utter awe shone in their eyes.

"*He* done it," whispered Monty. "All the time he was playin' dumb, he knew a way to stop the Injuns—"

"Yo' mean, make 'em bite the dust," corrected Slick solemnly.

"Bite the dust," agreed Monty. "He done it single-handed! Gents, I reckon we should'a knowed better'n to go mistrustin' o' a . . . *human!*"

Alex swayed in the saddle. A violent sickness gathered itself within him. And he reflected that he had caused a stampede, lost an entire herd of cattle, sacrificed all Hoka faith in the Terrestrial race for all time to come. If the natives hanged him, he thought grayly, it was no more than he deserved.

He opened his eyes and looked into Slick's adoring face.

"Yo' saved us," said the little Hoka. He reached out and took the sheriff's badge off Alex's tunic. Then, gravely, he handed over his Derringer and playing cards. "Yo' saved us all, human. So, as long as yo're here, yo're the town gambler o' Canyon Gulch."

Alex blinked. He looked around. He saw the assembled Hokas, and the captive Slissii, and the trampled field of ruin . . . why, why—they had won!

Now he could get to the *Draco*. With human assistance, the

Hoka race could soon force a permanent peace settlement on their ancient foes. And Ensign Alexander Braithwaite Jones was a hero.

"Saved you?" he muttered. His tongue still wasn't under very close control. "Oh. Saved you. Yes, I did, didn't I? Saved you. Nice of me." He waved a hand. "No, no. Don't mention it. *Noblesse oblige*, and all that sort of thing."

An acute pain in his unaccustomed gluteal muscles spoiled the effect. He groaned. "I'm walking back to town. I won't be able to sit down for a week as it is!"

And the rescuer of Canyon Gulch dismounted, missed the stirrup, and fell flat on his face.

"Yo' know," murmured someone thoughtfully, "maybe that's the way humans get off their hosses. Maybe we should all—"

POUL ANDERSON

Day of Burning

For who knows how long, the star had orbited quietly in the wilderness between Betelgeuse and Rigel. It was rather more massive than average—about half again as much as Sol—and shone with corresponding intensity, white-hot, corona and prominences a terrible glory. But there are no few like it. A ship of the first Grand Survey noted its existence. However, the crew were more interested in a neighbor sun which had planets and could not linger long in that system either. The galaxy is too big; their purpose was to get some hint about this spiral arm which we inhabit. Thus certain spectroscopic omens escaped their notice.

No one returned thither for a pair of centuries. Technic civilization had more than it could handle, let alone compre- hend, in the millions of stars closer to home. So the fact remained unsuspected that this one was older than normal for its type in its region, must indeed have wandered in from other parts. Not that it was very ancient, astronomically speaking. But the great childless suns evolve fast and strangely.

By chance, though, a scout from the Polesotechnic League, exploring far in search of new markets, was passing within a light-year when the star exploded.

Say instead—insofar as simultaneity has any meaning across interstellar distances—that the death agony had occurred some months before. Ever more fierce, thermonuclear reaction had burned up the last hydrogen at the center. Unbalanced by radiation pressure, the outer layers collapsed beneath their own weight. Forces were released which triggered a wholly different order of atomic fusions. New elements came into being, not only those which may be found in the planets but also the short-lived transuranics; for a while, technetium itself dominated that anarchy. Neutrons and neutrinos flooded forth, carrying with them the last balancing energy. Compression turned into catastrophe. At the brief peak, the supernova was as radiant as its entire galaxy.

So close, the ship's personnel would have died had she not been in hyperdrive. They did not remain there. A dangerous amount of radiation was still touching them between quantum microjumps. And they were not equipped to study the phenomenon. It is rare; this was the first chance in our history to observe a new supernova. Earth was too remote to help. But the scientific colony at Catawrayannis could be reached fairly soon. It could dispatch laboratory craft.

Now to track in detail what was going to happen, considerable resources were demanded. Among these were a place where men could live and instruments be made to order as the need for them arose. Such things could not well be sent from the usual factories. By the time they arrived, the wave front carrying information about rapidly progressing events would have traveled so far that inverse-square enfeeblement would create maddening inaccuracies.

But a little beyond one parsec from the star—an excellent distance for observation over a period of years—was a G-type sun. One of its planets was terrestroid to numerous points of classification, both physically and biochemically. Survey records showed that the most advanced culture on it was at the verge of an industrial-scientific revolution. Ideal!

Except, to be sure, that Survey's information was less than sketchy and two centuries out of date.

§

"No."

Master Merchant David Falkayn stepped backward in startlement. The four nearest guards clutched at their pistols. Peripherally and profanely, Falkayn wondered what canon he had violated now.

"Beg, uh, beg pardon?" he said.

Morruchan Long-Ax, the Hand of the Vach Dathyr, leaned forward on his dais. He was big even for a Merseian, which meant that he overtopped Falkayn's rangy height by a good fifteen centimeters. Long, shoulder-flared orange robes and horned miter made his bulk almost overwhelming. Beneath them, he was approximately anthropoid, save for a slanting posture counterbalanced by the tail which, with his booted feet, made a tripod for him to sit on. The skin was green, faintly scaled, totally hairless. A spiky ridge ran from the top of his skull to the end of that tail. Instead of earflaps, he had deep convolutions in his head. But the face was manlike, in a heavy-boned fashion, and the physiology was essentially mammalian.

How familiar the mind was, behind those jet eyes, Falkayn did not know.

The harsh basso said: "You shall not take the rule of this world. If we surrendered the right and freehold they won, the God would cast back the souls of our ancestors to shriek at us."

Falkayn's glance flickered around. He had seldom felt so alone. The audience chamber of Castle Afon stretched high and gaunt, proportioned like nothing men had ever built. Curiously woven tapestries on the stone walls, between windows arched at both top and bottom, and battle banners hung from the rafters did little to stop echoes. The troopers lining the hall down to a hearth whose fire could have roasted an elephant wore armor and helmets with demon masks. The guns which they added to curved swords and barbed pikes did not seem out of place. Rather, what appeared unattainably far was a glimpse of ice-blue sky outside.

The air was chill with winter. Gravity was little higher than Terrestrial, but Falkayn felt it dragging at him.

He straightened. He had his own side arm, no chemical slug-thrower but an energy weapon. Adzel, abroad in the city, and Chee Lan, aboard the ship, were listening in via the transceiver on his wrist. And the ship had power to level all Ardaig. Morruchan must realize as much.

But he had to be made to cooperate.

Falkayn picked his words with care: "I pray forgiveness, Hand, if perchance in mine ignorance I misuse thy . . . uh . . . your tongue. Naught was intended save friendliness. Hither bring I news of peril impending, for the which ye must busk yourselves betimes less ye lose everything ye possess. My folk would fain show your folk what to do. So vast is the striving needed, and so scant the time, that perforce ye must take our counsel. Else can we be of no avail. But never will we act as conquerors. 'Twere not simply an evil deed, but 'twould boot us naught, whose trafficking is with many worlds. Nay, we would be brothers, come to help in a day of sore need."

Morruchan scowled and rubbed his chin. "Say on, then," he replied. "Frankly, I am dubious. You claim Valenderay is about to become a supernova—"

"Nay, Hand, I declare it hath already done so. The light therefrom will smite this planet in less than three years."

The time unit Falkayn actually used was Merseian, a trifle greater than Earth's. He sweated and swore to himself at the language problem. The Survey xenologists had got a fair grasp of Eriau in the several months they spent here, and Falkayn and his shipmates had acquired it by synapse transform while en route. But now it turned out that two hundred years back, Eriau had been in a state of linguistic overturn. He wasn't even pronouncing the vowels right.

He tried to update his grammar. "Would ye, uh, I mean if your desire is . . . if you want confirmation, we can take you or a trusty member of your household so near in our vessel that the starburst is beheld with living eyes."

"No doubt the scientists and poets will duel for a berth on that trip," Morruchan said in a dry voice. "But I believe you already. You yourself, your ship, and companions are proof." His tone sharpened. "At the same time, I am no Believer, imagining you half-divine because you come from outside.

Your civilization has a technological head start on mine, nothing else. A careful reading of the records from that other brief period when aliens dwelt among us shows they had no reason more noble than professional curiosity. And that was fitful; they left, and none ever returned. Until now.

"So: what do you want from us?"

Falkayn relaxed a bit. Morruchan seemed to be his own kind despite everything, not awestruck, not idealistic, not driven by some incomprehensible nonhuman motivation, but a shrewd and skeptical politician of a pragmatically oriented culture.

Seems to be, the man cautioned himself. *What do I really know about Merseia?*

§

Judging by observations made in orbit, radio monitoring, initial radio contact, and the ride here in an electric groundcar, this planet still held a jumble of societies, dominated by the one which surrounded the Wilwidh Ocean. Two centuries ago, local rule had been divided among aristocratic clans. He supposed that a degree of continental unification had since been achieved, for his request for an interview with the highest authority had got him to Ardaig and a confrontation with this individual. But could Morruchan speak for his entire species? Falkayn doubted it.

Nevertheless, you had to start somewhere.

"I shall be honest, Hand," he said. "My crew and I are come as naught but preparers of the way. Can we succeed, we will be rewarded with a share in whatever gain ensueth. For our scientists wish to use Merseia and its moons as bases wherefrom to observe the supernova through the next dozen years. Best for them would be if your folk could provide them with most of their needs, not alone food but such instruments as they tell you how to fashion. For this they will pay fairly; and in addition, ye will acquire knowledge.

"Yet first must we assure that there remaineth a Merseian civilization. To do that, we must wreak huge works. And ye will pay us for our toil and goods supplied to that end. The price will not be usurious, but it will allow us a profit. Out of it, we will buy whatever Merseian wares can be sold at home for further profit." He smiled. "Thus all may win and none need fear. The Polesotechnic League compriseth nor conquerors nor bandits, naught save merchant adventurers who seek to make their"—more or less—"honest living."

"*Hunh!*" Morruchan growled. "Now we bite down to the bone. When you first communicated and spoke about a supernova, my colleagues and I consulted the astronomers. We are not altogether savages here; we have at least gone as far as atomic power and interplanetary travel. Well, our astronomers said that such a star reaches a peak output about fifteen billion times as great as Korych. Is this right?"

"Close enough, Hand, if Korych be your own sun."

"The only nearby one which might burst in this manner is Valenderay. From your description, the brightest in the southern sky, you must be thinking of it, too."

Falkayn nodded, realized he wasn't sure if this gesture meant the same thing on Merseia, remembered it did, and said: "Aye, Hand."

"It sounded terrifying," Morruchan said, "until they pointed out that Valenderay is three and a half light-years distant. And this is a reach so enormous that no mind can swallow it. The radiation, when it gets to us, will equal a mere one-third of what comes daily from Korych. And in some fifty-five days" (Terrestrial) "it will have dwindled to half . . . and so on, until before long we see little except a bright nebula at night.

"True, we can expect troublesome weather, storms, torrential rains, perhaps some flooding if sufficient of the south polar ice cap melts. But that will pass. In any case, the center of civilization is here, in the northern hemisphere. It is also true that, at peak, there will be a dangerous amount of ultraviolet and X-radiation. But Merseia's atmosphere will block it.

"Thus." Morruchan leaned back on his tail and bridged the fingers of his oddly humanlike hands. "The peril you speak of scarcely exists. What do you really want?"

Falkayn's boyhood training as a nobleman's son on Hermes

rallied within him. He squared his shoulders. He was not unimpressive, a tall, fair-haired young man with blue eyes bright in a lean, high-cheekboned face. "Hand," he said gravely, "I perceive you have not yet had time to consult your folk who are wise in matters—"

And then he broke down. He didn't know the word for "electronic."

§

Morruchan refrained from taking advantage. Instead, the Merseian became quite helpful. Falkayn's rejoinder was halting, often interrupted while he and the other worked out what a phrase must be. But, in essence and in current language, what he said was:

"The Hand is correct as far as he goes. But consider what will follow. The eruption of a supernova is violent beyond imagining. Nuclear processes are involved, so complex that we ourselves don't yet understand them in detail. That's why we want to study them. But this much we do know, and your physicists will confirm it.

"As nuclei and electrons recombine in that supernal fireball, they generate asymmetrical magnetic pulses. Surely you know what this does when it happens in the detonation of an atomic weapon. Now think of it on a stellar scale. When those forces hit, they will blast straight through Merseia's own magnetic field, down to the very surface. Unshielded electric motors, generators, transmission lines . . . oh, yes, no doubt you have surge arrestors, but your circuit breakers will be tripped, then intolerable voltages will be induced, and the entire system will be wrecked. Likewise telecommunication lines. And computers. If you use transistors . . . ah, you do . . . the flipflop between p- and n-type conduction will wipe every memory bank, stop every operation in its tracks.

"Electrons, riding that magnetic pulse, will not be long in arriving. As they spiral in the planet's field, their synchrotron radiation will completely blanket whatever electronic apparatus you may have salvaged. Protons should be slower, pushed to about half the speed of light. Then come the alpha particles, then the heavier matter: year after year after year of cosmic fallout, most of it radioactive, to a total greater by orders of magnitude than any war could create before civilization was destroyed. Your planetary magnetism is no real shield. The majority of ions are energetic enough to get through. Nor is your atmosphere any good defense. Heavy nuclei, sleeting through it, will produce secondary radiation that does reach the ground.

"I do not say this planet will be wiped clean of life. But I do say that without ample advance preparation, it will suffer ecological disaster. Your species might or might not survive; but if you do, it will be as a few starveling primitives. The early breakdown of the electric systems on which your civilization is now dependent will have seen to that. Just imagine. Suddenly no more food moves into the cities. The dwellers go forth as a ravening horde. But if most of your farmers are as specialized as I suppose, they won't even be able to support themselves. Once fighting and famine have become general, no more medical service will be possible, and the pestilences will start. It will be like the aftermath of an all-out nuclear strike against a country with no civil defense. I gather you've avoided that on Merseia. But you certainly have theoretical studies of the subject, and—I have seen planets where it did happen.

"Long before the end, your colonies throughout this system will have been destroyed by the destruction of the apparatus that keeps the colonists alive. And for many years, no spaceship will be able to move.

"Unless you accept our help. We know how to generate forcescreens, small ones for machines, gigantic ones which can give an entire planet some protection. Not enough—but we also know how to insulate against the energies that get through. We know how to build engines and communications lines which are not affected. We know how to sow substances which protect life against hard radiation. We know how to restore mutated genes. In short, we have the knowledge you need for survival.

"The effort will be enormous. Most of it you must carry out yourselves. Our available personnel are too few, our lines of interstellar transportation too long. But we can supply engineers and organizers.

"To be blunt, Hand, you are very lucky that we learned of this in time, barely in time. Don't fear us. We have no ambitions toward Merseia. If nothing else, it lies far beyond our normal sphere of operation, and we have millions of more profitable planets much closer to home. We want to save you, because you are sentient beings. But it'll be expensive, and a lot of the work will have to be done by outfits like mine, which exist to make a profit. So, besides a scientific base, we want a reasonable economic return.

"Eventually, though, we'll depart. What you do then is your own affair. But you'll still have your civilization. You'll also have a great deal of new equipment and new knowledge. I think you're getting a bargain."

§

Falkayn stopped. For a while, silence dwelt in that long dim hall. He grew aware of odors which had never been on Earth or Hermes.

Morruchan said at last, slowly: "This must be thought on. I shall have to confer with my colleagues, and others. There are so many complications. For example, I see no good reason to do anything for the colony on Ronruad, and many excellent reasons for letting it die."

"What?" Falkayn's teeth clicked together. "Meaneth the Hand the next outward planet? But meseems faring goeth on apace throughout this system."

"Indeed, indeed," Morruchan said impatiently. "We depend on the other planets for a number of raw materials, like fissionables, or complex gases from the outer worlds. Ronruad, though, is of use only to the Gethfennu."

He spoke that word with such distaste that Falkayn post-

poned asking for a definition. "What recommendations I make
in my report will draw heavily upon the Hand's wisdom," the
human said.

"Your courtesy is appreciated," Morruchan replied—with
how much irony, Falkayn wasn't sure. He was taking the news
more coolly than expected. But then, he was of a different race
from men, and a soldierly tradition as well. "I hope that, for
now, you will honor the Vach Dathyr by guesting us."

"Well—" Falkayn hesitated. He had planned on returning
to his ship. But he might do better on the spot. The Survey
crew had found Merseian food nourishing to men, in fact
tasty. One report had waxed ecstatic about the ale.

"I thank the Hand."

"Good. I suggest you go to the chambers already prepared,
to rest and refresh yourself. With your leave, a messenger will
come presently to ask what he should bring you from your
vessel. Unless you wish to move it here?"

"Uh, best not . . . policy—" Falkayn didn't care to take
chances. The Merseians were not so far behind the League
that they couldn't spring a nasty surprise if they wanted to.

Morruchan raised the skin above his brow ridges but made
no comment. "You will dine with me and my councillors at
sunset," he said. They parted ceremoniously.

A pair of guards conducted Falkayn out through a series of
corridors and up a sweeping staircase whose banister was
carved into the form of a snake. At the end, he was ushered
into a suite. The rooms were spacious, their comfort-making
gadgetry not greatly below Technic standards. Reptile-skin car-
pets and animal skulls mounted on the crimson-draped walls
were a little disquieting, but what the hell. A balcony gave
on a view of the palace gardens, whose austere good taste was
reminiscent of Original Japanese, and on the city.

Ardaig was sizable, must hold two or three million souls.
This quarter was ancient, with buildings of gray stone fantastically turreted and battlemented. The hills which ringed it
were checkered by the estates of the wealthy. Snow lay white
and blue-shadowed between. Ramparted with tall modern

structures, the bay shone like gunmetal. Cargo ships moved in and out, a delta-wing jet whistled overhead. But he heard little traffic noise; nonessential vehicles were banned in the sacred Old Quarter.

"Wedhi is my name, Protector," said the short Merseian in the black tunic who had been awaiting him. "May he consider me his liege man, to do as he commands."

"My thanks," Falkayn said. "Thou mayest show me how one maketh use of facilities." He couldn't wait to see a bathroom designed for these people. "And then, mayhap, a tankard of beer, a textbook on political geography, and privacy for some hours."

"The Protector has spoken. If he will follow me?"

The two of them entered the adjoining chamber, which was furnished for sleeping. As if by accident, Wedhi's tail brushed the door. It wasn't automatic, merely hinged, and closed under the impact. Wedhi seized Falkayn's hand and pressed something into the palm. Simultaneously, he caught his lips between his teeth. A signal for silence?

With a tingle along his spine, Falkayn nodded and stuffed the bit of paper into a pocket.

When he was alone, he opened the note, hunched over in case of spy eyes. The alphabet hadn't changed.

Be wary, star dweller. Morruchan Long-Ax is no friend. If you can arrange for one of your company to come tonight in secret to the house at the corner of Triau Street and Victory Way which is marked by twined fylfots over the door, the truth shall be explained.

§

As darkness fell, the moon Neihevin rose full, Luna size and copper color, above eastward hills whose forests glistened with frost. Lythyr was already up, a small pale crescent. Rigel blazed in the heart of that constellation named the Spear Bearer.

Chee Lan turned from the viewscreen with a shiver and

an unladylike phrase. "But I am not equipped to do that," said the ship's computer.

"The suggestion was addressed to my gods," Chee answered.

She sat for a while, brooding on her wrongs. Ta-chih-chien-pih—O_2 Eridani A II or Cynthia to humans—felt even more distant than it was, warm ruddy sunlight and rustling leaves around treetop homes lost in time as well as space. Not only the cold outside daunted her. Those Merseians were so bloody *big!*

She herself was no larger than a medium-sized dog, though the bush of her tail added a good deal. Her arms, almost as long as her legs, ended in delicate six-fingered hands. White fur fluffed about her, save where it made a bluish mask across the green eyes and round, blunt-muzzled face. Seeing her for the first time, human females were apt to call her darling.

She bristled. Ears, whiskers, and hair stood erect. What was she—descendant of carnivores who chased their prey in five-meter leaps from branch to branch, xenobiologist by training, trade pioneer by choice, and pistol champion because she liked to shoot guns—what was she doing, feeling so much as respect for a gaggle of slewfooted bald barbarians? Mainly she was irritated. While standing by aboard the ship, she'd hoped to complete her latest piece of sculpture. Instead, she must hustle into that pustulant excuse for weather, and skulk through a stone garbage dump that its perpetrators called a city, and hear some yokel drone on for hours about some squabble between drunken cockroaches which he thought was politics . . . and pretend to take the whole farce seriously!

A narcotic cigarette soothed her, however ferocious the puffs in which she consumed it. "I guess the matter is important, at that," she murmured. "Fat commissions for me if the project succeeds."

"My programming is to the effect that our primary objective is humanitarian," said the computer. "Though I cannot find that concept in my data storage."

"Never mind, Muddlehead," Chee replied. Her mood had turned benign. "If you want to know, it relates to those constraints you have filed under Law and Ethics. But no concern of ours, this trip. Oh, the bleeding hearts do quack about Rescuing a Promising Civilization, as if the galaxy didn't have too chaos many civilizations already. Well, if they want to foot the bill, it's their taxes. They'll have to work with the League, because the League has most of the ships, which it won't hire out for nothing. And the League has to start with us, because trade pioneers are supposed to be experts in making first contacts and we happened to be the sole such crew in reach. Which is our good luck, I suppose."

She stubbed out her cigarette and busied herself with preparations. There was, for a fact, no alternative. She'd had to admit that, after a three-way radio conversation with her partners. (They didn't worry about eavesdroppers, when not a Merseian knew a word of Anglic.) Falkayn was stuck in what's-his-name's palace. Adzel was loose in the city, but he'd be the last one you'd pick for an undercover mission. Which left Chee Lan.

"Maintain contact with all three of us," she ordered the ship. "Record everything coming in tonight over my two-way. Don't stir without orders—in a galactic language—and don't respond to any native attempts at communication. Tell us at once whatever unusual you observe. If you haven't heard from any of us for twenty-four hours at a stretch, return to Catawrayannis and report."

No answer being indicated, the computer made none.

§

Chee buckled on a gravity harness, a tool kit, and two guns, a stunner and a blaster. Over them she threw a black mantle, less for warmth than concealment. Dousing the lights, she had the personnel lock open just long enough to let her through, jumped, and took to the air.

It bit her with chill. Flowing past, it felt liquid. An enormous silence dwelt beneath heaven; the hum of her grav was lost. Passing above the troopers who surrounded *Muddlin' Through* with armor and artillery—a sensible precaution from the native standpoint, she had to agree, sensibly labeled an honor guard—she saw the forlorn twinkle of campfires and heard a snatch of hoarse song. Then a hovercraft whirred near, big and black athwart the Milky Way, and she must change course to avoid being seen.

For a while she flew above snow-clad wilderness. On an unknown planet, you didn't land downtown if you could help it. Hills and woods gave way at length to a cultivated plain where the lights of villages huddled around tower-jagged castles. Merseia—this continent, at least—appeared to have retained feudalism even as it swung into an industrial age. Or had it?

Perhaps tonight she would find out.

The seacoast hove in view, and Ardaig. That city did not gleam with illumination and brawl with traffic as most Technic communities did. Yellow windows strewed its night, like fire-flies trapped in a web of phosphorescent paving. The River Oiss gleamed dull where it poured through town and into the bay, on which there shone a double moonglade. No, triple; Wythna was rising now. A murmur of machines lifted sky-ward.

Chee dodged another aircraft and streaked down for the darkling Old Quarter. She landed behind a shuttered bazaar and sought the nearest alley. Crouched there, she peered forth. In this section, the streets were decked with a hardy turf, which ice had blanketed, and lit by widely spaced lamps. A Merseian went past, riding a horned gwydh. His tail was draped back across the animal's rump; his cloak fluttered behind him to reveal a quilted jacket reinforced with glittering metal disks and a rifle slanted over his shoulder.

No guardsman, surely; Chee had seen what the military wore, and Falkayn had transmitted pictures of Morruchan's household troops to her via a hand scanner. He had also passed on the information that those latter doubled as police. So why was a civilian going armed? It bespoke a degree of lawlessness that fitted ill with a technological society . . . unless that society was in more trouble than Morruchan had admitted.

Chee made certain her own guns were loose in the holsters.

The *clop-clop* of hooves faded away. Chee stuck her head out of the alley and took bearings from street signs. Instead of words, they used colorful heraldic emblems. But the Survey people had compiled a good map of Ardaig, which Falkayn's gang had memorized. The Old Quarter ought not to have changed much. She loped off, seeking cover whenever she heard a rider or pedestrian approach. There weren't many.

This corner! Squinting through murk, she identified the symbol carved in the lintel of a lean gray house. Quickly, she ran up the stairs and rapped on the door. Her free hand rested on the stunner.

The door creaked open. Light streamed through. A Merseian stood black against it. He carried a pistol himself. His head moved back and forth, peering into the night. "Here I am, thou idiot," Chee muttered.

He looked down. A jerk went through his body. "*Hu-ya!* You are from the star ship?"

"Nay," Chee sneered, "I am come to inspect the plumbing." She darted past him into a wainscoted corridor. "If thou wouldst preserve this chickling secrecy of thine, might one suggest that thou close yon portal?"

The Merseian did. He stood a moment, regarding her in the glow of an incandescent bulb overhead. "I thought you would be . . . different."

"They were Terrans who first visited this world, but surely thou didst not think every race in the cosmos is formed to those ridiculous specifications. Now I've scant time to spare for whatever griping ye have here to do, so lead me to thine acher."

§

The Merseian obeyed. His garments were about like ordinary street clothes, belted tunic and baggy trousers, but a certain precision in their cut—as well as blue-and-gold stripes and the double fylfot embroidered on the sleeves—indicated they were a livery. Or a uniform? Chee felt the second guess confirmed when she noted two others, similarly attired, standing armed in front of a door. They saluted her and let her through.

The room beyond was baronial. Radiant heating had been installed, but a fire also roared on the hearth. Chee paid scant attention to rich draperies and carven pillars. Her gaze went to the two who sat awaiting her.

One was scarfaced, athletic, his tailtip restlessly aflicker. His robe was blue and gold, and he carried a short ceremonial spear. At sight of her, he drew a quick breath. The Cynthian decided she'd better be polite. "I hight Chee Lan, worthies, come from the interstellar expedition in response to your kind invitation."

"*Khraich.*" The aristocrat recovered his poise and touched finger to brow. "Be welcome. I am Dagla, called Quick-to-Anger, the Hand of the Vach Hallen. And my comrade: Olgor hu Freylin, his rank Warmaster in the Republic of Lafdigu, here in Ardaig as agent for his country."

That being was middle-aged, plump, with skin more dark and features more flat than was common around the Wilwidh Ocean. His garb was foreign, too—a sort of toga with metal threads woven into the purple cloth. And he was soft-spoken, imperturbable, quite without the harshness of these lands. He crossed his arms—gesture of greeting?—and said in accented Eriau:

"Great is the honor. Since the last visitors from your high civilization were confined largely to this region, perhaps you have no knowledge of mine. May I therefore say that Lafdigu lies in the southern hemisphere, occupying a goodly part of its continent. In those days we were unindustrialized, but now, one hopes, the situation has altered."

"Nay, Warmaster, be sure our folk heard much about Lafdigu's venerable culture and regretted they had no time to learn therefrom." Chee got more tactful the bigger the lies she told. Inwardly, she groaned: *Oh, no! We haven't troubles enough, there has to be international politicking too!*

A servant appeared with a cut-crystal decanter and goblets.

"I trust that your race, like the Terran, can partake of Merseian refreshment?" Dagla said.

"Indeed," Chee replied. " 'Tis necessary that they who voyage together use the same stuffs. I thank the Hand."

"But we had not looked for, *hurgh*, a guest your size," Olgor said. "Perhaps a smaller glass? The wine is potent."

"This is excellent." Chee hopped onto a low table, squatted, and raised her goblet two-handed. "Galactic custom is that we drink to the health of friends. To yours, then, worthies." She took a long draught. The fact that alcohol does not affect the Cynthian brain was one she had often found it advantageous to keep silent about.

Dagla tossed off a yet larger amount, took a turn around the room, and growled: "Enough formalities, by your leave, Shipmaster." She discarded her cloak. "Shipmistress?" He gulped. His society had a kitchen-church-and-kids attitude toward females. "We . . . *kh-h-h* . . . we've grave matters to discuss."

"The Hand is too abrupt with our noble guest," Olgor chided.

"Nay, time is short," Chee said. "And clearly the business hath great weight, sith ye went to the length of suborning a servant in Morruchan's very stronghold."

Dagla grinned. "I planted Wedhi there eight years ago. He's a good voice-tube."

"No doubt the Hand of the Vach Hallen hath surety of all his own servitors?" Chee purred.

Dagla frowned. Olgor's lips twitched upward.

"Chances must be taken." Dagla made a chopping gesture. "All we know is what was learned from your first radio communications, which said little. Morruchan was quick to isolate you. His hope is plainly to let you hear no more of the truth than he wants. To use you! Here, in this house, we may speak frankly with each other."

As frankly as you two klongs choose, Chee thought. "I listen with care," she said.

Piece by piece, between Dagla and Olgor, the story emerged. It sounded reasonable, as far as it went.

When the Survey team arrived, the Wilwidh culture stood on the brink of a machine age. The scientific method had been invented. There was a heliocentric astronomy, a post-Newtonian pre-Maxwellian physics, a dawning chemistry, a well-developed taxonomy, some speculations about evolution. Steam engines were at work on the first railroads. But political power was fragmented among the Vachs. The scientists, the engineers, the teachers were each under the patronage of one or another Hand.

The visitors from space had too much sense of responsibility to pass on significant practical information. It wouldn't have done a great deal of good anyway. How do you make transistors, for instance, before you can refine ultrapure semimetals? And why should you want to, when you don't yet have electronics? But the humans had given theoretical and experimental science a boost by what they related—above all, by the simple and tremendous fact of their presence.

And then they left.

§

A fierce, proud people had their noses rubbed in their own insignificance. Chee guessed that here lay the root of most of the social upheaval which followed. And belike a more urgent motive than curiosity, or profit, began to drive the scientists: the desire, the need to catch up, to bring Merseia in one leap onto the galactic scene.

The Vachs had shrewdly ridden the wave. Piecemeal they shelved their quarrels, formed a loose confederation, met the new problems well enough that no movement arose to strip them of their privileges. But rivalry persisted, and cross-purposes, and often a reactionary spirit, a harking back to olden days when the young were respectful of the God and their elders.

And meanwhile modernization spread across the planet. A country which did not keep pace soon found itself under foreign domination. Lafdigu had succeeded best. Chee got a distinct impression that the Republic was actually a hobnailbooted dictatorship. Its own imperial ambitions clashed with those of the Hands. Nuclear war was averted on the ground, but space battles had erupted from time to time, horribly and inconclusively.

"So here we are," Dagla said. "Largest, most powerful, the Vach Dathyr speak loudest in this realm. But others press upon them, Hallen, Ynvory, Rueth, yes, even landless Urdiolch. You can see what it would mean if any one of them obtained your exclusive services."

Olgor nodded. "Among other things," he said, "Morruchan Long-Ax would like to contrive that my country is ignored. We are in the southern hemisphere. We will get the worst of the supernova blast. If unprotected, we will be removed from his equations."

"In whole truth, Shipmistress," Dagla added, "I don't believe Morruchan wants your help. *Khraich*, yes, a minimum, to forestall utter collapse. But he has long ranted against the modern world and its ways. He'd not be sorry to see industrial civilization reduced so small that full-plumed feudalism returns."

"How shall he prevent us from doing our work?" Chee asked. "Surely he is not fool enough to kill us. Others will follow."

"He'll bet the knucklebones as they fall," Dagla said. "At the very least, he'll try to keep his position—that you work through him and get most of your information from his sources —and use it to increase his power. At the expense of every other party!"

"We could predict it even in Lafdigu, when first we heard of your coming," Olgor said. "The Strategic College dispatched me here to make what alliances I can. Several Hands are not unwilling to see my country continue as a force in the world, as the price for our help in diminishing their closer neighbors."

Chee said slowly: "Meseems ye make no few assumptions about us, on scant knowledge."

"Shipmistress," said Olgor, "civilized Merseia has had two centuries to study each word, each picture, each legend about your people. Some believe you akin to gods—or demons—yes, whole cults have flowered from the expectation of your return, and I do not venture to guess what they will do now that you are come. But there have also been cooler minds; and that first expedition was honest in what it told, was it not?"

"Hence: the most reasonable postulate is that none of the starfaring races have mental powers we do not. They simply have longer histories. And as we came to know how many the stars are, we saw how thinly your civilization must be spread among them. You will not expend any enormous effort on us, in terms of your own economy. You cannot. You have too much else to do. Nor have you time to learn everything about Merseia and decide every detail of what you will effect. The supernova will flame in our skies in less than three years. You must cooperate with whatever authorities you find and take their word for what the crucial things are to save and what others must be abandoned. Is this not truth?"

Chee weighed her answer. "To a certain degree," she said carefully, "ye have right."

"Morruchan knows this," Dagla said. "He'll use the knowledge as best he can." He leaned forward, towering above her. "For our part, we will not tolerate it. Better the world go down in ruin, to be rebuilt by us, than that the Vach Dathyr engulf what our ancestors wrought. No planetwide effort can succeed without the help of a majority. Unless we get a full voice in what decisions are made, we'll fight."

"Hand, Hand," reproved Olgor.

"Nay, I take not offense," Chee said. "Rather, I give thanks for so plain a warning. Ye will understand, we bear ill will toward none of Merseia and have no partisanship—" *in your wretched little jockeyings.* "If ye have prepared a document stating your position, gladly will we ponder on the same."

§

Olgor opened a casket and took out a sheaf of papers bound in something like snakeskin. "This was hastily written," he apologized. "At another date we would like to give you a fuller account."

" 'Twill serve for the nonce." Chee wondered if she should stay awhile. No doubt she could learn something further. But chaos, how much propaganda she'd have to strain out of what she heard! Also, she'd now been diplomatic as long as anyone could expect. Hadn't she?

They could call the ship directly, she told them. If Morruchan tried to jam the airwaves, she'd jam him, into an unlikely posture. Olgor looked shocked. Dagla objected to communication which could be monitored. Chee sighed. "Well, then, invite us hither for a private talk," she said. "Will Morruchan attack you for that?"

"No . . . I suppose not . . . but he'll get some idea of what we know and what we're doing."

"My belief was," said Chee in her smoothest voice, "that the Hand of the Vach Hallen wished naught save an end to these intrigues and selfishness, an openness in which Merseians might strive together for the common welfare."

She had never cherished any such silly notion, but Dagla couldn't very well admit that his chief concern was to get his own relatives on top of everybody else. He made wistful noises about a transmitter which could not be detected by Merseian equipment. Surely the galactics had one? They did, but Chee wasn't about to pass on stuff with that kind of potentialities. She expressed regrets—nothing had been brought along—so sorry—good night, Hand, good night, Warmaster.

The guard who had let her in escorted her to the front door. She wondered why her hosts didn't. Caution, or just a different set of mores? Well, no matter. Back to the ship. She ran down the frosty street, looking for an alley from which her takeoff wouldn't be noticed. Someone might get trigger-happy.

An entrance gaped between two houses. She darted into darkness. A body fell upon her. Other arms clasped tight, pinioning. She yelled. A light gleamed briefly, a sack was thrust over her head, she inhaled a sweet-sick odor and whirled from her senses.

§

Adzel still wasn't sure what was happening to him or how it had begun. There he'd been, minding his own business, and suddenly he was the featured speaker at a prayer meeting. If that was what it was.

He cleared his throat. "My friends," he said.

A roar went through the hall. Faces and faces and faces stared at the rostrum which he filled with his four and a half meters of length. A thousand Merseians must be present: clients, commoners, city proletariat, drably clad for the most part. Many were female; the lower classes didn't segregate sexes as rigidly as the upper. Their odors made the air thick and musky. Being in a new part of Ardaig, the hall was built plain. But its proportions, the contrasting hues of paneling, the symbols painted in scarlet across the walls reminded Adzel he was on a foreign planet.

He took advantage of the interruption to lift the transceiver hung around his neck up to his snout and mutter plaintively, "David, what *shall* I tell them?"

"Be benevolent and noncommittal," Falkayn's voice advised. "I don't think mine host likes this one bit."

The Wodenite glanced over the seething crowd to the entrance. Three of Morruchan's household guards stood by the door.

He didn't worry about physical attack. Quite apart from having the ship for a backup, he was too formidable himself: a thousand-kilo centauroid, his natural armorplate shining green above and gold below, his spine more impressively ridged than any Merseian's. His ears were not soft cartilage but bony, a similar shelf protected his eyes, his rather crocodilian face opened on an alarming array of fangs. Thus he had been the logical member of the team to wander around the city today, gathering impressions. Morruchan's arguments against this had been politely overruled. "Fear no trouble, Hand," Falkayn said truthfully. "Adzel never seeketh any out. He is a Buddhist, a lover of peace who can well afford tolerance anent the behavior of others."

By the same token, though, he had not been able to refuse the importunities of the crowd which finally cornered him.

"Have you got word from Chee?" he asked.

"Nothing yet," Falkayn said. "Muddlehead's monitoring, of course. I imagine she'll contact us tomorrow. Now don't you interrupt me either. I'm in the middle of an interminable official banquet."

Adzel raised his arms for silence, but here that gesture was an encouragement for more shouts. He changed position, his hooves clattering on the platform, and his tail knocked over a floor candelabrum. "Oh, I'm sorry," he exclaimed. A red-robed Merseian named Gryf, the chief nut of this organization —Star Believers, was that what they called themselves?— picked the thing up and managed to silence the house.

"My friends," Adzel tried again. "Er . . . my friends. I am, er, deeply appreciative of the honor ye do me in asking for some few words." He tried to remember the political speeches he had heard while a student on Earth. "In the great fraternity of intelligent races throughout the universe, surely Merseia hath a majestic part to fulfill."

"Show us . . . show us the way!" howled from the floor. "The way, the truth, the long road futureward!"

"Ah . . . yes. With pleasure." Adzel turned to Gryf. "But perchance first your, er, glorious leader should explain to me the purposes of this . . . this—" What was the word for "club"? Or did he want "church"?

Mainly he wanted information.

"Why, the noble galactic jests," Gryf said in ecstasy. "You know we are those who have waited, living by the precepts the galactics taught, in loyal expectation of their return which they promised us. We are your chosen instrument for the deliverance of Merseia from its ills. Use us!"

§

Adzel was a planetologist by profession, but his large bump of curiosity had led him to study in other fields. His mind shuffled through books he had read, societies he had visited . . .

yes, he identified the pattern. These were cultists who'd attached a quasi-religious significance to what had actually been quite a casual stopover. Oh, the jewel in the lotus! What kind of mess had ensued?

He had to find out.

"That's, ah, very fine," he said. "Very fine indeed. Ah . . . how many do ye number?"

"More than two million, Protector, in twenty different nations. Some high ones are among us, yes, the Heir of the Vach Isthyr. But most belong to the virtuous poor. Had they all known the Protector was to walk forth this day— Well, they'll come as fast as may be, to hear your bidding."

An influx like that could make the pot boil over, Adzel foresaw. Ardaig had been restless enough as he quested through its streets. And what little had been learned about basic Merseian instincts, by the Survey psychologists, suggested they were a combative species. Mass hysteria could take ugly forms.

"No!" the Wodenite cried. The volume nearly blew Gryf off the podium. Adzel moderated his tone. "Let them stay home. Calm, patience, carrying out one's daily round of duties, those are the galactic virtues."

Try telling that to a merchant adventurer! Adzel checked himself. "I fear we have no miracles to offer."

He was about to say that the word he carried was of blood, sweat, and tears. But no. When you dealt with a people whose reactions you couldn't predict, such news must be released with care. Falkayn's first radio communications had been guarded, on precisely that account.

"This is clear," Gryf said. He was not stupid, or even crazy, except in his beliefs. "We must ourselves release ourselves from our oppressors. Tell us how to begin."

Adzel saw Morruchan's troopers grip their rifles tight. *We're expected to start some kind of social revolution?* he thought wildly. *But we can't! It's not our business. Our business is to save your lives, and for that we must not weaken but strengthen whatever authority can work with us, and any revolution will be slow to mature, a consequence of technology— Dare I tell them this tonight?*

Pedantry might soothe them, if only by boring them to sleep. "Among those sophonts who need a government," Adzel said, "the basic requirement for a government which is to function well is that it be legitimate, and the basic problem of any political innovator is how to continue, or else establish anew, a sound basis for that legitimacy. Thus newcomers like mineself cannot—"

He was interrupted—later he was tempted to say "rescued" —by a noise outside. It grew louder, a harsh chant, the clatter of feet on pavement. Females in the audience wailed. Males snarled and moved toward the door. Gryf sprang from the platform, down to what Adzel identified as a telecom, and activated the scanner. It showed the street and an armed mob. High over them, against snow-laden roofs and night sky, flapped a yellow banner.

"Demonists!" Gryf groaned. "I was afraid of this."

Adzel joined him. "Who be they?"

"A lunatic sect. They imagine you galactics mean, have meant from the first, to corrupt us to our destruction. I was prepared, though. See." From alleys and doorways moved close-ranked knots of husky males. They carried weapons.

A trooper snapped words into the microphone of a walkie-talkie. Sending for help, no doubt, to quell the oncoming riot. Adzel returned to the rostrum and filled the hall with his pleas that everyone remain inside.

He might have succeeded, by reverberation if not reason. But his own transceiver awoke with Falkayn's voice: "Get here at once! Chee's been nabbed!"

"What? Who did it? Why?" The racket around became of scant importance.

"I don't know. Muddlehead just alerted me. She'd left this place she was at. Muddlehead received a yell, sounds of scuffling, then no more from her. I'm sending him aloft to try and track her by the carrier wave. He says the source is moving. You move too, back to Afon."

Adzel did. He took part of the wall with him.

§

Korych rose through winter mists that turned gold as they smoked past city towers and above the river. Kettledrums rolled their ritual from Eidh Hill. Shutters came down off windows and doors, market circles began to fill, noise lifted out of a hundred small workshops. Distantly, but deeper and more portentous sounded the buzz of traffic and power from the new quarters, hoot of ships on the bay, whine of jets overhead, thunder of rockets as a craft left the spaceport for the moon Seith.

Morruchan Long-Ax switched off the lights in his confidence chamber. Dawnglow streamed pale through glass, picking out the haggardness of faces. "I am weary," he said, "and we are on a barren trail."

"Hand," said Falkayn, "it had better not be. Here we stay until we have reached some decision."

Morruchan and Dagla glared. Olgor grew expressionless. They were none of them accustomed to being addressed thus. Falkayn gave them stare for stare, and Adzel lifted his head from where he lay coiled on the floor. The Merseians slumped back onto their tails.

"Your whole world may be at stake, worthies," Falkayn said. "My people will not wish to spend time and treasure, aye, some lives, if they look for such ungrateful treatment."

He picked up the harness and kit which lay on Morruchan's desk and hefted them. Guided by Muddlehead, searchers from this household had found the apparatus in a ditch outside town and brought it here several hours ago. Clearly Chee's kidnappers had suspected a signal was being emitted. The things felt pitifully light in his hand.

"What more can be said?" Olgor argued. "We have each voiced a suspicion that one of the others engineered the deed to gain a lever for himself. Or yet a different Vach, or another nation, may have done it; or the Demonists; or even the Star

Believers, for some twisted reason. Morruchan's service too, they could know what the situation is."

"But," Falkayn objected, "they are scarcely so naïve as to think—"

"I shall investigate," Morruchan promised. "I may make direct inquiry. But channels of communication with the Gethfennu masters are devious, therefore slow."

"In any event," Falkayn said bleakly, "Adzel and I do not propose to leave our partner in the grip of criminals—for years, after which they may cut her throat."

"You do not know they have her," Olgor reminded him.

"True. Yet may we prowl somewhat through space, out toward their colony. For little can we do on Merseia, where our knowledge is scant. Here must ye search, worthies, and contrive that all others search with you."

The command seemed to break Morruchan's thin-stretched patience. "Do you imagine we've nothing better to do than hunt for one creature? We, who steer millions?"

Falkayn lost his temper likewise. "If ye wish to keep on doing thus, best ye make the finding of Chee Lan your foremost concern!"

"Gently, gently," Olgor said. "We are so tired that we are turning on allies. And that is not well." He laid a hand on Falkayn's shoulder. "Galactic," he said, "surely you can understand that organizing a systemwide hunt, in a world as diverse as ours, is a greater task than the hunt itself. Why, no few leaders of nations, tribes, clans, factions will not believe the truth if they are told. Proving it to them will require diplomatic skill. Then there are others whose main interest will be to see if they cannot somehow maneuver this affair to give them an advantage over us. And yet others hope you do go away and never return; I do not speak merely of the Demonists."

"If Chee be not returned safely," Falkayn said, "those last may well get their wish."

Olgor smiled. The expression went no deeper than his lips. "Galactic," he murmured, "let us not play word games. Your scientists stand to win knowledge and prestige here, your merchants a profit. They will not allow an unfortunate incident caused by a few Merseians and affecting only one of their folk . . . they will not let that come between them and their objectives. Will they?"

Falkayn looked into the ebony eyes. His own were the first to drop. Nausea caught at his gullet. The Warmaster of Lafdigu had identified his bluff and called it.

Oh, no doubt these who confronted him would mount some kind of search. If nothing else, they'd be anxious to learn what outfit had infiltrated agents onto their staffs and to what extent. No doubt, also, various other Merseians would cooperate. But the investigation would be ill-coordinated and lackadaisical. It would hardly succeed against beings as wily as those who captured Chee Lan.

These three here—nigh the whole of Merseia—just didn't give a damn about her.

§

She awoke in a cell.

It was less than three meters long, half that in width and height: windowless, doorless, comfortless. A coat of paint did not hide the basic construction, which was of large blocks. Their unresponsiveness to her fist-pounding suggested a high density. Brackets were bolted into the walls, to hold equipment of different sorts in place. Despite non-Technic design, Chee recognized a glow lamp, a thermostated air renewer, a waste unit, an acceleration couch . . . space gear, by Cosmos!

No sound, no vibration other than the faint whirr of the air unit's fan reached her. The walls were altogether blank. After a while, they seemed to move closer. She chattered obscenities at them.

But she came near weeping with relief when one block slid aside. A Merseian face looked in. Behind was polished metal. Rumble, clangor, shouted commands resounded through what must be a spaceship's hull, from what must be a spaceport outside.

"Are you well?" asked the Merseian. He looked still tougher than average, but he was trying for courtesy, and he wore a neat tunic with insignia of rank.

Chee debated whether to make a jump, claw his eyes out, and bolt for freedom. No, not a chance. But neither was she going to embrace him. "Quite well, I thank thee," she snarled, "if thou'lt set aside trifles such as that thy heart-rotten varlets have beaten and gassed me and I am athirst and ahungered. For this outrage, methinks I'll summon my mates to blow thy pesthole of a planet from the universe it defileth."

The Merseian laughed. "You can't be too sick, with that kind of spirit. Here are food and water." He passed her some containers. "We blast off soon for a voyage of a few days. Do you need anything?"

"Where are we bound? Who art thou? What meaneth—"

"*Hurh*, little one, I'm not going to leave this snugglehole open very long, for any spillmouth to notice. Tell me this instant what you want, so I can try to have it sent from the city."

Later Chee swore at herself, more picturesquely than she had ever cursed even Adzel. Had she specified the right things, they might have been a clue for her partners. But she was too foggy in the head, too dazed by events. Automatically, she asked for books and films which might help her understand the Merseian situation better. And a grammar text, she added in haste. She was tired of sounding like a local Shakespeare. The Merseian nodded and pushed the block back in place. She heard a faint click. Doubtless a tongue-and-groove lock, operated by a magnetic key.

The rations were revivifying. Before long, Chee felt in shape to make deductions. She was evidently in a secret compartment built into the wall of a radiation shelter.

Merseian interplanetary vessels ran on a thermonuclear-powered ion drive. Those which made landings—ferries tending the big ships or special jobs such as this presumably was—set down in deep silos and departed from them, so that electromagnetic fields could contain the blast and neutralize it before it poisoned the neighborhood. And each craft carried a block-house for crew and passengers to huddle in, should they get caught by a solar storm. Altogether, the engineering was superb. Too bad it would go by the board as soon as gravity drive and forcescreens became available.

A few days, at one Merseian g: hm-m-m, that meant an adjacent planet. Not recalling the present positions, Chee wasn't sure which. A lot of space traffic moved in the Korychan System, as instruments had shown while *Muddlin' Through* approached. From a distance, in magniscreens, she had ob-served some of the fleet, capacious cargo vessels and sleek naval units.

Her captor returned with the materials she had requested and a warning to strap in for blast-off. He introduced himself genially as Iriad the Wayfarer, in charge of this dispatch boat.

"Who art thou working for?" Chee demanded.

He hesitated, then shrugged. "The Gethfennu." The block glided back to imprison her.

§

Lift was nothing like the easy upward floating of a galactic ship. Acceleration rammed Chee down into her couch and sat on her chest. Thunder shuddered through the very blockhouse. Eternal minutes passed before the pressure slacked off and the boat fell into steady running.

After that, for a timeless time, Chee had nothing to do but study. The officers brought her rations. They were a mixed lot, from every part of Merseia; some did not speak Eriau, and none had much to say to her. She considered tinkering her life-support apparatus into a weapon, but without tools the prospect was hopeless. So for amusement she elaborated the things she would like to do to Iriad, come the day. Her part-ners would have flinched.

Once her stomach, the only clock she had, told her she was far overdue for a meal. When finally her cell was opened, she leaped forward in a whirlwind of abuse. Iriad stepped back and raised a pistol. Chee stopped and said: "Well, what happened? Hadn't my swill gotten moldy enough?"

Iriad looked shaken. "We were boarded," he said low.

"How's that?" Acceleration had never varied.

"By . . . your people. They laid alongside, matching our vector as easily as one runner might pace another. I did not know what armament they had, so— He who came aboard was a dragon."

Chee beat her fists on the shelter deck. Oh, no, no, no! Adzel had passed within meters of her, and never suspected . . . the big, ugly, vacuum-skulled bumblemaker!

Iriad straightened. "But Haguan warned me it might happen," he said with a return of self-confidence. "We know somewhat about smuggling. And you are not gods, you galactics."

"Where did they go?"

"Away. To inspect other vessels. Let them."

"Do you seriously hope to keep me hidden for long?"

"Ronruad is full of Haguan's boltholes." Iriad gave her her lunch, collected the empty containers, and departed.

He came back, several meals later, to supervise her transferral from the cell to a packing crate. Under guns, Chee obeyed his instructions. She was strapped into padding alongside an air unit and left in darkness. There followed hours of maneuver, landing, waiting, being unloaded and trucked to some destination.

Finally the box was opened. Chee emerged slowly. Weight was less than half a standard g, but her muscles were cramped. A pair of workers bore the crate away. Guards stayed behind, with a Merseian who claimed to be a medic. The checkup he gave her was expert and sophisticated enough to bear him out. He said she should rest awhile, and they left her alone.

Her suite was interior but luxurious. The food brought her was excellent. She curled in bed and told herself to sleep.

Eventually she was taken down a long, paneled corridor and up a spiral ramp to meet him who had ordered her caught.

He squatted behind a desk of dark, polished wood that looked a hectare in area. Thick white fur carpeted the room and muffled footsteps. Pictures glowed, music sighed, incense sweetened the air. Windows gave a view outside; this part of the warren proje^ted aboveground. Chee saw ruddy sand, strange wild shrubbery, a dust storm walking across a gaunt range of hills and crowned with ice crystals. Korych stood near the horizon, shrunken, but fierce through the tenuous atmosphere. A few stars also shone in that purple sky. Chee recognized Valenderay and shivered a little. So bright and steady it looked; and yet, at this moment, death was riding from it on the wings of light.

"Greeting, galactic." The Eriau was accented differently from Olgor's. "I am Haguan Eluatz. Your name, I gather, is Chee Lan."

She arched her back, bottled her tail, and spat. But she felt very helpless. The Merseian was huge, with a belly that bulged forward his embroidered robe. He was not of the Wilwidh stock, his skin was shiny black and heavily scaled, his eyes almond-shaped, his nose a scimitar.

One ring-glittering hands made a gesture. Chee's guards slapped tails to ankles and left. The door closed behind them. But a pistol lay on Haguan's desk, next to an intercom.

He smiled. "Be not afraid. No harm is intended you. We regret the indignities you have suffered and will try to make amends. Sheer necessity forced us to act."

"The necessity for suicide?" Chee snorted.

"For survival. Now why don't you make yourself comfortable on yonder couch? We have talk to forge, we two. I can send for whatever refreshment you desire. Some arthberry wine, perhaps?"

Chee shook her head but did jump onto the seat. "Suppose you explain your abominable behavior," she said.

"Gladly." Haguan shifted the weight on his tail. "You may not know what the Gethfennu is. It came into being after the first galactics had departed. But by now—" He continued for a while. When he spoke of a systemwide syndicate, controlling millions of lives and uncounted wealth, strong enough to build its own city on this planet and wily enough to play its enemies

off against each other so that none dared attack that colony—
he was scarcely lying. Everything that Chee had seen confirmed it.

"Are we in this town of yours now?" she asked.

"No. Elsewhere on Ronruad. Best I not be specific. I have
too much respect for your cleverness."

"And I have none for yours."

"*Khraich?* You must. I think we operated quite smoothly,
and on such short notice. Of course, an organization like ours
must always be prepared for anything. And we have been on
special alert ever since your arrival. What little we have
learned—" Haguan's gaze went to the white point of Valenderay and lingered. "That star, it is going to explode. True?"

"Yes. Your civilization will be scrubbed out unless—"

"I know, I know. We have scientists in our pay." Haguan
leaned forward. "The assorted governments on Merseia see this
as a millennial chance to rid themselves of the troublesome
Gethfennu. We need only be denied help in saving our colony, our shipping, our properties on the home planet and
elsewhere. Then we are finished. I expect you galactics would
agree to this. Since not everything can be shielded in time,
why not include us in that which is to be abandoned? You
stand for some kind of law and order too, I suppose."

Chee nodded. In their mask of dark fur, her eyes smoldered
emerald. Haguan had guessed shrewdly. The League didn't
much care who it dealt with, but the solid citizens whose taxes
were to finance the majority of the rescue operations did.

"So to win our friendship, you take me by force," she
sneered halfheartedly.

"What had we to lose? We might have conferred with you,
pleaded our cause, but would that have wrought good for us?"

"Suppose my partners recommend that no help be given
your whole coprophagous Merseian race."

"Why, then the collapse comes," Haguan said with chilling
calm, "and the Gethfennu has a better chance than most organizations of improving its relative position. But I doubt that

any such recommendation will be made or that your overlords would heed it if it were.

"So we need a coin to buy technical assistance. You."

Chee's whiskers twitched in a smile of sorts. "I'm scarcely that big a hostage."

"Probably not," Haguan agreed. "But you are a source of information."

The Cynthian's fur stood on end with alarm. "Do you have some screwbrained notion that I can tell you how to do everything for yourself? I'm not even an engineer!"

"Understood. But surely you know your way about in your own civilization. You know what the engineers can and cannot do. More important, you know the planets, the different races and the cultures upon them, the mores, the laws, the needs. You can tell us what to expect. You can help us get interstellar ships—hijacking under your advice should succeed, being unlooked for—and show us how to pilot them, and put us in touch with someone who, for pay, will come to our aid."

"If you suppose for a moment that the Polesotechnic League would tolerate—"

Teeth flashed white in Haguan's face. "Perhaps it won't, perhaps it will. With so many stars, the diversity of peoples and interests is surely inconceivable. The Gethfennu is skilled in stirring up competition among others. What information you supply will tell us how, in this particular case. I don't really visualize your League, whatever it is, fighting a war—at a time when every resource must be devoted to saving Merseia—to prevent someone else rescuing us."

He spread his hands. "Or possibly we'll find a different approach," he finished. "It depends on what you tell and suggest."

"How do you know you can trust me?"

Haguan said like iron: "We judge the soil by what crops it bears. If we fail, if we see the Gethfennu doomed, we can still enforce our policy regarding traitors. Would you care to visit my punishment facilities? They are quite extensive. Even though you are of a new species, I think we could keep you alive and aware for many days."

Silence dwelt awhile in that room. Korych slipped under the horizon. Instantly the sky was black, strewn with the legions of the stars, beautiful and uncaring.

Haguan switched on a light to drive away that too enormous vision. "If you save us, however," he said, "you will go free with a very good reward."

"But—" Chee looked sickly into sterile years ahead of her. And the betrayal of friends and scorn if ever she returned, a lifetime's exile. "You'll keep me till then?"

"Of course."

§

No success. No ghost of a clue. She was gone into an emptiness less fathomable than the spaces which gaped around their ship.

They had striven, Falkayn and Adzel. They had walked into Luridor itself, the sin-bright city on Ronruad, while the ship hovered overhead and showed with a single, rock-fusing flash of energy guns what power menaced the world. They had ransacked, threatened, bribed, beseeched. Sometimes terror met them, sometimes the inborn arrogance of Merseia's lords. But nowhere and never had anyone so much as hinted he knew who held Chee Lan or where.

Falkayn ran a hand through uncombed yellow locks. His eyes stood bloodshot in a sunken countenance. "I still think we should've taken that casino boss aboard and worked him over."

"No," said Adzel. "Apart from the morality of the matter, I feel sure that everyone who has any information is hidden away. That precaution is elementary. We're not even certain the outlaw regime is responsible."

"Yeah. Could be Morruchan, Dagla, Olgor, or colleagues of theirs acting unbeknownst to them, or any of a hundred other governments, or some gang of fanatics, or— Oh, *Judas!*"

Falkayn looked at the after viewscreen. Ronruad's tawny-red

crescent was dwindling swiftly among the constellations as the ship drove at full acceleration back toward Merseia. It was a dwarf planet, an ocherous pebble that would not make a decent splash if it fell into one of the gas giants. But the least of planets is still a world: mountains, plains, valleys, arroyos, caves, waters, square kilometers by the millions, too vast and varied for any mind to grasp. And Merseia was bigger yet; and there were others, and moons, asteroids, space itself.

Chee's captors need but move her around occasionally, and the odds against a fleetful of League detectives finding her would climb for infinity.

"The Merseians themselves are bound to have some notion where to look, what to do, who to put pressure on," he mumbled for the hundredth time. "We don't know the ins and outs. Nobody from our cultures ever will—five billion years of planetary existence to catch up with! We've got to get the Merseians busy. I mean really busy."

"They have their own work to do," Adzel said.

Falkayn expressed himself at pungent length on the value of their work. "How about those enthusiasts?" he wondered when he had calmed down a trifle. "The outfit you were talking to."

"Yes, the Star Believers should be loyal allies," Adzel said. "But most of them are poor and, ah, unrealistic. I hardly expect them to be of help. Indeed, I fear they will complicate our problem by starting pitched battles with the Demonists."

"You mean the antigalactics?" Falkayn rubbed his chin. The bristles made a scratchy noise in the ceaseless gentle thrum that filled the cabin. He inhaled the sour smell of his own weariness. "Maybe they did this."

"I doubt that. They must be investigated, naturally—a major undertaking in itself—but they do not appear sufficiently well organized."

"Damnation, if we don't get her back I'm going to push for letting this whole race stew!"

"You will not succeed. And, in any event, it would be unjust to let millions die for the crime of a few."

"The millions jolly well ought to be tracking down the few.

It's possible. There have to be some leads somewhere. If every single one is followed—"

The detector panel flickered. Muddlehead announced: "Ship observed. A chemical carrier, I believe, from the outer system. Range—"

"Oh, dry up," Falkayn said, "and blow away."

"I am not equipped to—"

Falkayn stabbed the voice cutoff button.

He sat for a while, then, staring into the stars. His pipe went out unnoticed between his fingers. Adzel sighed and laid his head down on the deck.

§

"Poor little Chee," Falkayn whispered at last. "She came a long way to die."

"Most likely she lives," Adzel said.

"I hope so. But she used to go flying through trees in an endless forest. Being caged will kill her."

"Or unbalance her mind. She is so easily infuriated. If anger can find no object, it turns to feed on itself."

"Well . . . you were always squabbling with her."

"It meant nothing. Afterward she would cook me a special dinner. Once I admired a painting of hers, and she thrust it into my hands and said, 'Take the silly thing, then,' like a cub that is too shy to say it loves you."

"Uh-huh."

The cutoff button popped up. "Course adjustment required," Muddlehead stated, "in order to avoid dangerously close passage by ore carrier."

"Well, do it," Falkayn rasped. "Destruction, but they've got a lot of space traffic!"

"Well, we are in the ecliptic plane, and as yet near Ronruad," Adzel said. "The coincidence is not great."

Falkayn clenched his hands. The pipestem snapped. "Suppose we strafe the ground," he said in a cold strange voice. "Not kill anyone. Burn up a few expensive installations,

though, and promise more of the same if they don't get off
their duffs and start a real search for her."

"No. We have considerable discretion, but not that much."

"We could argue with the board of inquiry later."

"Such a deed would produce confusion and antagonism and
weaken the basis of the rescue effort. It might actually make
rescue impossible. You have observed how basic pride is to the
dominant Merseian cultures. An attempt to browbeat them,
with no face-saving formula possible, might compel them to
refuse galactic assistance. We would be personally, criminally
responsible. I cannot permit it, David."

"So we can't do anything, not anything, to—"

Falkayn's words chopped off. He smashed a fist down on the
arm of his pilot chair and surged to his feet. Adzel rose also,
sinews drawn taut. He knew his partner.

§

Merseia hung immense, shining with oceans, blazoned
with clouds and continents, rimmed with dawn and sunset and
the deep sapphire of her sky. Her four small moons made a
diadem. Korych flamed in plumage of zodiacal light.

Space cruiser *Yonuar,* United Fleet of the Great Vachs,
swung close in polar orbit. Officially she was on patrol to stand
by for possible aid to distressed civilian vessels. In fact she was
there to keep an eye on the warcraft of Lafdigu, Wolder, the
Nersan Alliance—any her masters mistrusted. And, yes, on the
new-come galactics, if they returned hither. The God alone
knew what they intended. One must tread warily and keep
weapons close to hand.

On his command bridge, Captain Tryntaf Fangryf-Tamer
gazed into the simulacrum tank and tried to imagine what
laired among those myriad suns. He had grown up knowing
that others flitted freely between them while his people were
bound to this one system, and hating that knowledge. Now
they were here once again—why? Too many rumors flew
about. But most of them centered on the ominous spark called
Valenderay.

Help; collaboration—were the Vach Isthyr to become mere clients of some outworld grotesque?

A signal fluted. The intercom said: "Radar Central to captain. Object detected on an intercept path." The figures which followed were unbelievable. No meteoroid, surely, despite an absence of jet radiation. Therefore, the galactics! His black uniform tunic grew taut around Tryntaf's shoulders as he hunched forward and issued orders. Battle stations: not that he was looking for trouble, but he was prudent. And if trouble came, he'd much like to see how well the alien could withstand laser blasts and nuclear rockets.

She grew in his screens, a stubby truncated raindrop, ridiculously tiny against the sea-beast hulk of *Yonuar*. She matched orbit so fast that Tryntaf heard the air suck in through his lips. Doom and death, why wasn't that hull broken apart and the crew smeared into a red layer? Some kind of counterfield . . . The vessel hung a few kilometers off, and Tryntaf sought to calm himself. They would no doubt call him, and he must remain steady of nerve, cold of brain.

For his sealed orders mentioned that the galactics had left Merseia in anger because the whole planet would not devote itself to a certain task. The Hands had striven for moderation; of course they would do what they reasonably could to oblige their guests from the stars, but they had other concerns, too. The galactics seemed unable to agree that the business of entire worlds was more important than their private wishes. Of necessity, such an attitude was met with haughtiness, lest the name of the Vachs, of all the nations, be lowered.

Thus, when his outercom screen gave him an image, Tryntaf kept one finger on the combat button. He had some difficulty hiding his revulsion. Those thin features, shock of hair, tailless body, fuzzed brown skin were like a dirty caricature of Merseiankind. He would rather have spoken to the companion, whom he could see in the background. That creature was honestly weird.

Nonetheless, Tryntaf got through the usual courtesies and asked the galactic's business in a level tone.

Falkayn had pretty well mastered modern language by now. "Captain," he said, "I regret this and apologize, but you'll have to return to base."

Tryntaf's heart slammed. Only his harness prevented him from jerking backward, to drift across the bridge in the dreamlike flight of zero gravity. He swallowed and managed to keep his speech calm. "What is the reason?"

"We have communicated it to different leaders," said Falkayn, "but since they don't accept the idea, I'll also explain to you personally.

"Someone, we don't know who, has kidnapped a crew member of ours. I'm sure that you, Captain, will understand that honor requires we get her back."

"I do," Tryntaf said, "and honor demands that we assist you. But what has this to do with my ship?"

"Let me go on, please. I want to prove that no offense is intended. We have little time to make ready for the coming disaster and few personnel to employ. The contribution of each is vital. In particular, the specialized knowledge of our vanished teammate cannot be dispensed with. So her return is of the utmost importance to all Merseians."

Tryntaf grunted. He knew the argument was specious, meant to provide nothing but an acceptable way for his people to capitulate to the strangers' will.

"The search for her looks hopeless when she can be moved about in space," Falkayn said. "Accordingly, while she is missing, interplanetary traffic must be halted."

Tryntaf rapped an oath. "Impossible."

"Contrariwise," Falkayn said. "We hope for your cooperation, but if your duty forbids this, we two can enforce the decree."

Tryntaf was astonished to hear himself, through a tide of fury, say just: "I have no such orders."

"That is regrettable," Falkayn said. "I know your superiors will issue them, but that takes time, and the emergency will not wait. Be so good as to return to base."

Tryntaf's finger poised over the button. "And if I don't?"

"Captain, we shouldn't risk damage to your fine ship—"

Tryntaf gave the signal.

His gunners had the range. Beams and rockets vomited forth.

Not one missile hit. The enemy flitted aside, letting them pass, as if they were thrown pebbles. A full-power ray struck, but not her hull. Energy sparked and showered blindingly off some invisible barrier.

The little vessel curved about like an aircraft. One beam licked briefly from her snout. Alarms resounded. Damage Control cried, near hysteria, that armorplate had been sliced off as a knife might cut soft wood. No great harm done; but if the shot had been directed at the reaction mass tanks—

"How very distressing, Captain," Falkayn said. "But accidents will happen when weapons systems are overly automated, don't you agree? For the sake of your crew, for the sake of your country whose ship is your responsibility, I do urge you to reconsider."

"Hold fire," Tryntaf gasped.

"You will return planetside, then?" Falkayn asked.

"I curse you, yes," Tryntaf said with a parched mouth.

"Good. You are a wise male, Captain. I salute you. Ah . . . you may wish to notify your fellow commanders elsewhere, so they can take steps to assure there will be no further accidents. Meanwhile, though, please commence reentry."

Jets stabbed into space. *Yonuar,* pride of the Vachs, began her inward spiral.

And aboard *Muddlin' Through,* Falkayn wiped his brow and grinned shakily at Adzel. "For a minute," he said, "I was afraid that moron was going to slug it out."

"We could have disabled his command with no casualties," Adzel said, "and I believe they have lifecraft."

"Yes, but think of the waste; and the grudge." Falkayn shook himself. "Come on, let's get started. We've a lot of others to round up."

"Can we—a lone civilian craft—blockade an entire globe?" Adzel wondered. "I do not recall that it has ever been done."

"No, I don't imagine it has. But that's because the opposition has also had things like grav drive. These Merseian rowboats are something else again. And we need only watch this one planet. Everything funnels through it." Falkayn stuffed tobacco into a pipe. "Uh, Adzel, suppose you compose our broadcast to the public. You're more tactful than I am."

"What shall I say?" the Wodenite asked.

"Oh, the same guff as I just forked out, but dressed up and tied with a pink ribbon."

"Do you really expect this to work, David?"

"I've pretty high hopes. Look, all we'll call for is that Chee be left some safe place and we be notified where. We'll disavow every intention of punishing anybody, and we can make that plausible by pointing out that the galactics have to prove they're as good as their word if their mission is to have any chance of succeeding. If the kidnappers don't oblige— Well, first, they'll have the entire population out on a full-time hunt after them. And second, they themselves will be suffering badly from the blockade meanwhile. Whoever they are. Because you wouldn't have as much interplanetary shipping as you do, if it weren't basic to the economy."

Adzel shifted in unease. "We must not cause anyone to starve."

"We won't. Food isn't sent across space, except gourmet items; too costly. How often do I have to explain to you, old thickhead? What we will cause is that everybody loses money. Megacredits per diem. And Very Important Merseians will be stranded in places like Luridor, and they'll burn up the maser beams ordering their subordinates to remedy that state of affairs. And factories will shut down, spaceports lie idle, investments crumble, political and military balances get upset . . . You can fill in the details."

Falkayn lit his pipe and puffed a blue cloud. "I don't expect matters will go that far, actually," he went on. "The Merseians are as able as us to foresee the consequences. Not a hypothetical disaster three years hence, but money and power eroding away right now. So they'll put it first on their agenda to find those kidnappers and take out resentment on them. The kidnappers will know this and will also, I trust, be hit in their personal breadbasket. I bet in a few days they'll offer to swap Chee for an amnesty."

"Which I trust we will honor," Adzel said.

"I told you we'll have to. Wish we didn't."

"Please don't be so cynical, David. I hate to see you lose merit."

Falkayn chuckled. "But I make profits. Come on, Muddle-head, get busy and find us another ship."

§

The teleconference room in Castle Afon could handle a sealed circuit that embraced the world. On this day it did.

Falkayn sat in a chair he had brought, looking across a table scarred by the daggers of ancestral warriors to the mosaic of screens which filled the opposite wall. A hundred or more Merseian visages lowered back at him. On that scale, they had no individuality. Save one: a black countenance ringed by empty frames. No lord would let his image stand next to that of Haguan Eluatz.

Beside the human, Morruchan, Hand of the Vach Dathyr, rose and said with frigid ceremoniousness: "In the name of the God and the blood, we are met. May we be well met. May wisdom and honor stand shield to shield . . ." Falkayn listened with half an ear. He was busy rehearsing his speech. At best, he was in for a cobalt bomb's worth of trouble.

No danger, of course. *Muddlin' Through* hung plain in sight above Ardaig. Television carried that picture around Merseia. And it linked him to Adzel and Chee Lan, who waited at the guns. He was protected.

But what he had to say could provoke a wrath so great that his mission was wrecked. He must say it with infinite care, and then he must hope.

". . . Obligation to a guest demands we hear him out," Morruchan finished brusquely.

Falkayn stood up. He knew that in those eyes he was a monster whose motivations were not understandable and who had proven himself dangerous. So he had dressed in his plainest gray zipsuit, and was unarmed, and spoke in soft words.

"Worthies," he said, "forgive me that I do not use your titles, for you are of many ranks and nations. But you are those who decide for your whole race. I hope you will feel free to talk as frankly as I shall. This is a secret and informal conference, intended to explore what is best for Merseia.

"Let me first express my heartfelt gratitude for your selfless and successful labors to get my teammate returned unharmed. And let me also thank you for indulging my wish that the, uh, chieftain Haguan Eluatz participate in this honorable assembly, albeit he has no right under law to do so. The reason shall soon be explained. Let me, finally, once again express my regret at the necessity of stopping your space commerce, for however brief a period, and my thanks for your cooperation in this emergency measure. I hope that you will consider any losses made good when my people arrive to help you rescue your civilization.

"Now, then, it is time we put away whatever is past and look to the future. Our duty is to organize that great task. And the problem is, how shall it be organized? The galactic technologists do not wish to usurp any Merseian authority. In fact, they could not. They will be too few, too foreign, and too busy. If they are to do their work in the short time available, they must accept the guidance of the powers that be. They must make heavy use of existing facilities. That, of course, must be authorized by those who control the facilities. I need not elaborate. Experienced leaders like yourselves, worthies, can easily grasp what is entailed."

He cleared his throat. "A major question, obviously, is: With whom shall our people work most closely? They have no desire to discriminate. Everyone will be consulted within the sphere of his time-honored prerogatives. Everyone will be aided, as far as possible. Yet, plain to see, a committee of the whole would be impossibly large and diverse. For setting overall policy, our people require a small, unified Merseian council whom they can get to know really well and with whom they can develop effective decision-making procedures.

"Furthermore, the resources of this entire system must be used in a coordinated way. For example, Country One cannot be allowed to hoard minerals which Country Two needs. Shipping must be free to go from any point to any other. And all available shipping must be pressed into service. We can furnish radiation screens for your vessels, but we cannot furnish the vessels themselves in the numbers that are needed. Yet at the same time, a certain amount of ordinary activity must continue. People will still have to eat, for instance. So— how do we make a fair allocation of resources and establish a fair system of priorities?

"I think these considerations make it obvious to you, worthies, that an international organization is absolutely essential, one which can *impartially* supply information, advice, and coordination. If it has facilities and workers of its own, so much the better.

"Would that such an organization had legal existence! But it does not, and I doubt there is time to form one. If you will pardon me for saying so, worthies, Merseia is burdened with too many old hatreds and jealousies to join overnight in brotherhood. In fact, the international group must be watched carefully, lest it try to aggrandize itself or diminish others. We galactics can do this with one organization. We cannot with a hundred.

"So." Falkayn longed for his pipe. Sweat prickled his skin. "I have no plenipotentiary writ. My team is merely supposed to make recommendations. But the matter is so urgent that whatever scheme we propose will likely be adopted, for the sake of getting on with the job. And we have found one group which transcends the rest. It pays no attention to barriers between people and people. It is large, powerful, rich, disciplined, efficient. It is not exactly what my civilization would prefer as its chief instrument for the deliverance of Merseia. We would honestly rather it went down the drain, instead of becoming yet more firmly entrenched. But we have a saying that necessity knows no law."

He could feel the tension gather, like a thunderstorm boiling up; he said fast, before the explosion came: "I refer to the Gethfennu."

What followed was indescribable.

But he was, after all, only warning of what his report would be. He could point out that he bore a grudge of his own and was setting it aside for the common good. He could even, with considerable enjoyment, throw some imaginative remarks about ancestry and habits in the direction of Haguan—who grinned and looked smug. In the end, hours later, the assembly agreed to take the proposal under advisement. Falkayn knew what the upshot would be. Merseia had no choice.

The screens blanked.

Wet, shaking, exhausted, he looked across a stillness into the face of Morruchan Long-Ax. The Hand loomed over him. Fingers twitched longingly near a pistol butt. Morruchan said, biting off each word: "I trust you realize what you are doing. You're not just perpetuating that gang. You're conferring legitimacy on them. They will be able to claim they are now a part of recognized society."

"Won't they, then, have to conform to its laws?" Falkayn's larynx hurt, his voice was husky.

"Not them!" Morruchan stood brooding a moment. "But a reckoning will come. The Vachs will prepare one, if nobody else does. And afterward—are you going to teach us how to build stargoing ships?"

"Not if I have any say in the matter," Falkayn replied.

"Another score. Not important in the long run. We're bound to learn a great deal else, and on that basis . . . well, galactic, our grandchildren will see."

"Is ordinary gratitude beneath your dignity?"

"No. There'll be enough soft-souled dreambuilders, also among my race, for an orgy of sentimentalism. But then you'll go home again. I will abide."

Falkayn was too tired to argue. He made his formal fare-wells and called the ship to come get him.

Later, hurtling through the interstellar night, he listened to Chee's tirade: ". . . I still have to get back at those greasepaws. They'll be sorry they ever touched me."

"You don't aim to return, do you?" Falkayn asked.

"Pox, no!" she said. "But the engineers on Merseia will need recreation. The Gethfennu will supply some of it, gambling, especially, I imagine. Now if I suggest our lads carry certain miniaturized gadgets which can, for instance, control a wheel—"

Adzel sighed. "In this splendid and terrible cosmos," he said, "why must we living creatures be forever perverse?"

A smile tugged at Falkayn's mouth. "We wouldn't have so much fun otherwise," he said.

§

Men and not-men were still at work when the supernova wave front reached Merseia.

Suddenly the star filled the southern night, a third as brilliant as Korych, too savage for the naked eye to look at. Blue white radiance flooded the land, shadows were etched sharp, trees and hills stood as if illuminated by lightning. Wings beat upward from forests, animals cried through the troubled air, drums pulsed, and prayers lifted in villages which once had feared the dark for which they now longed. The day that followed was lurid and furious.

Over the months, the star faded, until it became a knife-keen point and scarcely visible when the sun was aloft. But it waxed in beauty, for its radiance excited the gas around it, so that it gleamed amidst a whiteness which deepened at the edge to blue violet and a nebular lacework which shone with a hundred faerie hues. Thence also, in Merseia's heaven, streamed huge shuddering banners of aurora whose whisper was heard even on the ground. An odor of storm was blown on every wind.

Then the nuclear rain began. And nothing was funny any longer.